THE HOLY WARRIOR

THE HOLY WARRIOR

GILBERT MORRIS

BETHANY HOUSE PUBLISHERS
MINNEAPOLIS, MINNESOTA 55438

Published by Bethany House Publishers
A Division of Bethany Fellowship, Inc.
6820 Auto Club Road, Minneapolis, Minnesota 55438

Printed in the United States of America

Library of Congress Cataloging-in-Publication Data

Morris, Gilbert.
The holy warrior / Gilbert Morris.
p. cm. — (The House of Winslow ; bk. 6)

I. Title. II. Series: Morris, Gilbert. House of Winslow ; bk. 6.
PS3563.08742H65 1989
813′.54—dc20 89–17568
ISBN 1-55661-054-8 CIP

To Johnnie, my wife

All things must have names, but no words can ever capture the essence of the best things. The word *wife*, for example, is a poor, frail substitute to describe the years of happiness, comfort, and support that the companion God gave me has brought into my life. Every year I say the same thing: *we have saved the best 'till last*—and so again, my heart, the old vows are echoing, so I must say once more—I love, honor, and cherish you as never before.

Perhaps such vows, such thoughts, and such words may be outmoded. If so, it only proves that our feelings have outlasted time and fashion, and I can only say—thank you for all you have given me.

No woman ever fulfilled the old words of the old Book better than Johnnie Morris:

> Who can find a virtuous woman?
> Her price is far above rubies.
> The heart of her husband doth safely trust in her.
> Her children arise up and call her blessed.
> Her husband also, and he praiseth her.

THE HOUSE OF WINSLOW SERIES

★ ★ ★ ★

The Honorable Imposter
The Captive Bride
The Indentured Heart
The Gentle Rebel
The Saintly Buccaneer
The Holy Warrior
The Reluctant Bridegroom
The Last Confederate
The Dixie Widow
The Wounded Yankee
The Union Belle
The Final Adversary
The Crossed Sabres
Valiant Gunman

GILBERT MORRIS spent ten years as a pastor before becoming Professor of English at Ouachita Baptist University in Arkansas and earning a Ph.D. at the University of Arkansas. During the summers of 1984 and 1985 he did postgraduate work at the University of London and is presently the Chairman of General Education at a Christian college in Louisiana. A prolific writer, he has had over 25 scholarly articles and 200 poems published in various periodicals, and over the past years has had more than 20 novels published. His family includes three grown children, and he and his wife live in Baton Rouge, Louisiana.

CONTENTS

PART ONE

THE MOUNTAIN MAN

PART TWO

THE PASTOR

PART THREE

THE MISSIONARY

THE HOUSE OF WINSLOW

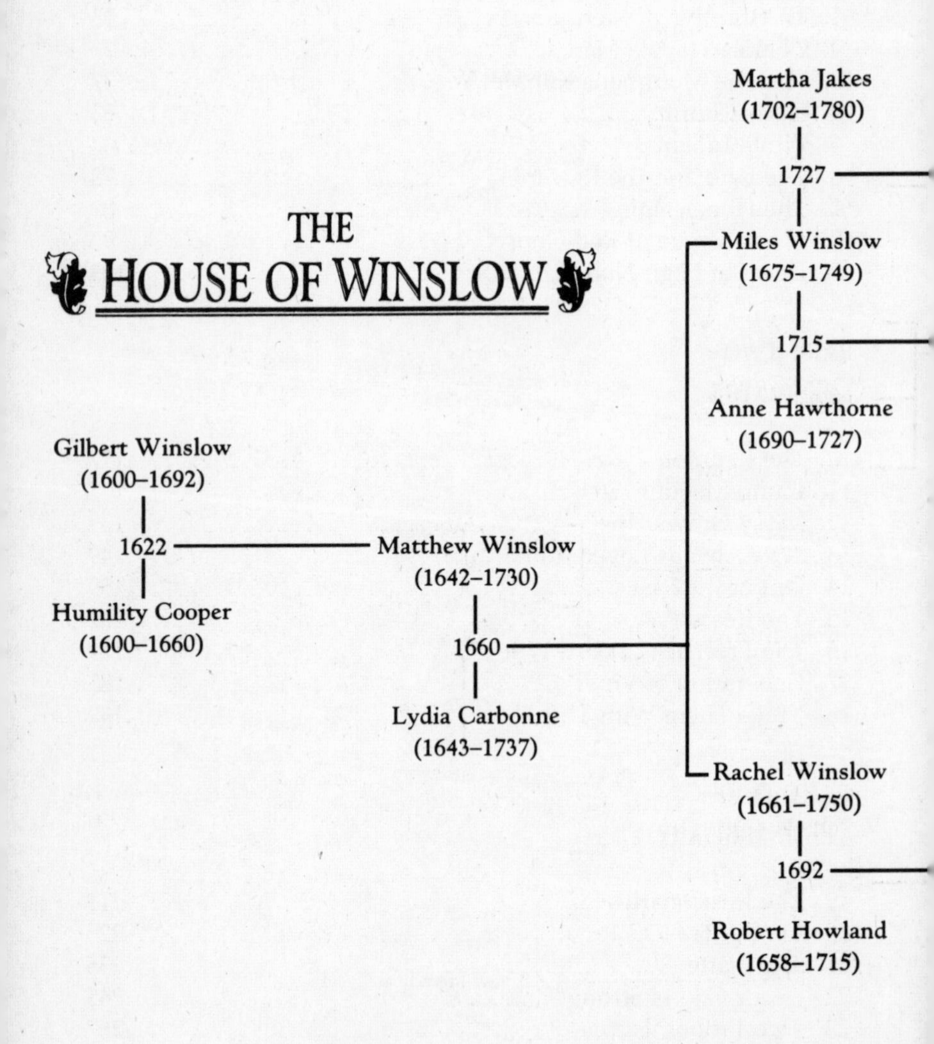

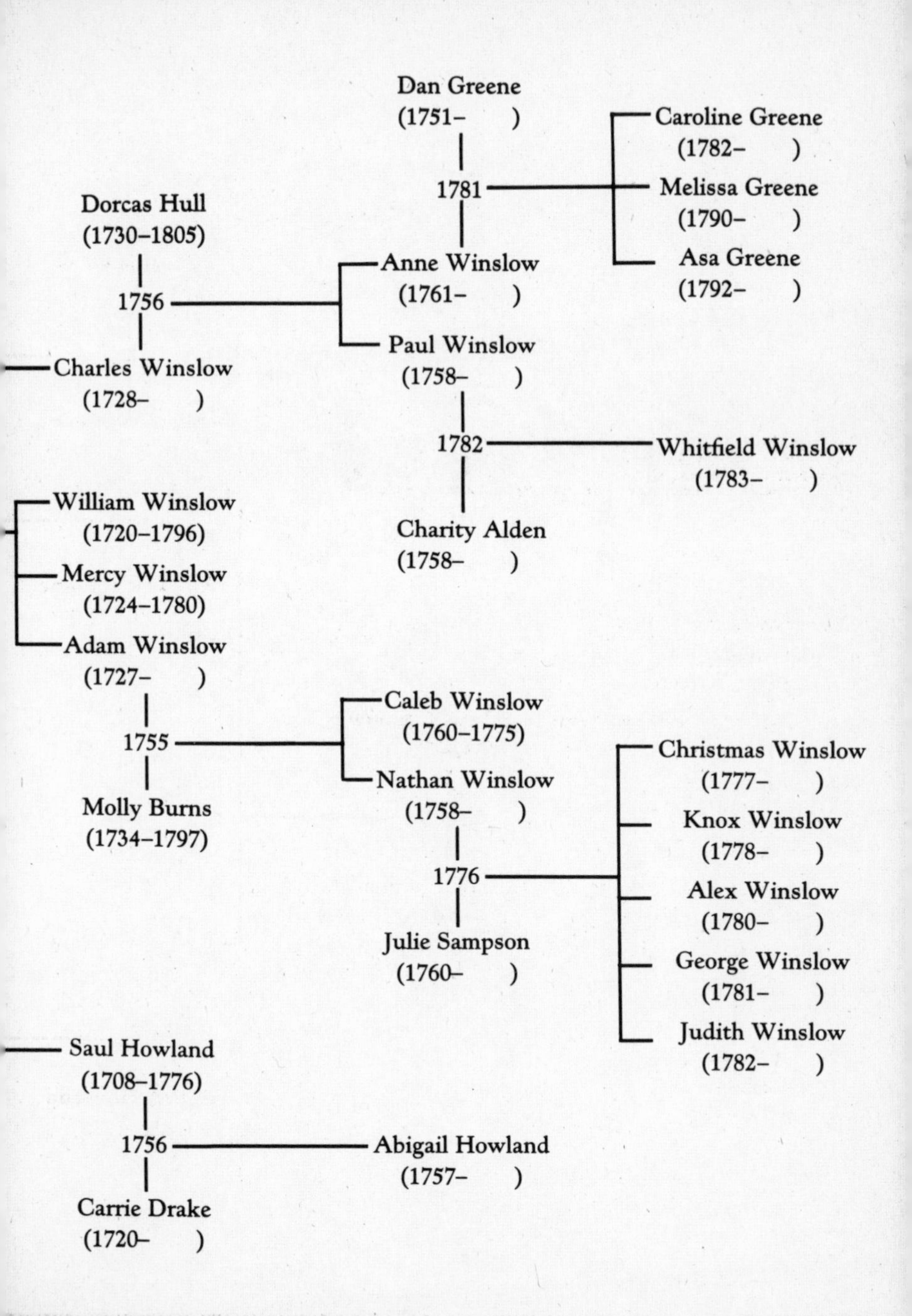
Dan Greene
(1751–)
1781
Caroline Greene
(1782–)
Melissa Greene
(1790–)
Asa Greene
(1792–)
Dorcas Hull
(1730–1805)
1756
Anne Winslow
(1761–)
Paul Winslow
(1758–)
Charles Winslow
(1728–)
1782
Whitfield Winslow
(1783–)
William Winslow
(1720–1796)
Charity Alden
(1758–)
Mercy Winslow
(1724–1780)
Adam Winslow
(1727–)
Caleb Winslow
(1760–1775)
1755
Christmas Winslow
(1777–)
Nathan Winslow
(1758–)
Molly Burns
(1734–1797)
Knox Winslow
(1778–)
1776
Alex Winslow
(1780–)
Julie Sampson
(1760–)
George Winslow
(1781–)
Judith Winslow
(1782–)
Saul Howland
(1708–1776)
1756
Abigail Howland
(1757–)
Carrie Drake
(1720–)

PART ONE

THE MOUNTAIN MAN

★ ★ ★ ★

CHAPTER ONE

The Captive of Merton

★ ★ ★ ★

Jonas Billings, the innkeeper of the Blue Swan, glanced up at the sound of the squealing hinge coming from the heavy oak door. The man who had pushed his way through the door stood there, looking over the taproom. An officer. Billings hurriedly finished serving a tall man with a pockmarked face and the highly painted woman perched on his lap, then turned to go, but he was caught by a hard grip on his wrist. "Wot's yer 'urry, Billings? That bloke can wait. Look at 'im all dressed up in 'is nice uniform!" He threw his head back and roared with drunken laughter, and the slender man with the pale face across from him grinned wolfishly.

"Wonder if 'is underwears got frills on it, eh, Bully?" the smaller man hooted.

"Might be I ought to find out," the other laughed. He kissed the woman lustily on the mouth, then gave Billings a rough shake. "Never mind 'im—and leave that bottle, you 'ear me?"

"Take it easy, Maitland," the burly innkeeper warned. Pulling his arm free, Billings made his point. "You've had enough. You want to wind up back in your cell?"

The big man swore and shook his fist in Billings' face. "Not likely! Not me! They'd 'ave to kill me first!" He took a huge drink from the tankard, glared around the room and bellowed, "Bully Maitland! That's me, and I've got a five-year thirst—so don't get in me way!"

Billings left the table and came to stand before the new customer. "Yes, sir, Captain," he said. "Can I get you something to drink?"

"I understand no one is admitted inside the prison walls after six. Is that so?"

The dark-haired man was of average height and wore the uniform of a Navy officer. His features were regular, even handsome, except for the large scar along his lower jaw that descended beneath his collar. His direct gaze never wavered as he spoke, and Billings knew quality when he saw it.

"I'm afraid that's the way of it, Captain. I take it you just come in on the stage? Too bad, sir!"

"You have a room?"

"That I do, and first class, it is." Billings smiled and moved toward the bar, saying, "Let me offer you a drink—on the house."

"No, but I'd like some hot tea—or coffee."

"Yes, sir, I'll have me wife fix you up a nice supper." He called out through a door behind the bar, "Betty, fix some of that beef and warm up some of the kidney pie. And hot coffee."

"My name's Winslow." He was looking up at a pair of fencing foils that were mounted over the bar. "Those are very nice."

"Aye, sir. Belonged to me grandfather, they did." He reached up and pulled the weapons down, placing them on the bar for the officer's inspection.

Winslow looked at them closely. "Do a little fencing yourself, I'd venture."

"I've done a bit."

Intrigued, he grasped the handle and stretched out his arm to examine the foil's balance. As he did so, he felt a hand on his shoulder and turned his head to look into the smiling face of the woman who'd been sitting on the loud customer's lap.

"Well, now!" she said saucily. "Give me a sea-going man every time! Like to buy me a drink, sailor?"

Winslow shrugged. "Better go back to your friend," he advised.

"Not likely!" the woman snapped angrily. " 'E ain't nothin' but a jailbird!" She moved closer, running a finger down the scar on his jaw. She lowered her voice to a coaxing whisper. "Come on, Love! I knows how to show a brave man like you a real good time!"

Winslow shook his head and was about to move away when a roar of anger made him wheel quickly.

"Steal my woman, will you!" Furious, Bully Maitland rushed across the room, his fist drawn back, and swung it hard at Winslow's head. Missing his target as the officer deftly moved to one side, the man crashed against the bar. With a stream of curses he straightened up, spying at the same time one of the foils near his hand. Snatching the weapon, he began to move toward Winslow. "Come on, Bill, we'll carve this pretty cove up! Use yer dirk!"

"You crazy fool!" Billings shouted. "You'll hang!"

The tall man seemed not to hear. He was joined now by his partner, who held a thin dagger in front of him in the manner of an expert knife fighter.

In a flash Winslow reached out, picked up a chair and threw it at Maitland, then stepped forward and picked up the other foil as the man fell. He stood there with a grim smile on his lips, waiting.

Maitland leaped to his feet, but paused at the sight of the foil in the officer's hand. Still, he was both angry and drunk enough to yell, " 'E can't 'andle us both, Bill! Git 'im from that side."

The two men moved apart and Billings yelled again, but they paid no heed. When they were on opposite sides of Winslow, Maitland yelled, "Stick 'im, Bill!"

The smaller man lunged with his knife. Winslow feinted to the side as his rapier flickered in the light. With a movement too fast to follow, the tip of the blade struck Bill's hand, sending the knife flying, and then flicked across his face, leaving a thin red line welling up with blood.

"Wot. . . !" Maitland gasped. It had all happened so fast, the bully seemed frozen to the spot. Recovering quickly, he started to back across the room, trying desperately to stave off Winslow's advance. It was useless, as Billings saw, for the officer was toying with the man. Time after time Winslow could have killed Maitland but did not drive his blade home. Finally, when the man's back was against the wall, his face white with fear, Winslow's blade caught the other's at the guard and sent it flying through the air. Just as quickly, Bully Maitland felt a cold steel tip tight against his throat.

"Nooooo!" he moaned with fear. "Don't! Don't kill me—please!"

Winslow dropped his blade. "Get out of here," he commanded his attackers coldly, then walked back to the bar, his face as calm as if he'd been reading the newspaper. At a word from Billings, the two men scurried out, followed closely by the woman.

"Sorry about that, Captain! The two of 'em just got out this morning. I reckon they over-celebrated."

Winslow looked at the door. "If I'd known that, I might have had a question for them."

"Something about the prison, sir?"

"Yes."

"Well now, you see that chap with the white beard? He's one of the guards—was, I should say. He's leaving on the morning stage." Billings hesitated, lowering his voice. "I know he's not got a dime. If you'd buy him a bit of supper, Captain, he could tell you 'most anything about Merton Prison."

"What's his name?"

"Bradley—that's all I know."

"Have your wife cook up another piece of meat—and do you have a room we could use?"

"Yes, sir. Shall I get Bradley?"

"Yes."

Half an hour later Bradley was stuffing food down his throat and washing it down with draughts of beer. Winslow let him finish, eating almost nothing himself. Finally he said, "If you're finished, I have a few questions for you."

"Yes, sir! Anything I can do!"

"Do you know a prisoner named Christmas Winslow?"

"Why, 'course I do, Cap'n!" Bradley took another drink of beer, then stared at his host. "Be you a friend of his?"

"A relative."

"Ah! I'm sorry for the lad!"

"What's the matter with him?"

"Been sick for months now." Bradley shook his head. "He's been gettin' worse for some time now, sir. He's not likely to make it—and it's sorry I am to have to tell you."

"I've come to get him out."

Bradley stared at him. "But—his sentence!"

"I have a presidential pardon signed by President Adams—and a personal letter from President Washington."

Bradley stared at him in awe. "Well . . . that oughter do it—though Hindleman will argue."

"Hindleman? He's the warden?"

"No, he's the Devil!" Bradley said, with a glint of anger in his eyes. "Thinks he's a little god in there, Cap'n! It's him has made the boy work out in the cold when he was so sick he couldn't walk. I tried to give the poor boy a break—but it was little I could do!"

Winslow nodded, reached into his pocket and took out two gold coins. "Here's something that may help, Bradley. I appreciate what you tried to do for the boy."

Bradley took the coins with a trembling hand. "Ah, sir! That's good of you!" Then he said, "Be careful, Cap'n! Hindleman hates to lose prisoners—one less for him to torment."

"I don't think we need be concerned about that, Bradley," the officer replied with a cold smile, and there was something in his dark eyes that made the other draw back a little.

"No, sir," he said with a broad grin. "I can see Warden Hindleman won't have his way this time!"

The Warden of Merton Prison was in only slightly better condition than the institution itself, Paul Winslow observed as he entered the shabby office. He had visited several naval prisons, and they were bad enough; but the dilapidated factory building that he had found settling into a bog twenty miles northwest of Boston was far worse.

Winslow was in a bad temper, having been forced to wait nearly two hours before the guard posted at the gate would admit him into the compound of the three-story square building. From there he had spent another hour in a vile-smelling room waiting for the privilege of seeing Warden Clement Hindleman.

Hindleman, he saw upon entering the office, was a grossly fat man, spilling out of his clothes on all sides. He had the flushed face and veined nose of a heavy drinker; although it was only eleven-thirty, he was well on his way to being drunk. The odor of whiskey was overpowering, and a jug sat on his desk—close to his fat hand.

"Well, wot is it?" the warden demanded. His voice was thick and his hand unsteady as he poured himself another glass of liquor, tossing it down his throat without waiting for his visitor's reply. He then shook his shoulders, gave Winslow a look of irritation, and raised his voice. "Well, speak up! I don't 'ave any business with the Navy!"

"You have business with me—if you're sober enough to take care of it." The soft answer cut like cold steel, causing Hindleman to sit up in his chair, a flush of anger coloring his cheeks.

"Your business, Cap'n!" he demanded. "And be quick about it—I'm a busy man."

Captain Winslow stared at him coldly, then reached into his inner pocket and pulled out a leather pouch. "This won't take long. Then you can get back to your whiskey."

Warden Hindleman snatched the pouch, ripped it open and stared at the single sheet of paper. He sat stock-still, and when he looked up his eyes were wide with shock. "Why—I can't let this man go!"

"Shall I tell President Adams and President Washington that is your answer?"

The officer's crisp reply struck the warden like a blow, and he cried out angrily, "There's procedures to be followed, blast ye!"

"In this case, here is your procedure: You will have Mr. Christmas Winslow placed into my charge in exactly one hour.

If not, I will have no choice but to notify the governor of Massachusetts that the warden of this place is an incompetent drunk! Then, Hindleman, you won't be so busy. In fact, you'll have plenty of time to get dog drunk all the time." He rose swiftly to his feet and said, "Perhaps I'll do that anyway—in addition to notifying the federal authorities. . . !"

"Now wait! Just wait, Cap'n!" Hindleman's face had gone pale, and he raised his hands in a gesture of pleading. "You don't have to jump down a man's throat that way! I just have to be sure of a thing like this!"

Winslow allowed him a minute to apologize, then said, "I need to be back in Boston by night. Have one of your guards take me to the prisoner."

"Yes, sir, Cap'n!" He got up and went to the door, shouting loudly, "Nelson! Take Captain Winslow to the hospital—see that the prisoner Christmas Winslow gets released into his custody. Here, you'll need that in writing."

As the warden scribbled a few words on a paper and handed it to Paul, he muttered, "Winslow's pretty sick. Might not be good to take him out in this bad weather."

"I think his chances are better with me than with you," the officer retorted, then whirled and followed the guard out of the office.

"Hospital's this way," the guard muttered. He led Winslow down a narrow hallway to a steel door guarded by two men. Inside, the room was very large, packed with men who stared at the visitor as he strode across the area. It was freezing, and most of the prisoners wore so many layers of rags that they looked grossly overweight. But their cheeks were hollow, and their huge eyes stared vacantly out of gaunt and hungry faces. Most of them were milling around, trying to keep warm, but many were lying prone, too weak to do even that.

They passed through another steel door that led to a rickety staircase. It shook alarmingly under their feet, and Winslow half expected the structure to crash beneath their weight, but the guard paid no heed. "This here's the hospital," he announced, opening the door with a key he pulled from his vest. "Ain't no doctor here 'cept on Wednesday. That's the medical assistant there. Name's Phelps. Used to be a doctor his own self—but he practiced on his own wife. Cut her throat, 'e did!" He laughed at his crude jest, then called out, "Phelps! This here gentleman has come to take Winslow with him. Get 'im all ready."

Phelps was a slight prisoner, with intelligent dark eyes, dulled with his condition, and he seemed to be almost too exhausted to speak. His voice was so thin that Winslow had to lean forward to hear him. "Let Winslow out? How can that be?"

"Bloke's been pardoned."

"Pardoned?" A slight smile appeared on Phelps' thin lips, and he shook his head. "Sir, you may have an official pardon—but I fear your man is past such things."

"What do you mean? Where is he?"

"I'll show you." Phelps led the way out of the large room—past a dozen men who lay on cots, covered to their chins with rough blankets—to a door at the far end. Opening the door for Paul, the doctor asked cautiously, "Are you a relative, may I ask?"

"Yes," Winslow answered. "How long has he been sick? What's wrong with him?"

Phelps motioned the man into the next room. "He's been sick for weeks. As to what's wrong with him—" He broke off and made no further answer. Winslow stepped inside and went at once to a bed beside the window where a man lay, and looked down at him.

He had met his second cousin only once, and that had been years ago. Nathan Winslow had moved his family to Virginia; after that he occasionally made the trip to Boston—where Paul lived with his family—but he had brought his family with him only once. Winslow remembered the boy, who had been thirteen, as a tall, healthy-looking youngster with a mop of red hair and blue eyes. Christmas had been quite wild even then, spending most of his time in the woods, for he was as skillful at hunting and tracking as most grown men.

But Paul could see no trace of this boy in the face of the man he looked at now. His cheeks were cadaverous under skin that was mottled gray. The sick man had a fever, and despite the bitter cold that settled in the room, there was a sheen of perspiration on his brow. Paul reached out and took the wrist, shocked at its thinness; the pulse was faint and irregular, and his shallow breathing could not hide the ominous rattle in his chest. "What's wrong with him?" he asked the assistant.

"Merton Prison is what's wrong with him, Captain," Phelps replied bluntly. "It started as a bad cold—and he was made to work in the cold and not given enough to eat. Got wet—which brought on a fever. Well, Hindleman says if they can stand, they work. So he went out in freezing cold with not enough to wear; went from bad to worse. Double pneumonia, I think, or consumption."

As the captain of a frigate, Paul Winslow had seen enough sick men to know about such things. Staring at the boy, Paul considered his best course of action. Move him? Could be risky, but desperate times called for desperate measures. Paul had learned through experience that sometimes it is better to "risk" the ship than to lie back and wait for something worse to develop.

He put the thin hand back under the blanket and turned to Phelps. "Put the warmest clothes you can find on him."

"You'll kill him if you take him out in this weather!" Phelps protested.

"He'll die if he stays here!"

Phelps nodded slowly, "You're right there, Captain. I'll get him ready."

Winslow left the room and called for the guard, who came running. "Have this man carried to the front gate at once. I'll have my carriage waiting." Barely waiting for the guard's "Yes, sir, Cap'n," Paul turned and made his way out of the prison.

The air was biting cold as he left the building, but Captain Winslow had planned the journey back to Boston as carefully as he planned a voyage of his ship, the *Constellation*. By now it had become second nature to him—ordering supplies, foreseeing emergencies. When his father had asked him to pick Christmas up and bring him home, he had spent considerable time rigging up the carriage for a sick man.

He had taken the largest closed carriage and removed the back seat so there was room enough for a tall man to lie down.

He'd had the servants bring a mattress down from upstairs, along with plenty of blankets. Aware that the cold would be his greatest enemy, Paul had ordered his servant Jason to tie blankets all over the interior of the compartment, forming a snug cocoon with thick walls of wool. *That'll keep the cold out. Be a lot warmer than that tomb he's been in,* Winslow thought as he pulled up to the front of the building.

It had taken six men to get the tall form down the stairs, and they were waiting with the sick man, who was muffled in blankets. "Put him in here, Sergeant," Winslow said, watching to make sure that they handled the unconscious man carefully. He pulled the fresh blankets over Christmas, throwing the filthy old ones on the ground, then got into the seat and whipped his horses up without a word to the guards. He passed by the guard at the front gate without incident; obviously, the man had been warned—by Hindleman, no doubt—not to give him any difficulty.

Glancing up at the sky, Paul saw that he would be hard pressed to get home by dark. He could not drive as rapidly as he had on the journey to Merton; the sick man would be shaken too badly. But he was prepared for that as well; it would take an army of bandits to get past the arsenal he had at his feet: two double-barreled pistols, an over-and-under shotgun, a Kentucky hunting rifle and a sword—all of which he used expertly.

All afternoon he drove steadily along the snow-packed road. He stopped twice to get hot broth from farmhouses, and was able to ladle a little of it down the sick man's throat. Christmas had opened his eyes once or twice, but he didn't seem to recognize anything. Paul made one last stop just before dark, at an inn a few miles from Boston. He ate a few bites himself, then went back to try to get Christmas to eat a little more. One spoonful of broth choked the sick man, producing a spasm of coughing. Paul held him tightly, and the coughing subsided; that was enough broth, he decided. As he was situating Christmas back in the carriage, Christmas's eyes flickered open. Paul saw at once there was a light of consciousness in them.

"Are you awake, Christmas?" Paul asked.

"Yes." Just that one word, but the eyes were fixed on Paul's face. He moved his lips slowly; he seemed to have difficulty speaking. Paul leaned closer, and finally heard him ask, "Where are you taking me?"

"I'm Paul Winslow, Christmas. I'm taking you home."

The eyes suddenly turned cold and the wide mouth closed like a trap. Christmas Winslow shut his eyes, and just before he passed out, Paul heard him say with finality: "I won't ever go home! I'll die first!"

Then his body went limp, and Paul gently laid him back and put the covers in place. He closed the compartment against the cold and mounted the seat. The moon was rising and the stars gave icy points of light in the fast-falling darkness. As Paul continued the journey, he mused over what he'd heard. He knew that Christmas Winslow had been a wild one—the black sheep of the family. Charles had told him that Christmas had renounced his family, and would have nothing to do with his parents.

Paul was grateful that his own son, Whitfield, had shown none of this rebellious spirit, though he could easily have inherited it. Paul's father Charles—and, indeed, he himself!—had been the wild ones in the family tree. Adam and Nathan had been the steady Winslows. But now this tall son of Nathan Winslow had gone bad, while Paul's own son gave every indication of being a good man. *No accounting where the dark side of the Winslows will crop up next,* Paul thought soberly.

This troubled him, and his face grew sad as he made his way into the city. By the time he pulled up in front of the stately house outside of Boston, it was almost midnight; but Jason, accompanied by two other servants, was out the door as soon as the carriage pulled up.

"You back, Captain," he said. Without being told, he moved toward the carriage and pulled the blankets from the opening. "We done got Mister Christmas's bedroom ready. Yo' pa is waiting fo' ya." Then he smiled and said, "You done bring the prodigal home, ain't ya now, Captain?"

Paul Winslow sighed and shook his head, saying as he turned to go inside to his father, "Yes, Jason—but he's a mighty reluctant prodigal!"

CHAPTER TWO

Charles Traps a Man

★ ★ ★ ★

When Knox Winslow arrived in Boston two weeks after Chris had been pardoned, his first visit with his brother proved to be quite a shock. He had been impressed with the stately home of his New England relatives, which seemed huge and ornate compared with his own home in Virginia. He had heard a great deal about Paul Winslow, whose rapid rise as a Navy officer made him something of a hero to many.

When he had first met his second cousin, he was a little shocked to see that Paul was not a large man, as he had expected of such a warrior; his own father, Nathan Winslow, could have knocked the trim officer down with one blow. But it was common knowledge that Paul Winslow was probably the best swordsman in America, and Knox could tell instinctively that the stories of the man's coolness under fire were not exaggerated.

"Well, Knox, how are your parents?" Paul Winslow had seen to it that the young man had been fed well; Charity had outdone herself with a meal of lobsters and homemade cornbread dressing. Then she had shooed them into the informal study—used by their son Whitfield for his own work. There the two men relaxed and drank hot coffee.

"Pretty well, sir" was Knox's immediate response. The

twenty-year-old son of Nathan and Julie was quick in most things, Paul decided. The officer prided himself in his ability to assess a man's character almost immediately; before he had known the young man half an hour Paul had said to himself: *Too bad the other one isn't of this cut!* For though Christmas was bigger and stronger, there was a decency and courtesy in Knox that the other lacked.

"They think a lot of you, Uncle Paul." The older man smiled. *Uncle Paul.* This manner of address was customary between the older and younger generations of the Winslow clan; although he was really more distantly related, Captain Winslow appreciated the affectionate title the boy had bestowed on him. After a brief pause, Knox continued. "Grandfather Adam is fond of your father, as well. He often tells us stories of when Charles was a boy."

As if the sound of his name had summoned him, Charles Winslow appeared at the door, and both men rose as he came in, leaning heavily on his cane. "Plague take it! I've got rid of that blasted idiot Cory! Now, let's have a drink of that good whiskey, Paul!"

"Dr. Webb says you shouldn't drink it, Father," Paul said evenly, but there was a grin on his face, and he allowed his right eyelid to fall in a sly wink as he glanced at Knox.

"He's a worse fool than she is! Now, obey your father, as the Good Book says. Reach me that bottle before that ebony witch comes in on her broomstick!"

Knox had told the truth: He had heard stories of Charles Winslow all his life—most of them unflattering. But his grandfather had said in his last conversation before Knox left, "You'll find my brother different from the man in the stories, Knox. All his life he's been his own worst enemy—and he tries to live up to the stories about himself. I've been praying for him for more than forty years, and God's not going to let that time be wasted!"

The old man, Knox saw, looked like a Winslow. His bright blue eyes and fair hair had marked many of the men of his family. But age had worn him down, and illness had taken its toll. As Charles slumped into a chair, aided by his son, Knox could see that the man was very ill. His eyes were the only thing about him that seemed alive—his eyes and his spirit, which flashed out as he commanded again, "I say get me that bottle! We'll see if this whelp can drink like a gentleman!"

Paul winked at Knox again, then pulled down a square crystal bottle and poured three small drinks in matching glasses. Charles threw his back and breathed a ragged sigh of pleasure, then shoved the glass forward. "Again!"

Paul bit his lip and a worried look appeared on his thin face. "You really shouldn't, Father. It's not good—you're not well!"

"Not good for me? You sound like that crazy doctor—and like Cory! I don't have long to hang around here, and I'm not going to get better—so fill that glass up and don't argue with me, son. I'm not one of your seamen, you know!"

A spark of amusement glinted in Paul's eye. "If you were, I'd have you keelhauled. You're more trouble than any man I ever saw. And if you don't stop pestering Cory, she's going to poison you." Cory was the middle-aged black servant who served as a nurse for his father; there was a running war between the old man and the black woman.

The second drink went down, and Charles Winslow smacked his lips. "Ahhhhh! Now that's fine-drinking whiskey." He looked at Knox with a light in his eyes and said, "Don't suppose any of Adam's brood ever gets to taste good liquor? I hear the whole tribe's got religion so bad they won't even eat an egg laid on Sunday."

Knox was unruffled; as his grandfather had warned, Charles's badgering was more bluster than substance. "Why, Mr. Winslow, I guess whiskey is pretty scarce at our house, for a fact."

"Not with your brother, though," Charles retorted, and his bright blue eyes flew to Knox's face. "Adam tells me the boy's drunk enough whiskey to float Paul's frigate."

"Well, sir—" Knox shifted uncomfortably, and could not think of anything to say. He loved his brother Christmas, and had spent a great deal of energy defending him against the attacks of others. He had several scars to prove it. Knox was not going to give this old man the satisfaction of agreeing to these accusations.

"Oh, never mind, never mind! Adam's always been a great letter writer, so I know more about you than you think." Charles smiled wickedly and added, "For example, you've always been jealous of your brother because he's a big, strong fellow, and you're a runt!"

Knox's face turned pale, for the truth of the old man's words hit him like a rock. "I can't help it if I'm small."

"You're not small, boy; you're just measuring yourself up against somebody else—and that's a bad thing sometimes," Charles warned. Knox was only marginally less than average height, and he was slight of build, but he had grown up in the shadow of his brothers, Christmas and George, both large men, and he had allowed the matter to prey on his mind.

"And you've always admired your brother—which bothers you a lot, because you know he's a no-good rascal."

"He's not that bad!"

"Yes, he is," Charles countered calmly. "It takes a scoundrel to know one, and I've spent enough time with Christmas Winslow to say with certainty that he's one of the rotten Winslows—like me."

"Like—like you, sir?" Knox had never met a person in his life who could admit to being a villain with such nonchalance. Most people, he knew, spent a great deal of effort trying to convince others that they were respectable. "My grandfather says you're not so bad."

"Your grandfather would make excuses for Judas Iscariot, boy!" Charles grinned, and slapped his frail leg with an equally thin hand. "Why, Saul Howland and I did our best to skin Adam Winslow out of every dime he had—and he never took a shot at either of us!"

"But, he says you saved his life once," Knox argued. "He told me how you jumped in front of him and took a bullet that was meant for him."

Charles Winslow dropped his head, and the silence in the room ran on so long that both Knox and Paul thought the old man had dozed off. But then he lifted his head and there was a quivering smile on his thin lips and a bright light in his bright eyes. "The only good thing I ever did for that man—and he's never forgotten it!" Then he seemed ashamed at showing weakness, and slapped his thigh again, violently. "Well, one good deed don't make a man decent. Your brother Christmas, he's probably done a few good deeds, but they don't make him a good man. Sure, he may be a fine hunter, an expert trapper. But that boy has broken your parents' hearts—and Adam's, too. Don't deny that, do you? No, you can't! Still, you think he's something just because he's big and strong—and as stubborn a sinner as he ever was."

"Father, you're being too hard on Knox," Paul finally protested.

"Got to be hard on him, Paul. Because he's got to be tough enough to help us if that fool boy upstairs gets a chance to live."

"Chance to live?" Knox straightened up with alarm. "He's not going to die, is he?"

"He's doing very poorly, Knox," Paul said. "We've had him here two weeks, and he's not made much progress. Dr. Webb tells us that he needs to get into a warm climate."

"Why, I'm taking him home with me, aren't I? Isn't that why Father sent me here?"

"Well, Adam sent you here to take the boy south, but Mr. Christmas Winslow, sick as he is, has made it abundantly clear that he'll die before he sets foot in his father's house. How's that for sense and gratitude, Mr. Knox Winslow?"

Knox bit his lip, for he had seen firsthand all the strife that had passed between his father and Christmas. Nathan Winslow was a strong Christian, a pillar of the church; when his firstborn son began to drink, it had broken his heart. He had tried to reason with the boy, but Christmas was blindly rebellious. The situation had rapidly deteriorated until Christmas had left home at the age of seventeen—vowing never to return. "You're too holy for me!" Knox had heard his brother shout as he ran out the door.

"I—I'll find a place for him," Knox finally said, with more conviction than he felt. His mind raced wildly, and he could not think of a single alternative.

"I've written Adam, boy," Charles said, and his voice was weary with strain. He leaned back and closed his eyes, his lips moving with effort. "You know my daughter Anne married Daniel Greene."

"Yes, sir. My folks think he's about the best man there is!"

"Well, I guess I'll have to agree—though I pitched a fit when my only daughter married a dirt-poor preacher. I don't mind telling you now that I was wrong. Dan's almost as good a man as your grandfather—and that's about the most I can say of anybody, I guess—"

"Whut's you doin' wit' dat whiskey!" A large black woman framed the doorway, her eyes big as moons. She swooped down on the old man like a hawk and pulled him to his feet. "Ah kotched you, didn't ah? And shame on you, Mistuh Paul! Letting yo' po' old fathah drink hisself into his grave! Fo' shame!"

"Guilty as charged, Cory," Paul Winslow said ruefully. "I'll be around to see you later, Father."

As the huge woman practically carried Winslow out, he turned and said, "Knox—boy, you pay heed to what my son tells you. It'll go hard for your brother otherwise."

Paul waited until they were gone, then said, "I've been writing to your father, and we've come up with a plan. Chris will never go to Nathan's house—but I think he'd go and stay with my sister and her husband."

"What can I do, Uncle Paul?"

"We'll have to trick him into it, Knox—but if you'll do as I say, we'll get him to agree."

"I'll do anything to help Chris!"

"All right. The first thing I'll do is to try to get him to go home with you. He'll fight that, as we already know. You join in with me, and we'll really put pressure on! Then, when the time is right, we offer him an alternative. He'll be against living with a preacher; but I believe by the time we get through with him, he'll agree to live with anybody to stay out of his father's house."

"It might work—if we let him think he's making the choice," Knox agreed. "You think Rev. Greene can put up with him?"

Paul Winslow thought back to the time when he had stood beside Dan Greene on a deck filled with dead and dying men, and he smiled and said, "Knox, I believe Dan Greene can handle just about anything that comes his way. Now, let's go up and we can start trying to trick your fool of a brother into doing something wise for a change!"

Knox followed Winslow upstairs, and the older man stopped before the door with a word of caution. "He looks pretty bad, Knox." Then he pushed the door open and the two men entered.

"Here's Knox, Chris. He's come to take you home."

Knox stepped inside the room, which had a high ceiling, with two large windows on one wall and a fireplace on the other. There was a smell of burning pine as a log crackled, sending a shower of sparks up the chimney. A man was sitting in a chair with a red and black blanket over his lap. For a moment Knox could only stare—the skeletal figure bore almost no resemblance to his brother. *That's not Chris!* he thought wildly. *They've made a mistake!*

He moved closer, and a bar of bright sunlight from the glass window fell across his brother's pallid features. "Hello, Chris."

"Hello, Knox." Chris had always had a lean face, but he looked like a living corpse, the flesh drawn and his blue eyes enormous in his shrunken face. The once-powerful neck was now nothing but bone and gristle, looking far too weak to hold up the large head. The full lips that Knox remembered were thin and had a bluish cast, and were drawn back from the teeth in a grimace.

"You look like the Devil, Chris," Knox blurted out.

"Don't I though?" A wheezy laugh came from the thin mouth, and Chris raised a hand, saying, "Look at that! Can't even lift a glass to my mouth!" Then he added without a pause, "And I ain't goin' back home with you, Knox, so keep shut about it."

Knox knew at once that Paul had the method that would work, so he sat down and for the next two days he nursed his brother and tried to talk him into going home. The nursing had no more effect on him than the persuasion—less, perhaps, because the more he urged Christmas to go home with him to Virginia, the more the sick man shook his head.

"He just cusses and says he'll go to hell before he goes back home," Knox told Paul and Charles.

"Got no sense, like I said," Charles snorted. He was having

one of his better days, and the color in his cheeks was high. "I think it's about time to spring our trap. Come along."

He led the way to Christmas's room and said loudly as he entered, "Well, I hear you'd rather go to hell than to live with your people. Just about what I expected, boy. You're not only a worthless scoundrel, you're dumb as a backwoodsman!"

Unexpectedly a smile lifted the corners of Chris's thin lips. Charles Winslow had made several visits, and his bluntness seemed to please the sick man. He nodded now, saying quickly, "You got me figured right. Only man in this place that's stubborner and meaner than me is you."

"Yes, but I'm not stupid, boy—that's the big difference between you and me."

"You wouldn't live in that house for ten minutes yourself," Chris grinned. "Father wouldn't let you have your whiskey."

Charles Winslow grinned back at the young man, rubbed his chin with his thin hand, then nodded. "In that, you're probably right—but if it were life or death, I guess I'd put up with it. At least long enough to get well. You're going to die if you don't get some sunshine."

"Who cares?"

"Why, I expect you do, boy," Charles shrugged. "You ain't as tough as you want people to think. Man will do a lot to stay alive."

"Maybe. But not that."

Charles stared at him. "Boy, I think it's rotten the way you hate your father. That's something you'll have to take care of yourself. But I have an idea that might help."

"What idea?"

"Go stay with my daughter Anne. She's a good nurse, and that Kentucky sunshine will get you well, I'd guess. That's what the doctor says, anyway."

"The Greenes?" Chris's brow wrinkled and he said in disdain, "He's a Methodist preacher, ain't he? It'd be like being home."

"No, it wouldn't. It's your father you hate, and you wouldn't be staying with him. The preaching might be pesky—but you'd not be at home. I reckon you're mean enough to make life miserable for Anne and Dan. Go on, boy, take what you want. Then walk off and leave them without a word of thanks. That's what a real tough man would do."

Chris turned his head to stare out the window. The snow was gone, and the landscape was brown and dead, like a carcass. No sign of life anywhere. He thought of the green hills of Virginia, and yearned to see flowers and grass, to feel the warmth of the summer sun. He had dreamed of it for two years in the tomb at Merton, and had not expected to see it again.

The three men waited, knowing that no words would move the man. Finally he said, "I'll go if they'll have me."

Charles snorted, "Sink me! I'm disappointed! I thought you'd be mean enough to stay here and die and put us to all the trouble and expense of burying you! Well, I'll go write Dan and tell him to double up on his praying. He'll need it with a heathen like you in his house!"

"Seems like his prayers don't amount to much, Mr. Winslow," Chris snapped as the old man turned to leave. "He's been praying for you for years, hasn't he? It don't appear to me he's made much headway."

Charles Winslow stopped, and all three men were surprised to see his eyes glistening with unshed tears. He stood quietly, trying to compose himself. "Well, Christmas Winslow," he said in a husky voice, "in that you may not be right. I've been a sorry man for most of my life—maybe not as wild as you, but bad enough. And now that the play's about over, I've been thinking how I'd do it differently. But there's no way to turn the page back . . ."

For a moment there was a tragic air about the old man; then he smiled and went on, a touch of irony in his voice. "I've had some powerful men of God praying for me—and women, too. Adam—and Molly, before she died. Your own people—even Paul here, who was about as bad as his father. But I've seen something in these Christians. Now that I've come to the end, I think all their prayers are catching up with me."

He turned to leave, and as he walked out the door, Paul hurried after him. Christmas remained silent, watching the retreating figures. Then closing his eyes, he said wearily, "Take me to Kentucky, Knox. I want to feel the sun."

"Sure, Christmas. We'll be there in no time."

Actually it was three weeks before Knox pulled the carriage up and pointed down at the small village nestling in a valley between two low-lying ranges. "That's the place, I reckon. Think you can make it, Chris? Won't take more than a couple of hours to get to the house."

"If I don't make it, bury me!"

"All right."

The trip had been slow, for the unexpected thaw made muddy rivers out of the roads, and time after time the wheels had mired down. The men stayed at inns, but those were few and far between on this route. Chris had done well for the first few days until he had come down with a fever that rose so high it frightened Knox. The doctor he had found at a little town called Brantly advised putting the sick man in the hospital, but Chris adamantly insisted, "Knox, don't stop! If I go into a coma, haul me on, you hear?"

Knox had lost the argument, and for many days he traveled only a few miles, spending most of the time trying to get food down Chris. But then, as quickly as it had come, the fever left, and Chris was sitting up to eat—pale as death and thin as a stick, but alive.

It was three o'clock when they pulled into the village and asked directions to the Greenes' place. The little house had a high pitched roof, and sat back off the road in a big meadow at the edge of the village. Cows grazed in the warm sun, and chickens clucked and scattered as Knox got down and went to the door. At his knock, the voices he heard inside stopped, the door opened, and a small woman with reddish hair, flanked by two small children, framed the doorway. "Knox Winslow?" she asked.

"Yes, ma'am."

"I'm Anne Greene. Is Christmas able to walk?"

"Just barely. He's been real bad, Aunt Anne."

"Bring him in. We've made a place in the small bedroom.

When he gets stronger you two can sleep in the loft."

"Yes, ma'am. I'll get him."

He went back to find that Chris had gotten out of the buggy and fallen flat in the mud.

"You fool!" Knox cried. "Why didn't you wait for me?" He was struggling to get the man to his feet when a voice came from behind him.

"Let me help you." A big hand reached across, and Chris's body seemed to rise into the air. Knox turned to see a muscular man with a brown face and very white teeth. He was dressed in brown knee britches and a white linen shirt. "I'm Brother Greene, Knox. I remember you well."

Knox got on the other side of Chris, saying, "I don't remember you, Brother Greene, but my mother's told me all about you."

"Well, I tried hard enough to marry her, Knox—but she favored your father, and that was that. Come now, Christmas, let's get you inside." The strength of the preacher was tremendous, for he practically carried the tall man inside and put him on the bed in the small room.

"Thanks . . . Parson." Chris's face was wet with perspiration, and it was difficult for him to speak. "Try—not to be a bother—too long."

"God is a great healer, Christmas."

There was a moment of silence; then Chris answered painfully, "Got to be honest—don't believe in God."

Greene seemed not to have heard the words, for he simply looked down and said, "I remember well the night you were born, son. I hadn't eaten a bite except for a piece of mule meat for two days. And cold! Never was a place as cold as Valley Forge in '77!" His eyes seemed to glow and he clapped his thick hands together. "Then your pa came running up to some of us and hollered, 'I've got me a boy!' Somehow General Washington heard of it—through Adam, I expect—and I'll be dashed if he didn't send enough deer for a whole meal!" He studied the sick man's face, saying quietly, "Not many men got ushered into this old world by His Excellency, Christmas."

"Did that really happen?" Knox asked in awe.

"Sure did. This boy here met just about all the great ones—though he doesn't remember it—Lafayette, Von Steuben, Mad Anthony Wayne. They all came calling on Christmas Winslow that winter."

Chris lay there, staring up at the square face of Dan Greene. Finally he shook his head. "I don't seem to have been worth the bother, Reverend."

Dan Greene leaned down and patted the thin shoulder with a thick hand. "You're not finished yet, Christmas," he replied gently.

"Can I nurse him, Pa?"

Knox turned to see the small girl standing in the doorway, an awkward looking child—all legs, arms, blond hair, and huge brown eyes.

The minister reached out and pulled her close, saying with a laugh, "Be good practice for both of you. This is my daughter, Melissa."

"No, I'm Missy," the girl insisted. She left her father's side and came over and with one small hand pushed Christmas's hair out of his eyes. "You won't be sick long, Mr. Christmas. I'll get you all well!"

Christmas Winslow smiled at the child through feverish eyes. "Are you old enough to be a nurse?"

"I'm eight," Missy answered. "That's old enough." She looked up and said, "I'll take care of him. You two can go now."

Greene laughed and led Knox out of the room. "She's a prudent one, isn't she now? Eight years old and runs the house!"

"I—I don't know how to thank you, sir!"

Greene put a friendly hand on the smaller man's shoulder. "God's not going to waste a man like that, Knox!"

CHAPTER THREE

"LET THE MOUNTAINS KILL ME!"

★ ★ ★ ★

"Never saw a March this mild." Dan Greene got to his feet, stretched, then glanced at Knox, who was sitting with his head back against the mud-chinked logs, eyes shut and mouth open.

"What—what'd you say, Dan?" he mumbled. His eyes were red around the edges and his stomach grumbled loudly—so loudly that he flushed with embarrassment at the smile on Greene's face. "Guess something I ate didn't agree with me."

"You and Christmas both," Greene answered idly, but there was a note in his voice that made Knox look up quickly. The younger man had learned over the past two months that the bulky minister might move slowly, but there was nothing slow about his mind. Knox realized guiltily that the minister knew that the raw whiskey he and Chris had downed at the tavern in the neighboring town of Little Fork was his problem—not anything he might have eaten. Yet there was no condemnation in Greene's tone or manner.

A streak of rebellion ran through Knox; he wanted the preacher to accuse him so that he could defend himself. "Chris and me, we got drunk last night," he said defiantly.

"Did you, Knox?"

The mild answer only irritated the boy more, and he got to

his feet, the sudden move sending a blinding pain through his head. It was so severe that he involuntarily grabbed his head with both hands and uttered, "Oh, Lord!" His stomach heaved, and he stood there, struggling to keep from throwing up.

"Does Christmas feel as bad as you do?"

The question sent another surge of guilt through Knox, for he knew that his brother's health was such that he had no business drinking at all. The two months the brothers had spent with the Greenes had been good for Knox, but Chris had mended hardly at all. The fever that had nearly killed him kept coming back, and despite the good home cooking, he could not eat as he should. Better to say, he would not, for as soon as he was able to get about, he had taken to visiting the tavern on the south edge of town. It was a rough place, little more than a large shed with a dirt floor and only one small window. Knox had gone with him—reluctantly, at first. "Chris," he had protested, "this is a putrid place! Looks like every no-account in Kentucky comes here to get drunk and raise the Devil!"

"My kind of place," Chris had muttered. "You get out of here, Knox. I don't want to drag you down."

Knox had been determined to get Chris off whiskey; unfortunately, it didn't work that way. Knox had not been a drinking man, but the small tankard of ale soon grew to two; and before long he was reeling as drunkenly as his brother when they made their way home. Knox had vowed time after time to quit, and Chris urged him to stay away. But somehow, Knox always went back.

Now he was sick and miserable. "Chris is going to kill himself one day, with all this drinking."

"I think that's what he's got on his mind. Seen a few like that, just so miserable and unhappy they don't want to go on." Greene turned to face Knox, and there was pain in his brown eyes as he added, "The thing that scares me is—sooner or later Christmas is going to realize that it's a lot easier to put a gun to his head than to kill himself by slow degrees drinking whiskey."

"He wouldn't do that!"

"Why wouldn't he, Knox? What's he got to live for?" Greene started to say something else, but at that moment Caroline, his sixteen-year-old daughter, came to the door.

"Breakfast is ready." She was a slight girl, not over five four, and her thin face was usually sober. She was not a beauty, but there was a quiet dignity in her face that would have been attractive if she had not chosen to wear her brown hair pulled back in an ugly roll. She wore dark and shapeless dresses, with little or no ornamentation; Knox guessed that was her idea of what a Christian girl should look like. She never missed a service, and after the first time she had tried to talk to Knox about his spiritual condition, he had shied away from her.

Missy was a different sort, as full of life and color as her older sister was deficient in those qualities. Knox smiled despite his splitting headache as the long legs of the girl came down the ladder that led to the loft. As usual, her soft voice dominated the small house. From the time she got up to the time she went to bed, she was either talking, singing or laughing. He had been shocked the first time he had heard her humming some tunes that he knew had bawdy lyrics—drinking songs, actually. Missy was blissfully unaware of what she was doing, for like a mocking bird she merely copied whatever she heard.

"Come on, Christmas!" She always called him that instead of "Mr. Winslow" or "Chris," and she was laughing as she jumped from the rung of the ladder to the floor. She reached up to pull at the feet of the man who was carefully and painfully creeping down after her. "Hurry up, now! I helped Mama make you some corn hoecakes and battered eggs for breakfast—come on!"

Knox smiled at the sight of Missy's blond head bobbing as she pulled the man toward the rough board table that took up most of the room in the parlor. The child was the brightest thing he'd ever seen, already reading books that would have given a much older child problems, and was in the center of every activity in the house. She had made a big toy out of Christmas, bringing him his meals and fussing at his bad manners. She was the one thing that would bring a smile to the face of the sick man. Once she had said in the midst of her babbling, "My favorite man in the Bible is Mephibosheth." Chris had stared at her, then burst out laughing. "Are you sure this isn't a midget you've got here, Preacher? Mephibosheth—who in the world is that?"

"He's the little lame boy, Jonathan's son, the one that David was good to," Missy informed him. "Don't you like to read the Bible, Christmas?"

"I used to," he had muttered, and left the room abruptly.

Now she was standing beside him, spooning a heap of battered eggs onto his wooden plate.

"Not so much, Missy!" he said quickly. In spite of his sickly condition, he had a slight smile for the child. "You say you made these hoecakes?"

"Yes, but Caroline made the jelly. It's muscadine, and it's real good!"

He took a cake, smeared it with the rich jelly, and tasted it. "This is real fine, Miss Caroline," he said. "You're a good cook."

Caroline had been pouring coffee into Knox's cup, and he noted the trembling hand and the flush that rose to her cheeks at Chris's words. Knox looked at her curiously. She didn't answer Chris, but there was a nervous smile on her lips. *Can't be!* Knox thought. *This female preacher can't be falling for a wild man like Chris!* But he kept an eye on her as he went on eating, and soon was convinced that it was true. She wouldn't be the first preacher's daughter to get silly over a bad apple, Knox reflected. He could think of several cases of such with no trouble.

Chris picked at his food, seemingly unaware of the conversation around the table; but when he realized that Greene was talking to him, he listened carefully.

". . . a letter from your father last week. He said that Doucett and Conrad would be passing through—in fact, they got here late yesterday afternoon."

"Who are they?" Chris asked idly. He was sitting back in his chair now, allowing Missy to fuss with his hair—"fixing it," as she called it.

"Two of the men that work for the company," Knox spoke up. "They came . . . after you left." There was a slight hesitation as he avoided mentioning the circumstances of Chris's leaving. "Father said he's going to send them up the Missouri to open new territory."

"They better have their scalps on tight," Greene remarked as he took a huge bite of biscuit and washed it down with a swallow of milk. "Those aren't tame Indians in that part of the world." He considered Knox soberly and added, "Far as I can make out, there's nothing *but* wild Indians up in that part of the world."

"You're pretty well right on that, but Father says it's worth the risk. First fur trappers that go in will make a fortune! Guess those two can handle it," Knox said, shaking his head in admiration. "They've traveled everywhere—and done just about everything. Both of them have been all the way up the Missouri and have convinced Father that they know what they're doing—that we can be the first to set up a trading post there. Wish Father would let me go with them."

"I know Lawrence Conrad," Greene informed him. "We fought together with Paul Winslow in the old days. Conrad was a good seaman. Never thought he'd leave the sea for trapping, but Nathan says the man is one of the best." Then he added, "They want to see you while they're here—said for you to come by the tavern tonight."

"Sure wish I could go with them up the Missouri, but I know Father'd never let me. Guess that settles it!" Knox grumbled.

Missy had been standing patiently by Christmas's chair, waiting for a chance to speak. With a deep breath, she blurted out, "You both are invited to my birthday party—it's tomorrow, and Ma's going to make me a plum cake." She paused, then added as an afterthought, "And you can bring presents if you want to."

Chris grinned. "Presents? What sort of present would you like, Missy? It's better if you just come out and say what you want, you know. You're more likely to get it that way."

Missy clapped her hands together and her brown eyes flashed. "I want a finger ring, like Mabel Durant!" she exclaimed.

"Missy, that's a little rich for a preacher's daughter," her father gently chided.

"You against women wearing jewelry, Reverend?" Chris inquired.

"Well, I was a Quaker for quite a spell, and none of the women wore any jewelry—except wedding rings, of course—but I don't see any harm in it myself. 'All things in moderation,' the Bible says, but . . ."

Embarrassed, the minister dropped his gaze, and at once both his guests realized that Greene was not battling with his conscience but with his empty pockets. Chris said quickly, "Well, I'll come to your party, Missy, and you can bet I'll have some sort of pretty for you—can't promise what, though."

"Goody!" Missy jumped up. "Remember, you promised to take me over to see the baby coon that Emily's pa cotched her."

He got up and the two went outside, the child reaching up to hold on to his hand as they picked their way along the muddy road. Watching them disappear, Knox shook his head. "Strange the way he takes to that child. He never was much with kids, Chris wasn't. 'Course, he always did like the girls . . ."

"Did he—ever have a steady girl?" Caroline asked, a studied look of indifference on her face. She stopped cleaning up the table long enough to look out the window at the pair.

"Oh, girls always liked him," Knox shrugged. "He just went from one to another—like a bee buzzin' from flower to flower."

"What do you think he'll do—when he gets well, I mean?"

"He's not going to get well if he doesn't quit drinking," her mother murmured quietly.

Knox turned to Rev. Greene. "You said Father wanted me to come home, but I can't leave Chris here."

"Looks like you'll have to. Nathan was pretty strong about it. But we'll look after Christmas the best we can."

Knox said no more, but he went around with a frown all morning as he helped Dan with the chores. When Chris came back with Missy and went up to his room to rest, Knox finished milking the cow and climbed to the loft. "Father says I've got to come home," he told him.

"Been expecting it, Knox."

"I can't do it, Chris!"

"You can't spend the rest of your life nursing me."

"But—"

"Look—" Chris broke off when a coughing fit doubled him up; the hacking stopped only after Knox gave him a glass of water. "Knox, you see what's going on. I'm not going to get any better."

That very thought had haunted the younger man, but he had

pushed it out of his mind. Shaking his head, he argued heatedly, "Shut up, Christmas! You ain't going to die!"

"We all are." A cynical smile touched the lips of Chris, and he looked at Knox with a knowing look on his thin face. "That prison did me in, I reckon. I won't go home as an invalid, Knox. And I won't get better, even if you stay. Go home—I don't want you around to watch me die."

Knox shook his head stubbornly, but the more he argued the more adamant Chris became. Finally Knox left and went downstairs. Dan was gone; anyway, there was no point in talking with him. Knox struggled with the problem all afternoon, until Chris appeared wearing his coat and hat. Suddenly a thought hit Knox and he stood up. "I'm going with you," he insisted. "I want to see Frenchie and Conrad."

"Come on, then. But it won't change nothing. You still got to go home."

The faded letters on the weatherbeaten sign spelled out "The Red Horse," though the crude drawing underneath looked more like a buffalo. The two men pushed inside the tavern. Knox spotted the trappers immediately. "Frenchie! Conrad!"

A game was in progress at the far end of the long, narrow building, but at the sound of Knox's voice, a squat shape quickly rose up from the group. "By gar! Look here who eet ees—the leetle chicken!"

"I told you not to call me that, Frenchie!" Knox protested, but he was cut off when he was seized around the middle and heaved into the air by the burly halfbreed. Christmas had never seen an arm with more power.

"Cut that out, you idiot!" Knox yelled.

Frenchie Doucett was almost as wide as he was tall; and dressed in smoke-blackened buckskins, he made a formidable figure, his bulging muscles rippling with each move. The man's broad face and dark coloring disclosed his Indian heritage. His wide smile, under a jutting brow and deep-set eyes, flashed yellow teeth large enough to crack walnuts. Hovering over this giant was a smell of sweat and smoke that seemed to permeate the atmosphere around him.

"Your papa, he say for me to give you thees"—he dashed to

the wall and plucked a rifle from the peg it hung on—"and your fine mama—she say give you thees!" Thrusting the rifle into Knox's hands, the big man grabbed the boy in a bear hug and planted a noisy, smacking kiss right on Knox's forehead. Then he stood back and roared with laughter at the boy's embarrassment as a howl rose from the crowd.

"Ah, leave him be, Frenchie." Another buckskin-dressed man by the name of Canby stood up and walked across to put his hand on Knox's shoulder. "This here young coon is full of fuss—looks ready to charge an elephant!"

"Con!" Knox smiled, pushing aside the flash of anger Canby's remark had sparked in him. "You look as bad as ever."

"Ma health is shot, boy, for a fact. Don't reckon I'll last through more'n two or three clean shirts."

The man's mournful words contrasted sharply with his appearance: medium height and lean as a panther. His face had been exposed to the sun so long that his naturally fair complexion was now permanently sunburned, including his long nose. His bright blue eyes were striking against the bronze of his skin.

Christmas was puzzled. What could be wrong with the man? Greene had warned him that Laurence Conrad was an odd one, and now Chris could see why. Conrad was at least forty-five, Chris knew, for the former seaman had been a shipmate of Greene's in the days of the Revolution. But the youthful look in his eyes belied his stooped shoulders. And despite his talk of ill health, the man was obviously still strong and hale.

"Ah, you'll bury all of us, you old pirate!" Knox grinned. Then he looked down at the gun in his hands. Holding it up, he exclaimed, "Why—it's Father's Pennsylvania rifle!"

"Shore is," Con nodded, a gleam in his eyes. He looked at Chris. "There's another one jest like it for you, if you be Christmas Winslow."

Chris stood there, stunned. He had not expected anything from his father. Con moved to the wall, took the other rifle and slipped it to his shoulder, sighting down the long barrel. "Same weapon Colonel Morgan's men carried in the war—'cept these is better. Got them fancy double barrel on 'em."

He held the rifle out, and Chris took it, somewhat awkwardly. There was no way he could refuse it, not with the crowd watching him. These weapons, he knew, had been made by William Antes and were highly prized. They carried one hammer, two frizzens, and two sets of sights. This doubled a man's firepower: after the first barrel was fired, the hammer was drawn back and the second barrel could easily be swiveled into place. Chris was painfully aware that any man in the room would have loved to own such a handsome rifle. He could not say a word.

"I say we 'ave a drink on eet!" Frenchie said and moved to the bar and pounded on it with his ham-like hand. Knox had been determined to drink no more, but in the hours that followed he was carried along by Doucett's breezy manner. Glass after glass of raw whiskey found its way into the young man's stomach; and in spite of all his good intentions, he was becoming very drunk.

Soon Knox and Chris were pulled off to a corner table by Doucett. There the ebullient trapper told them of the fortune to be made going up the Missouri, punctuating his tales with sweeping gestures of his mighty arms. He and Con had made the trip once, and his eyes gleamed as he said, "Beaver? My leetle chicken—you nevair see no beaver teel you get to Yellowstone country—*n'est pas,* Conrad?"

"That's true. Heap of critters, right enough. Brought back all we could stack in four bull boats. Reckon the Winslows gonna be filthy rich if that keeps up . . ." The middle-aged trapper trailed off, then tried to cover up his rare outburst of optimism. " 'Course, we probably won't do as good this time," he sighed. "If the Mandans or the Flatheads don't scalp us, we'll probably go over the Big Falls—if we don't git sick and die on the way, that is."

Frenchie chuckled. "You know heem, Knox. He always say what bad theengs gonna happen—but they nevair happen!" He went on to describe in glowing terms the breathtaking mountains, alive with an abundance of game, until Knox cried out, "Frenchie, I gotta go with you!"

"Your pa, he said you can go next time," Con said. "Him and your ma, they say as how you need to light a shuck and git yourself home right off."

Knox was drunk enough to blurt out what he wouldn't have dared to admit if sober. "They think I'm a baby!"

"Well, they ain't far wrong, boy!" Canby had come to stand beside them, a thin smile on his lips as he stared at Knox. "Why don't you get along to your mama now and let the menfolks get to their gamblin'?" Ignoring Knox's angry stare, he turned to Frenchie and added, "How about it? You want to lose any more money?"

Instantly, Frenchie snapped up the challenge. "Come on, Con! We skin thees one, eh? Leave heem like wolves leave a buffalo—wis nothing but ze bones!"

The game went on into the night. At first, Canby won a great deal of money from Doucett and Con. Chris sat at the table with a glazed look on his face, taking a roll now and then, but mostly just drinking. Knox drank more of the raw whiskey as the disappointment of having to return home ate at him.

Meanwhile, the darkness fell, and lanterns were lit, but the game went on. The tide turned, and Frenchie began raising the stakes recklessly. His winning streak allowed him to win back all the money he'd lost, and a good deal more besides. But Canby was a poor loser, and the higher the stack grew, the more he stared across at the halfbreed with undisguised hatred.

Finally, the largest pot of the game came, and it was obvious that Canby was sure to win it. He raised the stakes several times and then said, "Got you beat this time, breed!"

"Let's see your money, Canby!" Frenchie demanded, shoving another stack of coins across the table. His small eyes gleamed as he added, "Now we see what kind of man you are!"

Canby stared at him, and then looked into the small leather bag he used for his money. "I can't meet you—all I have is on the table. Wait . . ." He pulled a small pouch from his pocket, saying, "You'll have to take these, breed."

He handed the pouch to Frenchie, who unfolded the leather; two large white pearls rolled into his huge palm. Chris was impressed—but Frenchie wasn't. "Me—I don't want thees!"

"You have to take 'em!" Canby argued. "They're worth fifty dollars!"

"Not to me."

Chris spoke up. "Con, you know my father?"

Con stared at him, then nodded slowly. "Reckon so."

"I want fifty dollars. I'll pay it back if I live. If I don't—tell him it's what my funeral would have cost if I'd come home to die."

Conrad smiled. "Reckon Mr. Winslow would stand to that." He reached into his shirt and pulled out a bag. He struggled with the leather cord that held the mouth shut, but it was in a tight knot. "Blasted thing—does it every time!" he muttered. Drawing his knife, he cut the drawstring, putting the knife on the table beside his winnings. Extracting a few bills from the pouch, he handed them to Chris.

"I'll buy the stones, Canby," Chris offered.

"Done!" Canby grabbed the money, and Chris took the pearls from Doucett and placed them carefully in the pouch he'd taken from his pocket. Canby threw his leather cubes, and smiled at the result. "Beat that, breed!"

Doucett carelessly picked up the cubes, tossed them to the table contemptuously—and a strangled cry rose from Canby's lips as he stared at the dice.

"Looks like you lost, Canby," Con remarked quietly. He saw something in the man's unwavering stare he didn't like, so he said smoothly, "Fellers, let's us be gittin' to bed. We got to be outta here early in the morning."

"Well, you got plenty of money for the trip," Knox grinned as Frenchie raked the cash into his sack. With a short laugh, Knox rose to his feet, which were a bit unsteady from the whiskey. He looked at Canby and remembered the taunt the man had given him. "Looks like you're the baby here, Canby. I never seen a man took so easy as—hey! Look out. . . !"

Even the quick-eyed Con was taken off guard. Maddened by his loss, Canby was driven over the edge by Knox's needling. He plunged his hand into his coat and pulled out a pistol. Doucett saw it and threw himself to the floor.

But Canby had other plans. The pistol lined up, and the click of the pistol being cocked hit the nerves of every man in the room. Knox was frozen in place, staring down the barrel of the gun, certain he was a dead man. Canby couldn't miss—not at this range.

The shot never touched him. The pistol exploded, but the ball went into the ceiling as Canby fell backward, grabbing at the knife that was buried in his chest.

Laurence Conrad had seen many things in his lifetime, but nothing like this. He told Doucett later, "That Christmas Winslow—he's like a cat! He seen that pistol come out, grabbed my Green River blade off the table and planted it smack in that feller's middle! I was still standin' there, tryin' to move—and you was still wallowin' under the table. I tell you, Frenchie, a strikin' rattler is slow as mud next to that feller!"

The room exploded into a chorus of shouts. The innkeeper rushed over from behind the bar and bent over Canby, who had grown still. When the man looked up, his face was pale. "He's dead. You fellers had best get outta here. He's got friends over in the next town—and a bad pair of brothers. They'll be comin' for you."

"Self-defense," one man spoke up quickly.

"His brothers won't buy that—and you know it, Griffin," the innkeeper said. "They're a rough bunch—set a store by family. Better git!"

"Come on." Conrad reached down and calmly jerked the knife from Canby's body, then pulled at Knox. They gathered their rifles and walked out of the tavern. When they were out of earshot, he said, "We gotta git you outta here, Chris!"

"Got nowhere to go—but you men don't need to hang around."

Knox protested, "I'm not leaving you—and that's final!"

They argued with Chris, but he only replied wearily, "I can die here as well as anywhere."

Finally Conrad said angrily, "Chris, you're gonna have to git away! It'll mean trouble for Rev. Greene if you stay."

That caught Chris's attention. "Hadn't thought of that," he admitted.

"Come home, Chris!" Knox pleaded. The violence of the scene had sobered him, and his eyes appealed more eloquently than words ever could.

"No, I'm not going home, and *that's* final!"

Con stared at him intently, then spoke. "Well, that leaves it up to us, I reckon. We'll load you in the wagon and take you up the Missouri. The Sioux will take care of you—and won't charge a cent for the buryin'!"

Chris lifted his head and allowed his thoughts to wash over him. Even this prospect was better than the humiliation awaiting him at his father's house. "I'm ready," he murmured softly. "Let the mountains kill me!"

"Reckon that's possible," Con nodded. A hard light glinted in his eyes as he added, "We're goin' into country that the Injuns got all staked out. In ten or twenty years, mebbe, there'll be a line of trappers in there, takin' out the beaver. Right now, though, you won't see a white face—and it's a better'n even chance that you'll lose your scalp." He shrugged. "Always that way, I reckon. First come, first served—but in this case, it's a heap more risky."

"If you go—I'm going too!" Knox told Chris, and the stubborn set of his jaw warned the others that he could not be dissuaded. "You leave me, I'll follow," he stated flatly.

"No time for arguin'," Conrad said abruptly. "Let's git outta here quick. Frenchie, you git our goods together."

Chris turned to Knox. "We'll have to tell the Greenes." The two hurried to the house. Dan was a light sleeper and came into the small room when the boys entered; his face tensed as Chris told him the story. Knox went to the loft to gather their things.

"You don't have to go. The law's on your side," Dan said.

"From what I hear, these folks don't wait for law." Chris lowered his voice so that his brother could not hear him. "I'm afraid for Knox, Dan. They'll kill him if we don't get away."

"But his folks—"

"He won't go up the river. I'll tell the trappers to take him back home after I'm gone."

Conflicting emotions flickered across Greene's face. "Pretty sure you won't make it, eh, Christmas?"

"No—but I want Knox out of this." He squared his shoulders and said, "I want to see Missy."

"Go on in. She'd never forgive me if I didn't let you say goodbye to her."

Chris went into the small room carrying a lamp, and at one touch the girl was wide-awake. "Don't wake Asa up," Christmas whispered.

"What's the matter?"

"I—I can't come to your birthday party, Missy, like I promised."

"Why not, Christmas?"

"Have to go away on a trip—but I brought your pretty." He set the lamp down and pulled the small leather pouch from his pocket. Removing one of the pearls, he held it out to her. She took it in her palm, and the yellow lamplight caught the stone, making it gleam like a living thing.

"Oh, Christmas! It's so pretty!"

He watched her face, marveling at the fine structure of her bones and the quick intelligence in her eyes. "Your father will have it made into a ring or a necklace. I hope you think of me sometimes when you wear it."

"Do you have to go?" she pleaded. "When will you come back, Christmas? And where are you going—is it a long way?"

"It's a very long way—but I'll be thinking of my nurse as I go, won't I? Now, go to sleep."

"Can I keep my pretty?"

"Sure."

Holding the pearl tightly in one hand, she reached out with the other, beckoning him closer. He knelt beside her and she put an arm around his neck. The touch of her lips was light as a feather on his cheek.

"It's the best birthday pretty any girl ever got, Christmas!"

Feeling a lump rise to his throat, he got up and left quickly and found Knox standing ready with their gear. "The wagon's here," he stated.

"Preacher, I won't try to thank you," Chris said. "I sure wish I knew how."

"I'll be praying for you both," Dan replied simply. "Don't give up on God, Christmas. He's not giving up on you."

Dan's promise to pray stuck in his mind as he and his brother left. Knox got on the horse that Frenchie was holding, and Chris climbed into the heavily loaded spring wagon Conrad had driven up to the steps of the cabin. As they pulled out of the yard, the trapper heard Chris say softly, "Now—let the mountains kill me!"

CHAPTER FOUR

SIOUX COUNTRY

★ ★ ★ ★

"Guess if you ain't died yet, we might as well haul you upriver and let the Sioux finish you off."

Con gave a final jerk on a rawhide thong, grunting with satisfaction at the heavily loaded canoe. Stepping back to the small fire, he looked down at Chris, who was frying venison in a blackened skillet. "The good Lord must love sinners, Chris; thought you was a gone coon more'n once comin' from Kaintuck."

Chris glanced across the fire at the wiry trapper and grinned. "Guess you and Frenchie had more to do with that than the Lord, Con. I'd be underground by now if you two hadn't piddled around and nursed me along."

The trek from Kentucky to St. Louis could be made in a week of hard travel by most mountain men. But as soon as the party was out of the shadow of the Canby brothers, Con had said, "I ain't feelin' too pert, Frenchie. My constitution's hurtin' a little. Let's slow down and hope it ain't nothin' fatal."

"Where are you hurtin', Con?" Knox had asked.

"Wal, now, I sorta feel bad all over more than I do in any partic'lar place—but if we jest take it easy, I reckon my juices will git all balanced agin. Time we git to the river I'll be ready for trouble."

His talk had not fooled anyone, Chris least of all. He realized that Con was deliberately slowing the pace so that Chris would survive. His plan had been successful. The warmth of spring had fallen across the land, and the fresh breezes breathed new life into the sick man's lungs. For the first few days, he sat in the wagon, but soon he was able to walk alongside or ride the fine horse that Frenchie had brought along. Game was plentiful, and Con had picked up a few tricks of cooking that stirred Chris's appetite.

The trapper had brought down two mallards one evening, gutted the birds with a single slash of his knife, and plastered the carcasses with mud from the river's edge. Scooping a hole in the sand beside the fire, he'd pushed the burning embers into the bottom of the hole, laid the clay-covered birds in, and finished filling the hole with sand and the remainder of the campfire.

Chris had dropped off to sleep; he'd been sleeping like a baby since he'd been on the trail. The fresh air and the warm sun put him out like a dead man, healing his body and resting his mind. Later Con woke him and offered him what looked like a melon; Chris was startled when he felt how hot it was, until he remembered. It was one of the birds. Gingerly rolling the clay ball about in his lap, he began cracking it with the hilt of the Green River knife he'd begun wearing. The clay broke off readily, the feathers adhering to each piece, so that presently there was exposed the smooth browned body of the roasted duck.

When he'd bitten into it, the abundant juices tasted so delicious that Chris had torn at the steaming carcass, working from one end of it to the other as if attacking corn on the cob. Con had grinned and said, "Reckon you're gittin' well, Chris. Yore natural selfish instincts are comin' around. You didn't even once ask if anybody else wanted a bite of that bird!"

That had been three weeks ago, Chris realized as he handed Con a rich steak of venison dripping with juice. He looked down the bank to where Frenchie and Knox were loading the last of the canoes with trading goods, bit off a chunk of steak, and added, "I thought I'd be dead by now and you could send Knox home from here."

Knox and Frenchie came back, leaving the four Indians they'd hired to paddle upriver, and the two finished off the meal. Fog was rolling off the river, and Chris peered through it, trying to see upstream as the two mountain men talked about the trip. Tribes, such as the Omahas, Poncas, Loups, Pawnees and Sauks, were named and discussed—which would be friendly or unfriendly, trustworthy or thieving, kind or murderous. Outlandish yet wonderful names of places fell from the trappers' lips, inspiring the young men's imaginations—Cheyenne River, Bad River, Grand Detour, Knife River. Knox drank in every word, interrupting once to ask, "How long before we get to Indian country, Con?"

"Oh, mebbe two-three weeks we might see a few Pawnees. Look, here's the way our stick floats." He picked up a piece of bark and traced the river in the sand, noting various posts and other rivers that flowed into the Missouri.

"First, we paddle up past the Cannonball to Fort Mandan; then, if we ain't been drowned or taken a Pawnee arrow in our livers, we go past where the Knife River drops in. If we ain't kilt by the time we git to where the Yellowstone heads in, we got to decide if we want to follow it or go on up the Missouri to the Milk—or mebbe even on to the Great Falls." He dropped the bark and stood up. "But we got the first mile to go 'fore we git anywhere. Chris, you go with Frenchie. Knox, you do your best to keep from fallin' outta that Crow's canoe—name's Bull Man. Let's go to the mountains!"

They broke camp, and the four canoes, heavily laden with trade goods, drifted away from shore. Chris insisted on taking a paddle, but after an hour he was exhausted. "I feel like dead weight, Frenchie," he groaned, looking at his blistered hands and gasping for breath. "You can't paddle me all the way to the Yellowstone!"

"Ah, you be much bettair soon, you bet!" Frenchie was sitting in the rear of the canoe, effortlessly steering the craft upstream with powerful strokes of his paddle. He paddled all day, and when they stopped for camp late that afternoon, Frenchie looked as fresh as he'd been at dawn.

After a quick supper of fish that had been caught by one of

the Indians, Knox and Chris rolled into their blankets beside the fire. "Chris—I'm a goner!" Knox groaned. "Thought I was fairly used to work, but I ain't worth a pin at this paddlin'."

"You did better than me, Knox," Chris said gloomily.

"Both you lads will do good," Con encouraged them, speaking with an optimism that was unusual for him. He tempered it with his usual prophecy of gloom. " 'Course, we're probably gonna have bad weather tomorrow—but the good thing about that is that when the storms come, the pesky Indians won't be out so much."

Knox groaned and rolled over, hoping to find a position that would ease all his aching muscles at once. "I don't know about that, Con—but I'm gonna keep up with that fool Indian tomorrow, or die trying!"

"You deed good for first time, Leetle Chicken," Frenchie chuckled. "You, too, Chris. Every day you do a leetle more. By ze time we get to Cabanne's Post—that ees on ze Platte—you be in good shape."

Neither Knox nor Chris believed Frenchie, but the next morning they rolled out, ignoring muscles that screamed with pain and hands that blistered, broke, bled, then blistered again. Each day was a red-haze of pain for both of them, and the incredible boredom of twelve hours of sitting in a cramped position nearly drove them crazy. Day after day passed, and they made more progress than they knew.

By the end of the second week, Chris could sit upright, though he could not paddle a full day. His hands were no longer like raw meat, but had hardened with the beginnings of callouses. He was filling out, too, with stringy muscles on his arms and shoulders. Even the cough that had plagued him for so long was gone. Con noticed that the young man's face was filling out. "You're on your way back, Chris. Don't reckon I'm gonna have the pleasure of makin' your funeral speech," he teased, adding, "at least, not till we get to Sioux country."

Day after day passed, each day making Chris and Knox a little tougher, a little wiser. He was going to enjoy this, Chris knew. The past few weeks had rekindled a spark inside of him. He could feel his instincts sharpening—and his love for the woods returning—even as his body regained its strength. Some days the group made as much as fifteen miles; other days, when the winds and currents were contrary, not more than three or four. But that did not matter; apart from the sun passing overhead, signaling them to make and break camp, there was no sense of the passage of time. Once they stopped at a little tributary just a few miles south of the Platte. Con knew of a little beaver stream that was thick with beaver, and he took Knox with him, hoping to get the best of him. Chris, already a fair woodsman, was left behind.

"There's beaver here—see them cuttings and that li'l dam?" They were standing beside a small pond, and Knox spotted a wedge of ripples starting close to the bank. The point of the wedge came toward him and formed a whirling head, then turned and went the other way, sending more tiny ripples running out and whispering along the banks.

Knox followed as Con slipped along the shore, walking softly on the spring mud, keeping back from the water. Finally he found a spot that pleased him and laid his traps down. He leaned his rifle against a bush, cut and sharpened a long dry stick and cocked a trap, and then stepped into the water.

"That's cold," he commented. "Snow fed." Stooping, he put the cocked trap in the water so that the surface came a hand above the trigger. Next he led the chain out into deeper water until he came to the end of it. Then he slipped the stick through the ring in the chain and pushed the stick into the mud, putting all his weight to it. He tapped it with his ax to make sure the stick was secure enough, and waded back to the bank. Cutting a willow twig, he peeled it, and from his belt took the point of an antelope horn.

The odor of the oil inside, strong and gamy, assaulted their noses as the trapper removed the stopper. He dipped the willow twig into the medicine, replaced the stopper, and put the container back before he stooped again and thrust the dry end of the twig into the mud between the jaws of the trap. The baited end stuck about four inches above the surface of the water. Backing up, Con toed out the footprints his moccasins had left. With his hands he splashed water on the bank, drowning out his scent.

"Wal, that's all there is to it," he grinned at the boy who was carefully watching the trapper's every move. "You take that fork, Knox, and I'll take 'tother one. Let's git the rest of them traps set 'fore dark."

The cold of the stream took Knox's breath, but he set all the traps assigned to him, and the next day Con took him to run the line. The pond was still, but the stick from the trap Con had set was gone. "Ain't never had a beaver pull my stick loose—though I s'pose they's always a first time." His keen eyes ran over the pond until he found what he was looking for. "There we be." He led the boy to a clump of willows and Knox saw the end of the chain. Con stooped and seized it, pulling the beaver from the bushes. "It's a she beaver—in her prime," Con announced with satisfaction.

The animal crouched down where the trapper had yanked it into the clearing. It did not try to run, but just cowered there, trembling and shivering pitifully. Knox, who had never seen anything like this before, felt a little sick, and was thankful when the trapper killed the beaver.

"Been at work on her leg," Con commented. Knox saw that a little more and the beaver would have chewed itself free. He recalled how his father had once told him that animals will sometimes save themselves by sacrificing a limb in this fashion.

Con showed him how to skin her, cutting off the tail and slashing the castor glands to remove the oil inside (to replenish his "medicine") before they went on to the rest of the traps. They got two more, and only when they got back to the camp did Con say, "Took you a little bad, killin' the critter?"

Knox had a sober look in his eye. "She was so . . . so . . . *alive*! Then we came out of nowhere, and now she's just a pelt."

Con nodded and said thoughtfully, "Don't do to think about it too much, Knox. Man's got jest a few days here to pleasure himself. Don't do no good to think about the end of the line."

Chris looked up from the broken trap he was fixing. "That's what I've been saying for the last few years," he observed. "But it's a sorry way to live."

"Wal, you can always go the way your pa went—and that Greene feller. Them Christians all say the best is yet to come—

and sometimes I can believe it. Judgin' by what I've seen so far, it won't be hard for the good Lord to improve on't!"

The trapping had depressed Knox; he noticed that his brother was also very thoughtful when they all pulled out three days later, burying the hides to be retrieved on the trip downriver.

They sighted Indians on rare occasions—shadowy figures in the distance—as they passed the mouth of the Platte, which Frenchie swore was ten miles wide and two inches deep. After that, progress was slower. The summer heat hit, bringing buffalo gnats, mosquitoes and sandflies. They passed through the Vermillion River country, and two weeks later came to the White River and then to what Frenchie called the Grand Detour—a weird corkscrew gorge in which two of their canoes nearly capsized. Only the weight of their gear stabilized the crafts.

When they were out of it, the party made camp. "Now," sighed Frenchie, "she get a leetle bit dangerous."

"Why's that?" Chris asked.

"Thees ees Sioux country. Bad!"

"Lots of beaver," Con commented, "but nobody's had the guts to go get 'em."

Chris lifted his head and stared at Con, but said nothing. Later he left the camp and walked along the bank, staring at the stars in the summer sky.

"Something's bothering Chris," Knox whispered.

"I'd say you're right," he replied. Lifting his voice enough so Chris would hear, he called, "Chris, you better not be wanderin' around like you was back in Boston. Them Sioux is downright hostile."

Chris acknowledged the man's warning with a nod, then came and stood beside the fire, his face sober in the flickering firelight. He was silent, but the other men knew that he was struggling to say something.

He looks good, Knox thought, watching his brother. *He's filled out and seems strong and well.* But there was a strange look in Chris's eyes that worried his younger brother.

Abruptly, Chris sat down by the fire. "I'm staying here," he announced.

The three stared at each other, then back at Chris. Finally Con spoke. "Stayin' here? What's that mean, Chris?"

"Means just that." Chris smiled at their stunned expressions and said, "Leave me a few traps. You three go on to the Yellowstone. You can pick me up when you come back next spring."

"That's crazy, Chris!" Knox cried loudly. "Ain't you been listenin'? This is Sioux country!"

"Boy's right about that," Con agreed slowly. "Ah shore wouldn't want to try an' make it around them devils."

They all began arguing with him, but he cut them off impatiently. "I'm staying here. You can't keep me from it, so just give me what I'll need."

"But—why, Chris?" Knox pleaded. "Things have gone so good—here you're almost well, and we'd thought you'd die. Now why do you want to stay here?"

"Don't know." Chris shifted, then shrugged his shoulders and spread out his hands. "I can only tell you I've got to find out what I am. If the Sioux get me, then I reckon that's the way it was spelled out. If they don't—why, maybe I'll get a handle on some things. But live or die—I'm staying."

Con looked across the fire, a thoughtful look in his eyes. "Every feller has to go the way his stick floats," he said. "I'd say you've picked a mighty rough way to find out about yourself, Chris, but if'n you make it through a season on these here Sioux grounds . . . wal, ah reckon there ain't no quicker way to find out what you're made of."

At dawn the canoes were loaded, and Knox stared unbelievingly at Chris, who was standing alone next to the small pile of belongings they had left him. Pulling around a bend, Knox lost sight of the solitary figure, and the tears filled his eyes, blinding him to everything else.

Con was alongside, and he saw the boy bend his head, and he tried to assure him. "Don't give up on that brother of yours, Knox! I been watchin' him pretty close, and if he ain't a first-class trapper, I never seen one. Moves around like a ghost, and that's about half the secret in Injun country. If'n he keeps his hair, he'll be a real mountain man."

CHAPTER FIVE

WHITE INDIAN

★ ★ ★ ★

Watching the last of the four canoes disappear from sight, Chris was filled with an overwhelming sense of loneliness. He had to fight an impulse to run after them. *Now's not the time for second thoughts, I guess,* he decided. Instead, he set about moving his gear to higher ground. As he picked up his traps and his other gear and entered the thick grove of beech and oak that grew fifty yards away from the river, he mentally mapped out his next move.

He knew his only hope was to keep his presence a secret from the Indians. It was a miracle they hadn't spotted him already. As he made his way toward the higher ground, the traps jingled, and he was sure he would never make it. From what Con and Frenchie had told him, the Sioux knew this territory better than he knew the back of his hand. Clearly, his chances of survival were small. By white man's standards he was an adequate woodsman, but he was only visiting this wild country; the Sioux were immersed in it, as a fish is immersed in a stream or lake. If he wanted to survive, he must to do the same—forget everything he knew of "civilization" and join their world.

That would be difficult—just learning the wilderness lore was enough. At the same time, he was motivated by the fact that if the Sioux caught him, all was over. They were notorious for their cruelty to captives; his one firm resolve was to kill himself rather than fall captive to them.

As he went deeper into the wilderness, he grew strangely elated, less fearful. *Must have lost my mind,* he grinned as he moved upward through the brush. *Probably going to get scalped by the Sioux—and I just don't seem to be rightly scared.* Then again, he always had loved a challenge, reveling in competition with other men, just as he had loved to gamble—and this was the ultimate gamble. Everything was reduced to its simplest elements: live or die. None of society's subtle pressures were important now. And despite his slender chances of survival, he was suddenly filled with the deepest sense of satisfaction he had ever known.

He buried the traps wrapped in a piece of deerskin he'd gotten from Con, carefully obliterating all signs of digging. Before he left, he took a quick inventory of his gear, including a fine bow and fifteen arrows he'd obtained from Bull Man in exchange for his own pistol. Although he was not an archer, Chris was determined to master this weapon, for here the sound of a pistol shot could very well bring his own death as well as his prey's.

He picked up his sparse store of supplies and moved farther back from the river, in the direction of the small tributary where he'd seen Con and Knox go to trap the beaver. By noon he had scouted the terrain without catching sight of Indians. So he ate a piece of meat, washed it down with the cold water from the stream, and moved back into the deeper woods. *Got to learn to sit still and watch,* he thought, and was startled to discover how difficult it was to sit absolutely motionless for thirty minutes. His muscles grew stiff and it was a struggle to prevent involuntary movements. He'd still-hunted squirrels often, and had learned to stand motionless so long that they'd practically run over his boots. But this was different. Now it was not his dinner at stake; it was his life.

He made a fireless camp that night, finding a natural cave on the crest of a lofty knoll. He could lie in the mouth of the opening and catch a panoramic view of the woods that fell off toward the river bottoms. On the backside rose a sheer bluff of sandstone that afforded good cover from any approaching enemy. He lay there long after the full silver moon rose, listening to the echoes of a wolf howling down by the river. The peacefulness around him soon lulled him into a dreamless sleep.

Every day for a week, Chris made a stealthy journey, spanning out in circles from the cave; and by the end of that time, he knew the terrain well. Moving carefully as a fox, he slipped from tree to tree and avoided the open spaces whenever possible. He would freeze in one spot, totally immobile, and wait until the animals and birds resumed their activities. He became an expert in waiting, in turning himself into stone, and many times he could almost have reached out and taken game with his hands.

The week ended, and then another, and time was reduced to its simplest form—the light was day and the darkness night. Constantly he scanned the forest and sharpened his skill with the bow. While studying the wild creatures, Chris often spotted Indians far off, but he always faded back into the deep woods. He found wild berries, and learned to tolerate the small mussels from the river.

The weeks turned to months, and he broadened his range, finding on one of his silent stalks a large Indian camp about fifteen miles from his cave. He went to the camp's outskirts frequently, studying their activities, risking death for the sight. After some time he could recognize some of them, for they lived in the open, outside of the buffalo hide tepees they used for sleeping. The young men often had contests—running, wrestling, mock wars or drills with war spears and tomahawks. Among these young braves there was one who stood out from the others. He was taller than the rest, and always won at any of the contests. He wore a single eagle feather and a knife in a yellow sheath, and it was obvious that he was of some importance in the tribe.

Several times Chris was nearly discovered. Once he avoided a hunting party only by climbing a tree; it had been too late to run. The Indians moved by, speaking to one another in their guttural language, and he could easily have dropped his knife on the tall young Indian with the eagle feather and the yellow sheath.

A week later Chris had hidden himself near a small stream,

waiting for a deer. When three deer stepped out of the woods into the small clearing, he fitted an arrow into the bow and carefully took aim.

Zipppp! An arrow shot out of the woods at a point just upstream from where Chris knelt, stunned. He could clearly see the shaft of an arrow protruding from the body of the largest buck. The animal fell to the ground, then sprang up, mortally wounded, leaving a scarlet trail as he ran into the woods. Immediately, a short, stocky Indian wearing only a breechcloth leaped up from where he had been concealed by a clump of willows and dashed off in pursuit of the wounded animal.

Chris found his hands shaking with fear for the first time since he'd come to the Sky Country; if he had loosed his own arrow, he would have been an easy mark for the hidden Sioux warrior. He kept his place, and soon the Indian came tramping back, the deer draped over his shoulders. As he passed within a few feet of Chris, he could smell the strong odor of smoke and sweat from the man steadily making his way in the direction of the enemy camp.

Finally Chris rose and started to leave, then hesitated. Out of curiosity, he backtracked to where the Indian had hidden himself. Looking across the creek, Chris could clearly see the tree he had stood beside, and with a shudder he realized he had been directly in line of the Indian's sight. *Guess I've graduated. If I can be so still that a Sioux can't spot me, I must be pretty good!*

He was moving away when something on the ground caught his eye. Leaning over to pick up the object, he found himself holding a smooth piece of bone with a crude picture formed by lines of gold. He could make out a figure of a deer and then he saw what must have been a man hunting a deer. "Kind of pretty," Chris mused aloud. "That brave will miss it—probably come back for it sooner or later." The form and workmanship pleased him, so he stuck it in his shirt and took it with him.

He left the area, heading due north. More weeks passed, and the Sky Country began to grow on him. The peaks rose sharply, jagged and rough and inhabited with goats of a sort he'd never seen before. Then he swung east and found his first buffalo in the flat plains. They were huge shaggy beasts, seemingly unaware of him, and he brought one down with an arrow. He ripped the tongue from the carcass and ate it raw, having heard Frenchie say it was the best bite of meat the world afforded. He spent the rest of that day and a few more skinning the animal, then cutting up the meat and spreading it out to dry. After it had dried he wrapped the jerky in the buffalo hide and took it back to his cave.

For the next two months he wandered all over the Sky Country, his skills growing sharper as his body grew into a piece of fine-tuned machinery, strong and wily as any mountain lion. The air grew colder, and one day he was surprised to feel a cold touch on his cheek. "Snow!" he said. "Winter's caught up with me. I better get back to my place."

By the time he got back to the cave a week later, an early storm had hit, and he made it just in time to avoid getting frozen. He had made the buffalo hide into a bed, and as the ground swelled with the weight of innumerable snowflakes that packed themselves into blankets five feet deep, he felt as if he'd come home, sitting before a small fire, cooking a tender doe.

For a week it continued to snow, but he was warm inside the cave, and the doe was enough to last for a while when he supplemented it with pemmican. He would stare out at the flakes swirling in the wind and let his mind drift back to the time he had spent at the Greenes'. He particularly missed Missy. If he ever returned, he'd decided to give her the medicine bone he'd found. It was the sort of thing she would like; he could picture her eyes shining brightly as he gave it to her.

By the time he'd finished the deer, the storm had stopped. He put on a pair of winter boots he'd made out of a deerskin, rough but sturdy enough to keep the wet off his feet. Slipping some dried buffalo meat into his pocket, he hesitated. Then, for the first time, he picked up the rifle and left the cave, purposing to bring down a deer. It was risky, but he did not think he could get close enough for an arrow kill. He felt exposed as he moved down the slope—the only dark shape in that white world, the only motion in a frozen world of white stone.

The cold pierced him, but he grew accustomed to it. He broke through the crust in places, but for the most part it held his weight as he moved toward the river where he thought the animals might be seeking scrub leaves and willow bark.

He saw no game, nor did he see any sign of Indians. The snow was smooth and unbroken as he made a trail. *An Injun could follow my tracks back to the cave,* he thought. That fact troubled him, and he determined not to return until the snow melted or his trail was covered by a fresh snowfall. Finally the afternoon came on, and when the shadows of the trees grew long on the snow, he gave up his hunt. "Least I got this pemmican," he muttered. "Tomorrow I'll try upriver."

It was almost dark. Chris munched on the buffalo jerky while he hunted for a dry spot to get a little sleep. Suddenly he heard a sound that made every nerve in his body tingle—the sound a grizzly makes when it charges, and it was close!

He whirled to his left and through a screen of dead willows, he saw an Indian spring up, drawing his bow in the direction of the roar. The brave was facing away from Chris, seemingly unshaken by the frightening sight of a charging mammoth grizzly—its head down, revealing that unmistakable hump—not twenty feet away from where the man stood.

An arrow won't stop that critter! Chris thought frantically. Horrified, he watched the arrow leave the Indian's hand and bury itself in the chest of the bear; it didn't even slow the creature's pace. The wounded animal attacked the brave, who tried to avoid the charge by throwing himself to one side; but one swipe of the grizzly's paw caught him on the leg and sent him spinning through the air, landing on his back in a mass of hackberry bushes. He struggled to his feet, but the bear was over him, rearing high in the air, with his bloodied paw poised for another blow.

Without thinking Chris raised the rifle and sent a ball through the head of the beast, who fell to one side—but not before he had given another blow to the helpless Indian.

Quickly Chris swiveled the second barrel into place, then ran to where the bear lay still, with the Indian partially hidden underneath. The injured man raised his bloody head to stare at his deliverer. The claws had raked away part of his scalp—three crimson furrows seeped blood so rapidly it ran into his eyes.

Quickly Chris wiped the blood away, but it only welled up again; the cuts ran very deep. The brave struggled to crawl out from under the bear, but Chris stopped him. Pushing the carcass off, Chris could see the Indian's leg was severely hurt. With each pulsebeat the white snow turned red, and Chris knew that the big artery in the groin had been sliced.

Chris looked into those obsidian eyes and saw resignation—clearly the young man expected death. With a start, Chris recognized the tall young man with the yellow sheath. Even now the single eagle feather, covered with blood, lay on his head.

The eyes were black as night, but there was not a trace of fear in them as the young warrior stared back at him. He was only a couple of inches shorter than himself, Chris guessed, with a body that was sleek and powerful, like a panther's. With dismay Chris watched as the man's awful wounds poured his life out on the pristine snow.

Without warning the Indian raised his hands and started to chant —Chris had heard of the death song that Indians sang just before they died. Considering his options, Chris realized that if the Indian's wounds weren't closed immediately, he'd die from loss of blood.

Quickly, Chris leaned the rifle against a tree and moved beside the Indian who was trying to sit up. Taking him by the shoulders Chris forced him to the ground. The death song broke off, and the Indian struggled wildly. Chris's hands slipped on the wet arms and he hollered, "Be still, blast you!"

The voice seemed to take all remaining strength out of the brave; obviously the loss of blood already had done much damage. He lay back, his black eyes like twin dark tunnels as he watched the white man. Chris reached into his pouch and whipped out a bit of cloth and made a pad of it, putting the wad over the groin wound, then pushing down hard. He said nothing, and neither did the Indian. The silence was eerie as the deadly enemies stared into each other's eyes. There was a confused look on the face of the young Sioux.

"Here—you got to hold this, Injun!" Chris said, and saw that his words were at least partially understood. He took the Indian's hand and held it over the artery, pressed it down, and said,

"Hold that—or you're on your way to the happy hunting ground!"

While the brave watched, Chris pulled down a pouch he always carried on his shoulder on hunting trips and extracted the needle and waxed linen thread. Threading it, he checked the flow of blood and grunted with satisfaction. "Good!" Then he held up the threaded needle, and motioned to the Indian's head. "Got to patch you up. Going to hurt." He saw a quick intelligent glint in the eyes of the man, and there was a faint nod of the head.

Chris had never sewn up a wound, but he knew it had to be done or the man would be terribly deformed, for the scalp had been pulled forward so far that even the area close to his eyes was affected. There was no way to be gentle, so he went at it as best he could, pulling the matted scalp back and mercilessly driving the needle through the flesh. His own lips grew pale and perspiration beaded his forehead, but the Indian never flinched at what must have been excruciating pain. The ebony eyes watched him in an unnerving fashion as he worked, and Chris grew nervous at the stare. Finally he drew the last stitch and tied an awkward knot. "That's the best I can do—but it's better than having your scalp around your chin!"

The Indian said nothing, but stared silently at him. Chris looked at the wound that had cut across the young man's thigh and groin. "Bleedin's almost stopped." He pulled the blood-soaked rag away carefully and said, "Time for some more fancy needlework."

He sewed up the gashes in the leg, then checked the artery and was relieved to see that it was not bleeding at all. *Cold froze it, most likely,* he mused.

Chris stood up and wiped his hands on his shirt before he put the needle and thread away. He turned to look at the man. It was almost dark, but he could see that the Sioux's face was gray, and the eyes were glazing over.

"Got to get some kind of fire or you'll freeze to death," he said huskily. He pulled the Green River knife and began skinning the huge bear. He had never dressed a bear, but he observed grimly, "Just like a coon—only bigger." The knife was razor sharp, and despite his awkwardness he managed to get the pelt free, then turned the fur side up on the snow and carefully moved the wounded man on top of it. He pulled the excess over the man, and saw that the young warrior had finally passed out.

"Lost a heap of blood," he muttered. "Got to get him warm and get something into him."

He slashed away at the carcass of the bear and came up with what looked like the liver. Next he pulled the bearskin back and lifted the Indian's head up. The eyes opened and he accepted the raw meat without a word, chewing it methodically, all the while watching the white man intently.

Chris stayed awake all night, keeping up the fire and giving the wounded man a bite of liver from time to time, plus frequent drinks from the river. By morning he could tell that the Indian was becoming feverish.

He knew very little about wounds, but all day long he sat nearby, trying to keep the Indian from throwing off his covering in his delirium. Chris was afraid the brave would tear his stitches out as he thrashed wildly around, so he checked the groin wound often to be sure the bleeding hadn't started. By nightfall, he was exhausted, but he dared not sleep for fear that the injured man would need him. Consequently, he spent another night watching the restless brave. The next day was little better—until that afternoon when the eyes of the Sioux opened and he said something in a faint voice.

"What's that?" Chris asked urgently, but the eyes closed and he said no more. But that seemed to be a turning point, for the fever broke, and although Chris slept fitfully that night, when he woke up the next morning, the Indian was staring at him. He had crawled out of his bearskin and was sitting against a tree, his face pale but his eyes sharp, not dulled with fever.

"Well!" Chris grunted, pulling himself up stiffly. "Guess you decided not to die."

"Not die."

The words hit Chris like a blow, and he cried, "You speak English!"

"Little bit."

Chris stared at him, then pointed to himself. "Chris," he said, with a questioning look at the other.

"Running Wolf."

"Well, now, here we are chattering like a couple of fox squirrels." The young man's silence told Chris that the Indian brave had not understood the words, much less the humor. For months Chris had not spoken to a soul, and his speech seemed rusty. He covered his awkwardness by going to the carcass and hacking off two large chunks of meat. He rammed the meat on a sharp stick and pushed it over the glowing coals of the fire. Soon the two were eating the roasted bear.

They ate silently until finally Running Wolf paused and looked across at the white man. "You not kill me."

"Nope."

"Why?"

"You done nothing to me."

The simplicity of the answer puzzled the Indian, and he remained silent for a long time.

Running Wolf said no more, and soon he went to sleep, but it was not a fevered sleep. All day long he napped, waking only long enough to eat and to drink a great deal of water. He tried to stand, but found he could not walk. He stared down at the stitching in his leg and said with just a trace of humor in his black eyes, "Chris sew good—like squaw."

"Better be glad I do. It's all that kept your spirit inside. You'd be in the spirit land, Running Wolf, if this squaw hadn't sewed you up like an old moccasin!"

"Yes." The word carried no emotion, but there was a glint in his eyes as Running Wolf spoke.

Two days went by and each day the Sioux got stronger, but he was still too sore to walk. During that time, the two men carried on a conversation of sorts, with Chris picking up many words of Sioux. Running Wolf would listen for long periods as the tall white man spoke. The brave said little, only staring at Chris as if trying to understand.

On the fourth morning Chris awoke to find himself ringed by a silent circle of Sioux warriors. He glanced toward the tree where his rifle had rested, to find it in the hands of a short brave.

Running Wolf was awake, silently watching the reaction of the white man.

Tales of Sioux cruelty to captives flashed through Chris's mind, and he got to his feet, pulling the Green River knife from his belt. He was determined to die fighting. The short brave with the rifle said something to Running Wolf, and laughed roughly at the answer. He raised the rifle and Chris looked down the bore.

The others fell silent as Chris stood there, holding the knife. He was not afraid of death, though he had feared torture, as any man would. He looked over the bore at the man holding the rifle and spoke to him evenly. "You lost your medicine, Injun."

A puzzled look spread across the brave's face, and he glanced at Running Wolf, who spoke a few words in translation. He answered and lowered the rifle slightly. Running Wolf said, "This Four Dog. He say how you know him lose medicine?"

Chris reached over, opened the pouch and took out the bone charm. When he held it up a mutter of surprise arose from the group; Four Dog gave a sharp cry, abruptly shifting the rifle to point at the ground.

"I could have killed you, Four Dog, when you killed the deer by the fork in the spring. I let you live, but I took your medicine. Now it is yours again."

Four Dog stared at him, then swept the circle with a quick glance. He reached out slowly and took the charm. He said something with a tone of wonder, and Running Wolf smiled—the first time he had done so since Chris pulled him from under the bear.

"You are big medicine!" Running Wolf translated. "First, you save life of the son of Chief of The People. You kill the Father Spirit . . ." (Chris later learned that this was their name for the great grizzly) ". . . and take big medicine away from war chief." Running Wolf said something in Sioux and a mutter of agreement went up. Several of the group began cutting saplings to make a travois to carry the wounded man as Four Dog and Running Wolf engaged in earnest discussion, looking often toward Chris, who stood silently by.

Finally the travois was made and tied to one of the horses

that had been brought in from the woods. Running Wolf hobbled over to it, got in, and looked up at Chris. "You come with us." When he saw the question in the blue eyes of the tall man, he added, "You one of The People now. You white Indian!"

Four Dog carefully handed the rifle to Chris, then stood back, his eyes solemn and watchful as he fingered the medicine bone. There was a sudden flurry as two of the Indians appeared, mounted and leading other horses. Four Dog motioned to a short thick bay, which Chris mounted, and they moved out across the snow toward the camp.

A thought crossed Chris's mind, causing him to smile. *Wonder what Knox and them mountain men would think if they saw me now?* Running Wolf, facing Chris in the travois, studied his smile and wondered at the strange ways of the white eyes.

CHAPTER SIX

THE RAID AND THE REWARD

★ ★ ★ ★

The winter of '99 ravaged the land like a wolf, but finally the last of the ice melted under the warm March breezes. Running Wolf had been slow to heal after his wrestle with the grizzly. The right side of his face was pulled up as a result of the terrible head wounds, and the scars from the stitches still showed white through the bronze of his skin, but he still had his scalp. The leg had healed slowly, and Chris spent many of the long winter days and nights in the injured warrior's tepee, for the two had become fast friends.

Chris had brought in game with the long rifle when famine threatened to destroy The People; this, along with his feat of killing the bear and stealing the medicine of Four Dog, had placed him in a peculiar position for a white man. The Sioux called themselves "The People" as if they were the only race in the world—as if none of the others really mattered. Chris had never heard of a white man being allowed to live in the Sioux society, although young white children were sometimes taken captive and allowed to be a part of a slave class. In any case, no one could remember a white eyes becoming one of The People as Chris had.

He picked up the language quickly, for there was no one

except Running Wolf who spoke English, which had improved during their relationship. In addition to his hunting prowess, it was quickly discovered that Chris was one to reckon with at most of the tests of strength and endurance.

He was an honored guest in any tepee, and by the end of the first month, he could name every brave and most of the women, not to mention a great many children with whom he was a great favorite. Unlike the men of the tribe—who never seemed to notice the smaller children—the white warrior often joined them in their games, amused at how shocked the warriors were to see him rolling around with a host of small children screaming and clinging to his limbs.

"Bear Killer is a strange man," Four Dog said once as he sat along with Running Wolf and the chief of The People, Red Hand.

"All white eyes are crazy," Red Hand mused.

Running Wolf watched the game with amusement. "I wish all white eyes were crazy like Bear Killer. We'd have starved—many of us—without his long rifle."

"True," Red Hand admitted. "But he is not one of us. If war came with the white eyes, he would turn and be our enemy."

The other two were quiet, for they had both considered this very thing. The big white man had been one of them during the frozen winter, but what would he do when the earth warmed and The People had to fight as they always had?

The answer came a few weeks later. Grey Bull, the medicine man, announced that it was time for two of the young men to be admitted to the rites of manhood. "Tomorrow, Little Crow and Sixkiller will hang at the pole."

Although Chris could now communicate fluently in the Sioux tongue, he had never heard this term before. When voices rose at Grey Bull's words, he leaned closer to Running Wolf, seated beside him. "What's that mean—hang at the pole?"

"Hanging at the pole is the way a young boy becomes a full-fledged member of The People." Suddenly Running Wolf twisted his head and studied Chris. A thought had flashed into his mind, but he said nothing until the two of them had retired to his tepee.

Running Wolf's wife, a pregnant girl of about fifteen named Still Water, had supper waiting for them. She was a quiet girl, at least in public, but Chris had already discovered a streak of humor in her. As soon as she lost her awe of the white man, she had begun a campaign to fit him with a wife. Running Wolf was amused by her efforts. "Women are all alike—can't stand to see a man without a woman."

Hungrily Chris devoured the stew Still Water had prepared. She squatted beside the fire in order to refill his bowl before she spoke in coaxing tones. "You sleep cold, Bear Killer, and you have no lodge." She looked over the pot she was stirring with a gleam in her dark eyes. "I find you nice young girl. You sleep warm, eat good."

Chris grinned at her, his teeth white in the midst of the reddish beard that came down to his chest—a wonderfully luxuriant beard that was a source of amusement for some of the men of the tribe, though others were openly envious. "Guess I was born to sleep cold, Still Water. No woman would put up with me."

"Little Antelope would not run away too fast," she said, smiling into the pot.

Running Wolf spoke up angrily. "Be still, Woman! Bear Killer is not one of The People. He will go back to his own in the spring."

Chris gave him a quick look, trying to read the wooden features of the other. He shook his head, saying, "I may leave here, Running Wolf—if I'm no longer welcome—but I don't want to go back to my own people. I like the way I'm living now."

Running Wolf considered that, and then he put his hand on Chris's shoulder—a rare gesture that made the white man look up. "You could hang at the pole," he said quietly. "I would like for my brother to be one of The People."

Chris stared at him, and a strong desire to be a part of the tribe rose in him. "If I would do that—hang at the pole—would I be permitted to stay with The People?"

"It would give you a chance to prove yourself—but it is a hard thing, Bear Killer. Many men cannot do it."

"What does it mean—'hang at the pole'?"

Running Wolf pointed to several marks on his chest. "You see these scars? They come from hanging at the pole. The medicine man cuts into the muscles and ties rawhide thongs through the wounds. Then the young man is pulled up to hang in the air until he breaks the skin and falls to the earth. Sometimes the flesh is too strong—and they have to be taken down. Some never do it."

Chris said no more, but for a long time that night he lay awake, thinking about it. He had adjusted to life among the Sioux far better than he had dared hope—but this thing was the ultimate challenge. *If'n you make it through a season on these here Sioux grounds . . . reckon there ain't no quicker way to find out what you're made of . . .* Con's words rang in his ears.

In that moment he made up his mind to do it.

The next morning he said nothing to Running Wolf, but no surprise registered on Wolf's face when Chris stepped forward to join the two young men who were to be initiated that day. A murmur swept through the crowd when he moved toward Grey Bull, but it was a glad sound, and it made Chris smile proudly as he stood there. He noticed one very old man and a young girl standing beside Running Wolf. She was the prettiest squaw he'd ever seen, far slimmer than most, with eyes that were a light gray instead of the usual brown. Her features were finer and more delicate, so he knew she had white blood.

Grey Bull stared at the white man, then glanced toward Red Hand, who nodded slightly.

The ceremony took place under a large oak with strong limbs branching out about twelve feet from the ground. The pain was fierce when Grey Bull punched holes in the muscles of Chris's chest; and when he was hauled up, he felt as if a dozen knives were slicing him to pieces. The other two men were soon hanging beside him, and the ordeal began.

Later, when it was over, Chris could not remember the pain. It was as if he were outside his own body observing the spectacle. All day they had hung there, twisting slowly in the breeze, and the faces that turned to look up at him were burned in his memory. They kept well back, for it was to them a sacred thing, but he saw them clearly—especially the sharp features of Running Wolf, who stared at him without a flicker of emotion.

He heard everything going on around him as well, for it seemed that his senses had sharpened. That night as the cool breezes played over his body, he looked up, and it was as if he had never seen the stars so sharp and clear. Each of them was a separate dot of light, with its own shape and color, distinct from all the others.

Gradually Chris grew weaker. When he saw that one of the young men had succeeded in breaking free, he renewed his efforts, but his muscles were too thick and he could not tear loose. The next day the other young man fell heavily to the ground and was taken away, which left Chris alone. It was a long night.

The next morning he was not fully conscious any longer, and only faintly heard the voice that pleaded, "Bear Killer! Give up! Let me cut you down!"

But Bear Killer would not give up, and shook his head adamantly. With a great convulsive leap he jolted his body high, feeling the flesh tear as it came back down. He fell to the ground in a dead faint.

When he regained consciousness, he was in Running Wolf's lodge. By the light of a tallow lamp made of buffalo horn, he saw the face of the Sioux staring at him silently. The smell of bear grease was overpowering, and he knew that his wounds had been cleansed and plastered with it.

"You did well, Bear Killer."

Chris suddenly smiled and asked, "Am I one of The People?"

"You will be—when you steal the horse of one of our enemies." Running Wolf smiled, then added, "Every warrior wants to go on a raid with Bear Killer. You hung on the pole longer than any man ever did. You are good medicine."

"When do we steal these horses?"

"As soon as you are well."

The ordeal had taken more out of Chris than he thought. To make matters worse, one of the wounds in his chest became infected. He tried to ignore it, but Running Wolf shook his head, saying, "Bad wound." Still Water tried every remedy she knew, but in three days the wound was festering and he was running a fever.

Grey Bull came in and shook his rattles over Chris, but the next day it looked worse. Chris was lying on a buffalo rug and was burning up with fever. He heard Running Wolf and Still

Water arguing about something, but he couldn't wake up enough to make out what the argument was about. When he woke up he felt a cool hand on his chest, and opening his eyes he looked into the face of the young girl with the gray eyes.

She had a small knife in one hand and was about to do something to his wound, but stopped when his eyes opened. "I am White Dove," she said quietly. "I will make you well."

He later heard that the girl had a reputation for treating sicknesses that made Grey Bull rage with jealousy. Most of the Indians would send for the old man for the sake of his feelings, but often as not it was White Dove that came by later and treated them.

"I will have to open the wound and clean it out," she told him. Then she smiled. "It will hurt very much—but I have seen the courage of Bear Killer."

"Do it," he answered. As she began to work on the wound, he studied her face, which was very close to his own. The white blood was evident in her coloring—a smooth light copper—and in her fine features. Her nose and lips were much thinner than those of most squaws. She had the high cheekbones of the Sioux, but there was a roundness to her face, a fullness in her cheeks, that was unusual. There was a bronze sheen in her dark hair when the sunlight hit it, unlike the jet black hair of Sioux women. Her hair, thought Chris, and those strange gray eyes, made her one of the most strikingly beautiful women he'd ever seen.

Even the bulky elk robe she wore could not hide her trim figure, softly rounded by womanhood. Her neck was smooth and firm, and the hands were slender with tapering fingers.

She cleaned the wound deftly, then dipped her hand into a small clay pot and rubbed something cool and strong-smelling on his chest. The heat of it made him break into a feverish sweat.

"You will sweat the fever out tonight. This will make you sleep." She gave him a bitter-tasting drink and left the lodge.

"You will be better now." Running Wolf had been watching from the far side of the tepee. "White Dove is the real medicine man of The People."

"Who is she?"

A cloud passed over Running Wolf's eyes. "She is the daughter of my father's sister. She has been away since you came to The People. Her medicine is needed in other camps as well." He looked at Chris soberly. "Her father was not one of The People, as you saw."

"Who was he?"

"One of the white eyes who was captured as a child in a raid. When he grew older, he was made a slave. To our shame, the woman bore his child."

"What happened to him?"

"He was killed when the child was born. Everyone saw it was not one of our children."

"Her mother?"

"She died." The words were curt, forbidding any further question. "Sleep now, and you will soon be strong enough to take horses from our enemies."

The raid did not take place for three weeks, and Chris saw White Dove often. While he recuperated she came every day to Running Wolf's lodge to bring the herbal drink that made him rest and to apply the salve to his wounds. Later when he was able to walk he often encountered her as he wandered through the camp, and they would talk.

She was a bright girl who laughed easily, and she cast admiring glances at him when she saw the way he treated the children who constantly flocked around him. She was curious about him, as they all were; but it soon dawned on him that she was more vitally interested than the others because of her parentage. Though half white, she knew nothing about her father's people, and she would sit with him beside the small river as he fished, asking question after question about his life and about the land he came from.

One morning she asked, "Did you have many wives in your country?"

"Why, no," he replied with a smile. "I didn't even have one."

"Why? Is there something wrong with you?"

Her directness caught him off guard, and he laughed out loud. "Well, lots of reasons, White Dove—but mainly because I never loved a woman enough to marry her."

That brought on a barrage of other questions about courtship and marriage—clearly, marrying for love was a new concept to the girl.

The next day, late in the afternoon, they were walking beside the stream; he was carrying a small string of fish, and the air was still and warm.

"Tell me more." She stopped him by taking his arm and pulling him to sit beside her on a log. Her face was piquant in the red light of the sunset, and she said, "It is not this way with our people. If a man likes a woman, he goes to her father and offers horses. If the father thinks it is a fair trade, the woman is given to him."

"But what if she doesn't like the man?"

The question baffled her. "Not like him? She will belong to him."

Chris stood up, and she rose with him. Looking down at her, he smiled. "Well, where I come from, there's a lot more to it than that. Lots of visiting and kissing and—"

"Kissing? What is that?"

Impulsively he leaned over and planted a gentle kiss on her soft lips. "That is kissing, White Dove."

She blushed and touched her lips, then shyly looked up at him. "Does that mean you want me for your woman, Bear Killer?"

"Well . . ." He had been strangely stirred by the kiss and had a hard time forming a reply to her question. "You're a beautiful girl, White Dove. Any man would want you."

Her eyes dropped to the ground as she said simply, "No one wants me. No young man has ever come with horses to my grandfather."

With some discomfort Chris realized that it was because of her white blood, which the Sioux would see as a shame—no matter how well they had accepted him. "Some warrior will come one day," he said quietly.

"No." She walked quickly away, and he followed. The next few days, she was much quieter around him, and he thought of her most of the time. Once he tried to question Running Wolf, but without success; clearly, he would get no answers from this source.

The days passed, and by the time Four Dog led the war party out of the camp, the young men were bursting with excitement. Running Wolf had also come, but on a raid it was Four Dog who must be obeyed. This was made plain to Chris, who merely nodded.

It went so well that everyone was jubilant as they returned home. The Pawnees had been taken off guard; The People had killed at least five of their hated enemies and taken over twenty horses. Chris had gone mostly for the experience—until the Pawnees launched a counterattack, driving two young Sioux into a trap. In order to release them, Chris had been forced to shoot one of the Pawnee warriors with his rifle. His strange weapon with the long shot unnerved the Pawnee, who fled at once. On their way back to the camp, Four Dog came close and said, "You did well, Bear Killer. Our young men would have been killed if you hadn't driven the Pawnees away."

"Didn't do much. Rifle convinced them."

"One of those braves is my brother's son. He will be a great warrior. You will take two of the best horses."

So it was that Chris found himself with two fine horses, and the reputation of a hero as well.

"Now you can buy a squaw," Still Water whispered delightedly. "Take Little Antelope. She likes you."

But the white warrior was not listening, for on the way back from the raid, Chris Winslow had come to a decision. He never wanted to go back home—and the way to stay with The People was to take one of their women. As to whom that would be, Chris already knew which one he wanted.

The next morning when White Dove's grandfather went outside his lodge, his eyes opened wide to see two handsome horses—held by Bear Killer, his blue eyes bright in the morning sun.

White Dove heard her name called and came outside. She stopped dead still, staring at the horses, and at Chris. Then she nodded and said, "I will go with you and be your woman."

The match pleased no one, for everyone looked on Chris as good medicine—but now he was tied to a woman who was a symbol of shame to The People.

As the two lay in the lodge that night, White Dove tried to explain why the Sioux felt that way, but he would not listen. "I am Bear Killer, and you are White Dove, my woman. I don't care about your father or your mother. It's you I love."

Her hands caressed his face, and she whispered shyly, "I feel such—such love for you!"

He knew how difficult it was for a Sioux woman to say those words, and he held her close. "I'll always love you, White Dove!"

CHAPTER SEVEN

THE HOMECOMING

★ ★ ★ ★

It was almost dusk when the heavily loaded beasts plodded wearily into the corral bearing the sign WINSLOW FUR COMPANY over the gate. The three men pulled the huge bundles off the animals and wrestled them into the frame warehouse, then fed the horses and turned them into the small corral.

"Voila! And now, I got me a beeg thirst," Frenchie said. He shot a look at Knox and added, "You bettair go tell your family. We talk wis your papa tomorrow."

"All right," Knox nodded glumly. He left them arguing over which saloon to go to, and chose a frisky young buckskin from the corral. By the time he rode up to his home, the spring peepers were chirping loudly from the stream nearby and yellow lamplight streamed into the darkness from the windows of the house. As he got off the horse, he heard his mother cry, "It's Knox!" The announcement was followed by the sound of pounding steps on the porch where the family usually sat after supper.

The next instant he was almost knocked off his feet by his seventeen-year-old sister Judith as she flung her arms around him. Then his brothers George and Alex joined in by giving him enormous bear hugs. They were a demonstrative family. Knox felt his eyes get misty as the others moved aside and his mother stood before him, holding up her arms for his embrace.

At thirty-nine, Julie Winslow was still youthful in face and form. Her hair was as thick and curly as it had ever been, and only the streak of silver that began over her right eyebrow hinted at the passing of time. As she put her arms around his neck, Knox whispered, "I'm back, Mother!"

She stepped back and he could see her eyes glimmering with tears, but she only said, "You look like a wild man, Knox Winslow!" Then she looked back and, following her gaze, he saw the tall form of his father striding purposefully toward them.

Nathan Winslow, at forty, was in the prime of life. His reddish hair was thinning over his triangular face, but the light blue eyes had a youthful gleam in the lamplight, and the hand that gripped Knox's shoulder was strong. The only sadness Knox had ever seen in his father's eyes was when the man looked at his oldest son.

Nathan had taken over the fur trade of the Winslow business, and had done well at it. If anyone had asked for the best adjusted and steadiest man in Oakdale, the answer would likely have been, "Nathan Winslow." He had a beautiful wife, a prosperous business, a good family—with the exception of his eldest—and was a leader in the thriving Methodist church.

I'd forgotten how handsome he is, Knox thought as his father caught him in a tremendous bear hug that lifted the young man off the ground. "Hey, don't break my ribs!" he complained, but his heart was warmed at his reception; and as they moved toward the house, everyone was talking and laughing at once. Knox would have been totally happy, but he knew that the news of Chris would hurt them terribly. He had managed to send a letter or two with the Indians the company hired to bring the furs out, but all he had told his parents in those letters was that Chris had gone alone into Sioux territory and that they planned to rendezvous in the spring. He had not missed the glance that both his parents had taken toward the yard, hoping to see Chris there.

He sat down and his mother and Judith began putting food on the heavy oak table, as he'd known they would. He had refused to eat earlier with the trappers, knowing his family would want to feed him, and now he fell on the food hungrily: roast ham and baked sweet potatoes, and then baked turkey with a dressing made of walnuts and cornmeal. "I know I'm home now! This is a good sight better than the grub I've eaten the last year."

Nathan's eyes were bright with happiness as he measured Knox's form. "You've toughened up, Knox. Guess it's been pretty rough."

Knox nodded. "If it hadn't been for Frenchie and Con, I s'pect I wouldn't have made it." He stared around the table, shifted his shoulders uncomfortably, then said, "Chris is all right. He was at the rendezvous just below the Platte with the biggest, prettiest pile of beaver plews you ever saw."

"Praise God!" Nathan let his breath out with a gust of emotion, and his eyes closed as he leaned back, hiding his shaking hands quickly under the table, where they were safely out of sight.

"Tell us everything, Knox," George urged. Knox's younger brother was in that time of life when he was almost a man, but not quite. At eighteen, he was six feet tall, and had the same reddish hair and blue eyes as his father and Chris. He was different from any of his brothers, and the closest thing to a scholar that the family had produced. Although he was competent in the woods and was a good rider, he loved books better than anything else. "Why didn't he come with you?"

Knox hesitated, pulling at his curly beard nervously. He said finally, "I might as well tell you the way it is—" For days he had tried to think of a gentler way to break the news, and realized that the only way was to come right out and say it. "He's gone Indian, Father. Married a squaw. I don't think he'll ever be a white man again."

Shocked silence filled the room. As he stared down at his brown hands, he wished desperately there was some way to soften the blow, but there was none. Defiantly, Knox raised his chin and announced, "I know what people say about white men who marry Indians—but I don't give a hang! He's my brother and no matter what he does, nothing's going to change that!"

"Your loyalty to him has never wavered, Knox," his mother

said quietly. She'd taken the news better than his father had, Knox saw. She had always been a woman of great faith, hearing from God on the most minute things. It came as no surprise to him to hear her say, "God made me a promise the night Christmas was born. He told me that the child would be used in His service."

"Maybe that word was for George or Alex—or even Knox."

"No," Julie answered Nathan's gentle suggestion. "It was as plain a word as I've ever gotten, and it was about our firstborn."

Quickly Judith spoke up. "Tell us everything, Knox."

His story poured out: how Chris had been adopted into the tribe, and looked more contented than he'd ever been. When his mother asked about Chris's wife, he said, "Well, she was with him when he met us at the river. I can tell you this: She's the prettiest thing I ever saw—white or red! She's really only half Indian—her father was a white captive." When pressed to describe her, he said, "Well, she's got kind of a dusky skin, but not much redder than yours, Mother, when you stay out in the sun. Most squaws are kinda squat, but she's trim as a deer. Got black hair, but in the sun it's got a dark reddish glint and her eyes are gray, real big like."

"She'll put some good blood in the Winslows," Nathan remarked quietly. "I'd like to meet her."

"I wish you could, Father—but you'd have to go out there for that. Chris won't bring her here. He already told me that."

"Does she love him?" Judith asked, looking at him intently.

"You'd have to see it to believe it! Her eyes follow him wherever he goes—and he's just about as bad about her." He hesitated, then said in an off-hand way that fooled no one, "She's going to have a baby."

George looked startled. He started to say something, then closed his mouth as if he thought better of it. That was the reaction Knox had expected. *Having an Indian wife is one thing, but adding a Sioux to the Winslow line . . . that's different.* Knox could easily read his younger brother's thoughts. He'd had the same misgivings when Chris first told him about the baby, though Knox had been ashamed of the reaction and tried to push his prejudice aside. After all, he'd been closer to Chris than any of them—and besides, he had been around a great many Indians all year. He should have been able to accept the idea more easily.

"Our first grandson," Julie murmured with a soft smile. Turning to Nathan, she announced, "When you go to see them, I'm going with you."

"Haven't said I was going anywhere," he replied defensively. Then he grinned and reached over and took her hand. "But I never could fool you, could I? Well, I am going—but it's no place for a woman."

"How dare you say that to me, Nathan Winslow!" Julie's eyes flashed, and her voice was tart as she added, "If I could be a soldier in the Continental Army of the United States, I think I can make a trip to see my grandchild!"

She was referring, of course, to the time in her life when she had met Nathan. Knox had heard the story often. When Julie had been forced to flee from home after her father's death, she took desperate measures—disguising herself as a man. Nathan had found her freezing on a Boston wharf, and had saved her life. Thinking Julie was a young man, Nathan had encouraged her to enlist in the army. With his influence, she met General Henry Knox—young Knox's namesake—who discovered that the young "fellow" was an expert mapmaker and gave Julie a place on his staff.

Her identity remained a secret until she fell ill on the trip to Tyconderoga. There, she'd been left to get well at the home of Daniel Greene and his mother, who discovered her secret. When Dan learned the truth about the courageous young woman, he fell in love with her. Nathan did not find out about her secret until later, but when he did he also fell head over heels for her—after nursing his hurt ego for some time.

Nathan smiled. Clearly his wife's spunk had not diminished over the years. "I should know better than to try to stop you from doing something once you set your mind to it."

Looking at his parents, Knox was warmed by the love they had always demonstrated. "Chris said to give you his love, Father."

Nathan's face paled, and his mouth jerked involuntarily. The memory of the stormy scenes he'd had with Chris still ate at him. "I hope to make him think better of me one day. I've treated him badly."

"He's sorry about that time, too," Knox said, adding, "I've got to tell you all—I'm going back."

"To the mountains?"

"It's what I'd like to do." He wanted so much to make them see it as he did. "Look, you know that the fur trade is about done here. Not much left but rough fur. But I've seen enough beaver to make a million hats, Father! And there's nobody there now, except the English—and the Indians."

"I've been thinking that way for some time now," Nathan responded. "What's your plan, Knox?"

"Why, we move quick! Go in with as many men as we can get and establish forts along the river. We'll be there first—and believe me, it won't hurt to have a Winslow who's a member of the Sioux nation! Chris brought in the best furs we came back with!"

"Did he now?" Nathan looked across the table with renewed interest. "He trapped them himself?"

"Some of them—but the Sioux do it better. But he made us pay high. Not bead and trading goods, but real things. Things they really needed—rifles, shot, metal goods."

"It's only right," Nathan nodded.

"Sure—but most traders get their furs with whiskey. The stuff sure drives the Indians crazy, I tell you! But Chris wouldn't hear of it—he gave me a list and I'm taking the things back when I go."

He was not asking permission, his father noticed. Nathan admired this new-found confidence in Knox: a surer, deeper mark of manhood even than the black beard that covered his son's face. The year of hard living had tempered the boy, and now there was an air of independence in his face and in every action.

Nathan studied him, then said quietly, "I reckon you're right, Knox—I've been thinking the same thing. When we fought the Revolution, we were just a few colonies strung out along the coast—I'm sure even Washington himself never dreamed how God would pull together this great country of ours. Back then, all we thought about was freedom for ourselves—we never had a chance to think about growing west. But lately I've been thinking a lot about the western territory. It's the richest chunk of land on the face of the earth!

"And America will grow west—it's only a matter of time," Knox put in. "That's why I want to go back now. It's a big land, and I want to be a part of it."

They sat around the table and talked until Julie finally said, "Well, you won't be going back until summer, Knox. I've got that long to pray about it—and to get my husband used to the notion of taking me to see my grandchild." She got up and admonished, "You get to bed now—and tomorrow I'm taking the shears to that hair and beard. You look like a wild bear!" She stopped and gave him a quick look. "I suppose you told the Greenes about Chris?"

"Stopped on the way—Chris sent them all presents. They're worried about him."

He did not miss the pain in his father's response. "We all are, son—we all are."

The next few days passed quickly, and most of the time, Knox enjoyed being home. He was warmed by the avid curiosity that drew people to hear his stories of the western territory. This feeling of goodwill, however, was slightly ruffled after the church service his first Sunday home.

Rev. Josiah Landers was a fine minister, and welcomed Knox home from the pulpit. Afterward, when the church members gathered around Knox and his family to welcome him home, Deacon Simms' wife Martha overheard Julie say, "Our son Christmas is married now."

"Oh, how nice!" gushed Sister Simms. "Who is his bride, Sister Winslow?"

"Her name is White Dove."

Her quiet words fell like a bolt of lightning on the group, stunning them into shocked silence. In that moment Knox was proud of his parents' courage; he was well aware of the embarrassment Chris's marriage would probably cause them here.

"I see." Mrs. Simms cleared her throat and looked at Julie carefully. "Does that mean that he has married . . . an Indian woman?"

Julie's face was calm, and she smiled sweetly. "Why, yes. Our daughter-in-law is a member of the Sioux tribe. And you may wish us double joy, Sister Simms, because Chris and White Dove are going to give Nathan and me our first grandchild."

Sister Simms seemed to have trouble breathing just then, and gave something like a snort before she turned and stalked away, her back stiff. Mrs. Landers, the pastor's wife, had been on the outskirts of the crowd, but now she came forward and put her arms around Julie, saying with a smile, "Well, now! Isn't that fine? I'll be so jealous of you with a grandchild . . . and me wanting one so bad!"

Knox watched as the crowd divided itself into two groups: those who came forward to congratulate the family, and those that turned and walked away. The latter group, he noted, was much larger.

None of them mentioned the incident after it was over. Later in the week Adam came in from Boston, and after he had eaten dinner with the family and rested a bit, he went on a long walk with Knox. He listened carefully to Knox's story, as always, before he said anything. Finally, he observed, "It's a hard way Chris has chosen." The old man lifted his head and looked west as if he could see the mountains where his grandson was. "He's trying to run from God, Knox—but God will catch him sooner or later."

"Chris doesn't say much about God, Grandfather. Or if he does, he seems angry." Knox looked embarrassed, but he added, "Matter of fact, he's downright outspoken about his views on religion."

Adam smiled at him. "Men who run from God are angry men, Knox. Chris is like Jonah, I think. A reluctant prophet who has to be swallowed by some monstrous fish before he'll give in."

Knox spent much time with his family, for he knew that by summer's end he would be leaving for the mountains. The days sped by, turning into weeks, then months. Knox and his father worked long hours planning the trip, and it pleased him to see that his father trusted his judgment on many of the details.

Chris's name was seldom mentioned during this time. Then late one August night, Julie sat with her second son, talking about Chris and his wife and child. To her, the matter was simple: Her son had married a woman who would now give her a grandchild. Period. Her joy was not marred by racial prejudice. Knox had never loved his mother more than he did that night.

But there obviously was more that weighed on her mind. "Knox, are you a Christian?"

He stared at her, astonished. "Why, Mother, I've been a member of the church since I was thirteen."

She reached out and put her hand on his arm. "I know."

The silence grew uncomfortable, and Knox's face became flushed. He tried to speak, but all he could think of was the way he'd lived for the past year. Finally he whispered, "I—I've not done right always, Mother." Still she did not speak, but only looked at him, and he bit his lip, saying, "It's hard to be a mountain man and follow God."

"It's always hard to follow the Lord—no matter what you are."

With those words every excuse he could think of was stripped from Knox, and he dropped his head with the shame he could no longer bear. A momentous struggle was taking place in the young man's soul. And his mother, who saw it, could only sit by him, praying for her son as she never had before.

The next thing she knew he was weeping, his head in her lap. His mother listened quietly as her son poured out his heartfelt confession to the Lord, stopping only when his conscience accused him no longer. The battle was over.

The next day the change was evident; Knox's heart was so light that he even walked with a new spring in his step. His father, misunderstanding the source of his son's joy, was annoyed. "Blast it, Knox, the closer it gets to the time you leave, the happier you are! Can't you at least be a little sorry to leave us?"

Knox laughed and put an arm around his father. "I haven't had a chance to tell you yet, Father. Mother and I had a long talk last night, and I've made things right with God. It's made a world of difference—I was getting pretty far from Him."

Nathan smiled and gave Knox a hug. "Oh, that's it! Well, I'm happy for you, son—although I don't know why your mother didn't tell me. Your mother has been praying for you—for all her children—since before you were born. And when she prays, the very gates of heaven rattle. I've been on the receiving end of those prayers a time or two myself, come to think of it."

Julie appeared in the doorway, a smile playing about her mouth. "Breakfast is ready."

A few days later, Knox rode out with Con and Frenchie as his parents watched from the porch. The last they saw of him was when he stood high in his saddle and turned back to wave.

"I'll miss him, Julie," Nathan said wistfully. "If our boys keep going west, pretty soon we'll have to pack up and go, too."

He looked down and saw the tears in her eyes. "Aw, don't cry, Julie! He'll be back in the spring—and maybe he'll bring Chris and his family with him."

Julie did not answer. She stood quietly for a moment, looking at the trees that covered the pack train, and as she turned to go back into the house, there was a stoop to her shoulders and a pain in her eyes.

CHAPTER EIGHT

THE REVENGE OF RED GHOST

★ ★ ★ ★

The trapping party traveling up the Missouri that season went in eleven canoes instead of four, loaded to the gunwales with trading goods. Knox discovered he could now keep up with any of the others and remembered with amusement how pitiful he'd been at paddling only a year earlier.

This time Con and Frenchie would go on to the Yellowstone country once the group got to the White River, pausing only long enough to throw up a stockade, which they dubbed Fort Winslow. The single log building, surrounded by an eight-foot fence made of logs, would be used for storing the trading goods and the furs.

Already it was late in the season, so the men drove themselves to get the structure in place. When it was finished, Con and Frenchie departed with five of the canoes. "Keep your hair on, Leetle Chicken!" Frenchie laughed as they pulled out and headed north. "We'll 'ave more furs than you, I bet, when we come back!"

The winter was mild that year, and game was plentiful. The only time Chris had set for their rendezvous was "winter," so

Knox settled in the fort to wait. He and his Indian workers hunted and fished all day. Reading the Bible during the long nights, Knox wondered how he'd missed so much when he had read the book before.

On the night of December 25, he remembered it was Chris's birthday; and Knox kept an eye out for his brother, hoping to see him, but to no avail. Another two months went by before the white warrior materialized out of the woods, surrounding the fort with a party of mounted Sioux—more than forty of them. Knox looked up from his fishing just in time to see them walk their horses toward him. Sliding off his horse, Chris helped a woman with a baby down from her mount, then turned to his brother with a smile. "If we'd wanted your scalp, you'd never known what happened, Knox. Better stop picking daisies and pay attention if you want to live long enough to see your grandchildren."

Knox was embarrassed to have been taken off guard, but he was so glad to see Chris that he only grinned. "I was a mite careless, for a fact." Then he turned and said to White Dove, "What's that you've got?" He reached out, took the baby, and held the bundle in his hands. "Wow—how about that!" He looked down at the child, and had to smile at the blue eyes that gazed at him solemnly from a fat, dusky face. He laughed. "Well, I'll be dipped, Chris, if you ain't got yourself one fine boy! What's his name?"

"Dove named him Sky Blue Eyes—but I just call him Sky." He touched the baby's fat cheeks with a finger, adding, "Never thought I'd be one of those daddies that get silly over a baby, but . . ." His eyes twinkled.

Dove said something in Sioux, and Christmas chuckled. "She wants to know if you've got a wife. These Indian women get right down to basics fast."

"Tell her if she's got any sisters pretty as she is, I'm available," Knox replied with a grin at Dove.

Chris interpreted, and the tense look on Dove's face left. A smile curved her lips, and she reached for the baby as Chris announced, "Time for you to meet my people." One by one he named the solemn men who had dismounted and stood in a semicircle around them. "It'll take you a while to get to know them all, Knox. Guess you think like I did once—that all Indians look alike."

"I reckon they think we all look alike, Chris." He contemplated the silent stares of the Indians. "Well, we got nothing fancy to offer y'all, but we've got plenty of meat, so let's get the cooks cookin'."

Knox spoke to the Mandans, who had been watching the armed Sioux nervously, and soon they were scurrying around building cooking fires. The Sioux women began cutting elk, deer, and buffalo steaks and roasting them over the fires. They laughed and chattered loudly, excited over the pewter spoons and ladles—things they had never seen before.

When the men sat down to eat, Knox seated himself beside Chris in the midst of a circle of Sioux warriors who were relaxing and laughing as they ate. Knox told Chris about his trip home, making it plain that their parents were ready to welcome Dove and the baby.

Chris listened without comment as he ate, until Knox had finished speaking. "I figured they'd take it like that, Knox, though I don't imagine everybody would." Subtly shifting the subject, he asked, "How about Brother Greene and his family?"

"Why, fine as silk—except for Miz Greene. She's expecting again, and Dan told me she's not doing well." Then Knox's face lit up, and he slapped his leg and laughed. "That little girl—Missy, is it?— is a caution! She loved the moccasins you sent, and wears that pearl you gave her around her neck." He looked over at the pearl that adorned Dove's finger and said, "I see where the other one went."

"I had it made into a ring for her," Chris smiled. "Made it too small, so Dove can't get it off—but she claims she would never have taken it off anyway." He smiled briefly at the thought of Missy, then grew sober. "But I'll never go back, Knox. No way at all—so don't build the folks' hopes up."

"Guess they know that already—but Mother, she's set her foot down like she does sometimes when she gets a notion in her head. Told Father she's comin' to the mountains to see her grandchild if she has to paddle up the Missouri by herself. I think

Father was hopin' you'd make the trip just to spare her."

Chris looked down at his hands for a long time. He had, Knox realized, taken on the ways of the Indians at times like this. *He doesn't want me to see what he's thinkin'.* They sat like that for a time, each absorbed in his own thoughts. Knox shifted uneasily; there was something more he had to say to his brother, but he was not sure how Chris would respond. Chris looked up and noted his brother's discomfort. "What's gnawing on you, Knox?"

"Now don't get your hackles up, Chris. I been wonderin' about—well, about what you're going to do about God." Knox raised his hands hurriedly as if to defend himself. "Reason I asked—I been having a pretty hard time myself the last few years. I'd seen hypocrites like Miz Simms that gave me lots of doubts. Pretty soon I gave up . . . figured it was no use . . . I guess I lived pretty bad the last few years." His voice trailed off as he brushed his hair back from his forehead and stared off into the distance, struggling to find words.

"Then there's people like Grandfather and our folks, and the Greenes—I could tell what they had was real. Well, while I was home this time, I talked to Mother about it, and she helped me see it. And this time when I prayed, God was real inside me, too. I found Him in a way I never had before—and I haven't been the same since."

"I'm glad for you, Knox." He looked up sharply. Chris had a curious look on his face; his eyes were warm, but there was a familiar stubborn set to his lips. "Maybe religion works for some and not for others. It's not for me, Knox, and that's all there is to it."

Knox said no more; he knew it would do no good. Still, it saddened him to hear Chris's answer, knowing how much it would have pained his parents had they been there to hear it.

Later that night, there was a tribal meeting in the open space in front of the trading post, and for the first time Knox smoked an Indian pipe. At one point in the ceremony Four Dog spoke up, and although Knox didn't know what he was saying, the tone of the man's voice made it clear that it was something serious. The stocky Indian's face was grim and there was a light of anger in his black eyes.

Chris said, "He says it's not good for you to trade with the Pawnees."

"What should we do, Chris?"

"Better not trade with the Pawnees, I reckon."

"Red Ghost—he bad medicine," Running Wolf said in English. He had been following the talk as closely as he could, and now he shook his head and scowled. "He make vow, kill Bear Killer."

"What for?" Knox asked.

"I killed his son on a raid," Chris explained. "Now he's got to kill me to save face—though the Pawnees don't really need an excuse for fighting the Sioux. Red Ghost is pretty shrewd. He's using this to get his braves all worked up. Sent word to Running Wolf that if he'd hand me over to the Pawnees, Red Ghost would make peace."

Knox looked around at the hard faces of the Sioux, swallowed and inquired nervously, "Don't it worry you any, Chris—that they might do it?"

"They're my in-laws, Knox—and family means a lot to them. And the Sioux know Red Ghost wouldn't stick to his word. He'd carve me up, then find another reason to fight the Sioux."

Knox shook his head, worry clouding his eyes. "Wish you'd stay here with me, Chris. Hate to think of you getting scalped out there."

Chris looked across to where White Dove sat with her back to the wall, nursing Sky. "No way to stay safe in this world, Knox. A Pawnee arrow in your liver out here, or getting cholera in Kentucky—it's all the same in the end."

Knox said no more, for he knew it was no use to argue with the dark streak of fatalism that ran through Chris.

The next day the trading took place, and although the Sioux grumbled when they got no whiskey, most of them were pleased with the useful goods they received in exchange for the beaver pelts. They stayed the rest of the day and camped again that night; this time their meeting did not include Knox.

Chris came in later, and there was a sober look on his face. "What's wrong?" Knox asked.

"Some of the young bucks want to raid the Pawnees' camp.

Four Dog doesn't like it, but a war chief don't last long unless he gets plunder pretty regular. I'll have to go along, Knox."

"Do you have to go?"

"No choice," Chris shrugged. "I'm hoping we'll be able to hit the camp by surprise and get away with a few horses. Be all right to leave the women here? We'll pick them up on the way back to the village."

"Sure."

In less than an hour the war party was assembled. Just outside the fort, Chris stood beside Dove, saying, "Take care of Sky. I'll be back with a pony for him."

She lifted her face for his kiss, holding the baby up to him to be kissed as well. "Be careful. Don't try to count coup on Red Ghost."

Counting coup was an old Sioux custom by which many warriors lost their lives. It involved getting close enough to your enemy to touch him without killing him.

"Don't worry," he smiled down at her. "That's one mean Pawnee. If I catch a glimpse of that Indian's feathers, I'll show him how fast a white man can run." He kissed her again, then whispered in her ear, "Please . . . don't worry."

"I will wait for you." He turned and sprang onto the horse Sixkiller was holding for him. The warriors rode out, painted for war, while Knox stood beside Dove, watching them. *Hate to meet up with that bunch,* he thought.

The Pawnee camp was thirty miles away; Four Dog planned it so they would not get there until after dusk the next day. Cautiously, the war chief sent flankers out to be sure they were not seen, and when the group arrived at twilight they dismounted—leaving two braves behind to hold the horses.

After a long, careful stalk in darkness, they were caught off guard when they discovered that the camp had been moved recently.

"Not here!" Four Dog grunted in disgust. "We must wait till morning to find a sign."

"I don't like it," Running Wolf said quickly. "This is their ground. They may be setting a trap."

There was a long argument; the younger braves were impatient to follow the Pawnees. At last Four Dog made his decision. "Not good to follow them now. Later we will find them."

He led them back to the horses, and the warriors made a slow trip back to the post. The horses were tired, and they had to stop from time to time to rest them. It was after dawn the following day when they came out of the thick wood that blanketed the post on the south. The sun glimmered in the east, and Chris dozed off as he rode.

"Bear Killer—look!"

He jerked awake to see where Four Dog was pointing. An ominous column of smoke was rising into the sky. "That's the post!"

Frantically they dug their heels into the sides of their horses, spurring them to a run and sweeping along the edge of the woods. As soon as they wheeled their horses around the outcropping of sandstone that hid the post, they knew the worst.

The gates of the fence hung crazily on their hinges. Inside, the building was a blackened skeleton gutted by fire. The still figures on the ground enveloped Chris with fear as he fell off his horse and ran across the yard. The first body was just inside the wall. It had been scalped and riddled with a knife, but Chris knew who it was. Chris had known Curley well—the Mandan had been with him on his journey with Con and Frenchie. He gave the body a quick glance, and the horror mounted inside him as he noted the other bodies—all Mandans. Trying not to panic, he pressed in, calling for Dove.

An Indian woman lay across the threshold of the gutted building. Running to turn the body over, he was only slightly relieved. It was Little Fox, the wife of Four Dog.

He heard a faint cry, and his eyes flew in the direction of the sound. There was a figure slumped against the log wall. "Knox!" he cried, and picked his way across the corpse-littered ground as fast as he could to reach his brother.

Knox was tied to the wall with rawhide thongs. He'd been scalped and his eyes were filled with blood. There were four arrows protruding from his stomach, but he was alive.

Whipping out his knife, Christmas cut the thongs and lowered him gently to the ground. He wiped the blood from Knox's eyes, which fluttered open. "Glad . . . you made it . . . Chris," Knox whispered.

"Oh, Knox!" Chris's head whirled as if the earth had spun upside down. He could not think and he was trembling terribly.

"Red Ghost . . . came at . . . night."

"Where's Dove and Sky?"

"Took them. Said if you . . . want them . . . come . . . take them."

The blood seeped into Knox's eyes again, and as Chris wiped it away, he heard the cries of grief and outrage that rose as men found the bodies of their wives. He looked up to see Running Wolf and Four Dog staring down at Knox. Their faces were contorted with hatred.

"He knew . . . I was your brother." Knox struggled to speak. "Said . . . he'd have some . . . fun with me. Tied me up . . . used me for target practice." A spasm of pain doubled him up, and he clawed at the arrows. Chris held him down until the pain passed; then Knox said, "Gettin' dark, Chris . . . I'm goin' out . . . looks like."

Chris could only hold him, knowing there was no hope.

"Chris . . . don't fret about me . . . not your fault . . . promise."

Hoping to quiet his brother, Chris mumbled, "I—I promise."

The next words came so faintly that Chris had to bend low to catch them. "Tell Mother . . . I'm glad . . . we had our prayer."

"I will, Knox. Promise."

But Knox didn't seem to hear. "I'll be . . . waiting for you, Chris . . . waitin'." And with a sigh, Knox went limp. Seeing he was gone, Chris slowly lowered his brother to the ground. Madness glittered in his eyes when he looked up at the two men standing silently by. "We will have our women back, my brothers."

Four Dog said grimly. "My woman is dead—but Red Ghost will pay!"

"They leave a broad trail," Sixkiller spoke up. "And they will be back in their village before we can catch them."

A cry of rage ran through the warriors, most of them ready to mount and make straight for the Pawnee village, but Four Dog stopped them. His anger had not caused him to lose his head.

"They will be waiting," he shrewdly observed, "—and they have rifle guns they have taken."

"I will have my woman!" Running Wolf snapped.

"And I will have my wife and son," Chris said. "But Four Dog is wise. The Pawnees are many and we are but few—and they expect us. Have you not said many times, Running Wolf, it is a fool who does what his enemy expects?"

"That was the head speaking! My heart demands revenge!"

A sudden revelation hit Chris, chilling his blinding rage. Speaking with words as cold as ice, he said, "Four Dog—you are war chief, and I will follow you. But will you hear a thought that has come to me?"

"Let Bear Killer speak."

"Surely Red Ghost knows we will come—but he thinks we will follow blindly, carelessly. It may be that he will move slowly, spreading his band into two or three parts. When we come, he will close on the main body, and the others will close in and crush us."

Four Dog nodded. "That is so. But if we try to get ahead of them and catch them in a trap, the first thing they will do is kill our women."

Running Wolf looked at Chris. "What is your thought, my brother?"

"Go to the Pawnee camp now," Chris said. "There will be few braves there to watch the women and horses. We will take them captive, and when Red Ghost comes, we will make a trade—his women for ours."

A yelp of pleasure went up from Sixkiller and the other young braves, but Four Dog frowned. "Our horses are too tired. We can never get to the camp before them."

"We will ride them until they die. Then we will run." The simple declaration from the white man was met with a murmur of approval. He smiled and added, "Some of us will not make it, but I will attack the Pawnees if I am alone!"

A shout went up, and every warrior resolved not to be one who could not make the difficult journey. "We will go!" they shouted, and Four Dog nodded his approval.

"Two must stay to care for the dead," Running Wolf told

them. There was a cry of protest from the two he named, but he was adamant. "What shall we do with your brother, Bear Killer?"

Chris turned and went to kneel beside Knox's body. He reached out and held one hand lightly on the still cheek. *Knox . . . my baby brother . . .* He paid no heed to the tears running down his cheeks, for he was engulfed with many memories of his brother. *. . . always underfoot when we were growing up. But growin' up, you knew me better than anyone else . . . believed in me when no one else did . . .* His mind wandered back to a creek in Kentucky, where the two of them had been swimming one blistering hot summer. Knox had leaped to knock a cottonmouth aside that was ready to bury his fangs in Chris's leg. He thought of the times around their table at home, and of sitting for long hours at church beside him. *I'm sure gonna miss you . . .*

Awkwardly he stroked his brother's still face, then took a deep breath and got to his feet with a set determination. "Bury him beside the big oak that overlooks the river," he replied, mounting the horse that Running Wolf held. He did not look back as they rode out of the post.

The Sioux prepared the bodies of their dead—Four Dog's wife and two other women—wrapping them in blankets for the journey to the sacred burial ground on a high plateau near their village. They dug a grave near the oak beside the river, put the body of Knox in it, then carefully covered it over and destroyed all signs of digging so that neither wolves nor enemies could find the body.

A tall brave named Big Hand looked at the spot, and wondered aloud, "White men strange. They put their dead in cold, dark hole—when they could do as The People—lift them high in the sky for the sun and the stars to touch."

They searched the ruins for anything of value and found a case of rifles and a supply of powder and shot. When all was done, they put the bodies in a travois and started back to their village.

For several hours all was quiet in the yard of the trading post, and when dusk veiled the sky, a nervous buck stepped into the clearing, sniffing the air cautiously. He paused, ready to bolt, but curiosity caused him to come closer—close enough to peer through the broken gates. Nothing stirred, but the smell of death was still strong, so he snorted and fled the scene in that beautiful gait that is half run and half flight—leaving the darkness behind him.

CHAPTER NINE

DEATH AT HIGH NOON

★ ★ ★ ★

The raiding party flew the distance to the enemy camp at full speed, but by the time they got to the Pawnee grounds, it was obvious to the small group that had scouted ahead that they were too late for a surprise attack. Four Dog, who was among them, insisted that they pull back at once. "Red Ghost will be waiting now. We are too few for an attack." He sent Sixkiller to bring up the full strength of the tribe, and now there was nothing to do but wait.

Running Wolf looked bitterly in the direction of the camp. "The gods have struck us." He was not usually so cynical—normally he preferred to live close to the earth, letting life flow over him as it would. But not now. "I will not live and let this pass."

"Nor I, my brother," Chris answered. He looked at Four Dog and asked, "What does the war chief of the Sioux say?"

Four Dog answered slowly. He was a scarred veteran of many raids, and he knew the Pawnees better than any of them—especially Red Ghost. He sat there, a solid shape in the sun-speckled glade, alternately trying and rejecting plans, in the same manner as he would try different arrowheads for a shaft. His eyes were half shut as the war chief swayed slightly from side to side. At last he opened them and gave a short chopping motion with his hand. "The Pawnees will expect us to attack. They will have their scouts out already, and we cannot hope to get through their lines. But when would they expect us?"

"At night—or at first light" was Running Wolf's immediate response.

"So—we must attack when the sun is high! That is the soft underbelly of Red Ghost!"

Running Wolf pondered the idea silently, balancing the risk against the chance they would succeed. His eyes glittered as he nodded agreement. "It is so. All night the scouts will be thick around the village. But most will go back during the day to sleep. Even so," he warned, "we are too many to hide for long—and the Pawnees are coiled and ready to strike!"

"You will stay here for one week, Running Wolf," Four Dog said swiftly. "Hide by day, and by night try to learn all you can about the village. In one week I will have every warrior in the tribe ready to attack at the old camp below the bend in the river. You know it?"

"Yes."

"The Pawnees will not be expecting that. In seven days, meet us there." His thin lips twisted into a grotesque smile, and he lowered his voice, "We will find the soft underbelly of Red Ghost! Listen . . ."

He began to speak rapidly, relishing the looks of surprise that crossed the faces of the other two men. The old war chief's tactics had always been considered a bit unusual; while most Sioux in his position relied on brute force, Four Dog was noted for his cunning, his ability to catch his enemies off guard. Now he glowed with excitement, with expectancy, as he elaborated on his plan—his masterpiece. If it worked, he would be celebrated for many generations to come.

When he finished, there was a smile even on the stolid face of Running Wolf, and Chris said as he got up, "Four Dog is a great chief. We will feed the Pawnees to the wolves!" He turned and soon the band left, leaving Running Wolf alone in the glade.

Seven days later Four Dog led the band down the path that ran from the river. The thunder of the horses' hooves stirred a sleeping fox that lifted his head, sniffed, and faded into the timber. Only a few skeletal frameworks marked the site of an abandoned village; the forest had closed in quickly, covering the bare earth with grasses, and draping the broken pottery with vines and fallen leaves.

Four Dog pulled his horse up, and even as he did, a voice came from the edge of the timber. Running Wolf appeared, joining the braves as they dismounted.

"You come on time," Running Wolf said with a smile.

"And you are alive," Chris answered, relieved. "It occurred to me that your scalp might be drying on Red Ghost's belt."

"The gods were good." Running Wolf nodded seriously and regarded the braves who stood nearby, waiting. For a long moment he stared at them, then nodded. "It is strange to see The People looking so much like their enemies. If I had met you last night, Little Crow, you would be feeding the wolves right now!"

Little Crow gave a muffled howl and raised his rifle in a quick gesture. "I am a Pawnee! Beware!"

A laugh rippled over the group, and Running Wolf moved among the warriors, speaking a word to one, slapping another on the back. When he came to stand beside Four Dog, he said with approval in his voice, "It is well. We will fool them for a short time with your foolish plan!"

The plan was crazy; yet its sheer audacity was their only hope of success. Four Dog had done his work well—over and over, day after day, he had drilled his plan into his warriors.

"We will make ourselves look like Pawnees," Four Dog had said. "If we try to make a headlong attack, they will be ready—so we will come at them one at a time, dressed as they are!

"Running Wolf will know the ground. We will split up and move into the spots he says, in groups of two or three. We will wait until the night scouts of the enemy return to the village, until the sun is high in the sky. Then we will attack them—at the time when they will least expect it!"

"How do we get close to the camp?" asked Sixkiller.

"I will move toward the camp—very slowly, with my rifle tied on a thong behind me. I will stop and look off—or sit down and look at my foot. Most of the warriors will be either off hunting or sleeping after their night watch—only squaws and children will see us."

"What about the rest of us?" Little Crow demanded.

"You will have to choose your moment—but do not hurry and do not come close together."

"Sooner or later we'll be seen."

"Yes—but we must hope one of us will be close enough to kill the Pawnees that took our women! We must get them back! We must avenge their blood!"

Now as they prepared to take their places, Four Dog asked, "Running Wolf—where is the best place for Bear Killer to be? He must have many loaded rifles, for he never misses. Those that go in will only have spears and knives—until our brother can kill those that rush with the weapons from their lodges."

"I know a place," Running Wolf nodded, then stopped. "But how will he tell our warriors from the Pawnees? How can we keep from killing each other? In the heat of battle, what if I see Tall Deer and take him for the Pawnee warrior he looks like?"

"We have thought of a way," Four Dog said. "Every man has a red headband. As soon as we are discovered, we all put them on. Kill everything that moves—without a red headband." The light of battle was already in Four Dog's eyes. "Come, my children. We will slay the wife-stealers! Watch for me when the sun touches the highest part of the sky."

Running Wolf stooped and made a rough sketch on the ground, pointing out the best places for the braves to hide. One by one they melted into the woods until all but Chris were gone. "We will stay together," Running Wolf told him. "I will help carry the rifles."

Following Running Wolf through the woods was like trailing a ghost. More than once, they had to elude the enemy patrols that passed close by. *It'll be a miracle,* Chris thought, *if at least one Sioux doesn't get flushed out by the Pawnees.* His ears strained for the sound of a cry of alarm or of a shot, but they reached the spot that Running Wolf had selected without hearing anything out of the ordinary.

Settling down in the shelter of a grove of cottonwoods, neither of them said a word until dawn. As soon as the east began to turn gray, Running Wolf said, "Now," and led the way out of the trees. It was still too dark to see the village as Running Wolf continued on to a gully. Chris followed closely, the rifles bumping the back of his legs, as the Sioux turned and went along the gully for about three hundred yards. "This is your place—stay under those bushes until the attack, then rise up and shoot. You can see the lodges," he whispered. In the gathering light, Chris could see the shadowy outlines of the camp not two hundred yards away.

"Red Ghost's lodge is the one with a white buffalo hide over the door. Try to get him first."

With that he was gone, and Chris scrambled down the gully, which was about five feet deep and filled with gooseberry bushes that scratched his face as he ducked under them. He worked quickly, loading the rifles with great precision and carefully positioning them under the bushes. Taking one last look around, he ducked under the heavy bushes.

Time crawled. He heard horsemen coming and going for most of the morning, and once some boys came very close, evidently hunting for small game. They stood not ten feet from where he lay, caught up in a prolonged argument about which one of the young girls was the best, their ribald talk laced with laughter. Still joking among themselves, they moved on. Chris felt a wry smile appear on his parched lips: *Sound just like boys anywhere.*

At last the sun reached its zenith, and he risked another quick glance. He spotted Four Dog moving in, and his heart began to beat faster.

Four Dog had moved out of a growth of stunted timber not much higher than his head, and he ambled along idly, stooping from time to time to poke the stick in his hand down a hole. Chris glanced at the camp and saw that there were several squaws grinding meal, and two braves were sitting in front of a teepee, talking. There were children everywhere, playing games. Strangely enough, none of the Indians seemed to notice anything out of the ordinary, but a chill of dread swept over Chris. To him the whole plan suddenly seemed like a child's game—and doomed to fail.

A movement caught his eye, and he watched as two more of the Sioux shuffled unhurriedly out of the timber. Four Dog had stopped and seemed to be watching a hawk that was circling, but Chris knew he was keenly aware of every move of his own men and of the Pawnee camp.

The thing was well done, Chris conceded, and he began to relax. The Sioux did not bunch up as they idly closed in. They wouldn't be unnoticed for long, of course; there were too many men now in sight, but several of them were well within shooting distance, and Four Dog himself was less than fifty feet away from the first teepee—Chris's heart raced!

Four Dog had been discovered! A squaw, who had looked up nonchalantly from her work, had spotted him. She straightened up with a loud cry that brought the two bucks to their feet. One of them made a grab at a rifle that was leaning against a stump, but Four Dog's rifle materialized in his hands. With a single shot he killed the Pawnee.

From his hiding spot, the white warrior raised his rifle and shot the other brave, and seconds later he killed a short Pawnee who came running out of the adjoining lodge. Chris grabbed at one of the loaded rifles at his feet, throwing the discharged rifle on the bank of the gully. The air exploded with the war cries of the Sioux mixed with the screams of the squaws and the urgent cries of the Pawnee warriors who came bursting out of their lodges, weapons in hand.

The deadly accuracy of Chris's rifle made the difference, as Four Dog had hoped. His rapid fire demoralized the Pawnees, preventing them from banding together to defend themselves against the ragged line of Sioux racing out of the trees, crossing the level ground at a dead run.

Eleven times Chris fired, and eleven enemy bodies littered the ground, lying still or kicking feebly on the ground. The white warrior dropped the last empty musket and charged across the field with his knife in his hand. The village boiled with hand-to-hand fighting; the Sioux had fired their rifles and were closing in with spears, tomahawks, and knives. By this time some of the Pawnees had hit their targets and Chris saw Sixkiller go down. The brave who had killed him looked up to see Chris running toward him, and the Pawnee lifted the empty rifle to club the white man. Fearlessly Bear Killer fended off the blow with his left hand and slashed the Indian's throat with the knife in his right. The Pawnee crumbled to the ground, clutching his throat.

The battle rage that seized Chris was tempered by a coolness that enabled him to keep his eyes roaming the area, alert for a glimpse of Dove and Sky. He saw Still Water run by, hotly pursued by a Pawnee brave. The next thing Chris knew, an arrow had buried itself up to the feathers in the brave's chest. Grabbing her, Running Wolf shoved his woman toward the safety of the timber.

The tide was beginning to turn, for the Pawnee warriors who had been in lodges farther off were now putting up a stiff fight. Eagerly Chris scanned the mob for their leader until he spotted a tall brave who was forming up his warriors to take the charge of the Sioux. It was not Red Ghost. Chris dashed inside the lodge with the white buffalo robe over the door, finding only a squaw who drew herself up, defiance glittering in her dark eyes.

Hearing a noise behind him, he whirled and was almost brained by a war club that grazed his head and sent him sprawling to the ground. He hit the ground rolling, knowing that the next blow would kill him if he didn't move fast. Hearing the club strike the ground beside his head, he sprang up—knife in hand—to face the massive form of Red Ghost.

"I have your woman and your son," Red Ghost snarled, pulling a knife with his left hand, "and now I will have your life, Bear Killer!" Chris poised himself on the balls of his feet, weaving slightly, his knife grasped firmly in his right hand. He smiled and taunted, "Red Ghost is a weak chief. We walked into your camp and killed your braves as we kill puppies! It is easy to kill Pawnees—it was easy to kill your son. . . !"

Red Ghost was livid with rage; Chris was startled at how fast his opponent sprang at him. The white Sioux had no time to think, much less to swing his knife; only his catlike reflexes saved him as he fell back, dodging and falling as the club whistled through the air. The sounds of battle that raged all around him dimmed, and everything else faded from sight but the towering form of the Pawnee—and the club that descended again and again.

Got to get close, Chris thought wildly. Red Ghost had no fear of his opponent's knife, and Chris knew that his only chance was to leap on the other between swings. For the fraction of a second when the club was still, he must risk it all. If he misjudged the power and speed of Red Ghost again, his brains would be spilled on the hard ground, Chris knew. But there was no other choice.

He pretended to stumble, causing Red Ghost to put all his force into one last swing. The blow passed over Chris's head, and the force of it caught the large Indian off-balance.

Chris scrambled to his feet and lunged at Red Ghost, his knife held high. That was a mistake as well. With the speed of lightning, Red Ghost dropped his club and seized Chris's wrist with one hand, pulling his own knife from its sheath with the other. The Pawnee chief raised his knife to slash Chris, but found his wrist held in a grip of steel. Clearly, Bear Killer was much stronger than an ordinary white man.

The two men strained for advantage, every nerve in their bodies crying out, tortured muscles contorted with the effort. Now it was a matter of brute strength; the first to get a weapon free would kill the other—and both men knew it. Chris was several inches taller than Red Ghost, but the Indian was much bulkier, and his heavy muscles were like cables of sinew.

Chris could think of nothing now except hanging on to the wrist that held the Pawnee knife and, freeing his own knife, plunging it into the body of the other. Their faces were inches apart, but neither of them dared to speak or try to escape.

Chris's wrist was on fire as the fingers of Red Ghost bore down, and he felt the bones giving way, the nerves going dead. His own grip on Red Ghost's knife arm was weakening, and bit by bit he felt his opponent's power growing. In that moment, he knew that he was lost.

His eyes filled with triumph, Red Ghost taunted, "Is it so easy to kill the Pawnee, Bear Killer?" He laughed and added, "Call on your god—maybe he will help you!"

Chris stared into the cruel eyes of Red Ghost, knowing that this time his strength was not enough. It had always been enough before—a reserve that he could draw from to overcome his enemies. But now he could only watch helplessly as the Pawnee chief drew his knife slowly back, forcing his victim's hand with it. He had no strength left in his other hand, and his knife was held loosely in his fingers. Red Ghost saw this, and directed his attention to the knife he held, intent on killing the white man in his grasp.

Chris thought of Dove and Sky. Her face flashed before him, and then the blue eyes of his son, and their memory pained him far more than any knife could; for the warrior knew that once he was dead, his family would become slaves of the Pawnee forever. Just as the other's knife was about to be driven home, a thought leaped into his mind: *Call on me, and I will answer thee and show thee great and mighty things that thou knowest not.* The distant memory of the words he had overheard his mother read from her Bible echoed in his head. Those words had saved his brother George, who had nearly died of pneumonia years ago.

Impulsively, he cried out, "God! God, help me!"

Red Ghost's lips opened and he laughed—but his laughter was cut short as he realized that he could not lift the knife. The white man's grip had tightened. At the same time, the Indian felt a surge of strength leap through the right arm of Bear Killer. This time, the Pawnee chief could not hold off his attacker, who gave a loud cry and drove the knife deep into the thick body of Red Ghost, sending him writhing to the ground.

Chris knew he had not been responsible for the sudden power that had flowed through him. He stood there silently for a moment, trying to comprehend it all. *Guess there really is something to what Mother used to tell me.* When he looked up, the old woman was gone. Chris turned to join the battle.

"Wait!" Red Ghost was pulling feebly at something around his neck. "You kill me and my son," he gasped, holding up a rawhide thong—something was dangling from the end of it. "We are even, Bear Killer! I will sleep well—see?"

A pearl ring—Dove's wedding ring! He knelt and snatched it from the trembling fingers of the dying man. "You stole it from her!" he cried out.

"Yes! I cut off her finger after she was dead," Red Ghost said in triumph. His voice was feeble, and his eyes were dimming, but he roused himself to gesture toward the lodgepole, "You see? . . . what's left of her . . . her scalp . . . is on that lodgepole! I killed her—and the boy . . . too!" Coughing up blood, he gasped, "She would . . . not have me . . . so I killed . . . both. Fed them . . . to the wolves—"

A rattle sounded in his throat before he fell back, dead.

The conflict raging inside Chris drowned out the sounds of the skirmish outside. When he could stand it no longer, he turned and directed his gaze to the place Red Ghost had indicated. There—he saw it—a fresh scalp hanging on the pole. He forced himself to move closer and, trembling, he took it down.

It was the scalp of his wife; there was no Indian hair with such rich auburn lights. His eyes filled with an agony that would not wash away with his tears. The battle was forgotten, along with everything else.

When Running Wolf found him hours later, he saw the scalp-lock in his friend's hands. "My heart is hurt for my brother," he said quietly. After a moment, he asked, "What will you do now?"

Chris's eyes were fixed on the long strand of hair. Stroking it gently, he looked up to meet Wolf's gaze. "I must go to my people. They must know of my brother."

"Will Bear Killer come back to The People?"

Chris shook his head. "There is nothing for me to come back to." He turned and walked out of the Pawnee dwelling into the bright sunlight, across the bloody ground with his head down and his shoulders bent.

PART TWO

THE PASTOR

★ ★ ★ ★

CHAPTER TEN

THE REUNION

★ ★ ★ ★

Leaning over, Adam held his breath and listened. His brother's hoarse breathing broke off, and the awful silence in the sick man's room jangled his nerves. He glanced at Paul, who left his place by the bay window to stand by his father's bedside. Charles coughed and drew a deep ragged breath, and his eyes slit open.

"Father?" Paul asked quietly. "Are you awake?"

"Paul? Is that you?" The faded blue eyes searched his son's face; then he shifted his eyes. He smiled faintly and whispered, "Adam . . . I'm glad you're here."

"I've been waiting for you to wake up, Charles. How do you feel?"

"Well, for a dying man, not too bad." The wry streak of humor caused Adam and Paul to exchange bemused looks. "Actually, I feel like the ghost of Banquo at the feast, Adam. Why didn't you wait till I'd died to have the reunion?" He shook his head slightly. "Never mind. Who all is here?"

"Almost everyone, Father," Paul said. "Even William's son came all the way from England."

No one could remember who had suggested that the Winslow family needed a reunion, but now—after two unsuccessful attempts—it had come to pass. In 1801 and again in 1804 when

Jefferson was reelected, Adam had toyed with the idea; but nothing came of it until January of 1806. At that time Paul plowed ahead with his customary cool efficiency and pulled the family together at the old mansion in Boston where he lived with his family.

Charles closed his eyes for a moment, then opened them again. "Help me sit up, Paul." Braced against the pillows, the bedridden man looked at his brother. "You're looking very well, Adam." Charles's rough lifestyle had taken its toll. At seventy-eight, Charles was a skeleton, while Adam was still hale and healthy. "If I'd known I was going to live so long," he observed dryly, "I'd have taken better care of myself."

Adam smiled and put his hand, still thick and calloused, on top of Charles's thin one. "God has been good to us, Charles." He looked across the bed at the trim figure of Paul and nodded, "Your son's the rising star of the United States Navy—and that grandson of yours is a fine young fellow!"

Charles looked fondly at Paul, then nodded. "You're right—God has been good to me." He gave Adam a long look. "And if you hadn't looked out for us, Adam, we'd have been lost." Adam tried to interrupt, but Charles raised his voice over the man's protests. "No—it's true. You saved us when all the other Tories were thrown out of America penniless—and you—you did more, Adam." He hesitated, and his voice lowered into an almost confidential tone. "You helped me find God."

Adam felt a lump rise in his throat. He squeezed the thin hand. "I'm glad, Charles. Very glad!"

"Now—" Charles impatiently swiped at the tears in his eyes that threatened to spill over. "Tell me all about the family."

He listened while Adam and Paul gave him the news—the latest births, marriages, and deaths in the family. When he asked about the business, Adam said, "Better—much better than we'd ever hoped. It can't last, of course. Sooner or later the furs will be gone—or else the fops in England will stop wearing beaver hats and start wearing pot lids or some other such foolishness. But the last few years have been very profitable."

"Thanks to that grandson of yours, " Paul said.

"Whitfield is the man who makes it go." At twenty-three, Paul's son had proven himself to be a genius at figures. Under his management the Winslow Fur Company had expanded into an empire second only to that of the massive Hudson's Bay Company.

"Whitfield could not have managed the company if there had been no furs. It's been Christmas who's done that."

"Is Christmas here, Adam?" Charles asked. "I'd like to see him."

"You know Christmas, Charles," Adam shrugged. "He comes and goes like the wind. Never know when he'll come in—and then you never know when he'll decide to leave."

Charles saw the pain etched on Adam's face. "The boy's taken his loss harder than any man I ever saw, Adam. How long has it been now since his wife and son were killed?"

"Five years in July." Adam had been there the day Christmas had come back, his eyes empty, to tell them of Knox's death. He looked at Charles and said, "He's a driven man, Charles. He blames himself for his brother's death—that's why he's worked so hard for the company. He doesn't give a pin for money; he's trying to make it up to his parents for the loss of their son."

Adam paused, thinking of how Christmas had wandered restlessly since the death of White Dove and Sky. For a few weeks after his return, he had forced himself to take part in the business—mostly, Adam realized even then, to please Nathan and Julie. But it was no good. At last he had said to Adam and Nathan, "I'll get the furs; it's the one thing I can do."

Year after year, Christmas had gone into upper Missouri country, penetrating the deepest recesses of the Yellowstone and even into Canada, coming home once a year to bring the furs. He always became restless and unhappy on those visits, and he usually cut them short to get back to the mountains.

Paul interrupted, "Will he ever get over it, Adam?"

"I don't think he will, Paul—unless he finds the Lord." Adam bit his lip. "That's the miracle I've been praying for. Right now he's running—like a man possessed."

" 'Course, the business isn't suffering any by it; he knows the West better than any man in this country," Paul said, a sad smile on his face. "But it's as you say—he's running from God. Charity and I have often spoken of it."

Charles dozed off, and once again his breathing became ragged and uneven. The two men stepped outside. "He looks worse, Adam," Paul said with a worried frown. "I'll get Dr. Rawlings to come by this afternoon." The older man nodded agreement.

The two men descended the stairs, making their way to the outside arbor where they found Dan Greene and Nathan sitting and sipping lemonade. "Trust a Methodist preacher to sit around sipping lemonade whenever there's work to be done," Paul grinned. Pouring himself a glass, he sat down and asked, "You two still fighting about theology?"

Nathan stood and stretched, his tall frame still youthful and strong. He looked at Adam and half-jokingly suggested, "I wish you'd try to talk some sense into Dan, Father. About the revivals."

"He can't do that, Nathan, because he agrees with me," teased Greene. His hair was grizzled, but thick and curly as it had been at twenty-five, when he and Nathan had fought over which of them would marry Julie. Years of riding the long circuit in all kinds of weather had toughened him—but it had worn on him as well. His strong features were lined in the June sunlight, and his shoulders stooped.

"Well, Father, I don't see how you can give aid and comfort to the enemy. Every man of sense knows that these revivals are all based on emotion."

It was an argument of long standing, and although Nathan and Dan joked about it, the question of the validity of the religious movement that swept the southern states in 1800 was to both of them a serious matter.

Men of faith alluded to the Great Awakening that had shaken the nation, led by men like George Whitefield and Jonathan Edwards. When Asahel Nettleton graduated from Yale and began his work as an evangelist, it seemed that a new move of God was afoot.

Adam considered his son's remark, and it disturbed him. He knew Nathan to be a devout man, though he was unable to accept the camp meetings that had swept across the country like a wave. In August of 1801, Adam and Nathan had gone to Cane Ridge, Kentucky, to see for themselves what the excitement was about. They had been astonished how big it was; settlers came by the thousands with tents and wagonloads of supplies, prepared to camp out on the grounds until the meetings ended. No one had an exact count of the attendance, but Peter Cartwright, a Methodist clergyman, estimated between twelve to twenty-five thousand—remarkable indeed, considering the largest city in the state had less than eighteen hundred people.

Adam had been moved by the experience—but then, he had been converted under the preaching of George Whitefield. Even now, years later, he could remember every detail plainly, how he had "fallen under the power," as the phenomena came to be known. He had seen men and women cut down like ripe grain under the powerful preaching of Jonathan Edwards, so at the Cane Ridge meeting, he had not been shocked—but Nathan had.

Adam groped for words to make his son understand. "Nathan, tell me the name of the most powerful intellect that ever stood in an American pulpit."

"Why, Jonathan Edwards!"

"You are right—so think about this, son: His was the greatest mind in the church, and yet many times—many times!—when I was in his church at Northhampton, I saw almost every element that you fault the modern revivals for. I saw men and women shouting and shaking like a giant had hold of them; I saw them lying on the floor so thick a man couldn't walk between them. Edwards always said that—with a few exceptions—these things were of God."

Nathan replied, "I can't answer you, Father. If there are two men in this world I trust, it's you and Dan. Still, the Bible says that we must act decently and in order."

The argument had come full circle, so Adam changed the subject. "I hope Christmas gets here soon. He was supposed to be here two days ago. I still fret about him among those Indians."

"Maybe he'll come this afternoon," Nathan reassured him as they all got up to leave the arbor.

The afternoon passed, and the family gathered inside the spacious dining room. Adam sat at one end, with Paul and his wife Charity at his right. Their son, Whitfield, and his wife Alice were on Adam's left. Nathan's family took up a large section. The boys, Alex and George—aged twenty-five and twenty-six—sat on one side of Nathan; their twenty-three-year-old daughter Judith, a regal beauty, was seated beside Julie. Across from them Dan Greene and his wife Anne sat, their three children lined up beside them.

The Greenes' second daughter, Missy, was a tall girl, and at age sixteen was awkwardly trapped between girlhood and womanhood. Her blond hair was usually in need of combing; her brown eyes large and watchful. *She looks like a young colt—all arms and legs!* Adam thought, but he saw that the fine lines were there, and when she got past the leggy stage, she would have the graceful bearing that some tall women have.

At fourteen, Asa was a carbon copy of his father: thick black hair, dark eyes, strongly built. He was a stubborn boy, Adam knew, but not wild.

He gave their eldest, Caroline, a careful glance—she had always puzzled him. She was twenty-six years old, and one of the quietest girls he had ever met. She had built some sort of wall around herself, and Adam had never been able to get close to her.

There were others there, and Adam could name about half of the distant cousins—women who had changed the Winslow name for another. He looked down the table and was snapped out of his reverie when he heard Paul ask him to say the blessing.

Getting to his feet, he bowed his head. "Lord, how grateful we are for this food! Thank you. And we thank you for our family—earth's only wealth. We are thankful that we are not alone in this world, for you have given us to one another. Now we ask that every member of the House of Winslow will be a child of God—faithful to you, O Lord of all the earth!"

The hushed "amens" floated around the table. The lull was broken as they fell to eating, and the room was filled with laughter and talk. Adam said to Paul, "I'm glad you did this, Paul. It's right for families to be together again."

After supper the men retired to the large parlor and the

women all pitched in to help with the dishes. Paul and Charity kept two servants, but the sudden influx of relatives necessitated extra hands. Charity moved through the crowded kitchen, giving orders cheerfully and often stopping to show someone how to do something better. Coming up behind Missy, she looked down at the blue china dishes the girl was washing in a pan of hot soapy water. "Why, Missy Greene!" she exclaimed, "look at the food you left on this dish!" She shook her head, adding, "You must have your mind on something else, because you're surely not thinking of the dishes."

"She's mooning because Chris didn't come," Asa said with a grin.

No one expected the outburst the boy's teasing would incur. Missy's face went white—then red—and she turned and shouted, "You shut your mouth, Asa!"

The boy's eyes flashed, and a stubborn thrust of his chin accompanied his retort. "I don't have to shut up! Everybody knows you're plum silly over—ow!"

A ringing slap on the cheek cut him off, and for one instant he stood there, stunned, with the clear imprint of Missy's hand on his left cheek. He gave a howl and threw himself at her, and the two of them fell to the floor in a kicking ball of fury, yelling at the top of their lungs.

Caroline gave a cry of distress and tried to separate them, to no avail; she could only stand there, looking helpless. The sudden eruption of violence had frozen everyone else in place except Charity. Her years on ship had given her a great deal of experience with such things, for sailors are simple men, often childish and fights were not uncommon.

Her green eyes blazing with a mixture of humor and impatience, Charity grabbed the large pan of soapy dishwater and without hesitation dumped it over the pair, then stood back.

The sudden deluge caught both of them with their mouths open. Asa rolled around on the floor gagging and Missy managed to sit up, sputtering. Their fight was forgotten, but the water had flattened Missy's blond hair and it hung in her face in soapy braids. She stared up at Charity Winslow in bewilderment.

"Now, if you're through with your fits, clean up this mess, then go change your clothes." Though her aunt was only five feet five, Charity seemed to tower over Missy as the girl got to her feet. Drawing herself up, Charity berated the two children with iron in her voice. "I'm ashamed of you! If you were mine, I'd cane you both until you learned a few manners! Now get busy!"

Missy's fair complexion was pale as ivory as she knelt without a word to mop the floor. Asa, at her side, was also too cowed to speak. When the floor was clean, she turned and left the room, determined not to cry in front of the family.

She ran blindly to the room she shared with several younger relatives, and fell across the bed sobbing. Scalding tears rolled down her cheeks, and her whole body shook with the force of her crying. When she was calmer she got up and paced the floor, dreading the moment when she would have to go down and face those who'd seen her make such a fool of herself.

Missy is as sensitive as a girl without a skin! She'd heard her father say that once, and it was true. Her height made her feel ugly—she would gladly have given all her quick intelligence to be six inches shorter. She often compared herself—always unfavorably—with small, petite girls, and had driven her mother wild by habitually stooping to make herself seem shorter.

"I hate Asa! I wish he'd die!" she muttered, immediately feeling a wave of guilt wash over her. Unable to tolerate it any longer, she ran out of the room and found her way out a side door that opened into the arbor, taking a path that led into the woods. The day before, she and Asa had wandered here, where the banks of a small brook wound around the edge of the fields and into the deeper woods. She picked her way along the path to a natural dam that had created a pond about fifteen feet across, and seated herself on a large moss-covered rock. The silence seeped into her spirit, and soon she felt better.

An hour went by, then another. She watched a water snake slither down the far bank in a movement graceful and deadly, snatching a small frog in one swift strike. The snake swallowed his prey and wriggled out of the water not three feet from her foot, its body swollen with the dead frog.

The moon edged across the sky unnoticed, and still she sat there, as if she were a part of the rock. She saw an owl cruise over, and she watched a nervous doe hover over her spotted fawn that staggered on absurdly long legs. The mother drank, coaxing her fawn to do the same before they melted into the dark wood.

Rustling leaves behind her startled Missy, gripping her with an unknown fear. Panicking, she turned around to see a large black shape appear against the background of the foliage less than ten feet away. *It's a bear!* The thought chilled her.

She leaped to her feet and made a wild lunge for the path, but her foot slipped on the moss, and she fell sprawling and helpless as the dark shape loomed closer. "Go away!" she cried out, desperately rolling over to kick at the bear.

"Go away? Why, here I've come halfway across the country and now you tell me to git?" The shape grinned at her.

"Christmas!" Missy scrambled to her feet and flung herself into his arms, her relief causing her to forget herself. "You scared me to death! I thought you were a bear!"

"You're not the only one who's scared," Christmas told her, the smile disappearing from his lips. "Your mother is about crazy with worry, child!" There was an edge in his soft voice as he added, "You ought not to worry her, Missy, her being so poorly."

The gentle rebuke was a blow to the girl, and tears sprang to her eyes. Dropping her head, Missy turned and trudged blindly down the path, speechless. To her, a reprimand from Christmas was ten times worse than from anyone else. She had looked forward to his arrival for so long—and now this!

"Wait!" he said, running after her. He stopped her and gently turned her around to face him. There was gentleness in his eyes. She had always been his pet, and it distressed him to see her hurt. "It's not so bad as that."

"It is! I've acted like an idiot!"

"Me too, Missy—lots of times," he laughed softly. "I heard all about it. You and Asa fought like wildcats, so Charity said."

"Did she say what we fought about?" Missy felt her face get hot.

"No. Wanna tell me about it?"

"Oh—it was nothing."

"Guess little brothers are just a pain in the neck sometimes."

"I'm such a fool!"

Christmas looked at her thoughtfully. Missy had grown two inches taller since he had seen her last year. The high point of his yearly trip east was the time he spent with the Greenes, and watching Missy and Asa grow up was a pleasure that carried him through the long winters in the mountains. He was fonder of her than he knew, and now he wanted to ease her grief.

"Go on and feel bad then," he grinned, "but I can tell you something that'll make you feel better, I bet. Matter of fact, I'll bet you what I got in my pocket against a big hug and a kiss that I can make you whoop and holler in ten seconds."

"Bet you can't!"

"I'm coming home with you and I'm gonna stay there two months and you and me—we're gonna get a sample of every bird's egg in the country, and I'm gonna teach you how to shoot like a mountain man!"

"Christmas!" she exclaimed, her face beaming with joy—as he had hoped—and her brown eyes widening in delight.

"See? You lose," he said. "Now, give me that hug and kiss—then we better get back before they send out a search party."

She threw her arms around him and he smiled, thinking, *This won't last long. Someday soon she's going to grow up and be too big to hug.*

Assuring himself that that time was still far off, he let her lead him back to the house, chattering and pulling at his hand.

CHAPTER ELEVEN

CAMP MEETING

★ ★ ★ ★

Years later, the Greenes never referred to those months as "the summer of 1806." It was always "the summer Chris stayed with us."

On July 4th of that year the Greenes had a big celebration dinner to welcome their guest. After the meal, Chris left the room, returning with a rifle in one hand and a small sack in the other. Setting down the rifle, he took something out of the sack—a powder horn, Asa saw, and a shot pouch—and picked up the handsome rifle again. Asa eyed it longingly, thinking it was a gift for his father, and paled when Chris held the rifle out to him. "You can't be a mountain man without a rifle, boy." Asa was speechless. His hands trembled as he took the heavy gun, running his fingers down the barrel, caressing the smooth stock. His throat was thick and tears stung his eyes. Not wanting Chris to notice and think he was a baby, Asa turned away with a husky "Thanks."

Chris grinned and clapped Asa on the shoulder and explained, "I'm never around anybody but Indians at Christmastime, so I decided this Christmas'll be on July 4th." He fished around in the sack and handed a package to Caroline. "Hope you like this, Caroline. You're hard to buy for, but maybe this will please you."

Caroline's gift was a fine leather book with HOLY BIBLE in gold letters across the front. Her fingers gently traced the words. "It's beautiful, Christmas," she said softly. "I'll treasure it always."

The bulky package Dan unwrapped was a volume of Rev. Charles Wesley's sermons—something he'd always longed for. The bindings were all calf leather, and the paper was thick vellum. "Why—these must have cost a fortune, Christmas!" he exclaimed.

He handed Anne a small package, saying, "This isn't Indian made, Anne. Came from over the water."

Chris watched her as she removed the paper, and he was saddened by how thin and wan she looked. She had been such a pretty young woman when he had first met her, but her last pregnancy had almost killed her, and she never recovered her strength after losing the baby. Nothing seemed to relieve her nagging cough, and she was unable to do hardly any work.

"Why, Christmas! It's the most beautiful thing I've ever seen! Look, girls—a pearl case."

They admired the delicate mother-of-pearl case, finely worked with gold wire, and then Chris said, "Well, that's all—oh, except this." He handed Missy a length of braided leather, saying, "You like to ride so much, I thought you'd like an Indian-made bridle. This one was made by a Sioux woman named Still Water—made of elk hide she chewed herself to make it soft."

The Greenes cast furtive glances at each other. It seemed unfair that Chris would give Missy such a small gift when he had given the rest of them such expensive things. Even Asa felt bad and tried to console her. "Hey, Missy, that's really a nice bridle." The others, somewhat embarrassed for her, admired it loudly.

But Missy was delighted with her present. "Thank you, Christmas!" she smiled. "You always think of the best gifts for us!"

"Oh, it's not much," Chris shrugged. "Say, did you notice there's no bit for the horse's mouth? Gotta be a pretty fair rider to control an animal with an Indian bridle. Come on—we'll try it out on the mare."

"All right."

Leaving the house together, they heard Asa clamoring to fire the rifle. Dan, who had not lost his interest in guns since his younger days, gave in and took his son down the road to find a safe place—away from the house—for shooting practice.

Watching her brother proudly carrying his rifle, Missy said, "What nice gifts!—much nicer than what we usually get for Christmas."

"It's little enough, Missy. I've taken a lot more from the Greenes than I'll ever be able to pay back." They came to the barn, and Chris put his hand on the bolt, swinging the door back. "Let me get Lady out for you."

"All right." Missy was perfectly capable of getting the mare, but it pleased her to have Chris do it. She turned the bridle over in her hands, examining the finely worked leather, and did not look up when she heard the sound of the horse's hooves. Still toying with the bridle, she walked closer to where Chris stood, glanced up, and froze in her tracks.

It was not Lady that Chris had led out. It was a beautiful chestnut stallion!

"Here's the rest of your present, Missy," Chris said quietly, handing her the hackamore he'd slipped over the neck of the animal.

She took the reins without looking at Chris, for her eyes were filled with the beauty of the horse. He was young, but very tall and rangy. His eyes were large and his coat glistened under the rolling bands of smooth muscles as he stamped the ground.

Chris moved back to lean against the barn, savoring the sight. Somehow he knew that even when he grew old, he'd still be able to pull this scene up from the place old dreams lie—the tall girl, leggy and strong, with the dying sun putting red lights in her blond hair, looking up with wonder at the powerful colt.

He was pulled out of his reverie when Missy turned and looked at him with enormous eyes that were brimming with tears. "I—I can't ever thank you enough. . . !"

Embarrassed, Chris shifted his weight and pushed himself

away from the wall. Brusquely, he told her, "Well, you've got to teach this horse a few things, Missy. He's got a mind of his own, and he's big enough to make life miserable for you if you don't show him who's boss."

"What's his name?"

"Whatever you call him."

She thought hard before saying, "When he runs, I bet it sounds like thunder. What's the Indian name for thunder, Chris?"

"Wah-tee-nah."

She mulled it over, then shook her head. "No, it'll just be Thunder." On the heels of that decision a new thought occurred to her. "Will you teach me to ride him—like you taught me to shoot?"

"Do what I can—but you're a natural rider, Missy. You ride like you're a part of the horse—just like the Sioux."

The compliment made her blush, and she ducked her head. "I—I don't ever give you anything, Christmas. You always bring me such wonderful presents, but I never give you anything."

He stirred uncomfortably, "Ah, Missy, when you get older, you'll find out that to us older folks, the best present is to give a youngster something and watch them enjoy it. Come on, it's time you took your first ride on Thunder!"

The rifle for Asa and Thunder for Missy—those were milestones in their young lives. For Asa, everything was dated "after I got my rifle." As for Missy, the stallion became her clock; everything else fit in around the times she was feeding, grooming, and riding him. So the days sped by, and the dark streak that had been such an obvious part of Chris's manner disappeared; the long hours he spent teaching Asa to shoot and Missy to care for the horse were like balm. One Monday morning Dan remarked to Caroline, "Christmas is going to the camp meeting over at Cane Ridge with me on Friday."

"Did you make him agree to go, Father?"

"Not a bit of it!" he said emphatically. "Matter of fact, when I mentioned that I'd be preaching there, he asked if he could go with me. There's been a lot of prayer for this meeting, Caroline. If the power falls again like it did back in 1801—could be that Chris gets converted. You pray on that."

"Yes, of course. Are we all going?"

"Your mother's not up to it. Someone will have to take care of her."

"I'll get Mrs. Rollins to stay with her. Mother likes her so much—and it'll be good for Sister Rollins, too."

That Friday the Greenes pulled into the Cane Ridge campground where the meeting was to be held. Chris had said little on the journey, and now he looked around the area, half-angry with himself for coming, half-wondering why he had asked to go in the first place. Over the past five years he had tried to put God out of his mind, until last winter when he'd been snowed in with Con and Frenchie for over a month in a tiny line shack.

The only reading available had been Con's greasy, worn New Testament. Though Con prided himself on his cynicism, secretly he admired men who seemed to know God, and so had carried the New Testament wherever he went, reading it from time to time. Chris had read a few chapters of John's gospel, and was surprised to discover that the simple story of Jesus gripped him as nothing else ever had. Something broke within him, and the words seemed to leap from the pages with dramatic intensity. Totally absorbed, Chris would read for fifteen hours at a stretch—much to Con and Frenchie's consternation—hardly pausing long enough to eat. When the thaw came, Chris threw himself into getting the furs back to the east. Still, the words of the little New Testament echoed in his mind night and day.

Now he had come to Cane Ridge—out of curiosity, mostly. He had no intention of making a fool out of himself, like some of the others he had heard of. Chris watched without comment as Dan waved and greeted almost everyone they passed. The place hummed with activity, and he noted stages erected in a clearing of the woods about a hundred yards from a small meeting house. On one of them stood a fat man who was already preaching to a large crowd. When they stopped the wagon and made their way through the crowd, they encountered several more of these platforms, all manned by fiery preachers who drew the attention of the swelling mobs around them.

"Why so many pulpits?" Chris asked.

"Gets you closer to the people in smaller groups," Dan answered. "Whitefield preached to ten thousand at times—but not many men have the voice for that."

"Are these all Methodist folks?"

"Oh no!" Greene began to identify the speakers and their organizations. "That's Brother Hayes, and he is a Methodist—but over there, the skinny man with the jug ears? Rev. Tyler, a Baptist—and next to him, Rev. John Hamilton, a Presbyterian—"

Dan was interrupted several times by men who greeted him respectfully; one very muscular young man by the name of Peter Cartwright welcomed Chris with a bone-crushing handshake. "Well, glory!" His intense black eyes sized the frontiersman up as if he were a prize steer. "You are a big one, Brother Winslow—just the man to preach the word in these parts!"

"Didn't know size was a qualification for the ministry, Brother Cartwright," Chris grinned.

"Maybe not in Boston," Cartwright replied, "but here a minister has to handle whatever comes."

Dan said carefully, "I've heard some talk about the Winston boy, Brother Cartwright. Folks are saying he's here to make trouble."

"God forgive the lad," Cartwright returned steadily. "We must have order—I will pray that there is no trouble."

He turned and walked away, and Dan laughed. "There's nobody like Peter Cartwright!" Then, "Well, I must leave you, Chris. Watch out for Caroline and the children, will you?"

But it was Caroline who took charge of them all, settling the sleeping arrangements and getting Asa and Chris to build a cooking fire so she could prepare dinner and get them presentable to go to the meeting.

"That sister of yours, she's a hummer!" Chris whispered to Missy as they made their way to the meeting.

"I guess church is all she cares about," Missy shrugged. She and her brother had been to many camp meetings with their father, and they seemed unimpressed with all the excitement, but Chris was as jumpy as he had ever been in his life. The camp was well lit by fires and lanterns; ministers occupied every stage, and the immense crowd milled around them.

Caroline led them to one stage after another, briefly commenting on the speaker: "That's Brother Satterfield—good preacher, but weak on the doctrine of sanctification. . . ." She stopped and pointed at one platform. "Look! There's brother James McGready!"

"Is he good?" Chris asked with interest.

"Why, he's been used of God more than any other man at camp meetings!" Caroline said with admiration. "There'll be some people hard hit by his message!"

Although he was of only average height, McGready's voice was overpowering, and Chris had no trouble picking up the subject in the middle of his sermon—hellfire. The magnificent voice roared like thunder:

" . . . he died accursed of God, and when his soul was separated from his body, the black flaming creatures of the deep began to encircle him on every side. As the fiends of hell dragged him into the eternal gulf—roaring and screaming—the Indians, pagans, and Mohammedans stood amazed and upbraided him, falling like Lucifer from the meridian blaze of the threshold of heaven, sinking into the liquid boiling waves of the flaming abyss . . ."

Suddenly a woman right in front of Chris gave a piercing scream and fell to the ground. McGready did not even pause, but the sound seemed to trigger a reaction, for all around the stage people were dropping to the ground. Some of them toppled like trees, falling stiffly where they stood, making no attempt to break their fall. Others seemed to lose their strength and melt to the earth. Alarmed, Chris glanced at Caroline and saw that her eyes were closed, a satisfied smile on her lips. Asa was watching it all with the avid curiosity of a fourteen-year-old, but Missy simply stood with her head down, showing no reaction at all.

Chris felt uncomfortable about the whole event. The preaching was much as he remembered as a boy, but the people's reaction . . . it was so . . . unnatural. He fervently wished he had not come, but now there was no way out. What seemed like hours later, Caroline led them to another area. There a preacher named Barlow was cutting the air with his hands and running up and down the platform, shouting at the top of his lungs.

Chris did not want to be there, and was relieved when Caroline said, "Asa, you and Missy need to go to bed. Do you want to stay a while and hear some more exhortation, Christmas?"

He saw that she wanted him to do just that, but he said, "I'm pretty tired myself," so she turned and led the way to the wagon.

Lying in his blanket that night, he thought again of Knox. His brother's faith contrasted so sharply with the waves of emotion he had witnessed that day; he had difficulty making sense of it all. The stars did their great dance overhead, and he lay there most of the night wondering why God seemed so far away.

The next day brought more of the same. Dan preached until he was hoarse, and as Chris listened he realized he liked Greene's preaching best. By the end of the fourth day he would go to hear no other minister—until Dan asked him to go hear Peter Cartwright.

Chris enjoyed the way the thick-set preacher spiced up his sermons with illustrations from life. He was absorbed in one of these stories when a tall, strong-looking young man in a ruffled shirt began to heckle Cartwright loudly. "Tim Winston! Now, he's a bad 'un!" Chris heard a man beside him mutter.

Abruptly Cartwright stopped preaching and stared boldly at the young man. "Mr. Winston, you are disrupting the service."

The young man guffawed. "Listen, Cartwright, I'm sicka you and your preachin'. Seems to me you cain't know all that much about hell anyway, see'n as you never been there. Maybe ya oughta jest go there yourself! Then come back and tell us about it."

Fire in his eyes, Cartwright jumped off the platform and made his way toward young Winston as the crowd parted. The young man's smile faded a little with every stride the preacher took; and when he stood before Winston, the young man cursed and drew back his arm. With panther-quickness the preacher's arms shot out.

The next thing Winston knew he was sitting on the ground, his arms pinned at his sides. As the crowd looked on, Brother

Cartwright made his point. "I said be quiet. I'll not have this service disrupted again. Not by all the demons in hell—and most certainly not by you. God forbid it."

The people standing nearby watched nervously, fully expecting the young man to leap up and thrash the preacher. But lowering his gaze, the heckler studied the ground in silence, and did not move when Cartwright released his grip and strode back to the stage, resuming his sermon as if nothing had happened. Winston left at once. Afterward Chris made his way up to shake hands with the preacher. "Brother Cartwright, I admire the way you took care of that troublemaker—I can't say I've met many preachers who would have handled it the way you did."

Cartwright looked up at Chris with a twinkle in his eyes that disappeared when he asked, "Are you a man of God, Mr. Winslow?"

"No," Chris swallowed.

"At least you are an honest man," Cartwright replied gently. He put a hand on Chris's shoulder. "I will pray that you will meet God tonight. You are a strong man, son, but that is your weakness. Your pride has kept you running from God—but I feel that He will find you soon!"

The preacher walked away, but his words echoed over and over in Chris's mind, and he wanted to run. But there was nowhere else to go, and since this was the last night, it would not be fair to the Greenes to ask them to leave now. So he kept on the outskirts of the crowd, trying to ignore the cries of the people calling out to God all around him.

Later that night on his way to the wagon, he passed by a stage where not more than ten or twelve people were gathered. A small man was speaking very softly. Chris would have kept on walking, but one phrase of the man's sermon drifted to his ears, and he stopped. It was one of the first verses that had burned into his brain when he had picked up Con's New Testament the previous winter: *Ye must be born again*.

Chris stared at the man, thin and seedy-looking with a receding chin. A tale of long, hard poverty and failure was etched on the man's face, and his weak voice was evidence that he had little ability as a speaker. But Chris could not push aside the earnestness of his message: *Ye must be born again.*

Chris wanted to run, but stood rooted in place looking up into that man's face. In that moment something began to happen inside—and it frightened him. He had always been in control of his life, and now he felt that control slipping away. His knees were weak and Chris felt as he had once when he'd gone without food for five days in the Sky Country—lightheaded, and filled with thoughts that arose from another source.

Is this you, God? he thought wildly, his brain spinning. He thought of Knox, of his parents, and of the wild life that had brought him nothing but emptiness. As if for the first time Chris really saw himself—who he was, the things he had done—and he was horribly ashamed of what he saw. Overwhelmed, he sank to his knees, sobbing uncontrollably. He was embarrassed and wanted to stop, but he could not. The other words he remembered reading began to fill his memory, "Repent . . . have faith . . . believe in me . . ."

Religion he had known—but this was different. Somehow he knew that God was with him in a way that made him terribly afraid. And then he seemed to hear a voice that said, "Come to me—and I will give you rest!"

Until then Chris Winslow had not known how tired he was. The years had taken their toll, and though his body was strong, inside he was worn out—exhausted. He had a great longing for just one thing: "Yes, Lord! Give me rest!"

The lights and the noise seemed to fade as the weariness slipped away, leaving him fresh and strong. He felt as though a crushing burden had been lifted. "Thank you, God! Thank you!" He raised his hands to heaven and shouted with joy.

When Chris looked up, he found Dan looking at him with a broad smile.

"Dan—you'll never guess what happened!"

"Oh, won't I? It's written all over your face! Praise the Lord, brother—it looks as if after all your running, God has caught you at last!"

The three Greene children stood silently behind their father. Missy and Asa stared wide-eyed, unsure what to make of it all; Caroline, overjoyed, seemed unaware of the tears coursing down her cheeks. Peter Cartwright, walking past the group, caught sight of Chris's face, ran up to them and pulled Chris to his feet, wrapping him in a big bear hug.

"Brother, God has done a work in your heart! Isn't that so?"

Once Chris was able to (Brother Cartwright's greeting had knocked the breath out of him), he tried to answer. "I . . . don't know what happened . . . but something is gone . . ."

"That's your sin!" Cartwright cried out, and he gave Chris a hearty blow. "It's gone! You're a free man, Chris Winslow!"

"Glory to God!" Dan said, his face beaming.

"Father in heaven," prayed Cartwright, "we thank Thee for what Thou hast done in this man's life. We commit him now to Thee, for Thy service, and trust Thee to lead him into the work Thou hast for him. May he serve Thee with his whole heart, and never forget what Thou hast done for him this day. In Thy Son's most precious name, amen!" The group echoed, "Amen."

"I don't claim to be a prophet, Brother Winslow," Cartwright continued. "But I've seen lots of men get saved, and from time to time I get a feeling—and I've got it right now—about you!"

"What kind of feeling?"

"I believe God is calling you to be a preacher, Chris Winslow!"

CHAPTER TWELVE

MISSY GROWS UP

★ ★ ★ ★

The sun seemed to be stuck in the sky. Missy had changed dresses twice, then in total frustration put on the original. Ever since her father had come home with a letter and a smile on his face, saying, "Christmas is going to be on the Kentucky circuit!" she had lived for the day her friend would be there. The three years Chris had studied for the ministry at Yale under Timothy Dwight had lasted for eons, but this morning he was coming home!

She stopped pacing the floor long enough to peer in the small mirror over the washstand. Critically she studied her features: large wide-spaced brown eyes shaded by thick lashes under brown, arching brows, a generous mouth—which she thought far too wide—and blond hair that tumbled in thick masses like a crown, framing her oval face. With a disgusted sigh, she wheeled from the mirror, muttering under her breath, "You're nothing but a fat ugly old cow!" She hated her looks (when she thought of them at all, which was seldom). She had always admired Caroline's regular features and trim figure, and longed to be small and neat like her sister.

At five feet eleven inches, the younger of the Greene sisters was very tall for a woman, and full-figured as well; only the largest and tallest young men had given her a second glance, and she had cried herself to sleep many nights bemoaning her appearance. Actually, she was not "a fat cow" at all; a life of ceaseless outdoor activity had pared away any excess weight, and for her height she was a beautifully shaped and healthy young woman.

Picking up a small wooden box from the table, she opened it and took out a packet of letters tied with a blue ribbon. They were all brief and showed the signs of much handling. She could have recited them by heart. She picked up the first one.

September 10, 1807

Dear Missy,

I am at Yale now—feeling as out of place as a Sioux medicine man at a Methodist camp meeting! Peter Cartwright may have been right about God calling me to preach, but all the struggles I've had—even just this first week—really make me wonder if I'm doing the right thing. Almost all the other students are young and have studied Greek and Hebrew and theology at school. And here I sit, a thirty-year old mountain man, in a class with twenty-year-old scholars, feeling like the biggest fool God ever made!

I'd give anything to just chuck it all and come running back and see you and Thunder—just to ride out to the old lake where we caught the big catfish! But I can't quit now—so you pray for me, y'hear?

Love,
Christmas

Missy thought back to that summer when Christmas had gotten converted. She'd been so happy that he was saved—but how she'd cried when he'd announced that he was going to Yale to study to be a minister. She skipped through the letters, selected another and opened it.

March 4, 1808

My dear Missy,

I have thought of you often during the long winter months. I am sorry that I haven't written more often, but my head is as thick as an anvil, and I have to work three times as hard as the other students to keep up. Your letters have been so good for me! You have a flair for telling things in such a way that I can see it happening—like when you won the race against the Hodgkins boy and his mare! Maybe when I come home next time, you and Asa and I can go to the mountains. I get lonely for the hills, Missy, and this life is so confining! But it will be over soon, and I can begin preaching.

Then she skipped to the last letter in the pack.

March 11, 1809

Dear Missy,

Finished—at last! I can't believe that my studies are over and that I'll be home in two months! It's been harder than I ever thought it would be—but it's over.

I will see you in May—but I wanted to warn you that Caroline has told me about your sweetheart, Tom Cantrell. (I'm a little hurt that you didn't tell me yourself, but I suppose a grown young lady doesn't tell such things to gray-haired old uncles like me!) I may as well warn you, I'm going to give the young fellow a good examination and a heart-to-heart talk. I think too much of my Missy girl to have her throw herself away on some worthless scoundrel!

Seriously, your father tells me that the young man is acceptable in every respect, and when I arrive home, I'll congratulate him on getting the finest girl in the world!

Love,
Christmas

She gave her head an impatient shake and snorted "Tom Cantrell!" before she heard Asa yell from the front yard, "He's comin'! Christmas is comin'!" She threw the box down and dashed out of the room, her eyes flashing—and then remembered that she was a grown woman now, so she slowed down and forced herself to go out on the porch at a more sedate pace to join the others.

Christmas was three hundred yards away when he saw them on the porch waiting. Lifting his hat, he gave a wild cry and spurred his horse to a run. He pulled the big bay up and leaped to the ground, his face flushed but alive with pleasure. Except for two visits, the last a year ago, he had not left Yale, and Missy's heart leaped at the sight of him as he grabbed Asa in a bear hug, lifting the boy off the ground. Dan gave him a hug, and he carefully put an arm around Anne's frail shoulders, saying, "Anne, it's good to see you!" Caroline stood at the foot of the steps, and he broke through her reserve by leaning down and kissing her cheek, saying warmly, "Caroline! I've missed you!"

She colored at the unexpected kiss, reached up to touch her cheek, and her eyes were bright as she said, "I'm glad you're home."

Missy came down the steps, thinking that he'd greet her as he did Caroline—but with a whoop he seized her in his powerful arms and swung her around in a wide circle, crying out, "Who's this girl? What's happened to my little Missy?"

She had been too big for anyone to pick up for a long time, and she felt like a child in his arms; still, it annoyed her that he would treat her like Asa. She wanted to be treated like a woman.

He put her down but kept his arms around her; looking up so far into a man's eyes made her feel very strange. For the first time since childhood she felt delicate—feminine—and her anger fled as he stooped to give her a sound kiss on the cheek, then held her at arms' length, smiling and shaking his head.

"The little girl I left behind has grown into a beautiful young lady!" he said. "But I still mean to take you and Asa to the mountains—even if you are a grown-up lady!"

"Oh, Christmas!" she cried, "when can we go?"

"Now wait just a minute, Rev. Winslow." Dan spoke up, his face mock-solemn. "If you haven't learned at Yale that Methodist preachers don't go to the woods with single young ladies, then Timothy Dwight has gotten much too liberal. You'll have to take the young lady's father along if you want to go traipsing all over the woods!"

"Done!" Chris laughed, fondly looking from one face to the next. "It's good to be home."

He has changed a little, Missy thought, watching him follow her parents into the house. His face was paler than she remembered— the three years of studying inside had done that, no doubt—but he looked no older, and he was as energetic as ever. Still, his eyes had lost the wild gleam that she remembered, and his manner was calmer, less intense.

The afternoon passed quickly, Dan and Chris sitting on the porch most of the time. The others came and went, stopping now and again to listen to their conversation, which was all about the seminary. Dan listened carefully as Chris spoke with warmth of Timothy Dwight. "He's a wonder, Dan. When he took over as the president of Yale, there were only a handful of students who were converted. Most of them were pretty close to being infidels. But Rev. Dwight started in fighting deism and skepticism—and revival broke out."

Dan gave Chris an odd look. "Did you meet Dwight's father?"

"Oh yes. He's a grand old fellow—big as the side of a barn. He came to see his son pretty often."

"Did you know he had a fight with your grandfather once?"

"A fight! Over what?"

"Over which one of them would marry Mary Edwards—the youngest daughter of Jonathan Edwards." Dan laughed at Chris's shocked expression. "Adam wanted to marry her, but he lost out to young Dwight."

"If he had married her—my grandfather would have been Jonathan Edwards!" Chris exclaimed.

Dan laughed and said, "Never mind, Christmas. I think you got some of your better qualities from your grandmother, Molly."

All afternoon neighbors came by to greet the new minister, and Caroline sniffed, "Look at that, Missy! Ellen Jennings come to call—and she hasn't been to church twice running in years!"

Missy looked at the attractive girl who stood beside Chris, gazing up at him with a dazzling smile. Ellen was the youngest daughter of Ellis Jennings, a wealthy landowner. "She's pretty," Missy observed, and felt a twinge of jealousy stir when the girl laughed and reached out to touch Chris's arm. After all, Ellen was a petite girl, and seemed totally at ease with men—two qualities Missy envied.

Finally the Jennings left, and Ellen called "We'll expect you next Tuesday evening, Rev. Winslow!" as she drifted down the steps beside her father.

"Beautiful girl," remarked Dan, grinning at Chris as he led the younger man inside the house. "Her father's quite influential in the Methodist world. Gives more money than anyone. If a preacher were to get Jenning's girl, I guess that minister could find himself in one of the biggest pulpits in the country."

Caroline walked into the room just in time to overhear her father's last remark, and was visibly annoyed. "I doubt that Ellen's fitted to be a minister's wife, Father. Supper's ready." With that, she swept back into the kitchen.

Both men stared after her. Christmas observed, "The life of a preacher's wife is not an easy one, for a fact. Guess there're not many women who'd be willing to live like that." He rose from his chair and followed Caroline.

That evening he asked Missy to go for a ride, and they saddled and rode until dark in the foothills. Coming back, he said, "I always wondered how you'd figure out a way to ride in a dress. You sure treed that coon! Real practical—and you look nice, too."

Missy felt the red creep into her cheeks. "Thank you, Christmas." It had taken her months to convince her parents to permit her to make her own riding suit, complete with a split skirt that was full enough to satisfy the demands of modesty, while enabling her to continue to ride with a conventional saddle. Normally, women rode side saddle, but Missy revolted against that idea. In her mind the skirt was a much better solution to the problem.

They turned down an old path that led through the forest of large hardwoods and dismounted at the creek that bubbled over smooth, moss-covered stones. "Oh, Missy, am I glad to be here!" Christmas exclaimed. "College just about got the best of me."

She had taken off her shoes and was dabbling her feet in the brook. *Sure is a pretty sight,* he thought, admiring how the dappled shadows fell on her cheeks. "I'm glad you're here too, Christmas. It was lonesome without you. Every time I rode Thunder, I thought of you and how we'd do this when you got back."

The minutes flew by as they drank in the sounds of the wood. At last Chris stirred and said, "We have to get back. Your mother said that young Cantrell was coming to sit on the porch with you tonight."

She ignored the teasing light in his eyes, tossing her heavy mane of hair so that it fell down her back. "He's too short" was her cryptic remark.

He stared at her in surprise. "Didn't know there was a height requirement for a young man."

"There isn't—if you're small, like Caroline—or like Ellen Jennings. But if you're a giant like I am—"

She didn't finish her sentence, for he had reached out and turned her around, gripping her shoulders. "Missy," he chided her sharply, "that's not fit talk!"

To her horror she felt her eyes fill with tears, which she blinked away furiously, saying, "It's true! I'm a—a giraffe!"

"You've never even seen one of those critters—and I don't want to hear you talk so!" His eyes flashed in the falling darkness. "What would your father say? What I hear you saying is that you're not satisfied with your looks—and that's what the Bible calls vanity, Missy." His rebuke cut her, and she dropped her head, biting her lower lip. "What if you'd been born blind—or crippled? I've seen women who'd give anything to look like you!"

"What do you know about it!" Missy blurted out, raising her head to meet his gaze. "You don't know what it's like. When I was growing up the boys never paid attention to me like they did to other girls. They treated me like a boy, just because I was big and strong and could run fast. Well, that's fine when you're twelve years old—but when you get to be sixteen and are nearly six feet tall, it's awful! What do you think it feels like never to get asked to parties because you tower over all the boys your age? I—I'm nineteen years old—and no man has ever wanted me—because I'm so—big!"

Before she could choke out the last word, her body was racked with sobs and tears were running down her cheeks. She turned blindly toward the horses, hoping to get away, but Chris caught her arm and turned her around. He pulled her close in a comforting hug, and she leaned against him, unleashing the unshed tears of a lifetime. She had never spoken to a soul as she had to him, and now that her secret was out, she could only lay her head on his shoulder and weep.

Christmas stood there, patting her shoulder gently. *My*

Missy. All these years I've known her—I can't believe that I never once saw this coming! he thought. When the sobs lessened, she took a deep breath and drew back. He took a handkerchief from his pocket and handed it to her, groping for the right words to say to her. After she had wiped her tears and returned his handkerchief, he said slowly, "Missy, I'm sorry I hurt you. I can be mighty self-centered at times, but I would never knowingly hurt your feelings for the world."

"It's all right," she murmured quietly.

"No, it's not. All I can say is this: To me you always seemed—just right. Just what a girl ought to be. I—I never once thought that you could be unhappy with yourself—because to me you're beautiful."

She shrugged and avoided his eyes. Forcing a smile she said, "I—I guess we'd better go home." Then, "Don't think of this time, Chris. I never cried over it before—and I promise not to bother you with it again."

"No!" he returned sharply. "It's no 'bother' to listen to the problems of people we love."

She threw her head back and looked up at him with a strange expression. "I'll remember that." Then they mounted and rode slowly back to the house. Dan saw them come in, noticing that Missy looked a little troubled, but thought little of it—though Caroline did. As they prepared for bed that evening, she asked casually, "Did you have a nice ride with Christmas?"

"It was fine." Missy said no more, but her silence spoke volumes to her sister. Caroline did not press her, but after they were in bed she asked, "Are you going to marry Tom?" Christmas had met the young man that night, and had been pleasantly surprised to see that he was not a dwarf, as Missy had implied. Cantrell was a well-built young man only an inch or two shorter than Missy—soft-spoken, with steady gray eyes and a quick mind. "I like him," he'd commented to Missy after Cantrell left.

There were several other young ladies in the area who shared Chris's opinion, as well. Missy liked Tom—but not enough. "No," she sighed. "I told him so tonight." Caroline did not speak, but Missy could feel her unspoken disapproval. *She thinks I'm a fool, but I can't help it!* She remembered earlier days, simpler days, and she cried out silently:

O God, why do we have to grow up?

CHAPTER THIRTEEN

"I'VE ALWAYS LOVED YOU!"

★ ★ ★ ★

By the time Chris had been home six months, Missy knew that she was in love with him. She also realized bitterly that he would never think of her as anything more than a young girl he was very fond of—and she withdrew from him in a manner that confused and hurt him. Trying to smooth things over, he began seeking her out quite often. Usually he would appear on his big bay, saying, "Let's work these horses out, Missy." They would say little during those rides, but she was aware of a change in him.

He was gone most of the time, preaching—with some success—in the most backward parts of Kentucky. Worn thin and dusty he would appear from time to time at the Greenes' home. They all noticed that at those times Ellen Jennings managed to be very much present, sitting in the front row of Dan's church where Chris was always asked to preach, leaning forward attentively as he spoke.

"She'll get him, for sure," Martha Shipton said. She was Missy's close friend, a lively girl of seventeen. "Mark my words, he gets a little closer every time he comes here! Did you see them with their heads together at the social last night? If they'd been any closer, they'd have been wearing each other's clothes!"

Missy had to smile at the way Martha put it, but she had not failed to notice that Chris spent much of his free time with Ellen. "I don't think he'll ever marry," she said finally. "He lost his wife and baby, you know, and once he told me that he didn't mean to have another family. Too hard when you lose them, he said."

"Bosh! Men talk like that, but you just watch, Missy—they'll be married in six months. Then he'll be made pastor of some rich Methodist church—and that's about the last we'll see of Rev. Chris Winslow!"

"I've got to go home, Martha."

"How's your mother?"

"Not well." Missy rubbed her forehead wearily. "She's not able to get out of bed at all now—and with Caroline so busy helping Father with the church, I have to take care of her."

"I'll help you," Martha offered instantly. "Why don't I come over tomorrow?"

"It's good of you, Martha, but Mother's gotten a little . . . hard to please. Maybe when she's better."

She returned and took care of her mother's needs, then cooked supper for herself and Asa. He was subdued, fearful of what his mother's sickness might mean, and for once he went to bed early without argument.

Missy was washing the dishes when she heard a horse leave the road and come to the house. Drying her hands, she went to the door and opened it to find Chris there. "Why, I didn't know you were back," she uttered in surprise. "Come in—supper's still warm."

"Maybe just a cup of coffee, Missy," he replied. He followed her to the kitchen, sat down wearily in a chair and sipped the hot black coffee. "How's your mother?"

"She was better last week, but yesterday she had a bad spell. She can't keep anything down—and the cough is worse."

He put the coffee cup down, stared at it, then lifted his eyes. "Missy, she's very sick."

"I know. She's not going to live." She sat down and rested her chin on her hand, brushing back a lock of hair from her forehead with her other hand. "She slips away a little every day."

Chris nodded sadly, thinking again—as he often did—of how bright Missy'd been as a child. "Do you remember when you took care of me—when Knox brought me to this house just about dead?"

Missy's features softened with a smile. "I remember—you were my 'patient.' I remember holding the cup so you could drink the soup, and even feeding it to you, a spoonful at a time. When your fever went up, I'd put cool, wet towels on your forehead. And when you got better, I'd take you for short walks to the creek." Her eyes brightened. "I still have the bird egg collection you gave me."

"Do you now? I'd like to go again. Maybe we could get that woodpecker egg I promised you. I never did get that one, did I, Missy?"

She stirred and there was a sadness in her voice. "I don't know, Chris. That was a long time ago." Their eyes met and held across the table.

"I hate to bother you with this, Missy, but I got bad news today—"

"Remember what you told me, Christmas," Missy interrupted. " 'It's no bother to listen to the people you love.' Especially when they have a problem. What's wrong?"

He smiled at her sadly, then pulled a letter from his coat pocket. "I got a letter from my father." He hesitated. "My grandfather died two weeks ago."

"Oh, Chris!" She quickly put a hand on his arm. "I'm so sorry—I know how you loved him."

"Well, he was eighty-two, and he went easy. Father put it all down in the letter."

"Could I hear it, Chris?"

"Why—of course, Missy." He unfolded the sheet of paper and scanned the letter for the place he wanted as she watched his face in the lamplight. It pained Missy to see him like this; obviously the news had cut him deeply. Though Adam was her great-uncle, she herself did not know him that well. Finding his place, Chris began to read aloud:

"He was never in any pain, son, and we are grateful for that! For the last week, he slept most of the time; though when he did awaken, his mind was perfectly clear. The night before your grandfather died, he woke up and said, 'Nathan—who's here?' I said, 'Just my family, Father. See—here's Julie, and Judith and the boys.' He looked at us all—me, your mother, and the children, and then he shook his head. 'No, I heard Molly.'

"That shocked us all at first—we thought he was losing control. Then he saw the looks we were giving each other, and seemed to read our thoughts. With that old smile, he assured us, 'Don't worry, I'm as clear-headed as a dying man can be, Nathan. It may be that none of you heard her—but I did.'

"I asked what she said, and he just smiled again and shook his head. 'I've missed her so much,' he whispered. 'It won't be long now.'

"Father laid back with his eyes closed, and I thought he was gone, but then he opened them again and began to talk. He told story after story of the Winslow family, how each one of the Winslow clan had added to the legacy of the family name. When his own father died—Miles Winslow was your great grandfather, Christmas—Father said, 'My father had always loved Charles best, but when he died he whispered to me, "You are the best of the Winslows, Adam!"—it wasn't true, of course!' Then he told us how proud he was of us all—and I especially want you to know what he said about you, Christmas: 'Chris has been a grief to you, Nathan, but he'll be a man that you and all the family will hold up with pride!'

"That was almost all, son. He closed his eyes and seemed to be resting. Ten minutes later his lips moved, and when I bent down, I heard him say, 'I'm coming. . . !' and when I looked up, he was gone."

Chris stopped reading and refolded the letter, replacing it with hands that were not quite steady. Putting his hands on the table, Chris rested his forehead on them, saying, "I've given Father a lot of grief—and all the rest of them as well!"

Missy rose and went to him, putting her arms about him and pulling his head to her bosom as she might have done with Asa or with a hurt child. His shoulders shook with grief, and she stroked his hair, making comforting sounds. When he grew still, she released him and lifted his chin, his cheeks still wet with tears. "Adam Winslow was a very wise man, Christmas," Missy murmured quietly. "And he was very proud of you."

Laughing shakily, Chris did not try to refute that. "You're a strong woman, Missy." He studied the tabletop for a moment before looking up, where she was again seated across from him. "I'm going to Virginia," he announced. "It's too late to see grandfather—and I couldn't go back when Charles died last year—but I need to spend some time with my family. When I come back, I'm going to be pastor of the Pineville church."

"You're not going to ride the circuit?" she asked in surprise.

"No. The bishop asked me to take the church. He says I may go on the circuit later, but he thinks I need experience as a pastor first."

"It'll be different," she responded. "But you'll be close, so we can see more of you."

He rose and paced the floor, deep in thought. Then as though a decision had been made, he stopped by her chair and put his hands on her shoulders. Missy looked up at him, not knowing why he did that until he asked her, "Would you go with me, Missy—to Virginia?"

"To Virginia?" Her head swam in a confused muddle. "Why do you want me to go to your home?"

His grip on her shoulders tightened. "The bishop thinks a pastor should be a married man."

The room seemed to shift, and Missy reached up and grabbed onto Chris's arms to steady herself. Once in her life she had fainted, when one of her friends had cut herself badly—and she had that same lightheaded feeling as she looked at him. Her thoughts raced wildly, and she could only stare at him, sure that she must have misunderstood what he said.

"Missy," he urged quietly, "I know it's crazy, and I don't have any right to ask a young woman to share the life that's in front of me. Will you let me tell you what's happened?"

"Chris—I don't know. . . !"

He put his finger on her lips, saying soberly, "I had a wife once—and I never thought I could love another woman. And when I left to go to Yale, in my mind you were just a little girl. Even when I came back, that was what I thought. But something happened the evening we took a ride to the creek." He shook his head. "When I put my arms around you that night and held you close, I did it because I was sorry to see you so unhappy, and wanted to comfort my little girl. But at that point I realized something: you were not a little girl anymore! You remember how I told you that to me you were everything a girl ought to be, Missy? I'd like to change that now—to me you're everything a woman should be."

She looked up at him with trembling lips and whispered, "I've always loved you, Chris!"

He pulled her into his arms and kissed her gently, and they stood close together for a long time, lost in the wonder of it all. Finally she drew back. "But I—I can't marry you. Not with Mother so sick."

"I know. I can wait, if you'll have me."

She hesitated. "Are you sure you want me?"

"Yes. I've fasted and prayed about it for months!"

She smiled and asked mischievously, "When did all this fasting and prayer take place—while you were running around with Ellen Jennings?"

"I'm a handy man, Missy," he protested innocently. "I can do lots of things at the same time."

"You just want to marry me because the bishop said you had to," Missy teased.

"That's better than the reason you're marrying me!"

She looked puzzled and he laughed. "You just love me because I'm tall!"

They stood there for a long time, talking lightly, happily. Missy finally said, "They'll think we're both crazy, Chris."

He grinned and bent down and kissed her again. "Maybe we are. I'll have a word with your father as soon as he gets back. He'll probably run me off with his shotgun."

"No. He thinks there's nobody like you." She touched his cheek and whispered, "That's what I've always thought, too—but I never believed it would turn out like this!"

He stroked her hair, loving each moment. After a while, he murmured softly, "I don't want to leave, but I must. I'll see you tomorrow, Missy."

Three days later her father came home, and when Chris walked in that evening after supper, Missy's heart skipped a beat. Her mother was asleep and Asa was off running a trout line, so only Caroline was there.

Chris drank coffee while Dan filled him in on the details of the meeting. He was nervous, and Missy found that she could barely sit still. Caroline got up and took some sewing out of her box. Returning to her seat, she sat quietly, listening but not entering into the conversation.

Dan wound up his story, saying, "Well, it was a grand time—a grand time! The Lord moved in power, and I found myself wishing you were there." Then settling back comfortably, he asked, "What have you been doing, Christmas?"

There was an awkward silence, and Caroline looked up swiftly. Her hands grew still as she saw the tense look on Chris's face, and Missy had an overwhelming urge to jump up and leave the room.

"Dan, I—I've got to tell you something, and it's not easy," he began. After a pause Chris went on hurriedly, "I've asked Missy to marry me, and she's agreed if you approve."

The silence was almost palpable, and Missy shut her eyes, clenching her hands into fists. She had seen Caroline's face go pale as paper, and could not look at her again.

Dan stared at Chris as if he could not believe what he had heard. "Why—it's pretty sudden, isn't it?"

"Not as sudden as it seems, Dan. I loved White Dove so much that when I lost her, it tore something out of me. I had no notion of marrying again. But something happened." He smiled and looked across the table at Missy. "I found a woman who filled that empty spot. I love Missy, and I always will."

"Missy?" Dan looked at his daughter, noting the pale face and the nervous hands. "Is this what you want?"

"Yes." For the life of her, Missy could say no more, but she managed a tremulous smile at her father.

Dan looked down at his hands and thought hard, while the others waited. When he lifted his head there was a smile on his lips. "Every father wants his girl to get a good man—and as far as I'm concerned, you are the best man I could trust with Missy."

"Oh!" Missy leaped up and flew to her father, nearly knocking the chair over as she flung her arms around him.

"Well—don't strangle me, girl!" he protested helplessly. Pushing her off, he got to his feet and put his hand out. "She'll be a helpmeet to you, Chris."

Caroline put her sewing down, came over to Missy and put her arms around her, saying evenly, "You'll be very happy, Missy." She turned and looked at Chris, speaking in that same tone. "She'll be a good wife to you, Chris." Then she walked back to her chair and picked up her sewing. "I'll see if Mother is all right."

When she left, Chris remarked, "Caroline is a fine girl. I wonder why she's never married?"

Missy's eyes met her father's, and she knew they were thinking the same thought: *He really doesn't know that Caroline loves him.* But when she started to say something, Dan gave her a warning shake of his head and said, "Someday I think she'll find the right man. But when have you planned to marry?"

"When Anne gets better," Chris replied. "Missy won't leave until then."

Dan shook his head and said with characteristic honesty, "We all know that Anne will never get off that bed unless God performs a miracle. You two have a work for God, and it would be a mistake to put your wedding off for any reason. And you mustn't feel guilty, either of you. God puts men and women together, and that's all there is to it."

"I'd like Missy to spend some time with my folks," Chris told Dan. "I've let them down so much that it would mean a lot to me to show them I'm doing this thing right."

"I believe they would be very pleased—"

"But I can't leave my mother to go for a visit," Missy broke in.

"Then they'll have to come here," Chris decided. "In fact, I think Mother would jump at the chance—and that means Father will agree too." He rose and walked to the door. Turning back, he said warmly, "You've always been like a family to me. Now I'll be a real member."

After Chris left Dan said to Missy, "It's the most wonderful thing I could have wished for you—but . . ."

"I know. What about Caroline? I—I wanted to say no to Chris, but I love him so much!"

Dan put his arms around her, and his eyes filled with pity. "Every one of us has to carry a special load of grief. I'm carrying mine now with your mother. Someday, Missy, you'll have yours—but now it's time for Caroline to bear hers. Scripture tells us that 'the heart knoweth its own bitterness, and a stranger does not meddle therewith.' Love Caroline—more than you ever have, Missy. God will see her through. She loves Him, and He honors those that honor Him!"

If a bomb had gone off in the church, it could not have caused more excitement than when Rev. Greene stood up and announced the engagement of his daughter Melissa to the Rev. Chris Winslow. An audible gasp rippled across the room, and when the crowd was dismissed, they swarmed around Missy. Martha Shipton's eyes were reproachful as she gripped Missy's arm and hissed, "I hate you, Missy! Not a word to me, your best friend!" Her mock-scowl was replaced with a smile as she hooked her arm in Missy's, saying contentedly, "But now you'll tell me everything!"

Poor Tom Cantrell looked as if he'd lost his life's savings, but he put up a bold front, coming up to say, "Well, you picked a big one, Missy. I always knew you'd find someone more your size than I am!"

Missy laughed out loud and gave Tom a better hug than he'd ever gotten in the two years he had doggedly pursued her. "You do have a way with words, Tom!"

She was relieved to see Caroline come to stand beside her, smiling slightly as she spoke of the match. Missy managed to give her a hug, saying, "Caroline, I—I'm so happy." Then the bride-to-be was pulled away by a group who were demanding the right to have a bridal shower for her.

When Chris came over the following Tuesday, he grinned

when Missy asked him how his congregation had taken the news.

"I suppose 'mixed emotions' would best describe it. The elders were all relieved, the mothers with eligible daughters were affronted, and the eligible daughters mad as hops."

"Oh, Chris, how awful!"

"I suppose—though your father warned me that it would be like that." He grinned again, a twinkle in his eyes. "It's nothing, though, compared to what's in store for you!"

"Christmas Winslow—whatever do you mean?"

"My parents will be here in less than a month."

"Oh, Chris! I'm scared to face them!"

"You should be, stealing their firstborn!" he teased. "No, seriously—you'll do fine. The funny thing is, Mr. Jennings practically forced the church to buy a nice old house for a parsonage last month."

Her eyes sparkled and she laughed in delight. "I'll bet he had the lady all picked out who was going to live in it!"

"Couldn't say—but the lady who is going to live in it is far more beautiful than the lady Mr. Jennings had in mind!"

Missy laughed, and with a warm feeling of possession, she reached up, pulled his head down, and kissed him. "You are a charmer, Brother Winslow!"

He squeezed her in response. "As I started to tell you, my folks can stay in the parsonage—and you and Mother can fix it up. They've got plenty of money, so soak them for all the traffic will bear!"

"You're awful!" she scolded.

"I have always been pretty awful," he agreed. "But I'm tall!" And he smiled at her, saying, "It's going to be fun being married to you, Missy!"

CHAPTER FOURTEEN

OUT OF THE PAST

★ ★ ★ ★

"It's beautiful, Missy," Julie said, standing back to admire the two-story house shaded by three towering elm trees. The two women had been to the general store to pick up the curtains that Julie had ordered from Lexington. For weeks they had worked on the house, ever since Nathan and Julie had arrived.

Standing at the white picket fence, Missy looked with pleasure at the house, and slipped her arm around Julie, saying, "How can we ever thank you for all you've done for us?" She laughed and added, "I'm not good enough for Christmas—but you'll have to put up with me anyway."

"Nathan and I are so happy about it, Missy. God gave me a word when Chris was born that he would be a preacher." She sobered and Missy saw the fine features, still youthful, grow pensive. "It's been a long wait, but I praise the Lord for calling him—and for giving him a good wife to share his labors."

"It's been good to see Chris and his father together."

"Another miracle," Julie remarked, and looked with a smile toward the side of the house where the two men were putting in a new bay window for the dining room. "Nathan's been a new man since Chris changed. I've never seen him so happy." Then she laughed and said, "Well, if we're going to get these curtains up before the wedding, we'd better get at it!"

"Oh, it's a long time yet—almost two weeks!"

"Slow as I am, it may take that long." The two women went inside and worked steadily on the curtains for the next few hours. At noon they all paused to eat lunch under the large apple tree in the backyard. It was late July, and no rain had fallen, so the cool shade was welcome. They dined on cold chicken, potato salad, biscuits dripping with yellow butter, and cool milk chilled in the spring, topping the delicious meal off with a fresh peach pie that Julie had baked.

Chris licked his fingers, leaned against the tree, and said, "I hope you'll stay around long enough to teach Missy to cook and bake, Mother. Why, last week I gave the dog a piece of bread she had made, and he wouldn't even touch it!"

"What! How can you say such things—after all the awful stuff you ate in the mountains?"

"What awful stuff are you talking about?" Chris winked at Nathan and went on innocently. "We ate good food all the time."

"Good food! You ate raw liver—and buffalo tongue, and all sorts of terrible things."

"Sounds all right to me," Nathan replied good-naturedly. "Never had any buffalo tongue, but it sounds tender. Wonder why we don't eat the cow tongue? Might be the best part."

"He'd eat shoe leather if you put it in front of him. He was always that way. Knox was the finicky one." Julie was able to say her son's name easily now, Missy noticed, and was touched by it. It had not always been that way, she knew. Chris had told her about Knox's death, and how the whole family had been devastated by it—especially Chris, who had struggled with feelings of guilt that intensified his grief. It took years before he was able to forgive himself for his brother's death.

"He was pretty picky when we were growing up, but in the mountains he ate like everybody else," Chris told them. "Once we ran out of grub in the middle of winter, except for some deer that had spoiled bad. We finally had to eat it, even though it was downright green—"

"Hush up, Chris!" Julie cried, throwing up her hands. "I don't want to hear such things!" She looked at the house and sat back, smoothing her dress over her knees, a contented expression on her face. "The congregation has done a lot to get this house together. It shows how much they love their pastor."

"And they've taken to the pastor's bride-to-be," Nathan smiled. "Even Brother Jennings and Sister Smiley have had to give in."

"Sister Smiley could talk the legs off a stove!" Julie commented tartly.

Chris snorted. "You two have learned more about this congregation in a month than I have since I've been here."

"People are alike, Chris," Julie said. "Every church has its saints and its sinners. Those you think are worthless will sometimes prove to be pure gold; others who are prominent will pull the wool over your eyes and you'll be fooled. Of course, there will be those who are merely religious, but they will fold when the trials come."

"I think you're right, Mother," Chris responded soberly, a thoughtful look in his eyes. "You never know people until they get in the fire, do you? What we are is covered up by our manners—until we get hurt. That's when we let what we're like inside come out."

Missy rose and began clearing away the lunch things, thinking about how much she enjoyed the conversation. She had never been so happy in her life. Every day she and Chris grew closer. He was stronger spiritually than she was, and she was sorry she had not spent more time reading the Bible. It wasn't too late, however, for it had become a joy to sit down with Chris and read the Scripture and pray together. Never before had she had anyone she could really open her heart to, and every time they talked she learned more about herself. Missy finished gathering the lunch dishes and leftovers, and she and Julie returned to the house.

Moments later she heard Chris's excited shouting outside, and she and Julie dashed to the window.

Missy looked in the direction he was pointing to see a man dismount and approach the house, where the men were relaxing on the porch.

"It's Con!" Chris cried excitedly. "Did you send for him, Father?"

"Why, no—matter of fact, I thought he and Frenchie were upriver," Nathan replied in a puzzled voice. "They were supposed to build a new post on the Milk River. I wonder why he's back."

"Con, what in the world are you doing here?" he asked. "Anything wrong?"

The trapper had aged considerably since Chris had last seen him. He was thin and had few teeth left, but there was still the same light in his eyes. He grinned, saying, "Nathan, you're gittin' as fat as a sucklin' pig!" Then he gave Chris a sharp look. "Well, I always knowed you'd never make it as a mountain man, Chris." He sighed and leaned against a white column. "But when I heard you'd hit the glory trail and gone to preaching, I say to Frenchie, 'It's a disgrace what a man will do to git hisself outta work!' "

"Con, you old pirate!" Chris responded joyfully, slapping the old man's thin shoulder. "I'm going to get you converted if it's the last thing I ever do."

"Too late."

"It's never too late to get right with God, Con."

Con's wrinkled face broke into a broad grin. "I mean I done did it already, Chris. Made the mistake of listenin' to a preacher feller named Cartwright, and I'd be blasted if he didn't jest talk me into it! Them words I've been readn' all these years finally took."

Chris stared at him. "Are you serious, Con?"

"Yep. I'm a new creature, Chris—and Frenchie hates it! I don't say nothin' to him about his sinful ways, but he's got so's he feels guilty when I'm around. Says I've got so holy he's afraid to spit in my presence!"

"That's wonderful, Con!" Chris responded warmly. "I've been praying for you and Frenchie."

Just then the women emerged, and Julie said, "Why, Con, it's good to see you."

"Howdy, Miz Winslow." He gave Missy a sharp look. "You shore did grow up nice and tall!"

Missy laughed. "I sure enough did. What's more, you can't

take Chris back with you this time, Con. I've got him all tied with my apron string!"

Everyone but Con laughed. Puzzled, Julie asked, "What's wrong, Con?"

The trapper shifted his feet nervously, looked at Chris, and cleared his throat. "Chris—I got something to say to you. Might be best if you heard it by yourself."

Chris stared at him, then said quietly, "Whatever it is, Con, my parents and Missy can hear it."

"It's your say, Chris." He paused, looking carefully at Chris. "I been up in the Snake country, Chris. Went plum on up into Canada. Thought I'd see if they was a chance of puttin' a post up there."

"The Hudson's Bay Company would never stand for that," Chris said.

"Yeah, I know that. Guess I just wanted to see the country again 'fore I settle down. Anyway, I followed the Milk up above Fort McKenzie, and then I crossed the mountains and turned north. I'd heard that there was a pile of beaver to be had somewhere around there, so I followed the mountains—and I swear I never even knew when I hit Canada! Well, it was like most tales you hear, Chris—there wasn't much truth to the tale; it wasn't really beaver country. Wal, I figured I'd jest see some new country, so I started east, crossed the mountains again—and I hit a village right at the foot of them. First I thought they was Snakes, like over west of the mountains, but they wasn't. They was Pawnees."

Chris stared at him. "Never heard of any Pawnees that far north."

"Me neither, but that's what they was." Con grinned humorlessly and scratched his head. "Fact is, they sorta caught me off guard—but I didn't mention that I was part of the Winslow Company. They ain't forgot you wiped out Red Ghost and lots of their relatives a few years back."

"How'd you get away, Con?" Nathan asked.

"Mostly by promising to come back with everything they asked for, Nathan. They want guns and whiskey, 'course; and I made them such big promises, they let me go. But while I was there, I seen something, and I come right here to tell ya, Chris."

A strange hollow feeling gnawed in the pit of Chris's stomach. "What was it, Con?"

"I seen your boy, Chris!" Con slapped his thigh and lifted his voice, "I swear to God, it's him!"

A shocked silence enveloped the group. Chris licked his lips. "But—he's dead, Con!"

"That's what that Injun said," Con nodded. "But he lied. I was there fer jest two days, and as they was lettin' me go, this young boy come runnin' out. One of the bucks grabbed him and hauled him off, and I seen they'd been keepin' him hid from me."

"What did he look like?" Chris asked.

"Why, he looked like you! He was wearing Injun garb—but I seen his face plain as I see yours right now. His skin was too light to be all Indian."

"Lots of Indians with white blood."

"Shore—but how many of 'em have reddish hair and eyes blue as that sky up there?" Con shook his head, and his voice rang with certainty. "He's got the same sort of face as you—wide forehead that narrows down like . . . jest like yours."

Chris stood motionless, his eyes fixed on Con. Then he nodded and turned to Missy and his parents. "It can't be—but I'll have to go see for myself."

Missy could not speak, and she felt Julie's arm go around her, giving her the strength to respond. "Yes. You go see the boy, Chris. The wedding will have to wait."

"Will the bishop let you leave, son?" Nathan asked.

"I think he will—but I'm going, in any case."

"I'll be goin' with you, Chris," Con said. "And Frenchie, he's bound to tag along."

Missy asked, "But Chris, even if he is your boy, how will you get him? The Indians won't let him go, will they?"

"No. When they adopt a white child, he's like one of theirs. If it is Sky, I'll have to take him any way I can."

"You don't think we could ransom the child?" Nathan asked. "If it's just a matter of money—"

"Only ransom they'd take is Chris's scalp," Con broke in.

"Them Pawnees is real good haters—and they got long memories. If they knew we was after the boy, they'd knock him in the head to keep Chris from gettin' him!"

Chris had no doubt about that. Their was a grim light in his eyes as he spoke to Con. "You need to rest. We'll pull out at dawn."

"How—how long will it take, Chris?" Missy asked.

The others, seeing the two needed to be alone, turned to go into the house. "You can sleep here tonight, Con," Nathan told him.

After they had left, Chris said, "Let's walk a bit, Missy." She followed him off the porch. He said nothing until they came to a clump of trees that hid the house. Then he stopped and put his hands on her shoulders, searching her face.

"I know this must be hard on you."

"It's all right," she murmured, resting her head against him as he took her in his arms and held her close. "You've got to find out. If he's your son, bring him back. He'll be our boy."

Her words brought a warm light to his eyes and he kissed her softly. "I knew you'd say that—though most women wouldn't. But you have to understand, Missy, he's an Indian. That's all he's known. It'll be hellish for him, being pulled out of the only world he's had. Like as not, it'll be as bad for you."

"I'm not afraid, Chris." She raised her head and gazed steadily at him. "God will help us. Go get Sky, and I'll be waiting for you!"

As they turned to go back to the house, Missy thought again of what her father had told her the night that Chris had asked for her hand: *Every one of us has to carry a special load of grief. Someday, Missy, you'll have yours.*

Chris left the next morning. Dan took him aside briefly, saying, "Don't worry about things here, Chris. I'll see to it that your church is taken care of. Just be careful—don't get yourself killed. I don't know what Missy would do if something happened to you."

The two men headed for the Missouri. Despite his age, Con didn't seem bothered by the difficult journey. They reached the fort on the upper Missouri in two weeks—record time—and six days later they stepped out of the canoe to be greeted by Frenchie Doucett. "Ah, my friend!" He grabbed Chris and gave him a tremendous hug. "You 'ave come for your boy—and Frenchie Doucett, he ees ze one who will help you." He gave Con a contemptuous snort. "Thees one ees too old. We leave him here weeth ze women."

Con gave him a beatific smile. "You heathen! I brung Chris all this way to see you git religion."

Frenchie sobered, and shrugged. "I theenk it weel be much bettair if we don' 'ave too much religion till we finish weeth zem Pawnees!"

"It's going to be real tight. I don't think either one of you should go," Chris said.

"If them Pawnees git one look at that red hair and blue eyes of yours, Chris, it'll be too late to pray," Con warned. Then he added, "But let's look on the bright side of it—if they scalp us, there won't be no expensive funerals to pay for!"

They left at once, taking only their rifles and what food they could carry. It took a week of hard traveling, the last few days only at night, to avoid any chance of being seen.

"There's the camp," Con informed them. They stood on a rise, looking down into a valley where a large collection of lodges lay against the foothills.

Chris studied the camp for a minute before he announced, "It'll take a miracle to even locate the boy—much less get him out." But he felt a surge of sudden faith. "Let's see what kind of medicine we can make!"

CHAPTER FIFTEEN

THE RESCUE

★ ★ ★ ★

"If we could jest git sight of that young'un," Con complained, "mebbe we could grab him and run."

The three men were hunched over a small fire—one of the few they'd allowed themselves during the four days they'd scouted the Pawnee camp. A brush fire had filled the air with smoke, and they saw their opportunity to roast a small deer that Frenchie had brought down a great distance from the enemy camp. Since the Pawnee dwellings lay in an open space far from the trees that covered the hillside, the men had not dared to get close enough to identify the boy.

Chris tore at the meat, chewed slowly, then answered, "We'd not make it, I'm thinking. The boy would slow us down—since I'm pretty sure he wouldn't go willingly—and the Pawnees know the trails better. We'll have to take the river. Break in the bottoms of all the canoes but the ones we take. If we can get a good start, we might make it."

The other two considered it; then Frenchie said, "Me, I like zat bettair." He was a born boatman and felt much safer in a canoe than on foot. "I tell you somtheeng, Chris—we bettair not fool around much longair. Zem Pawnees, they find us pretty soon, you bet."

It was a thought that all of them had entertained, but none had dared to voice it until now.

Con spoke up. "I been ponderin' this business, and jest 'fore dawn it come to me." The aging trapper looked very worn, and Chris realized, *Why, Con must be over sixty now!* "I ain't really up on this prayin' business, Chris, but I asked the Lord to give me some kind of direction—and He done it!"

"You mean God, He speak to you?" Frenchie demanded, skepticism in his sharp eyes. "I know zees releegion make you crazy!"

"Didn't hear a word," Con said with an air of confidence about him that made the hopes of both men soar. "Jest had a thought that fell on me—and I can't shake it. Anyway, it's the only shot we got, so I hope it's the good Lord speakin'."

"What is it, Con?" Chris asked.

"Why, it's plum simple. These Injuns know me. When I left I told them a passel of lies about how I'd be back pronto with guns and whiskey to trade. Only way I could get away. Wal, I'm back—and all I got to do is go in and dicker with them. Be sure to spot that boy if I hang around and keep my eyes open long enough."

"Con, that's too risky," Chris objected.

Con laughed. "My land, Chris, we been in tighter spots than this a heap of times! This'll be easy. When I get the young'un pinned down, it'll take some doin' to get him loose—so you two think on that while I'm palaverin' with them redskins down there."

He picked up his rifle and Chris rose and said quietly, "You don't have to do this, Con. He's my boy."

Con regarded him, and replied, "I'm about at the end of the trail, Chris, and I ain't got but one regret. Never had me no boy." A faint sadness clouded his faded eyes. "Seems like a man ought to leave something that'll last after he's gone. Mebbe the boy will think of ol' Con once in a while. No matter what, it'd be worth it."

He blinked his eyes and grinned. "'Sides, if this don't work, Frenchie, at least I won't have to worry about eatin' no more of your cookin'!"

Frenchie stared at him, his face serious. "You come back safe, an' I'll make ze beegest steak dinnair you ever seen! Go weez God, my friend."

"Con—thanks," Chris said.

He would have said more, but Con cut him off. "You stay put. When I spot the boy, I'll sneak off somehow so's you can go spoil the canoes, Frenchie. Then you and me will go in an' git 'im, Chris."

With that he turned and left, and the two watched him walk away. "Zat ees one brave man," Frenchie commented. "I theenk he won't do it, Chris."

For the next three days the two dared not move, for if they were taken the Pawnees would know that Con was lying. They stayed in the same spot, not knowing when he might appear—though the possibility that he would come during the day was small.

Sometime after midnight on the fourth day Chris and Frenchie caught the sound of someone running, and they leaped to their feet, rifles ready. Then Con appeared, and cried, "I got him located, Chris! And the main bunch rode out this morning on a buffer hunt!"

"Thank God you're all right!" Chris said, giving the old man a hug.

"Jest quit slobberin' all over me," the old man responded testily. "We gotta git ourselves outta this spot. Frenchie, pick the two best canoes and put the rest out of commission. Take all our gear and have that boat ready to go—jest in case we stir up a hornet's nest. You ready, Chris?"

"Sure. Frenchie—if we're not there by dawn, don't wait, you hear?" He clapped the burly Frenchman on the shoulder, then ran to catch up with Con, who had disappeared into the darkness.

They circled the village and paused in the outer edge of the trees, looking down on the lodges. A pale sliver of a moon shed a feeble light on the flatland. "That's the one—right there," Con said, pointing.

Chris nodded, thinking of the time nine years earlier when he had led the attack on Red Ghost's village. *Seems like once in a lifetime would be enough to have to do something like this.* Shaking off the memory, he voiced his thoughts. "I don't see any easy way to do this—we better go over the game plan right now."

"The hard thing is gonna be the first minute in that lodge, Chris," Con told him. "It'll be dark, prob'ly—unless they got some sort of oil lamp burnin'—which they do sometimes. But we can't count on it. And not all the men went on that hunt—so we gotta assume that there'll be at least one Pawnee brave in there—mebbe more. If him or his squaw lets out one beller—it's hello Mister Gabriel!" He pulled something out of his coat and held it up. "Picked up some rich pine. There'll likely be a camp fire with hot coals. It's risky, but I say we light the pine, make a jump into the lodge. Them Injuns will be blinded by it—at least, they better be! It'll give us one chance to put them down before they can make a squawk."

Chris grinned in the darkness. "Glad you're on my side, Con." Then he said, "You light the pine and make the jump into the lodge. I'll take care of the rest of it."

Con took a deep breath, saying quietly, "Wal, we're in the good Lord's hands." Then he moved out of the trees and Chris followed. They dropped to the ground, crawling silently across the beaten earth, pausing once as Con pointed to a smoldering campfire. Rising to his feet, Con moved to stand next to it, and thrust the rich pine torch into the coals. The resin caught at once, bursting into flame, but he left it there until it was burning steadily. He looked back at Chris, who had moved to stand in front of the lodge, waiting for a signal.

Chris pulled his knife from the sheath, gave a short nod, and Con jerked the burning brand out of the coals and ran to the entrance. Without hesitation he pulled the flap back and leaped inside, holding the torch high.

Chris was right behind him, his eyes searching the lodge. The flickering blaze highlighted the bulky forms along the walls of the lodge. One of them stirred, and Chris leaped, knife raised, and found himself looking into the eyes of an old Indian woman. She opened her mouth to scream, so he hit her head with his left fist. As she fell sideways he caught a movement to his left. He wheeled and saw a thick-bodied Indian diving at him. Chris was off balance, but Con rushed in and hit the Indian over the head with a war club the trapper had picked up.

Pushing the Indian off him, Chris looked up in time to see Con leap to one side. A small figure had appeared out of the shadows, and Chris scrambled to his feet and made a wild grab at the assailant. He caught a handful of leather and jerked backward—it was another woman; he knew by the size and by the braids down her back. He clapped his hand around her mouth, and she began to kick and claw at him. He caught her wrist with his free hand, gave a tremendous squeeze, and heard a knife strike the floor of the lodge.

"Look out, Chris!" Con hissed. Still holding the struggling woman, Chris felt a small body strike against him, and at the same time a voice cried out something in Pawnee. *He'll raise the camp!* Desperately, Chris struck out with his left hand, catching the boy in the temple. The boy was driven to his left, unconscious. Chris was afraid he had killed the lad, for although he had softened the blow, he knew he was a powerful man.

"Hold this squaw, Con!" Chris swung the woman around, trading her for the torch Con held. The old trapper grabbed her, holding her mouth tightly.

"Have to put her out!" Con whispered.

"No! Just hold her!" Chris knelt beside the boy, and was relieved to see the chest rising and falling. He put his finger on the throat and felt the pulse pumping strongly. It was too dark to see much, but one look at the face told him that the boy was half white. He thought he could see a flash of red in the hair, but the blue eyes that had convinced Con were closed—even at that, it was too dark to tell.

He picked up the boy and turned to Con. "We'll have to tie her up and gag her."

"No time—and she'd make a noise somehow. I don't like it no better than you, but it's her or us, Chris!"

An agony of indecision held Chris motionless, and then a dog barked in the distance, and he almost nodded to Con, who had drawn his knife. Then the woman's eyes were framed by the flickering light of the torch he held, and he knew he could not do it.

Her eyes were large and beautiful, with a plaintive quality in them that he could not ignore. She was trying to say something but the words were muffled by Con's hard hand. Then she flung up her left hand—and pointed to it frantically with her right.

The ring finger of her left hand was missing!

Chris cried hoarsely, "Con! Let her go!"

"Chris—!"

"Let her go—it's Dove!"

Con stared at Chris as if he had lost his mind, then slowly took his hand away; but the knife in his other hand was raised and placed along her neck. "You jest keep nice and quiet," he whispered.

Chris could see her clearly now—older and very thin, but her eyes had not changed.

"Bear Killer!" she cried softly.

"I—I thought you were dead!" he managed to say. His mind reeled. "Red Ghost—he showed me your scalp—and your ring!"

There was a sudden sound of movement in the distance, somewhere in the village, voices and dogs yelping. "Chris! We got to git outta here!" Con urged.

Chris shook his head. "Let's go! I'll carry the boy. Dove, you go with Con."

She tried to speak, but there was no time to argue. Con jerked her around and pulled her outside, hissing, "Douse that light, Chris!"

Chris tossed the torch down, snatched up the boy and plunged outside, blinded by the darkness. Dawn was only a thin line of light to the east, and his eyes had adjusted to the torchlight so he could not see Con or Dove. The voices were getting louder. Recklessly he plunged across the open, barely able to pick up the two figures ahead of him running for the timber.

Suddenly a yell of alarm ripped the air, and the dogs cried out. Others joined in, and when he was still a hundred yards from the timber, he heard the sound of other voices.

"They're on to us!" he said, catching up with Con. "Make for the river!"

It was a deadly footrace; both men were sure that the Pawnees would head straight for the river, knowing it would be the best path for the raiders to follow. As he followed Con and Dove's fleeting forms along the well-beaten trail, Chris hoped that Frenchie had done his job.

They were halfway to the river when Chris heard the sounds of pursuit. *Going to be close!* he thought. The light was coming fast, and as they ran around a bend in the path, he glanced back and thought he saw the flash of sunlight on steel. His breath was coming in short spurts and he saw Con stumble and almost drag Dove down with him; but when they topped a rise, they saw Frenchie, holding his rifle in his hands. He waved to two canoes behind him and cried out, "Come on!—We go!"

With legs almost like rubber, Chris stumbled down the bank past Frenchie, and put Sky in one of the canoes. He glanced back to see that Con had fallen—and spotted a small group of Pawnees atop the hill.

As Chris dashed back to pull Con to his feet, one of the Indians raised his rifle, but Frenchie dropped him with one shot. The other Indians split to each side as Frenchie stopped and pulled another rifle, taking cover behind the trees.

"Get heem in thees boat!" Frenchie yelled, and Chris half carried, half dragged the winded man, shoving him into the boat as a shot from the trees knocked bark from the gunwale of the canoe not five inches from his hand. He heard Frenchie's rifle bark in response. Leaping out, he saw Dove standing on the bank staring at Sky in the canoe.

"Get in the canoe, Dove!" he shouted. As she jumped into the canoe, he seized the last loaded musket from Frenchie. "Get out of here—I'll hold them off!"

Frenchie leaped in the boat, and with a few powerful strokes drove the canoe into the stream, where the current took him. "Come on, Chris!" he yelled.

Holding his rifle steady, Chris paused beside the canoe where Dove crouched low over Sky, who was beginning to stir. An arrow whistled close beside Chris's ear, followed by a shot that dimpled the water at his feet. He knew they would soon pick him off, so he leaped into the boat and shoved the canoe forward, dropping the rifle and grabbing the paddle with the same motion. He propelled the canoe toward the middle of the river, hearing the cries of rage and the ragged volley of arrows whistling through the air. One of them pierced the top side of the canoe, and another tore the leather of his left legging, drawing blood but not penetrating the flesh.

Three scattered shots whizzed past him, so he dropped his paddle, seized his rifle, and whirled in time to drop a tall Pawnee who was taking a direct sight on him. The Indian's rifle flew up and exploded, the ball passing so close to Chris's head that he flinched. Dropping the rifle, he poured every ounce of strength into getting the canoe out of range. There were no more shots, and he was thankful that they were safe for the moment. Frenchie slowed enough to allow Chris to catch up with him. "Chris! Con took a ball!" he called out.

"Is it bad, Frenchie?"

"Don' know. I theek maybe yes!"

"We'll pull to shore—soon as we gain a little distance," Chris said grimly.

They paddled hard, and Chris saw that the boy had regained consciousness and was sitting in front of Dove. Her hands were on his shoulders and his eyes were blue in his bronze face. They were hard eyes, Chris saw; there was nothing in them but a burning hatred. Once Dove leaned over and said something to him, but he shook his head angrily, never removing his eyes from Chris's face.

"Over here!" Frenchie called, and paddled his canoe into a small opening in the thick bushes that rose six feet out of the water. Chris followed and saw that the quick eyes of the riverman had seen the tiny natural harbor that was shielded from the other side by the vegetation. By the time Chris was able to pull in, Frenchie had beached his canoe, picked up the limp body of his friend, and carried him to a dry spot.

Jumping out of the canoe, Chris went to where Frenchie was pulling Con's leather shirt up, seeing the small round hole high on the left side of the back. He caught his breath and his eyes met Frenchie's, who shook his head silently.

Carefully Chris rolled Con over and for a moment he thought the man was dead. Then the eyes opened, and Con looked up. He opened his mouth to speak, but could only cough, and a stream of crimson ran out of his mouth and down his chin.

Must have pierced his lung. Chris wiped the old man's mouth, and knelt beside him with a helpless feeling. Even if the finest doctor in the world had been there, he could have done nothing. Frustration and guilt ran through him. *God, why did it have to be now—right when we almost made it!*

"Chris. . . ?" Con's eyes were open, and his voice was faint. "We got the boy?"

"We got him, Con."

"Wal—that's all right then." He lay quietly, his eyes studying the faces of the two men; then he whispered, "Frenchie, I been with you—a mighty long time, ain't I?"

"Yes, my friend," Frenchie managed to say. He put his hand on Con's and said hoarsely, "You and me—we 'ave been—ze best of friends, always."

"Reckon—there's somethin' you can do for me."

"Anything!" Frenchie answered fiercely.

Con smiled, his eyes fixed on Frenchie. "Don't think—I'm gonna enjoy the pearly gates—without you bein' there. Sure would like—to know you'll be comin'."

Frenchie's face contorted with the effort to contain the tears, but it was no use. "I will do my best—our Chris, he will help me."

"That's—good . . ."

Con's face relaxed, and he seemed to sink. But in a moment he opened his eyes and reached up a hand. Chris seized it, and the old eyes considered him; then he whispered, "Good thing about this . . . Chris . . . I went out . . . doin' something . . . that will last. Don't grieve . . . and don't let Sky . . . forget . . . me . . ."

His eyes closed and his body went completely still, and his hand limp. Chris laid it carefully across the old man's chest, then rose and turned toward the river. Dove was alone! He lunged toward the canoe, and saw a head bobbing as Sky forged across the river with determined strokes. Throwing himself into the stream, Chris reached the boy in a few powerful strokes. He ignored the fists that struck at him, gathered the fighting boy, and hauled him to the shore.

Reaching the bank, Chris held him down, saying in Sioux, "Why did you try to get away? I'm your father, boy."

"Black Elk is my father," Sky retorted.

"It is no use, Bear Killer." Chris looked up to see Dove standing beside him. "He has been taught to hate you. He is Pawnee—and he is too old to change. He will never be your son."

Chris looked at her, shocked. "What about you, Dove? You are my woman."

She dropped her gaze. "I—am no longer White Dove. I am the slave of Black Elk."

Then Chris understood the reason for her shame. The role of wife and mother was the only respectable status Indian society offered a woman. Had Black Elk made her his wife, her life might have been bearable. As his slave, he could use her as he wished, and share her with his friends—or even those who were not his friends if they gave him gifts.

Chris put his free hand on Dove and said, "Nothing has changed between us. You are my woman. We will go to my home, far away from the Pawnees."

She shook her head silently, and Chris did not argue. He released his son, who did not move or acknowledge him in any way, and spoke to Frenchie. "Let's bury Con here by the river." They moved to the place Chris had indicated and began digging the grave. When it was prepared, they put Con's body in the ground and covered it with stones and dirt. After the last stone had been placed, the two men stood beside the fresh grave.

"Ze bes' friend I evair had," Frenchie uttered quietly. Then he looked at Chris questioningly. "You really believe he ees weeth God, yes?"

"Yes."

Frenchie's shoulders lifted, and he said, "So—you have one beeg job—to get thees mountain man ready, no?"

Chris put his arm around the burly shoulders and prayed for his friend that God would change Frenchie's life—and make him ready for heaven. Then they all got into the canoes and paddled around the bend—out of sight of Con's last resting place.

Sky did not try to escape again, but his hate-filled eyes did not waver from Chris's face as the canoe swept them closer to the world Sky did not know. *Good thing Con didn't see this,* Chris thought. *Getting Sky out of the Pawnee camp cost Con his life—but I wonder what it's going to take to bring back my son.*

CHAPTER SIXTEEN

THE PREACHER TAKES A WIFE

★ ★ ★ ★

Asa came running into the house, calling loudly, "Missy! Father! It's Chris—he's comin' down the road in a wagon!"

It was almost dark outside, and Dan was lighting the lamp on the parlor table. Glancing up, he saw Missy's face brighten. Both of them had secretly been worried about the mission. "Thank God!" he smiled, feeling a burden lift from his shoulders.

Missy ran lightly out the door. Following quickly, her father came to stand beside her and Asa at the edge of the road just as the wagon drew close enough to make out the faces. "He looks all right," Missy murmured, and she gave an embarrassed laugh. "I've been thinking all kinds of things."

"Look—he's got a boy with him!" Asa exclaimed, and would have run to meet the wagon that had turned off the main road toward the house, but Dan held him firmly by the shoulder.

The horses pulling the wagon were exhausted and scarcely able to lift their hooves. It seemed to take forever before Chris said, "Whoa up."

Missy searched his face and saw that he was bone-tired, and his eyes were filled with unhappiness. She shifted her gaze to the boy who sat upright beside him, and was startled at how much he resembled Chris—the same blue eyes and wedge-shaped face; and even in the pale twilight she could see the reddish glints in his long hair. He was looking at her steadily, with an unfriendly air. Bravely she stepped forward and said warmly, "Chris, I'm so happy you're back—and this is Sky?"

Chris nodded shortly. "Yes." He climbed down from the wagon and she went to him, but he did not put his arms around her as she expected, so she stood there awkwardly, sensing the tension in his body and the trouble in his face.

"Glad you made it, Chris." Dan spoke carefully, studying the pair. "We've got something still warm to eat. Bring Sky and—"

Chris held up a hand, cutting him off. With an iron constraint in his voice that made them all stare at him, he said evenly, "You know all these years I thought my wife and son were dead—but I was wrong. I took one look at Sky and knew he was mine—" Then his voice faltered, but he took a deep breath and moved to put his hand on the side of the wagon. Looking straight into Missy's bewildered eyes, Chris continued. "I found my wife was alive, too. She took sick on the way back from the Pawnee camp."

As his words sank in, the blood drained from Missy's face. For weeks she had been apprehensive, wondering how she would be able to love a strange boy as a son. She never dreamed it would end like this.

"I'm sorry, Chris," she heard herself say. "But I know how happy you must be that she's alive."

In that moment Dan was terribly proud of this tall daughter of his. He had watched her blossom into a vibrant, beautiful woman as her engagement to Chris had drawn her out of childhood. Her world had narrowed to her coming marriage—and now as it fell to pieces before her eyes, she was able to take the blow, saying what needed to be said.

"Better bring her into the house," he said quickly.

Chris hesitated. "Maybe I shouldn't have brought her here," he voiced, "but she's pretty worn out. I've got to get to my church, and I didn't want to leave her with strangers."

"Of course," Dan responded. "You'll have to have some help with her, Chris. Caroline is over at Clarenton at a meeting, but I'll go fetch her—"

"No," Missy broke in impulsively. "She's looked forward to that meeting so much after being tied down so long." She turned to Chris. "Mother died two weeks ago."

He winced and looked at the ground; when he looked up, there was pain in his eyes. "She was very good to me. I'll miss her."

"She was glad to go, Chris," Dan told him. "She'd been wanting to for a long time." Apprehensively he looked at his daughter. "Are you sure—?" he began, but she cut him off.

"It'll be all right. Caroline is a very good nurse. We can sleep in one of the spare bedrooms until . . . your wife is better. And we'll take care of Sky until you're ready to take him home."

As Missy went into the house to get Dove's room ready, Asa—who had taken in every word—edged closer to the wagon, peering over the side to see a woman lying on some blankets. Her eyes were closed, and her thin, dark face was covered with perspiration. He studied the skinny boy as well, who wore buckskin leggings and moccasins—and nothing above the waist except a necklace made of some sort of sharp teeth. The bronze face turned to meet Asa's stare with a hostile expression that made the white boy blink. "Good to have you here, Sky." Asa tried to make him feel welcome, but there was not a flicker of understanding in the Indian's startling blue eyes.

"He doesn't speak much English, Asa," Chris spoke up. "It's going to be hard for him to adjust to a new life—and I'm counting on you a lot."

"Sure," Asa replied, stepping back from the wagon uncertainly.

"It's been a rough trip, Dan—we lost Con. Took a stray shot just after he got us out of the camp. Hard for me to think of it—him dying for my family." He straightened his shoulders, then added, "After we got away from the Pawnees, we split with Frenchie. He was hard hit, losin' Con. They were like brothers. The trip down the Missouri wasn't bad—but Dove took sick."

"What's wrong with her, Chris?"

"Mostly ten years of hell on earth, I reckon. She was a slave with the Pawnees, and there's nothing worse than that. They took Sky in and adopted him—but bein' a slave in an Indian camp is a fate worse than death. They work 'em to death, feed 'em scraps—or nothin'. Usually they don't last more'n five or six years."

Dan glanced at Dove, puzzled. "But you thought she was dead. You said once that you knew she was gone because that Pawnee had her scalp and her ring."

"He did." Chris's lips contracted, and anger flashed in his eyes. "Dove told me about it on the river. When the Pawnees attacked our camp, Red Ghost took a fancy to Dove and claimed her for his slave. When she resisted him, he beat her bad, and took her anyway. But she fought him every time he got close to her. The other bucks laughed at him, told him he was no man. When they got back to the camp, they all got drunk to celebrate the raid. Red Ghost was like most Indians—goes crazy when he gets whiskey. He went for Dove, and when she fought him in front of everybody, he picked up a club and hit her in the head—and then he scalped her in front of them all and cut her finger off to get her ring."

"If he was mad enough to scalp her, I'm surprised he let her live."

"He was too drunk to know," Chris explained. "They all thought she was dead, I reckon, but she come around. When Indians scalp a white man, they take the whole scalp, but with another Indian, they just take the scalp lock—cut a circle of skin about two inches in diameter and take it with the lock. You can't see it because her hair's so thick, but Dove's got a bald spot where the hair was taken."

"When Red Ghost saw her alive," he continued, "he sold her and the boy to Black Elk, a buck from another branch of the Pawnees from up north. That's where she's been all these years." He shook his head, and his eyes clouded over. "It was Red Ghost's idea of revenge to let me think they were dead."

"A strange and terrible thing," Dan murmured softly. "Well, let's get her inside."

Chris went to the back of the wagon and scooped up Dove in his arms, gently carrying her into the house, followed closely by Sky. In Dove's room, Missy had folded the covers back, and now pulled them over the frail body after he put her down. Chris remained standing beside the bed, looking down at Dove's face. Suddenly he turned to face Missy. "I can't let you do this!"

"I'm not doing it for you, Chris," she replied quietly, and her face was pale but fixed on the still form under the blankets. "I'm doing it for me."

Instantly he knew what she meant, and the two of them walked without another word into the kitchen. "I'll unhitch the team, Dan," Chris said.

He turned to go, and Missy quickly joined him. "I'll help you."

Asa watched them move toward the barn, then looked at his father with bewilderment.

"Missy and Chris—they'll never get married?"

"Chris has a wife, Asa."

"But—they're not really married, are they? I mean it was just an Indian thing; it wasn't real—you know, legal—was it?"

Dan put his hand on Asa's shoulder and said, "To a man like Christmas Winslow, it's a real marriage, Asa. He told me that once. Said she was his wife just as much as if they'd stood up in front of a hundred preachers with a piece of paper."

Asa mulled that over, and as his active mind probed the future, doubt furrowed his forehead. "Most people around here don't like Indians. I heard you say that the members of Brother Sawell's church ran him off because he married a German woman who didn't speak English much. It's gonna be hard for the preacher at the church to have an Indian wife and son."

The same thought had been on Dan Greene's mind. Much as he loved the people at his church, he knew that Asa had accurately laid the problem bare. There were no preachers with Indian wives, and the sturdy minister's face was grave with unspoken doubts.

Outside, neither Missy nor Chris spoke as he led the team to the barn. The silence and the tension grew unbearable. When they got to the barn, Missy turned to face him. "We have to talk, Chris. Tell me all about it."

He told her the details of the rescue. She cried when he told her of Con's death, and listened silently when he related how Sky had tried to run away. Finally he said, "I never dreamed it would come to this, Missy. But now that it's come, I'm bound to do what I can for her and the boy."

She avoided his eyes. "It'll be hard, Chris. You know better than I do about how some people hate all Indians. Even church-going folks. You'll have trouble with the congregation."

"Yes." Then he said, "I still think you're making a mistake, Missy—nursing Dove, I mean," and for the first time since they'd left her house, he turned and looked at her fully. "There's going to be a hard time for Dove and Sky, and for me, of course. But no one expects you to . . ." He sought for a word, couldn't find it, then shrugged. "Listen to me, Missy. I've got no choice but to marry Dove legally and make a home for her and the boy. But there'll never be a time when I won't love you."

His quiet confession broke her control, and she bit her lips to keep them from trembling. Tears blurred her vision, but she blinked them away. As a child Missy often irritated her family with her single-minded approach to life. Once something caught her attention, everything else was put aside, closing the horizons of her world until that single passion occupied all her attention. Collecting birds' eggs, reading, riding Thunder—she had filled her life with those things. But when she fell in love with Chris, she became so absorbed with thoughts of him and the life they would share together that she ached with happiness. And now it was over. Gone.

She wanted to run away, to lose herself in the warm darkness, but she was too strong for that.

After a long pause she said, "Christmas?"

"Yes, Missy?"

For the last time her hand reached out and touched his shoulder, and when he turned his head to look at her, she spoke in tones as gentle as the breeze that moved her blond hair off her forehead. "I'll always love you—but I'll never be a burden to you."

He knew they would not have a moment like this ever again. Hardly aware of what he was doing, he slowly put his arm around her, and she let herself be drawn into his embrace. His kiss was gentle, and she took it, then pulled back, saying, "Goodbye, Christmas."

A sense of unbearable loss overwhelmed him. "Goodbye, Missy." And they left the barn and returned to the house—silent as the stars that glittered overhead.

CHAPTER SEVENTEEN

GENERATION OF VIPERS

★ ★ ★ ★

Despite the best that Dr. Miller could do, White Dove's condition did not improve during the weeks Missy cared for her. She lost weight, and it was a constant struggle to get her to eat. Dr. Miller came often, and on the third week Missy followed him outside, away from the house. "She's a little better, isn't she, Doctor?" she asked. Dr. Miller, a heavy man with a full beard and sharp black eyes, fingered the heavy watch chain that dangled from his vest as he considered the question. "I'm not happy with her progress, Missy. She's still pretty weak, but I think it'll be safe to move her to Pineville by the end of the week."

"She's scared to death of us."

"Well, that's understandable. She's been jerked out of the only life she's known—and thrown into another world, completely foreign to her," Dr. Miller explained. "To make matters worse, the treatment she suffered while she was held captive by that hostile tribe of Indians was just about enough to kill any woman—so it's no wonder that now she's weak and confused. But she'll come around. Just give it some time." The doctor directed his sharp gaze at her. "Besides, it seems to me that White Dove is not the only one who has had to make some . . . adjustments lately. Guess you know the whole town's talking about you, the way you've been taking care of Brother Winslow's wife. It's—well, I must say it's pretty unusual."

Missy said, "Caroline has done as much as I have."

"Caroline wasn't going to marry the woman's husband," the doctor returned pointedly. "Most of the congregation in Pineville expect Rev. Winslow will send the woman away as soon as she's well. They think you're waiting around, hoping he'll marry you when that happens."

"Anyone who says that doesn't know Christmas Winslow!"

A small smile flitted briefly across Dr. Miller's face. "They don't know you either, I think," he replied soberly. "But I know them, Missy. You've got to try to prepare Chris for what's coming."

"You're sure there'll be trouble?"

Miller's eyes were half closed as he looked toward the house, which he regarded for a long moment; then he shook his heavy head. "I'm not a religious man myself, but I know the folks in that congregation pretty well. People can't hide much from a doctor. Most of them are fine, but there's enough meanness in a few sorry members of the church to destroy anything they don't like. Hate to see Rev. Winslow hurt. He's a fine man. Most men wouldn't have stuck with the woman." Changing the subject, he said, "Try some of that thick broth—and bring her over to Pineville on Friday."

"I'll tell Brother Winslow," Missy promised as she went back into the house to prepare a pot of the soup that Caroline had recommended for Dove. When it was done, she put a bowl of the broth on a tray, along with a cup of fresh milk, and left the kitchen to feed Dove. She found her awake, looking very small in the huge bed. "Now—you're going to sit up and eat every bit of this soup, Dove!" she said cheerfully, placing the tray on the small oak table beside the bed. She reached around the sick woman's thin shoulders and helped her into a chair. There was no fear now in Dove's eyes, as there had been for a long time, and Missy thought, *Well, she's not scared to death of me, at least!* She pointed to the tray beside Dove and urged, "Now, you eat this fine soup, Dove, while I change the bed."

As she busied herself with the work, she sang a hymn—one

of Dr. Watts'. She began to whistle it as she tucked the clean linen sheet under the featherbed mattress, breaking off mid-note when she heard a voice coming from the chair.

"Good—ver' good."

"Why, bless me!" Missy exclaimed, for it was the first time Dove had spoken in English. She looked at the bowl and said with a laugh, "You ate almost the whole thing, White Dove—that's real fine!" She handed her the cup of milk and added, "Now, you drink all of this."

As White Dove obediently drank the milk, Missy saw that her cheeks were not flushed, and she reached out and put a hand on the sick woman's forehead. She remembered the first time she'd done that, how Dove had flinched, her eyes filled with fear. Now she didn't move, but her strange gray eyes were fixed on Missy's face. "You don't have any fever," Missy said with a smile. "Your eyes are clear, too. Maybe you could walk just a little bit—be a pleasure to get out of that bed, wouldn't it, now?"

She spoke reassuringly as she helped White Dove out of the chair. "Careful, now," she cautioned, feeling the small figure weave as Missy led her across the floor. *She's so small—like a child!* Missy thought, putting her arms around the thin shoulders. Slowly she led the woman back and forth. Then hearing the front door open and close and footsteps coming down the hall, the two women looked up to see Chris in the doorway.

He stopped abruptly and took in the scene with pleased surprise. "Well, praise the Lord! You look fine, Dove!" He came and took her by the shoulders, leading her back to the chair. Missy stepped back, watching Dove's eyes brighten at the sight of her husband, her hands reaching out for his. She said something in Sioux, to which Chris nodded and answered in kind. Turning to Missy he asked, "What did Dr. Miller say?"

"He thinks she's doing much better. Said you could take her home on Friday if she doesn't have a setback. Look—she ate all her soup, and the fever's gone."

"I go—out?" Dove looked up at Chris, then motioned toward the window.

"Better take it easy," Chris replied. "Tomorrow I'll take you outside."

Dove glanced at Missy, and her eyes grew warm. "Missy good to sick woman . . ." Her words were choked off as she began to cough spasmodically, and Missy hurried to her side.

"Better rest for a while," she said, and gently helped Dove into bed. To Chris she added, "If you'd like to sit by her for a while, I need to go to the store."

"All right." He picked up the worn black Bible from the washstand and pulled the chair to Dove's bedside. "She doesn't understand much," he conceded, "but she likes to have me read."

"The psalmist said, 'The entrance of thy word giveth light,' " Missy responded. Picking up the tray, she turned to leave the room, saying, "Father and Caroline took Sky with them over to Nettleton." Nettleton was a small village five miles north of Pineville where Dan was attempting to start a new church. Caroline had been going with him for several months twice a week to teach a small group of children Bible stories.

"He been all right?"

"Yes." She left the room, feeling guilty about her answer, for it was not the truth. While Dove's health had been a concern, it was her ten-year-old son who had nearly driven them all wild. Rejecting every attempt of friendship they offered him, Sky stubbornly refused to communicate with anyone, speaking only to his mother—in Sioux, of course. He would sit on the floor in her room, his back against the wall, ignoring everyone else. When he was forced to leave her room, he did so sullenly, resentfully.

Asa rushed into the kitchen, out of breath. "Missy, can I have some liver for trotline bait?"

"I guess so, Asa. Are you going to take Sky with you?"

"No! There'll be enough snakes in the river trying to bite me without taking another one along!" Asa grumbled. "He just stares at me as if he'd like to cut my throat!"

"Asa!" Missy chided him halfheartedly. She knew Asa had tried hard to break through the barrier Sky had erected between them, and that his attempts to make friends with Sky had been a total failure. "Don't be angry with him, Asa. Right now Sky sees us all as his enemies. But if we show him love, he'll learn to trust us."

"Trust us! Why, he hates the air we breathe, Missy! He'll run off first chance he gets—and I hope Chris has sense enough to let the varmint go!"

Wisely, Missy did not argue with the boy, but she put her arm around him and gave him a hard squeeze. "Never mind, Asa. You've tried so hard—and I'm proud of you for it."

He ducked his head at the praise, then gave her a rough hug.

"Goodness, Asa! Don't crack my ribs!" She shoved his unruly black hair back from his forehead and smiled. "I'll help you set the trotline this afternoon. Some blue catfish steaks would be real good for a change—and it'll be fun."

"Sure!" he grinned happily, then remembered the harsh words he had spoken earlier, and tried to set things right. "Guess mebbe we can take Sky with us."

"That'd be fine. Soon as they get back from Nettleton, we'll go."

She went to the store and made a few purchases, and when she came home she saw the buggy hitched in front of the house. Inside, she found Chris talking to her father and Caroline. She moved around quietly, putting the groceries away as she listened to them. After a few minutes of general conversation, Chris asked, "How's the Indian mission over in Nettleton, Dan?"

"Oh, mighty slow! A hard bunch over there! It'll take a move of God to get them stirred." He sipped his cold cider. "Like plowing new ground, Chris—except for Caroline's work with the children. That's going better than the rest of it put together."

"You always could handle children better than anyone else, Caroline."

Chris's compliment brought a faint touch of color to her cheeks, and Caroline said quickly, "Oh, they're starved for attention, that's all." She changed the subject hurriedly. "Sky behaved very well, Chris. He sat still as you please while I told stories. I think he understands more English than he lets on. I wouldn't be surprised if he's hiding behind his language. It's as though he thinks as long as he doesn't have to talk to us, we can't get close to him." She smiled and added, "But I may have found a way to get him to talk. I've been asking him how to say things in his language. It seems to please him for some reason—and I like it, too."

"Not many Sioux here for you to use it on," Chris grinned at her. "Just me and Dove and Sky."

Caroline went on. "I've been thinking that someday—" She broke off. "Oh, it's just a thought."

Missy caught her father's sharp glance at Caroline, and both of them knew that it was not what her older sister had intended to say. "I'm going out with Asa to set the lines. Would you see to Dove, Caroline?"

Caroline agreed at once, and Chris spoke up. "Reckon you and Asa could use some help? Been a long time since I pulled a monster cat off a hook."

"Why—of course." Missy had not been alone with him since he had brought Sky and Dove back, and she would have refused, but could think of no way to do it gracefully. "Asa will like that very much."

The deep hole in the river was six miles upstream, and it was after five before they got there and tied their horses to saplings. Asa had begged for a boat, and Dan had traded some blacksmith work for a ten-foot dugout that was just right for running lines. Asa kept it well concealed in a cutback, under a canopy of vines and willows. By the time the four of them reached the place, Asa was jumping with excitement. "Let's go bait up before it gets dark, Chris!" he cried, running back to where Chris had begun to make a small fire. Chris had gathered a few sticks of firewood and was lighting it with some black powder and his flint and steel. He struck a spark, and the powder caught with a puff of smoke, and the punk he'd put under it began to glow.

"That's fine, Chris," Missy told him. "You go with the boys and bait up. I'll build the fire, and we'll have some supper when you get back."

"All right," he agreed and left.

Missy was glad to see that for once Sky was alert, his eyes bright and happy as he got into the dugout. She quickly gathered some wood, built the fire up, then walked along the riverbank, enjoying the cool air beneath the large water oaks.

The sun dropped behind the tree line, turning the river to molten gold, and she went back to the campsite and put the coffeepot on. By the time the coffee brewed, the darkness had closed in, and the stars reflected their glittering lights in the river. Soon she saw the dugout come up the river and pull into the bank.

"Coffee's ready," she called. "How about some bacon and eggs?"

"Hey, that sounds good!" Asa exclaimed, and he carried on a running conversation with Chris as she cooked the meal. When it was done, they sat around the fire, eating hungrily. "Wonder why stuff tastes better when you're camping out?" Asa wondered aloud. Without waiting for an answer, he began urging Chris to tell a story about the mountains. Missy leaned against a tree, sipping a cup of strong black coffee and listening to him spin out a tale of an improbable bear hunt. The night's shadows played against the light of the fire, and she noticed how full Asa's face was, and how lean and hollow the other two seemed. Sky had the same thin nose and high-cheeked face as Chris, and as he sat back in the shadows Missy saw that he was studying his father's face covertly. Neither did she miss the puzzled gleam in his dark eyes as if there was something he could not understand, and from time to time he would duck his head and stare into the fire.

It was only a little after eight when Asa suggested, "Let's go run the lines."

"Too soon," Chris told him. "Those big fellows won't be stirring until midnight when the water cools off. You'll just scare them off if you go pulling the baits up."

But Asa was impatient, and begged, "Let Sky and me go, Chris. We can re-bait the hooks—and maybe we'll get one big enough to fry up."

"Well—I guess it's all right, seein' as you can't sit still," Chris decided. He said something to Sky, and the boy got up at once and followed Asa to the boat. As they moved down the river to the lines, the sound of Asa's voice came floating back on the still air, and then the silence of the night closed in again, broken only by the cry of a distant screech owl.

Missy was uncomfortable. There was nothing she could say that would not rake up old memories, so they sat there in silence, watching the glittering track of the river as the reflection of the stars was broken into flakes of light. Finally Chris spoke. "I'm glad Dove's better. It's been a weight on me, Missy, having to ask you and Caroline to take care of her." He waited for an answer, but none came, and he went back to staring into the fire.

When he could stand the silence no longer, Chris got up and walked to the riverbank, making a tall shape against the sky as he stood there. Missy forced herself to turn away, not giving into the impulse to follow him, to throw herself into his arms. *But . . . I know he loves me!* her heart cried out. She sat with her back to the fire, staring into the dark shapes of trees that blotted out the sky; then, because it was so dark and because Chris could not see her, she bent her head and the hot tears ran down her cheeks. When at last she looked up, she saw that he had not moved. Taking a deep breath, she thought, *Now I've cried for us. Lord, let me never weep again. Thy will be done!*

Sky and Asa brought back a large bullhead weighing over twenty pounds. It was obvious Asa had enjoyed himself, but both Missy and Chris said little after the trip. He spent most of his time with Dove and Sky, and she found excuses to be away from the house a great deal. On Friday, Dove was strong enough to walk to the buggy, and it was a relief to see them leave.

Caroline had surprised them all by announcing that she would go help Dove for a few days. Watching the buggy disappear, Dan said to Missy, "I'm glad Caroline went to help out for a spell—and I'm glad you didn't." He said no more for a while, but he was concerned about his younger daughter. She had lost weight and there was a soberness in her manner that bothered him. *Have to keep her busy,* he thought. Then breaking the silence, he went on. "I've got a notion about your sister."

"What?"

He rubbed his chin and shrugged. "Just a notion. She's been getting Sky and Dove to teach her Sioux. Wouldn't be surprised if she's thinking about doing mission work among the Indians sooner or later."

Missy considered the idea. "Perhaps. Caroline did mention the American Board of Missions in Boston. She's been getting some letters from them, and she's written some, too." She looked at her father and asked, "What would you say if she went?"

"I don't know," Dan answered thoughtfully. "She's a strange girl, Missy. Nothing really seems to interest her 'cept church things. You know, I've had a thought or two myself about mission work—especially since Chris came and told me about the way things are."

"You'd think of going to the Indians?"

"Oh no, I don't think so. It's no life for you and Asa, though it's a work that'll have to be done, Missy. But God help those who go first. Not all of them will die in bed."

She patted his arm. "You'd go to the moon to preach if there were any way to get there!" She smiled briefly. "I wonder how Chris and his family are doing—I'm worried about them. You haven't heard how the church took to Dove and Sky, have you?"

Dan decided not to worry her further, although he had heard rumors. "They'll come around," he promised.

For the next month, Caroline came and went, spending more time with Dove than she did at home. She gave glowing reports of how well Dove was feeling, and was proud of the progress she herself was making in language study; but she said little about how the congregation had responded to their pastor's family. It was obvious to both Dan and Missy that things weren't good.

Three weeks after she went home, Dove was well enough to go to church. Dan was edgy, and surprised Missy by saying, "I asked Brother Evans to preach the sermon tomorrow morning. I'm going over to Pineville for the service. Maybe you'd like to come along."

"No, I'll stay here. I've promised my class a little tea after service. You can tell me about it when you get back."

He left early the next morning. At church, Missy listened as Brother Mott Evans, one of the deacons, struggled through a sermon on the beast and the false prophet in Revelation. There was to be no night service, so she read some of *Pilgrim's Progress*, though she practically knew it by heart. Later she went for a ride on Thunder. She had just put the stallion out to pasture and started back to the house when she saw her father coming down the road. He was driving at a fast clip, sending clouds of dust boiling over the road behind him; and when he got to the house, he slammed the brakes and called "Whoa! Blast you!" in an angry voice.

She hurried to meet him, and one look at his square face told her that he was hopping mad. "What's the matter?" she demanded.

He clenched and unclenched his fists, his face flushed with anger, and it was obvious to Missy that he was keeping his wrath bottled up by sheer willpower. Finally through clamped teeth he said, "Bunch of hypocrites! Generation of vipers! God could do no better than to open the earth and swallow their miserable carcasses—the whole lot of 'em."

"Stop that!" Missy cried. "Tell me what happened."

He shook his shoulders and passed a trembling hand over his forehead. When he spoke it was with a controlled tone. "The church was full. Lots of people there that never show their faces except on Christmas and Easter. Just came to see the show, I guess!" Agitated, he clenched his hands again and continued. "It was a terrible thing. Chris came in a little late, and he had Dove and Sky with him. They were both all dressed up in new clothes—looked real nice, but Dove was scared to death. Never felt so sorry for anyone in my life."

"Then what? Why was Dove so frightened?"

"Well, Chris asked me to preach, and I did, but nobody listened. They were all like buzzards on a roost—staring at Dove and Sky like they were some sort of animals. You could almost feel the hate, Missy! Well, when I finished, I made a little speech. Told them how God had been gracious enough to restore their pastor's family—but they weren't listening. After I announced that there'd be a little reception at the parsonage to welcome White Dove and Sky, I gave the benediction, and then it happened."

"What?"

"Why, Missy, not ten people came by to welcome them! We

sat there, waiting. Soon Martha Shipton and Dr. Miller came, and he's not even a Christian. Some more welcomed them, but it was mighty embarrassing, sitting there with all the cake and punch—and so few came."

"Do you think Dove understood?" Missy whispered.

"Of course she understood!" Dan bellowed. "She sat there all dressed up with Sky beside her, and she held her head high, I tell you! But she knew she was being rejected. So did the boy."

"How dare they treat her so!" Missy cried angrily. "How . . . did Christmas take it?"

"How do you expect?" Dan snapped. "He looked like a volcano—looking for someone to strike out at. Instead, he just stood there with a smile on his face and an empty light in his eyes. God help us!"

"What will happen now?" Missy asked quietly.

Dan shook his head, sorrow lining his face. "God knows, Missy—but I'm writing to Bishop Asbury tomorrow. Chris is in big trouble—and sooner or later, there'll be pressure put on the bishop to have him removed." Still fuming, he snapped the reins and drove off to the barn, and she could hear him muttering as he went: "Generation of vipers!—Generation of vipers!"

CHAPTER EIGHTEEN

"TAKE THEM WITH THEE!"

★ ★ ★ ★

"Peter Cartwright to see you, sir."

Bishop Francis Asbury was a serious man, but a smile touched his thin lips as he said, "Better stay by the door, Roberts—in case Brother Cartwright gets out of order."

The small-built secretary replied, "I'd not be surprised. Two weeks ago over in Delaplane two rowdies tried to break up the service. Cartwright jumped off the platform, laid one of them flat on his back, and offered to do the same to the other one unless he behaved." Roberts laughed aloud, adding, "I don't know if either of them got saved, but they got a good dose of Methodist hellfire-and-damnation preaching."

Asbury shook his head in mock-despair, but could not hide the glint of humor in his gray eyes. "Well, well, Cartwright is what he is. Send him in."

Cartwright entered, and Asbury motioned the preacher to a chair. *He breaks every rule in the clergy code book,* the bishop thought, *but he preaches the gospel to the poor.* Cartwright's commitment to an anti-elitist form of ministry compelled the feisty preacher to serve—tirelessly and at any cost—the widely scattered and highly mobile population of the United States. The dynamic of the church, Asbury knew, was contained in the simple and straightforward message Cartwright proclaimed: People are free to accept or reject God's grace. Men such as he streamlined the gospel, avoiding theological and ecclesiastical wrangling. This message was proclaimed unstintingly—indoors and out, seven days a week, and under the most adverse conditions.

"Well, Brother Asbury, I suppose you received my letter," Cartwright began as soon as he was seated. His chin jutted out pugnaciously, and he thumped the arm of his chair with a hard hand.

Asbury nodded and picked up the letter from among the papers on his cluttered desk, his eye falling on a paragraph he had marked:

> I awfully fear for our beloved Methodism. We multiply colleges, universities, seminaries, and academics. We multiply our agencies and editorships, and fill them all with our best and most efficient preachers. And by doing that we localize the ministry—and secularize them as well. If we continue, we will bid itinerancy farewell; and when that happens, we will plunge right into congregationalism, leaving off precisely where all other denominations start. Only when all our ministers follow their appropriate calling—namely, to preach the gospel to a dying world—will we be in the will of God. Tying a minister to a college or an office is like forcing a man to ride a race with the reins of his horse's bridle tied to a stump!

He writes much as he preaches; the style suits him, Asbury thought as he looked up. *Blunt, caustic, and bold. Peter is right in many ways—and the rest of us are wrong.* But he could not afford to act on this knowledge, to threaten the structure. There were not enough men like Cartwright to carry on the work. Aloud, he said, "I am praying over your proposal, Brother Cartwright—but surely you see that as much as we need men in the field, they need to be trained first!"

Cartwright's gaze clouded over, as though he was forming his answer and was struggling with a thought. At last he spoke. "Of course, Bishop. Many of our church problems now have their roots in untrained ministers, but—"

Agitated, Cartwright jumped to his feet, strode to the window and gazed outside. When he began to speak again, it was in a subdued voice, quite unlike his own robust tones. "Remember in the early days, Bishop? When God called a man to be a Methodist preacher, instead of hunting up a college, he hunted up a hardy pony of a horse, and packed up his library: a Bible, a hymn book and the Discipline. He started out with a text that never wore out or grew stale: 'Behold the Lamb of God that taketh away the sins of the world.' Through storms of wind, hail, snow and rain; over hills and mountains, through swamps, and around swollen streams he went. He would lie out all night—wet, weary, and hungry, holding his horse by the bridle all night so it wouldn't bolt. He had his saddle blanket for a bed, his saddlebags for a pillow, and his coat for a covering." He closed his eyes, remembering. "We slept in dirty cabins on an earth floor, ate roasting ears of corn for bread, drank buttermilk for coffee. But the message was always the same: 'Behold the Lamb of God.' " Opening his eyes, he fixed his gaze on the bishop, who had stood wordlessly nearby. There were tears in the old circuit-preacher's eyes as he whispered, "Under such circumstances, who in these days would say, 'Here am I, Lord, send me'?"

Asbury felt his own heart cry out at the words, and he rose from his desk and went to put his arm around Cartwright's shoulders. "We will pray. There are still men—and God is still calling them."

They prayed and then the two spoke for an hour about plans for the future. Finally Asbury said, "I must leave for Boston on the afternoon stage. If there's nothing else. . . ?"

Cartwright squared his shoulders, and there was a light of battle in his eyes. "You must do something about Pineville, Bishop!"

Asbury frowned, trying to remember, and Cartwright prompted him. "You've had correspondence from the leaders of the church—and I wrote you a letter last month."

"Yes, yes! I remember now. That's the case of Brother Winslow. He married an Indian woman."

"Yes, and now the church won't accept her and wants to be rid of him." Cartwright's face was flushed, and he put up one thick hand in a squeezing motion. "I'd like to pinch their heads off!"

"We can't do that with every congregation that disapproves of their pastor, I'm afraid." Asbury shook his head. "He'll have to be relocated. You know better than I the strong feelings against Indians in the West."

"And do you think it will be better for the man and his family in the East?" Cartwright demanded angrily.

"Well, in all honesty," Asbury spoke sadly, "I fear not. But the church will be destroyed if he stays."

"Good riddance!"

Asbury regarded him thoughtfully. "We are all frail human beings, Peter. Perhaps the day will come when an Indian wife will be acceptable—as we grow more into the stature of the Lord Jesus. But we must deal with our people as they are—not as we would like them to be."

Asbury bowed his head in deep thought. Cartwright stood silently until the bishop looked up and noticed a determined look on Peter's face. "I have been much in prayer over a matter for some time—and I feel that this situation is part of an answer from the Lord. You know of the meetings at Williams College?"

Cartwright brightened. "Of course! The American Board of Commissioners for Foreign Missions! They're beginning to send out missionaries."

"Send Winslow and his wife overseas?"

"No—send them to her people." The novelty of the idea excited Asbury, and he spoke rapidly. "Why, it's ideal! The man is already accepted in one of the tribes—he speaks the language—he's been a trapper, so he's hardy and can take the hardships."

Cartwright was smiling broadly. "Wesley didn't make you bishop for nothing, sir! It'll be a pioneer work—and it'll open up the far west to the gospel of Jesus!"

"Sit down, Brother," Asbury said. "We have work to do. Roberts! Roberts! Get yourself in here with plenty of paper!"

Dr. Miller did not like the looks of it at all, but he kept his fears to himself as he settled back in a chair by the bed and said,

"Well, Rev. Greene, this isn't the first bellyache you've had—and it won't be the last."

Dan's face was pale and covered with a fine sheen of perspiration as he lay looking at the burly doctor. He had lost weight since the pain in his stomach had forced him to stay home, and it showed in his hollow cheeks and eyes that had sunken into his wide face. Ignoring the pain, he had gone to a camp meeting twenty miles away, but was forced to come back when the pain grew more severe. Caroline and Missy had put him to bed immediately and, ignoring his protests, sent for Dr. Miller.

Dan grinned with an effort and his voice was raspy as he replied, "That's all you doctors are good for. To think you've come all the way over here to tell me I have a bellyache—and I already knew that!" A spasm of pain made him catch his breath and grab at his middle.

Dr. Miller's sharp eyes watched him; then he shook his head. "I don't know what it is, Dan. If I did, I'd tell you. We doctors don't know much. We can set a broken leg or do some bleeding. Things like this, you just can't always tell. Whatever it is, it'll probably go away. Most things do." He rose to his feet, saying, "I'll leave some laudanum for the pain."

"Thanks, Doctor," Dan said. "Don't forget to go by and see Mrs. Landers, will you? And it would be nice if you could stop by the Bakers. I know there's nothing you can do for Will, but it would make Erma feel better if you'd leave some pills or something."

"I'll see them. I have to go over to Shady Grove tomorrow—be there for two days, but if you get worse, send Asa to get me."

"Guess I'll last till you come back through on Thursday," Dan told him, and he closed his eyes as Miller left the room.

"How is he, Dr. Miller?" Caroline was at the fireplace, cooking. She put down the spoon she was holding and walked to where the doctor was standing. Missy looked up from where she was sitting on a stool, peeling potatoes.

"I don't like it," he answered. "It may be just stomach cramps—or something he ate—but this has been going on for nearly a week, so I doubt it's that." He opened his bag, gave them the drug, and told them to send Asa for him if their father got worse.

"We'll trust God to heal him," Caroline said.

Miller did not respond, but gave her a direct look and asked, "What do you think about Rev. Winslow's leaving the church?" It had been two weeks since Winslow had announced that he was leaving to do mission work among the Indians, and people had talked much about it. The doctor himself thought it was a good decision, but he was curious about the Greenes' reaction. He did not look at Missy, but it was for her he was most concerned.

"I think it's wonderful, Doctor!" Caroline responded. Her thin face lit up and there was warm approval in her voice. "It's the field that Brother Winslow and his wife are best suited for."

"I suppose that's true."

"Have you heard when they're leaving?" There was no trace of emotion in Missy's face that Miller could see. "I suppose it'll be soon?"

"The new minister will be coming in two weeks, Jennings told me. Can't imagine the Winslows staying longer than that—not after—" He broke off abruptly, then said, "Put three drops of the laudanum in a cup of water—more if the pain gets worse. I'll be back on Thursday."

After he left, Missy got up and walked back and forth across the small room, her face tense. "I can't help being afraid for Father," she worried.

"I know, Missy," Caroline answered. "I feel the same way. It's not an ordinary stomachache." She brushed her hair off her forehead and added, "I've prayed until I don't know what else to say to God. It's like speaking to the air—and that frightens me," she whispered. "Always before when I've prayed, I knew God was there, listening—but now—"

Just then Asa came in asking what the doctor had said, and his face grew long when he heard that his father was no better. Missy put a comforting arm around him, hoping to take away some of the fear that gnawed at him, but her reassurances sounded weak—even to her.

It was a terrible night. Despite his efforts, Dan Greene could not help but groan, and though he tried to muffle his voice, it carried to the three young people sitting in the kitchen. No one was able to sleep. Finally when the groans grew louder, Asa asked, "Can't we do anything for him?"

"I'm afraid to give him more laudanum," Caroline replied. "If he doesn't get better by morning, we'll send for Dr. Miller and—"

Suddenly they were interrupted by their father's call, and all three went quickly to his room. Dan was holding his stomach with both hands and gasping in pain. "Send for Chris!"

Missy said, "We'll get Dr. Miller, Father!"

"No—Christmas! Get Christmas, Asa!"

"Take Thunder, Asa—tell Chris to hurry!" Caroline urged him.

Both women stayed with their father, bathing his face, and soon they heard Asa leave on Thunder, riding at a dead run. Caroline and Missy made Dan as comfortable as possible and then waited. The minutes passed for what seemed like hours. Finally they gave him a heavy dose of the pain medicine and in twenty minutes he fell into a fitful sleep.

The ticking of the clock punctuated the slow passage of time, and by the time they heard the pounding of hoofbeats on the road, Dan had roused out of the drugged sleep, and was doubled over with pain, his eyes wild and feverish.

They heard the front door open, and soon Chris appeared in the doorway, his hair wildly blown by the ride. He rushed to stand beside the bed, and the sight of Dan twisting in pain made him drop to his knees. "Dan! Dan!" he cried out, and his voice seemed to cut through the agony of the sick man.

"Christmas. . . ?" he gasped, and reached out one hand. Chris seized it and held on tightly. "I was afraid you—wouldn't make it," he whispered.

"Dan, God is able—!"

"No! It's time for me to go—the Lord has—told me so."

Asa came into the room just in time to hear the words, and he gave a cry and threw himself beside Chris. Dan's eyes cleared, and he said in a stronger voice, "Help me up." Chris pulled him to a sitting position, resting the man's back against the headboard. Dan took a deep breath and went on. "Better—much better."

"Dr. Miller's on the way, Dan," Chris told him.

Dan's eyes were bright in the sunken sockets; obviously he was in terrible pain. But his voice, though weak, was steady. "No time. Want to—ask you something, Christmas."

"Anything, Dan!"

As though he had not heard Chris, Dan paused, regarding each of his children in turn, and rested his hand on the shaking shoulder of Asa, who was trying most manfully not to cry. "Asa—God knows I hate to leave thee—but thee will be all right—God has told me so."

Her mind in a whirl, Missy noted absently that he had slipped into his Quaker speech patterns, the speech of his youth. She moved to the other side of the bed, and Caroline followed her; they both knelt and clasped his free hand.

The terrible lines of pain faded from his face as he turned his head to look at his daughters. His breath came in shallow, quick spurts. "Caroline—my dear child!" She sobbed, but he continued. "God has been thy—life." He struggled for a moment, then said, "He is calling thee—follow Him—to the Indians."

"You know, Father?" she smiled through her tears. "It's what I must do!"

"Yes—I know. God has told me—" His eyelids fluttered, and a tremor shook his body. "Chris!" he cried. "Thee must take them with thee—all my children!"

Chris stared at him. He glanced at Missy and Caroline, then at Asa. "Dan, I'll take Caroline. She'll go anyway—but it wouldn't be right for Asa and Missy. Uncle Paul would be glad to have them!"

"No—no! God has told me that thee must take them! Thee must!—Promise!" he gasped.

Chris could not think clearly. He could not bring himself to make such a vow to Dan, for he knew how hard the life would be on Missy and Asa.

Then Asa cried, "I'm going with you, Chris! I'll run away if you won't take me!"

Chris looked at once toward Missy, and her face, though wet with tears, was set stubbornly. "Father, if Chris will have me," she said, "I'll go help with the work."

Chris felt the grip of Dan's hand growing slack and he heard him whisper, "Promise—take them with thee!"

"I'll take them, Dan!" he promised, giving the hand a squeeze. "Did you hear me? I promise!"

Dan opened his eyes and looked for the last time around the room. "You have been my good children always," he sighed. And then he closed his eyes and slipped away, a gentle smile on his lips.

Chris stood up slowly, shaken. As he looked at the three young people beside the bed, the enormity of the promise he'd made hit him. He was incapable of breaking such a vow, but to take these three into hostile Indian country was a crushing burden—and he knew it would get heavier as time went on.

Chris stepped outside and stood on the porch for a while, and then he heard the door close. He turned to see Caroline, Missy, and Asa come out of the house and wait for him to speak. *Already it's started,* he thought grimly. Aloud he said, "You heard me promise your father. I intend to keep my word—but none of you promised him. I want all three of you to pray over this thing like you've never prayed over anything before."

Caroline replied calmly, "It's my calling from God, Chris. I've been trying to find a way to tell Father for weeks now."

Missy crossed her arms and spoke quietly. "I don't have a word from God on this—but I know my father heard from the Lord. I'll do what he asked."

"Me, too, Chris!" Asa whispered. "It's what he wanted."

As if those words released him, in that moment Christmas Winslow felt the presence of God as he rarely had before. It was as if God were saying to him, *Don't be afraid—I will help you*. He let the silence run on, enveloping him peacefully, and murmured with finality, "God's will be done!"

PART THREE

THE MISSIONARY

★ ★ ★ ★

CHAPTER NINETEEN

THE MISSIONARIES

★ ★ ★ ★

By the time faint red streaks illuminated the sky, Asa had been up and dressed for an hour. The excitement of leaving home for the mountains had filled him for days, and now, peering out the window, he could make out the faint outlines of the two wagons that held all their goods. Smiling, he thought of the arguments that Missy and Caroline had carried on with Chris, begging him to let them take this and that favorite piece. Chris had been adamant. "Take what you please, but it'll have to go in these two wagons—that's all the boats will hold."

A door slammed below, and Asa whirled around. "Come on, Sky! It's time to go!"

He grabbed his rifle and shot pouch and bolted for the door, but stopped when he saw that Sky had not moved from where he sat cross-legged on his bed, regarding Asa solemnly. The two had spent much time together in the past five months, but as far as Asa could tell, they were no closer than when Sky had first come.

Asa stood poised at the door, eager to leave. "Aw, Sky, for cryin' out loud—ain't you even a little excited about goin'? Good night! Your father's takin' you back home!"

"He is not my father—Black Elk is my father." The harsh

words echoed the flash of anger in Sky's eyes. He got up off the bed and brushed past Asa. "We'd better go."

Asa shook his head and followed him out of the room. Outside, they found Chris loading the last few things into the wagons. "We can help, Chris," Asa offered. He leaned his rifle carefully against the wall and waited for instructions. Sky stood by, stoically observing.

"You can go put the harnesses on the horses, but watch out for that mare," Chris called after them as they headed for the barn. "She's a little frisky." He watched them go, painfully aware that, as usual, Sky had said nothing to him. Although he was loathe to admit it, Chris knew that he was much closer to Asa than to his own son. His failure to get through Sky's armor hurt him more than anything ever had. Shaking his head, he went back into the kitchen, where the women were almost running into each other as they made the final breakfast in the small room.

His eyes went at once to Dove, who was carefully turning hoecakes on a skillet before the fire. She met his gaze and smiled weakly, and he felt the same doubt that had beset him for weeks, for she looked pale and sick in the dim lamplight. He tried to remember the fresh beauty of her face as it had been when he'd first seen her, but the memory had almost gone. Her cheeks were sunken now, and the hair that had been so sleek and black was now dry and touched with gray here and there. Her skin, which had been smooth and clear, was rough, and there was only a spark of life in her eyes. Trying not to let his concern show on his face, he went to her and took the pan out of her hands, saying, "I'll do that. You sit down and drink some coffee."

"I'm all right," she protested, but she sat down anyway. As she began to sip the coffee, Chris saw that her hands were trembling, and her high cheekbones had a touch of unnatural red that was almost certainly fever. He hoped that she was not too sick now to travel. The first few months she had been there, he had often told her: "This country is too low and damp, Dove. Bad for anyone with a cough. But when I get you back to the mountains, you'll get better."

To which she had always responded, "It will be good to be

back home, Bear Killer—Chris." She never complained, but he had seen that she would never adjust to the white world.

As he turned the cakes, Chris thought about the change in White Dove. The years of slavery had crushed her spirit so badly that she lived for only one thing: "If it had not been for our son, I would have killed myself, Chris!" she had told him. "I wanted to die—but I lived so that in some way I could help him."

Although they shared the same room, from the time Chris brought her home he never touched Dove, never loved her as a man loves his wife. Sensing the fear in her when he came near, he treated her with kindness, recognizing that her reaction was the result of brutal treatment by callous men. He had said, "You've been badly hurt, Dove. I want you to rest and take care of yourself—until I have my young wife back again."

At once she knew he understood, and gratitude filled her heart and overflowed in tears. She had learned to endure rough treatment stoically, but she did not know how to handle his tenderness. "That girl is gone, Chris," she told him, but he had laughed and said, "Just you wait!"

Her health had improved markedly, but she was still not her old self, and tired easily. Chris was disturbed by this new sign of illness. He sighed, setting the skillet down. Not wanting to take such a long journey unless he was sure it would be safe for her, Chris sent Dove back to their room to lie down while he went for the doctor.

Upon examining her, Dr. Miller led Chris out of the room. "I wish she could have been rescued earlier, Rev. Winslow," he told Chris privately. "I'm afraid she'll never be as strong as she was before. Your wife is very ill."

"What do you think it is, Doctor?"

"Almost certainly consumption."

"I—I thought that might be it. Will a different climate help?"

"Well, we'll certainly hope so. Should help some." But there was little assurance in Miller's tone, and Chris knew that Dove was in serious condition. He had spent long hours praying for her to improve and for Sky to open up to him, but in neither case did he see any visible results.

Missy overheard the two men talking, and went into the next room and patted Dove softly on the shoulder. "I'll fix you a good breakfast—some of those battered eggs and some honey for your hoecake," she said. "Why don't you get up and get dressed again?" After the doctor had gone, she told Chris, "You go get the boys; we're almost ready to eat." She finished cooking the food, and by the time Chris returned with Asa and Sky, she and Caroline had the table set and the piping-hot food spread out. "The last meal in this house," Missy reminded them as she took her seat across from Chris.

"Will it be hard for you to leave here?" he asked.

"No—it was a good home—but now that Mother and Father are gone, it's just another house," Missy answered.

Caroline's face was animated. "It's going to be a good life."

"Let's hope so . . . but it'll be the last meal you'll have in a house until we get to St. Louis," Chris remarked.

"I'm so anxious to meet the missionaries," Caroline said. "I wish Bishop Asbury had told us more about them." The bishop had written Chris, informing him that a small group of volunteers had been formed to work among the Indians, and that they would meet in St. Louis no later than the first of July.

"What was the name of the minister who's heading the mission?" Missy asked.

"Rev. Aaron Small. He's giving up a prosperous church in Georgia," Chris stated. "Bishop Asbury speaks highly of him. He's done some mission work with the blacks in his area."

Finally the meal was finished, the pots and dishes cleaned and packed, and the teams hitched to the wagons. As they all assembled around the wagons, Chris asked, "Sky, you think you can handle that team?"

For once Sky spoke with some excitement. "Yes! I can drive."

Chris nodded. "Let's go to the mountains then."

He helped Dove into one wagon, then Caroline, as Sky and Missy got into the other. Two riding mounts were tied behind each wagon, and Asa mounted Thunder. Chris spoke to the team and the wagons moved away from the house. As they passed the grove he looked back and saw that despite her brave words, Missy was dabbing at her eyes. Dove, who had been watching, said quietly, "She will be lonely."

"For a while. But it's good for you—getting away from this place. You'll get rid of that cough in the mountain air."

Dove did not reply, and he did not speak about it again. They reached the main road, turned west and settled down for the long journey to the mountains.

The trip to St. Louis was sheer joy to Asa; even Sky smiled from time to time as they made their way across the country. It was a dry June, and the sun was hot; but every night they camped beside rivers or small streams, stopping early enough to make a good evening meal. Missy and Caroline sunburned, then tanned under the hot sun, but both of them seemed to thrive. The fresh air and sunshine—along with the exercise of the trail—made Asa say, "Gosh! You two look bettern' you ever did!"

Chris smiled. "Time we get to the Rockies, you two'll be so pretty we'll have to guard you day and night. I'd wager those poor trappers won't ever have seen anything so beautiful as you girls!"

Caroline flushed scarlet, but Missy sniffed, "I've seen your trappers, Christmas Winslow. I'd just as soon cuddle up to a grizzly bear."

Chris laughed at the remark. "I expect you're right. Bear would probably smell better—and have better manners, too."

Dove did not fare well on the trip. She coughed a great deal, and although she tried to walk beside the wagon sometimes, as the others did, it soon became too much for her. Saying little, she would sit beside Chris for long stretches before she was forced to get inside the wagon and rest. Missy often drove Chris's wagon, freeing him to roam ahead on his horse looking for game, and the two women became close.

Missy was never sure that Dove understood that she and Chris were to have been married. But if anyone had mentioned the fact to her, the small, thin woman never alluded to it. *Well—once, perhaps,* Missy conceded. Late one afternoon they had been sitting alone in the wagon while Chris and the boys were ahead hunting. Missy had been half asleep, lulled by the rocking of the wagon, when Dove said softly, "Your God will give you a good man, Missy, for the one you have lost."

Startled, Missy turned to look at Dove, and saw a certainty in the dark eyes, a kind of wisdom that she'd never seen before. *So, she knows about Chris and me.* It occurred to her that there might be tension over the knowledge, but she was mistaken. Dove never again mentioned it, and spent most of her time talking about Sky and what could be done to help him.

"He will be neither white nor Sioux," she whispered to Missy once. "Neither will claim him."

"Oh no!" Missy said quickly. "Chris is a noted warrior, isn't he? Sky will be accepted because of that."

Dove shook her head. "He says that Black Elk is his father. The Pawnees taught him well to hate Bear Killer."

"We must pray that he will learn to love his real father, Dove."

There was a silence and Missy saw that Dove was considering her through half-closed eyes. "How I wish all Christians were as kind as you—but they are not."

This was the first time Missy had heard Dove hint about how much the rejection of Chris's congregation had hurt her. Laying her hand on the thin arm, Missy said, "I know. It's not right—but listen to me, Dove. Anyone who really loves God would love you, too."

With all her heart Missy longed to win this woman to the Lord, to convince her that all Christians were not like the ones she had met so far. But she knew that words were useless, and wisely did not press the point, praying for the day when Dove would see the reality of Jesus acted out in the lives of His followers, and respond. As she drove she continued to pray silently for Dove and Sky, and urged the horses forward when she saw Chris and the boys ahead.

Two days later they reached St. Louis, a bustling town on the banks of the Mississippi. Chris inquired the way to the Methodist church, and found it without difficulty—a two-story red brick structure with a high steeple and the first stained-glass windows Chris had ever seen. A lanky man was cutting grass in the front and he looked up as the wagons stopped.

"Expect you must be Rev. Winslow," he said. He pulled his

shapeless felt hat off in greeting, exposing a homely face. "Rev. Small told me to wait till you came." He put a hand out, and though he was thin as a rail, the meaty hand that took Chris's closed with a tremendous grip. "I'm Barney Sinclair, Reverend."

Chris liked the face, plain as it was. Sinclair was about thirty, with a receding hairline, large ears that stuck out, and a pair of faded blue eyes. "Are you one of the missionaries?" Chris asked.

"Oh no!" Sinclair said quickly, shaking his head. "I'm just goin' along to help Rev. Small out." The thought of being taken for a minister seemed to embarrass him. "The pastor of the church, he had to go out of town, so I've been waitin' to show you our camp, Reverend."

"Is it far, Barney?"

"Down by the river," he nodded. "'Bout two sightings and a dog bark. Mebbe I can drive that team for you?"

"Sure."

Sinclair followed him to the wagons and ducked his head when he was introduced, not looking either Missy or Caroline in the eye, but gave Asa and Sky a big grin. He climbed onto the wagon and Chris sat between him and Dove. When Chris introduced him to Dove, Barney pulled his hat off again and gave her a smile and a nod. "Real pleased to know you, Miz Winslow." Sinclair was, Chris saw at once, an expert driver, with a look of capability in the large hands that belied the apparent frailty of his lath-shaped frame. *Tough as a buffer hide!* Chris thought. *If the rest of them are like this, we might make it*. "Where you from, Barney?" he asked aloud.

"Well, I guess I'm from all over more than I am from any particular place." Barney flicked the reins, adding, "Spent the last five years on a two-hoss farm on the backside of Virginia."

"How'd you get yourself in with this missionary crowd?"

The question seemed to bother the lanky driver. He shifted on his seat, considered the sky, then shrugged his bony shoulders. "Well, Reverend, to tell the truth, I always liked church, even when I was a sinner. Went to meetin's every chance—even was a feeler fer a spell."

Chris looked puzzled. "Don't recall hearin' that word before, Barney. What's a 'feeler'?"

"A feeler, Reverend? I guess you ain't been around Baptists much. When we go down to the river to baptize, it's the feeler's job to go out and feel around for a good place to baptize folks—see there ain't no deep holes or such like."

Chris smiled. "You're a Baptist? How'd you get in with the Methodists?"

"Well . . ." Barney hesitated and turned his eyes on Chris. He studied him carefully, then nodded as if satisfied by what he saw. "To tell the truth, I guess the name don't matter much to me, Reverend. Like I said, I always liked church. Went to the big camp meetings: after the hymns were h'isted heavenward, there was all sorts of courtin' and horse tradin' and such goin's-on, whilst the blessed and the saved gorged themselves on basket dinners spread out on waist-high tables! It was a lot of fun—and two years ago I went to a meetin' over near Lynchburg, and met the Lord somethin' powerful.

"You were converted?"

"Me? Oh, my Lord, I got a case of the jerks at that meetin' that liked to have killed me!" The "jerks" occurred when worshipers were "struck down" by the power of the Holy Spirit—jerking and twisting in spasms that sometimes lasted for hours. Chris had some reservations about such things, but was loathe to say so to the lanky Sinclair. "I went out and when I come to, I was prayed for, and it was then I got all tangled up with God."

"Never heard it put just that way, Barney," Chris smiled.

"Well, it was the best thing that happened to me—but servin' God ain't no easy thing. You asked me how a Baptist got in with the Methodists. Well, don't say a word about this to Rev. Small, but the Lord put it in my heart to go to the savages, and when I found out there wasn't no Baptists headed in that direction—I became a Methodist."

Chris chuckled at the simplicity of his answer. "Well, Barney, I'll keep your secret—although I don't think the Sioux will be particularly interested in the theological implications of water baptism." Then he grew serious and said, "But it's dangerous, Barney. I'm not sure any of you folks know how bad it can be. It's hard living."

Barney looked down at his big hands and made fists out of

them. "As fer hard livin', I ain't never known nothing else. And no matter how dangerous it is, I reckon the Lord God can look out for me better than I can look out for myself."

"I say amen to that." Chris nodded. "What about the others? Are they pretty tough?"

"They act like they're agoin' for a picnic in a Boston city park! I tried to tell 'em different—but then I ain't never been there myself, so it was a waste of time. Maybe they'll listen to you. At least, Doc Spencer says so."

"Tell me a little about them, Barney."

"Well, Rev. Small, he's the leader. Not a big man, but shore knows a lot. Seems pretty confident, even though he's not been west any farther than the rest of us—'cept you, of course. He's a bachelor. Doc Spencer is a fine man, but he was raised in Philadelphia and don't know one end of a cow from another—and his wife is kinda dainty. Real nice, but can't see her livin' in a cabin with a dirt floor. There's Karl and Ellen Shultz. He's a big, strong man—and she's pretty stout her ownself. Good man with tools. Got two kids, Anna and Max, 'bout fifteen. Then there's Rev. Tennyson and his wife. He's a furriner from over the water. Shore can sing! Him and his wife was both teachers in Boston. And last is the Moores. His name is Thad. Hers is Bessie. Got a couple of kids. That's it, more or less, 'cept fer me and two other single men—Neal Littlejohn and Leon Prince."

Chris tried to imagine the group Barney had described surviving in hostile Indian country, and shook his head grimly. "Well, they'll be in for a shock, I'm afraid. A Pawnee with his war paint on won't see the difference between a minister of the gospel and any other white face."

"Reckoned so," Barney agreed. "One of the reasons I come was that folks always said I was too careless-like. Always laughing and never taking things serious." He studied Chris a moment before he flashed a quick grin and said, "I reckon headin' into Sioux country with this bunch is likely to add some sobriety to my moral character—don't you reckon, Reverend?"

"Like as not, Barney," Chris nodded, vaguely wondering if the tall, skinny fellow was indirectly trying to prepare him for something.

Sinclair took them to the river and pulled up beside a cluster of several wagons. Women were busy around a campfire and the smell of cooking meat was in the air. A short man walked toward them as Chris jumped out of the wagon. "Rev. Winslow? I'm Aaron Small."

"Glad to meet you, Brother Small." The preacher was a short chesty man with a blunt face and a full set of whiskers. Chris turned and helped Dove down, saying, "I'd like you to meet my wife Dove."

There was a slight alteration in Small's black eyes that Chris did not miss. *Guess he doesn't like me having an Indian wife.* Recovering, Small gave a short bow. "My pleasure, Sister Winslow."

"And this is my son, Sky." Again the eyes flickered. "Fine looking boy."

"And this is Caroline Greene, and her sister, Melissa, and their brother, Asa."

Small drew himself up to his full height, but still was not quite as tall as Missy. He smiled at them both. "A pleasure! A great pleasure! We have looked forward to this—I've heard such good things about your father!" He shook his head and added quickly, "Such a loss! But"—he smiled again and drew his shoulders back—"The work must go on. I'm sure he'd be pleased to see you having a part in this great endeavour to carry the gospel to the savages." Chris winced slightly at the last word, but Dove's face was expressionless.

He bustled around, calling the names of the rest of the party who came forward to meet the newcomers. Chris found they were pretty much as Barney Sinclair had described them.

John Spencer was a tall fine-looking man of thirty-two; his wife Lorene was younger, very small with a fair complexion and large blue eyes.

Karl Shultz was almost as tall as Chris, and much heavier. He was like a draft horse, massive and slow to move and to speak. *Too big for a man—and not big enough for a horse* was the way Barney had put it. His wife Ellen was a well-formed woman, tall and attractive with dark hair and eyes. At fourteen, Anna was much like her; while Max, a year older, was like his father, muscular and blond.

"And this is Robert Tennyson and his wife Helen. They are our musical arm." Tennyson was small but wiry. He had been a coal miner in Wales, Chris learned later, and the arduous labor had molded his upper body into a compact mass of muscle. He was a fine tenor; and his wife, dark and rather plain, was a talented pianist.

"Brother Moore and his good wife Bessie." Moore was a small, thin man with mousey hair and the squint of a nearsighted man. *Been a clerk all his life,* Sinclair had said, and he looked the part. His wife was overweight, and her fair skin was already burned and peeling. *A good woman—but she's got a tongue long enough to set in the parlor and lick the skillet in the kitchen!* Chris chuckled under his breath, remembering Barney's remark.

The single men came forward: Neal Littlejohn, a heavy-set man with a cheerful face—and a nose that made Chris suspect he had been a heavy drinker—and Leon Prince, a man of average height who hid his features behind a massive beard.

"Well, let's have supper," Small said after introductions were made, and the group moved toward the wagon. The meal was good and Small did most of the talking. He was full of "the mission," and as he talked Chris eyed the size of the wagons, noting how heavily they were loaded.

When the meal was almost over, talk turned to the trip that lay ahead of them. "I know it will be hard," Small remarked, and he waved toward the wagons, "but these wagons are the best that money could buy—specially built just for this mission work. Gift of a wealthy manufacturer in New York—a convert of mine."

Swallowing hard, Chris put his plate down and stood up and stared at the wagons. He was speechless as he thought of the distances and obstacles that lay ahead of them.

"Brother Small," he said slowly. "Let me understand you. Do you mean you intend to take these wagons overland to the Yellowstone country?"

"Why, certainly!" Small stopped and stared at Chris. "There's never been any question about that."

"Well, I'm afraid I'm going to have to question it," Chris said; and instantly he saw Small's eyes grow hard and his shoulders set defensively. "This train will never make it. Not in those wagons. We'll never make it—it's never been done."

"Oh, I don't think we need worry about that, Brother Winslow." Small waved his hand, adding, "This is God's work. He will see that we get there."

Chris stared, incredulous. "When Lewis and Clark were commissioned by President Jefferson to chart the purchase this country made from Napoleon, they could have gone any way they wanted, because the government was paying all expenses. But, as I'm sure you know, they refused to go overland. They took small boats up the Missouri in 1803. And even with hardened French boatmen and little baggage, they had trouble."

Small settled back on his heels and rocked slightly. Clearly, this was to be a test of wills. With a stubborn set to his jaw, he said loudly, "No doubt, but there is now a way overland. You've not heard of it, I dare say."

Chris thought of the miles of desert, the steep canyons, the upthrusting Tetons, and shook his head. "I don't know who's been talking to you, but he's wrong."

At that moment a horseman appeared, coming out of the grove that grew fifty yards back from the river. "Here's our guide, Brother Winslow." A sudden sly smile touched Small's full lips. "He tells me you two are acquainted."

Chris stiffened as the rider stopped his horse and slid to the ground. He was a tall man, heavy in the shoulders and in the flanks. The worn buckskins he had seemed molded to his muscular build, and he wore a trapper's round fur hat and a pair of moccasins. He was a virile man, full of animal strength and energy that seemed to spill over as he moved. He stopped and stared across the fire, and the buzz of conversation stopped abruptly until the lastcomer broke the silence. "Hello, Winslow."

"Hello, Ring."

He remembered Ring Tanner well. Years ago the two had narrowly avoided a fight at his first rendezvous. Tanner had drawn a smaller man into a fight, then whipped him unmercifully. But when he started to kick at the man, Chris had offered himself as a substitute. "C'mon, Ring—pick on someone your own size," he'd said, and for a moment he saw the desire flare in Tanner's eyes. Only the size of Chris—and his reputation—had made Ring back down. Chris had heard several times later that the bully had boasted about what he would do to him the next time they met.

"This is the man who says he can guide you across the desert to the Yellowstone? Don't you believe it," Chris stated flatly, staring into Tanner's eyes.

"He comes highly recommended."

"You always was a sorehead, Winslow," Ring Tanner retorted. "You got a big reputation, but at least I didn't have to marry no squaw to get my beaver!"

For one instant a red rage flared in Chris's eyes, clouding his judgment and inducing Tanner to unsheathe his knife. Small cried out, "Here! None of this! Winslow, I'm ashamed of you! A minister of the gospel acting in this fashion!"

Chris took a deep breath, then nodded, forcing himself to say, "Sorry." He looked at Tanner, determination in his eyes. "You can take your people overland if you like—but I'm going to hire a keelboat for my family."

"I'm afraid that's not possible," Small said smoothly. "I have a letter for you from Bishop Asbury. He says that you will submit yourself to my orders. If you do not, you will no longer be a Methodist minister."

Chris looked at him, stunned. "I'll pray about it, but I can tell you now, neither Tanner nor any other guide can get these wagons through." Then he added, "We'll camp downstream. Perhaps we can find some way to fix things."

He walked away, followed by his family, and as soon as they were out of hearing, a loud debate sprang up. Some were fearful of what Winslow had said, but Tanner insisted, "He don't know nothin'. He ain't never been through that desert like I have. But he's a stubborn one. He won't go."

Rev. Small stroked his chin and nodded. "Oh, I think he will, Tanner." He smiled, adding, "He values his calling—and Bishop Asbury made the matter clear. Winslow will go, or give up the ministry—and he'll never do that!"

CHAPTER TWENTY

ON THE TRAIL

★ ★ ★ ★

"I can't make this decision alone." Chris looked around the small fire at each face. The air beside the river was still and heavy, so that the smoke curled upward slowly as if reluctant to leave the blaze. The other camp, only a hundred yards away, was quiet. Dove usually said nothing, but she nodded slightly, and said, "The man is foolish. Even The People would not start across the great dry space now. There is no water for the horses—and the enemies are many and cruel." Then she stopped herself. "But you know this. I will go if you say."

"Why don't we just let them go their way and we'll go ours?" Asa asked. "They ain't none of our business—"

"Asa, I think Chris feels they really are our concern," Missy broke in. She was sitting with her legs drawn up, her chin resting on her knees in a childlike fashion. Her eyes were enormous in the firelight. "And he's right," she added. "Aside from the fact that Bishop Asbury has given a direct commission, they're our fellow Christians—and I think they need Chris more than they know."

Chris studied her a moment, then looked at Caroline. "It's got to be unanimous. Caroline, do you have a word from the Lord on this?"

"Oh no!" Caroline shook her head. "But," she went on, reaching out and touching Missy's shoulder, "Missy is right. We can't desert them—even if they're wrong."

The stillness that followed, briefly interrupted by a coyote's call rising in a series of yips, could almost be felt. Sky was sitting back from the fire, as usual, distancing himself from the rest of the group. He studied his father's face with a puzzled expression.

"I don't understand," he remarked at last, breaking the silence. Chris turned quickly to look into the eyes so much like his own. "The big man, he hates you—and the little man is keroti." He moved his head slightly from side to side and asked Chris, "Why go with them to die?"

Chris smiled at the description of Aaron Small, and when Missy asked what keroti meant, he explained offhandedly, "Well, it's a bird, Missy—a very small bird with lots of feathers. It puffs itself up, swelling out and strutting, trying to look bigger than it really is." Missy giggled and Chris added quickly, "Not that I'm criticizing Brother Small, of course."

Caroline gave a rare smile that made her face almost beautiful in the warm light of the fire. "We are bound not to speak evil of anyone, especially of the Lord's anointed, but . . ." She paused, searching for a kind way to put what was in her mind. "Brother Small has been very effective in his work—but he has not realized how different this mission is going to be. He'll come to himself, I'm sure."

Once again Sky spoke. "The big hunter—he will not change."

Chris looked swiftly at his son, surprised by Sky's insight, but nodded in agreement. "That's the trouble, son. Ring Tanner is bad medicine. He was up in the Milk River country with Tom Sellers and Milt Cannon in the dead of winter. Tom fell into a crevice and broke his leg. Well, that was rough—Milk River's a bad country, especially in winter. Most partners would have built a hut and toughed it out till spring. But Tanner took off. Milt stayed, and he got out all right. But the point is this: If trouble comes, Tanner won't stick."

"Then it's decided," Caroline stated. "If he's that kind of man, the people need you more than ever, Christmas."

"I think Caroline is right, Chris," Missy agreed.

The boys were silent, and Chris turned to Dove. He studied her thin face. "It's your say, Dove. The trip by boat would be a lot easier for you."

White Dove's face was softened by the glow of the fire, and she smiled. "You must decide. I will go with you."

He sat there, a big shape in the flickering light, and then he got up abruptly. "All right. We'll go with them—but we're gonna have to pray like we've never prayed before. Better get some sleep. It's going to be a hard trip—but we won't leave for a few days." He gave a short laugh, adding, "First item in the morning is, I go to Brother Small and eat humble pie."

True to his word, after breakfast Chris walked over to the other camp. He knew exactly what he would say, having racked his brain the night before in order to find the right words to smooth things over. Every eye in camp was on him as he approached the leader. "Brother Small, we would like to join your wagon train if you will have us." The preacher drew himself up, and the light of pride in his eyes assured Chris that his little speech had done its job.

"Certainly—certainly!" Small replied, with a magnanimous wave of his hand. "We all make mistakes, don't we? And I must say that your spirit of humility is a thing that's good to see in a minister of the gospel!"

"When did you plan to leave?"

"As soon as possible!" The man turned to go.

"I'll have to trade my horses for oxen," Chris informed him. "These were fine for a short trip, but they won't do where we're headed. Oh, and Brother Small . . ."

The preacher turned back to look at him.

"Brother Small," Chris said quickly, "it seems to me that some of your wagons are overloaded—and I know ours are. It might be good to take care of that here where we can sell the surplus. Be better than tossing it out later."

Small generously conceded, and for the next two days a continuous debate went on as to what should go and what should be sold. Soon Chris discovered that the party had enough to supply a general store, including an over-supply of bacon, flour and beans, plus an enormous quantity of useless articles: pins and needles, brooms and brushes, glass beads and hawkbells, jumping jacks and Jews' harps, rings, bracelets, pocket mirrors, pocketbooks and boiled shirts. "Looks like a flock of birds building nests," Chris remarked to Barney.

Finally the preparations were complete and at dawn they pulled out. Missy recorded the first weeks in her log:

> July 12, 1811: We left at five, just as the sun came up. Rev. Small led us on a big white horse, but by noon he seemed to have had enough and got off. I noticed he could hardly walk, he was so saddle-sore, and rode on a pillow for the rest of the day. We've gone only twelve miles, but I'm sure we'll do better as the trail toughens us up.
>
> July 26, 1811: We left Independence, Missouri, this morning. Now we are in The Great American Desert. Nothing between us and the Yellowstone except a few small trading posts and one or two army forts. We are truly in the hands of God—but He is able!
>
> August 14, 1811: It is late and I am very tired. I write this by the light of a candle. Tired as I am, I want to put something down while it's still fresh. We have become a little tougher now, and I will write what happened today as a sample of our days on the trail.
>
> We got up this morning at four A.M., and made fires out of buffalo chips. There is no wood to speak of, so the chips are the only fuel we have. It made me a little sick to have to touch them, at first, but Barney made us all laugh by calling them "prairie pancakes." I don't know what we'd do without his good humor! The women cooked breakfast while the men hitched the teams. After breakfast Rev. Small led Bible reading and prayer. This morning he managed to insert a sermon into the middle of his prayer, and we got a late start.
>
> The hunters go out in front of the train, usually about five miles. They watch for water, too, which is already a problem, and will get worse, Chris says. Most of us walk beside the wagons to make it easier on the oxen, but it's fun, too. There are lots of beautiful wild flowers to pick.
>
> Dove walked for about an hour this morning, and it put some color in her cheeks—until she had a coughing spell and had to ride for the rest of the day. I pray constantly for her to be healed.
>
> At noon we stopped to eat a cold lunch and rest the animals. One of our wagon wheels almost lost the iron rim, and Barney Sinclair fixed it. He's such a shy fellow. Caroline went over to

talk with him while he worked, and it flustered him so much he nearly hit his nose—instead of the wheel—with the hammer! Caroline told me later that she had to keep the conversation going; he didn't seem to know how to talk to her. But he's a good man. Fixed the wheel like he fixes everything else that goes bad. Now it works like a charm.

Stopped by a little stream for the night's camp. Drew the wagons in a circle, made fires and cooked a good meal. After supper Barney got his fiddle out and played. Such a cheerful sound! Mr. Tennyson sang some sad Irish songs. He has a beautiful voice. Caroline and I sang some hymns, too.

Chris is worried. I can tell. I asked him why he looked so glum when things were going so well, and he said, "This is the easy part. We hit the Platte soon, and that's when we can stop sleeping easy."

The days seem to flow into one another. The enormous open sky and the immense spaces in every direction have made us draw closer to one another. We have become so much of a team. By the time our party crossed the Big Blue, a tributary of the Kansas River, and turned toward the Platte River, there were few secrets left among us.

Asa has fallen madly in love with fourteen-year-old Anna Schultz—a phenomena that borders on the brink of insanity to Sky. He tried to talk Asa out of his mooning by saying, "She's only a girl, Asa. She can't even throw straight!"

They were a week past the Blue River when Sky cornered Chris and asked, "Will you teach me to shoot?"

Chris, who had just bent over to pick up his rifle, stopped abruptly with surprise. This was the first time his son had asked him for anything since leaving the Pawnee camp, and though Chris felt it might be a sign of Sky's acceptance, Chris knew better than to overreact. And so, swallowing the surge of joy that ran through him, he shrugged and said, "Do what I can."

The two of them walked through the short grass without speaking. In an hour the wagons looked small in the distance, and Chris stopped. "Guess this is good enough. Got your rifle loaded?" For the next hour he tutored the boy in the art of long-range shooting. Sky had been too proud to ask for help, and he had picked up many bad habits. Still, he had a natural hunting ability; for once he had learned to follow the few simple techniques Chris showed him, Sky was able to send the slugs where he wanted them. His eyes glowed when he hit a white stone no bigger than his fist at one hundred yards.

Chris nodded. "That rifle's a mite heavy for you now, Sky, but in a year you'll be handling it like it was a straw." He let his hand drop on the boy's shoulder just for one instant. "You've got a good eye and a steady hand."

Sky's blue eyes dropped to the ground as he mumbled, "Thanks." *Well, it's a start,* Chris thought. Every day the boy would appear just as Chris got ready to go. "Want to hunt a mite?" Chris would ask. Sky would shrug carelessly, "Might as well."

All of this did not go unnoticed. Missy sat beside Dove one time, watching with her as the man and boy went out together. "That's good—isn't it, Dove?"

"Yes," Dove nodded, and gave a rare smile. "He is like his father."

"He's like both of you. Best looking boy I've ever seen. I . . . I'm glad he's opening up to Chris."

Caroline was walking along beside the last wagon, which Asa was driving, and she too had seen the pair leave. It pleased her so much that she kept her eyes fixed on them and did not notice the gopher hole in her path. She stepped into it and was thrown sharply to the ground with an intense cry of pain. She called out, but the bawling of the oxen drowned her out. She tried to stand, failed, and fell again.

"Miss Caroline! You all right?"

She looked up to see Barney Sinclair's homely face as he dropped to one knee beside her, his anxious eyes searching her face. In spite of the excruciating pain in her left ankle, she had to smile. "Well, Brother Sinclair, you finally did speak to me—even if I had to break my leg to get you to do it!"

Barney's face burned, but he grinned. "I'm a bit gun-shy around ladies, fer a fact. Especially . . ."

"Especially what?"

"Well—especially . . . p-pretty ones!" he stammered, then added quickly to cover up his confusion, "We're gettin' left behind, Miss Caroline. Can you walk atall?"

"I—I don't know, Barney—" She grasped his hands as he pulled her to her feet. "Let me hold on to you!" she said. Since her eyes were on her feet she did not see the expression of alarm that swept across his face as she held him tightly around the middle. "Don't let me fall!" she cried out, forcing him to put his arm around her waist. She tried to walk, but each step on her left foot was agony, and she bit her lip to keep from crying out.

Seeing her white face, Sinclair stopped. "Here, this won't do, Miss Caroline! Ain't nobody seen you fall but me, I reckon. You set here and I'll go git a wagon."

"No!" Caroline's terror of immense spaces attacked her with thoughts of wolves and creeping Indians. "Don't leave me alone, Barney!"

"But, Miss Caroline. . . !" Barney protested. Watching the wagons rolling farther away, he came to a sudden decision. "Don't want to be forward, but I got to git you to the wagons."

"Barney!" Caroline cried out in alarm as he reached down and swooped her up in his arms. "Barney—you can't carry me! I'm too heavy!"

"Heavy? Why, Miss Caroline—you don't weigh near as much as a yearling calf, and I've packed them fer a mile many a time." In spite of himself he began to relax, laughing. "Don't mean to compare you to a calf—but you sure are little!"

It was Caroline's turn to blush, for he was holding her close, his arms under her legs and around her back. Caught in that awkward situation, she didn't know what to do with her arms. Should she let them dangle or put them around his shoulder? With an embarrassed laugh she decided on the latter, saying, "I feel like a fool!"

He was walking at a fast pace, closing with the wagons, which were still fifty yards away, and both of them were painfully aware of their embrace. Caroline's soft form in his arms was doing strange things to Barney's mind. He could smell the faint odor of some delicious scent, lavender he thought, as the breeze caught her hair, brushing it against his lips. Her cheek was smoother than he had thought possible, and the curve of her lips more beautiful than anything he'd ever seen.

Caroline, too, was disturbed, bothered by the sensations that ran through her, and she was relieved when they reached her wagon. Keeping in step, Barney lifted her over the tailgate as easily as if she were a child. She bit her lip as the injured ankle took her weight, but she looked out at once, saying, "Thank you, Barney. I would have been terrified if I'd been left." Impulsively, she put her hand out—and, just as impulsively, he took it. "You're very strong!" she exclaimed.

He was walking along behind the wagon, oblivious to the fact that he was talking easily to an attractive woman for the first time in his life. Until now, his experience with women had been limited to dance-hall girls who left him cold with their bright smiles and empty eyes. Barney was well aware of his lack of good looks, and had learned to avoid rejection by not putting himself in situations where it was a risk, or by cutting himself down—beating them to the draw, so to speak.

"Well, fer a feller skinny as a snake, I reckon I'm fairly stout. Good thing, too, since I ain't got much upstairs."

Caroline replied indignantly, "Don't talk like that, Barney! I've seen you fix things that no one else could. You play the fiddle better than any man I ever heard. And Asa tells me you know the name of every flower and bird in the world."

He stared at her, then shook his head. "Aw, Miss Caroline, a feller picks up stuff like that just by livin', but I can't . . ."

His mouth clamped shut and his ears turned red. Suddenly he bolted around the side of the wagon and was about to disappear, but she called out swiftly, "Barney—wait! Come back!" He stopped, looking back with an unhappy light in his eyes, and fell in behind the wagon again. "What is it you can't do?"

Caroline was mystified at the misery in Barney's face. Several times he would open his mouth to speak, only to shake his head and clamp his lips shut. Sweat covered his face, and she could see that his large hands were clenching and unclenching nervously. "Barney—what on earth is it? Nothing can be so awful!"

"Yes—yes, it is!" he gasped hoarsely, and he took his hat off and wiped his forehead with his sleeve. He pulled the hat down firmly on his head, gritted his teeth, then said loudly: "I can't read!"

"Why—Barney. . . !"

"Can't read a sign to say what town it is. Can't write no more than my name. Can't read the Bible. That's the worst of it—can't even read the Word of God!"

Sinclair's eyes were misty, and Caroline's heart went out to him. She once again held out her hand and as he took it, blindly, she said, "Barney—I'll teach you to read."

"Oh, Miss Caroline, I couldn't learn! I'm too old!"

"Nonsense!" Her voice was sharp but her eyes were warm. "When I fell down and you helped me up, did I say, 'No, I'm too old'?"

"No—you said, 'I'm too heavy.' "

"And I was wrong, wasn't I? Are you too proud to sit under a woman's teaching—is that it?"

He shook his head in protest. "No!"

"Then let me help you—as you've helped me." Her voice was soft and she saw the yearning in the homely face. "By the time we get to the Yellowstone, you'll be reading the third chapter of John. I promise. Will you let me teach you?"

He dropped his head and drew his sleeve across his eyes. Then his hand tightened and he looked up with a mixture of wonder and joy on his face. "If you could teach me to read—maybe I could be a preacher someday. That's what I really want more than anything else!"

Caroline looked at him intently, seeing not the quick-witted humorous outside that he showed the world, but the sensitive spirit lying beneath.

"We'll start tonight after supper, Barney," she said simply.

CHAPTER TWENTY-ONE

THE PLATTE

★ ★ ★ ★

From the Big Blue crossing, the trail ran north to meet the Platte, then turned west to follow its south bank. "Nebraska," the Indians called it, meaning "flat and shallow," while the French dubbed it with an equivalent word: the "Platte." Both names did descriptive justice to the river's broad band of flowing silt. Barney reckoned its measurements graphically: "My law, Chris—it's a mile wide and an inch deep: too dirty to bathe in and too thick to drink!"

They saw Indians fairly often, but always at a distance. When Small asked Chris about the danger of an attack, he answered, "Not likely. This valley is in a kind of neutral ground between the Pawnees to the north and the Cheyennes to the south. But we better put out a guard from now on."

Ring disagreed loudly. "No need of that. Not till we get to Pawnee country anyway." He grinned wolfishly, adding, "Reckon the Pawnees will come callin' for your hair, Winslow. I heard about how you took Black Elk's woman—and he's a bad 'un."

"Not likely Black Elk will be this far south," Chris shrugged. "He won't know I'm here." The answer, he saw, did not satisfy

Small, but there was nothing else to say. "The big problem is water and grass—not Indians."

Small looked at Turner. "I thought you said there was plenty of grass and water, Ring."

"Told you we should have left a month ago, but you wouldn't listen," Ring returned, putting his tough gaze on the smaller man.

The rebuke ruffled Small, and his face grew red. "It's your job to provide for the wagon train, and you've not been doing too well since the buffalo thinned out. I suggest you bring in some antelope or deer."

"They've skedaddled to the high country," the trapper shrugged with an air of nonchalance. In truth, he was touchy about his failure to find game, and added roughly, "If I can't get game, there ain't none to be got. You say 'amen' to that, won't you, Brother Winslow?"

Chris studied him, ignoring the taunt that always lay beneath Tanner's words. He turned to Small. "Guess I can go bring in fresh meat today."

"You sayin' you're a better man than me?" the big hunter bridled, his face tense. He was like a wild animal, flying into a fighting fury the instant he felt threatened.

Chris said evenly, holding Tanner's eyes, "You're just twisting your own tail, Ring."

"I allus said you was more brag than do! Bet you my rifle against yours you don't bag a deer or an antelope by sundown."

"Wouldn't care to bet." They were standing slightly away from the morning fire, in full earshot of the rest of the party. Chris turned his back on Tanner and walked to his wagon. "Want to go, Sky?" he asked.

Sky nodded and picked up his own rifle; then Missy said impulsively, "Would I be in the way?"

"Come along. Be a change for you—but put a bonnet on."

The three of them saddled and left, leading a packhorse, and Small grumbled, "That girl is too free in her ways. Not right for a single woman to go off like that with a married man!"

Caroline, seated beside Barney, was so absorbed in Barney that the remark went unnoticed. Barney had been eating with one hand and holding a reader in the other. Already he had waded through several beginning readers that the Tennysons had furnished, and Caroline had been amazed at his progress. She was a natural teacher, was so absorbed with teaching that she did not realize how deep her interest in Barney Sinclair went. Missy had hinted at it once: "Better watch out, Caroline, or you'll have a suitor." Caroline had merely laughed, but sometimes when their hands touched as they held the same book, it sent a quick shock through her. It did not seem to occur to her that for the first time in her life she was spending long hours with a man she truly liked.

Barney looked up when Small commented about Missy, and said, "You notice how Rev. Small watches Missy?"

"Why—no, I haven't."

"He's got a real case on her. Surprised he ain't started courtin' her."

"It wouldn't do him any good," Caroline replied. "He's too short, and besides . . ."

Barney had learned somehow of Missy's engagement to Chris, and he nodded understandingly. "She's a fine girl. None finer—'cept maybe her sister!"

Caroline giggled, something she was doing more often these days, and her eyes sparkled. "You're going to be a dangerous man with the ladies, the way you talk, Barney!"

He grinned and stood up to stretch, pointing toward the tiny figures to the east. "Reckon we'll have fresh meat tonight."

"You think Chris can do it?"

"Why, Caroline, Christmas Winslow is all sorts of a feller! He ain't much fer talk, but when he sets out to do a job, he's stubborn as a blue-nosed mule!" He looked fondly across the plain to where the trio had disappeared in a line of willows that marked a small stream. "Yes, ma'am, I'd trust Chris to fill the smokehouse!"

Unaware of the attention they had drawn, the three reached the small stream. After tying the horses, Chris said, "Sky, I'm going to loaf and let you do all the work."

Sky looked around at the empty space that fell away into the distance, and shook his head. "Nothing to shoot."

Chris took his Green River knife and cut one of the skinny saplings growing beside the stream. He sharpened the end of it, then pulled a strip of red cloth from his pocket and tied it to the other end. Handing it to Sky, he pointed to an outcropping of rock half a mile away. "Go stick this flag in the ground over by that rise, then get behind that rock—and keep your head down."

He gave no more instructions, but Sky obeyed, heading out at a trot. For a moment Chris watched his son with a pleased grin, then turned to Missy. "We might as well get comfortable, Missy. There's a little shade over there on that bar." They walked across the nearly dry bed, having to wade only about six feet across the shallow summer-shrunken stream, to a canopy of scrawny trees no more than eight feet high. Chris cleared the small rocks away under the trees, then sat down on a single large one and watched as Sky trotted out and set the flag. Missy eased herself down beside Chris.

"Why in the world did you tell him to do that?" she asked.

"Watch and learn," he said. Removing his hat, he let the slight breeze cool his forehead. He kept his eyes half closed, but they were never still, always moving from point to point across the terrain as his muscles relaxed and he leaned back against one of the stunted trees.

Missy did watch, but it wasn't the terrain; it was the wind blowing his hair. "Your hair's too long," she remarked. "Why don't you have Dove cut it for you tonight."

"All right."

They sat there for half an hour, saying nothing. Finally she lay back and closed her eyes. Almost at once she fell asleep, and was startled when he spoke quietly, "Missy, wake up."

She sat up quickly. "What's wrong?"

He pointed to where Sky was hidden and she saw three small antelope nervously approaching the flag that was whipping in a brisk breeze. They would come closer, their long necks outstretched, stamping their tiny hooves nervously, then bolt—only to return at once to the flag.

"Why are they doing that?" Missy whispered.

"Just curious."

Suddenly the silence was broken by a shot, and the largest animal was knocked to the ground. Sky came running out, crying, "I got him!"

"Come on," Chris said, pulling Missy to her feet. "We'll bring that one in and let him get another." When they reached Sky he was kneeling beside the antelope, stroking the horns. His eyes were wide with admiration as he looked at his father. "Bear Killer is also a hunter of antelope!"

"Don't have to be much of a hunter for this," Chris grinned. He picked up the carcass with a grunt. "They say curiosity killed the cat—but it works on these critters, too. They don't learn very fast. Hour or so, and they'll be back to look at that flag. You want to get another one, Sky?"

"Yes!"

They left him and went back to the shelter of the shade. All morning they stayed there, enjoying the solitude and the silence. Just before noon, Sky got the second animal, and then he begged to get one more. "I guess one more will be enough for the whole train," Chris responded. "Need to get back for supper."

All afternoon they waited, relaxing under the trees, napping from time to time, and talking hardly at all. It was almost three when Chris spoke up. "Have to go soon."

"It's been nice, Chris. Thanks for letting me come."

She was sitting beside him on the large rock, and when she turned to speak to him, their faces almost touched. Her nearness made him aware of her softness. She was relaxed and happy, her dark brown eyes quiet and her blond hair streaked with the sun. She had loosened her hair, and now it lay in abundance over her shoulders, framing her face. Chris had never seen Missy look so beautiful, so intensely feminine. She smiled and put her hand on his arm, saying, "It's been a wonderful day."

Her touch and her presence struck him powerfully, and he was stirred by old memories of another time spent together . . . the time when she was to be his wife. The temptation was almost more than he could stand. Perhaps that was why he did what he did. It was an involuntary movement as he put his arms around her, pulling her to him, then kissed her softly. She did not draw back nor heed the still small voice that seemed to be making a protest.

He kissed her once more, his pulse racing. In that moment his conscience was seared and he released her and hastily stood up. Catching the hurt in her eyes, he said in a hoarse voice, "Missy! I'm sorry!"

With a trembling hand, she pushed her hair back, unable to speak. She looked away, absorbed in thoughts of her own for a long time. Finally she stood up and murmured gently, "It's all right, Chris. I—I guess we knew this wouldn't be easy. I shouldn't have come."

She could see the pain and frustration reflected in his eyes. "It's a hard thing," he acknowledged, "but God can give us the strength we need. He has to or—" The crack of Sky's rifle was a welcome distraction, and they hurried away from the shade.

Overjoyed at the successful hunt, the travelers celebrated that night. They camped early and the smell of fresh meat cooking was so strong you could almost taste it. Ellen Schultz had Karl unload the cast iron stove, and with the small supply of wood she baked six apple pies. The Spencers brought out a small keg of cider—everyone brought something—and when they had eaten till they could hold no more, they lay back and listened to Barney's fiddle singing in the night air.

Only Ring Tanner did not join in the fun. He ate none of the fresh meat, but drank steadily and sullenly from a jug. As the night wore on and his tongue got looser, he began to make comments about Indians. Although his eyes were fixed on Dove and Sky, everyone knew the remarks were directed at Chris, who grew tenser by the moment.

Casually Barney sauntered over to Chris, letting his words fall quietly. "Watch out fer Ring. He said before, he's goin' to tree him a coon. And he was lookin' at you. Don't fight him, Chris."

"Do all I can not to."

But Tanner got louder and he shuffled over to the Schultz's stove, his eyes red-rimmed with drink. "Be glad when we get to Mandan country," he said, raising his voice loudly. "Mandan squaws are the best there is. Long legged and *real* friendly-like."

"Tanner, that will do!" Small commanded. "There are ladies here."

The big man leered at Chris. "Guess you got your share, didn't you, Winslow." He grinned. "Black Elk mebbe got the best of that squaw, but she's still—" Chris stood up.

"I'd think real careful how I finished that if I were you." The warning was spoken softly, but there was something dangerous in Chris's tone that made the others look at one another nervously—although Ring was too drunk to catch it.

"That squaw? Why she bedded down with half the Sioux nation, Winslow!" Tanner jeered.

Sky was standing back in the shadows, his eyes black as midnight. He stepped closer to the big trapper, and his voice rang clearly in the air. "You lie!"

Big as he was, Tanner was fast as a cat. He took two long steps and caught Sky with a blow of his open hand that slammed the boy back against the wagon. Then with a wild yell he rammed Chris with the full force of his weight.

A hard fist caught Chris high on the temple, setting off an explosion in his brain, and driving him to the ground. He remembered to double himself over to guard against the kick he knew was coming. Tanner's foot struck Chris in the small of the back, and he managed to grab the leg and give it a twist. Tanner fell, giving Chris time to get up and give his head a shake to clear it. The second time Tanner came at him, Chris struck him in the stomach, jerking the man's feet out from underneath him as he broke backward, half bent over. Tanner hit the ground, twisting like a cat, and scrambled to his feet.

"Here's my coon!" he yelled, and made a forward run, which was cut short when Chris stooped low and clipped Tanner across the waist. Gripping the man by the legs, Chris stood and threw his opponent sideways onto his back. Chris waited for Ring to get up; then he swung at him but missed as Tanner dodged and struck Chris full in the mouth, ripping his mouth with the force of the fist. Staggering, Chris took a kick to the kidneys, rolled against Tanner's legs and brought the man down. Falling on Ring, Chris thrust his knee into the man's belly and his forearm over Tanner's windpipe, and pressed down hard. Tanner's fingernails slashed across Chris's face, leaving long welts as he thrashed around, trying to unseat the preacher. Chris raised his right arm and clubbed Tanner's neck. The man went limp, and Chris shoved himself to his feet.

"Come and get your coon, Ring," he taunted. For a moment Chris's tall, dangerous shape swam before Tanner's dulled eyes. The man knew he was beaten. Tanner pressed his lips together, feeling bile rise to his throat as Chris motioned toward the circle that had formed. "Let him out of here."

They all watched as Tanner got up and moved painfully toward his horse. He shakily put the blanket on it, every movement slow and careful, then crawled up and sat down, bone-weary. He kicked the animal forward and pulled at the rifle that was in a scabbard.

The sound of a cocked pistol made him reconsider. Chris had pulled his weapon and trained it on the man. "Go on—ride out, if that's what you want, Ring."

As much as he wanted to shoot this Indian-lover, Tanner knew he didn't have a chance. "I'll kill you, Winslow!" he snarled; then he turned his horse and disappeared into the darkness.

Chris never wavered, holding the gun steady. His beaten nerves cried out and his legs quivered. His mouth was bleeding, his ear and face had been raked by Tanner's fingernails; the broken skin across both rows of knuckles made it hard to grip the gun. It wasn't until the sound of the horse's hooves died off that Chris relaxed enough to look at his son. "Are you all right, Sky?"

"Yes." The boy came closer and looked up at Chris with a burning light in his eyes. Dove approached Chris and took his hand gingerly. "Let me clean your wounds."

Chris allowed himself to be led away. When the two were out of earshot, Barney expressed his thoughts to Caroline and Missy. "They was both tryin' to kill. I wasn't surprised at Ring—but I didn't think Chris would git that crazy!"

"He had no choice!" Missy's voice was harsh and she discovered that she could not stand up. She sat down again quickly and squeezed her eyes shut, resting her head in her hands.

Barney's eyes scanned the darkness that had swallowed the trapper. "Have to keep a guard all the time, now. Tanner's mean—low down as a snake in a wagon track."

The others were talking rapidly, and Small wrung his hands. "He'll have to come back! We're lost without him."

Schultz shook his head. "He is no goot, dat von! Better he is gone!"

Spencer looked over to where Dove was tending to Chris's cuts and bruises. "Looks like it's up to Christmas," he remarked. "We're all babies out here."

Tennyson nodded. "That's about right, John. Far as I can see, nothing Tanner said about this trip has worked out. I wish we'd gone by boat the way Brother Winslow said."

The words affronted Aaron Small, and he retorted angrily, "Tanner will be back! He won't desert us!"

"He left his partner to die," Lorene Spencer told him. "Why would he do any different for us? Especially now . . ."

The group continued to argue, most of which Chris could hear as Dove worked on his wounds. "I'll get a hot stone and wrap it for your mouth." She smiled proudly. "You fight for us."

"Sure."

In the dim light he could see the traces of her early beauty. She touched his bruised lips and smiled again, then went to get the stone.

Chris hurt all over. And it only got worse when he thought of what would happen in the days to come. He was the only one who fully grasped the trouble they were in; and he watched the small group milling nervously around, looking at him covertly from time to time, with some impatience. *I reckon now they expect me to get them out of this mess—they must think I'm a magician.* The odds were heavily against them, he knew, but there was no turning back. He raised his eyes to the pale stars and whispered, "Lord God, if we get out of here alive, it'll be your hand—not mine— that delivers us!"

CHAPTER TWENTY-TWO

"YOUR GOD IS STRONG!"

★ ★ ★ ★

The Platte lay a hundred miles behind them, and Missy found herself longing for it. "It wasn't much of a river," she said to Chris late one afternoon, "but at least it was wet!"

"Another week and we'll hit the Sweetwater," Chris replied. "From there it's not far to the Popo Agie—then we've got it made."

"Sweetwater—what a nice name for a river!" she murmured.

Chris rested his hand on the steel rim of a wagon wheel, removed it quickly and stared at his palm. "It's a nice stream—but I'd settle for just about anything in the way of a creek right now. We lost two more oxen today—one of Spencer's and one of the Moore's. That means no spares left."

He relaxed and seemed reluctant to move. "Wish we'd get a breeze. This heat is hard on Dove—she looks awful pale."

"She won't eat, Chris. If we could just get a break in the weather."

"Not much chance of that, but when we hit the Sweetwater, we'll turn north. It'll be cool in the Tetons, and by the time we get to the Yellowstone, we'll be on high ground. Least then it'll be cool at night." He drew his shoulders back, took a deep breath, and said, "Guess I better give Barney a hand with Moore's wagon."

He walked over to where Barney and Thad Moore stood, staring down at a broken wheel. "Ain't no way to fix it, Thad—not without a forge," Barney sighed.

Moore's face, always thin, was now little more than a skull. The trail had worn him down and his nerves, never strong, were thin as wire. There was a rising note of fear in his voice as he cried, "What'll I do! It's all we got!"

"Take it easy, Hoss," Chris encouraged quietly. He put his hand on Moore's shoulder, shocked at how fragile the man was. "There's a way out of this somehow, I reckon."

"Never should have come to this godforsaken place!" Moore choked, tears filling his eyes. He was not far from falling off the edge, Chris saw. The worst was, Thad was not the only one acting like this. It was time to tighten up.

The women finished cooking the steaks from one of the oxen that had played out, and they washed the meat down with sips of the tepid water from their shrinking supply. It was early, and the stars glittered overhead, but the wind was hot even at night.

Brother Small led in a service: he was not the same man who had started the trip. He had lost weight and looked ill. The hardships seemed to have shaken his confidence; for once he did not preach an hour-long sermon, but read a psalm, then asked Tennyson to lead in some hymns. Their voices sounded thin and reedy on the air, and when the last note faded, Small said, "We will pray for deliverance. God is our only hope."

The prayers were urgent, and Chris knew that it was time to make his move. After Small dismissed the meeting, Chris announced, "Before we break up, I think we better talk a bit." Everyone looked at him expectantly as he continued. "We're going to have to make a few changes."

"What sort of changes?" Small frowned. He was jealous of his position, well aware that he had lost prestige. It was to Christmas Winslow that everyone looked, and Small resented it.

"We've lost a lot of animals, Brother Small," Chris answered, "and we're going to lose more. Don't want to discourage you, but the stretch ahead of us is bad."

"Worse than what we've just come through?" Spencer asked.

"Water's scarce—and we're pretty well whittled down, Doctor. It's rough country, and some of the wagons are going to fall apart."

"Can't do much without tools and a forge," Barney added. He looked across the fire at his friend. "What you got on your mind, Chris?"

"Have to strip the wagons down. Get rid of everything we can do without," Chris explained. "All the furniture and farming tools—anything we can do without."

"I don't have any frills in my wagons, Brother Winslow. Got rid of everything that could be spared before we started." Aaron Small drew himself up like a gamecock, his back straight and his black eyes defiant.

Chris dreaded the confrontation that was brewing, but could not back down. "Brother Small, you're our spiritual leader—but much as I dislike having to do it, I'm going to have to insist that you join the rest of us in stripping down to the bare essentials."

"I am down to that!"

"No, sir, you have hundreds of pounds of books, as all of us have seen."

"I can't leave my books out on this desert."

"If you don't, you may have to leave your bones here, Aaron!"

The blunt words drove the color from Small's face, and he stammered in protest, but one look around the circle told him it was no use; he would get no support from the others. He was an intelligent man, knew that he could not press the issue without losing face, so he quickly changed his tactics. "Well . . . maybe I was hasty! This is a crisis—so I will submit to whatever is necessary."

"That's generous of you, Brother Small," Chris rejoined. "We'll take the best of the wagons, and those we leave we'll strip for wheels and parts. And with fewer wagons we can alternate the teams—give them a chance to rest, so it won't be so hard on them. And with fewer oxen it may be easier to find a place for grazing."

"What about water, Chris?" Tennyson voiced the chief fear of all of them.

"We're all believers here, and now is the time to trust the Lord God," Chris replied, and his eyes glowed with confidence. "Here's the plan. Three of us will go ahead looking for water. We may not find a river like the Missouri, but I believe God will supply what we need." He looked over the men, considering the prospects, then shook his head. "No—I better do the scouting."

"You can't cover enough ground, Chris," Barney argued. "Let me go."

"You're needed here," Chris said firmly. Then a thought struck him and he added eagerly, "My boys and I will do the scouting. That all right with you and Asa, Sky?"

Asa blinked, unable to believe his ears. "Sure it is!"

Sky nodded slowly, saying nothing.

"Why, they're just children!" Small exclaimed. "You can't ask them to do a dangerous thing like that!"

"Boys grow up pretty fast out here," Chris returned evenly. "Now, let's get these wagons stripped down."

There was a flurry of activity as each family began to sort through the wagons. Cries of distress arose from the women as their men placed treasured items of furniture on the growing pile. Aaron Small's face was a study in misery as he laid book after book beside his wagon. "I'm sorry, Brother Aaron," Chris said quietly, taking the minister aside. "I know what your library means to you."

Small looked up and tried to smile. Holding up his large black Bible, his voice choked. "I've still got the one that counts, Brother Winslow!" Then he dropped his voice and asked quietly, "Are we going to make it, Chris?"

It was the first time the stocky minister had ever used his first name. By stripping Small of his library, God had stripped the man of his pride as well. *All things work together for good . . .* , Chris realized, and thought the better of the preacher. "We'll make it, Aaron. You'll be mightily used to preach the Word to the Indians."

"I—I trust that is so."

At last the sorting was complete. They all gathered to stand in front of the large pile. A silence fell as they stared at the goods, until Ellen Schultz spoke up. "Ve are all alife. Let us tank Gott dat ve leaf only tings here." Chris said later as he lay beside Dove, "I was proud of them, Dove. They're green, but they're learning to trust God."

She coughed—she had been coughing a great deal lately, Chris thought. When she was able to speak again, she said, "I was proud of you, Chris. When you speak of your God, there is something that makes people believe."

He rolled over and looked at her face in the moonlight. *Your God.* It troubled him that she never spoke of her own belief. Though he would never try to force God on anyone, he longed to see some response in her. Her eyes were closed, and her chest rose and fell in a regular rhythm. She looked very young and vulnerable in the dim light, and he reached over and caressed her shoulder. She opened her eyes, startled. He had not done such a thing often.

"Dove, what about God? Do you believe in Him?"

White Dove lay there quietly, thinking. When she first came to live with him, she had expected that he would force her to pray to his God, but he had not. She thought back over the months of her sickness, how kind he had been—and how undemanding. Her years of slavery had seared her emotionally; in order to survive, she had forced herself to feel nothing. Except for Sky, she had known nothing of love since the day of her captivity.

Chris had released her from physical bondage, but her inner release had taken more time. She was still very sick, she knew, but Dove was not afraid of death. What tormented her instead was the deadness she felt inside. She would do anything to escape that! All the years of loneliness rose up and she whispered, "You have been so good to me!—and to Caroline and Missy." Tears flowed down her cheeks. "I do not know your God, Chris. Tell me."

He wiped her tears and began to tell this woman, his first love, of his love for Jesus Christ. She had heard it all in church many times. But there in the quiet darkness, listening to the sound of his voice and feeling his hand on her head, it finally become real.

When she had heard it all, she said, "I want your God to be my God, Chris." And for the first time in her life, White Dove opened her heart to God, pouring out all the pain and fears inside her. "And he has heard me, Chris!" she told him later. "Jesus Christ is in my heart, now! He is real—I know He is real!"

He held her all night, his own heart full with a joy that he could not express. When the dawn came, he bent his head and kissed her.

"Now I know what Solomon meant when he called his wife 'My sister and my bride'!"

The group got up before dawn and ate a meager breakfast. Between mouthfuls Chris instructed, "Head due north, Barney. Soon as we find water, one of us will be back to guide you to it."

"Watch yourself, Chris," Barney warned. Then he grinned, adding with a streak of wry humor, "Looks like you got yourself a volunteer."

"What?" Chris turned and found Missy standing beside Thunder along with Asa and Sky. "What's this?" he demanded.

"Four can cover more ground than three."

He noted the stubborn set of her lips and said reluctantly, "I reckon you're right." He motioned to the boys. "I'll take the east flank, Asa you search to the west. Go about five miles. Missy, you and Sky spread out between us. Look for pockets of water trapped in hollows of the rock, a moist creek bed—anything wet. If it looks like enough for the train, fire one shot, wait two minutes, then fire another." He hesitated. "Don't have to tell you this is Indian country. Not likely a band would be here this time of year, but just one wandering buck is all it takes. So keep your eyes open all the time."

They left as a gleam of light broke over the prairie. Chris worried about them, but there was no other way. He got off his horse when he was about five miles away, and walked along the burned, parched earth. All morning he walked, taking sips from his water bottle, but finding no trace of a creek. About two that afternoon he was about to swing farther east when he heard a shot far off to the west. He counted out the seconds, and sighed with relief when the second report sounded. Jumping on his horse, he raced off in the direction of the shot.

He found the three "scouts" waiting for him. "I found it, Chris!" Asa yelled, pointing to the pool of water that was trapped in the saucer-shaped depression of a rock formation. Chris clapped young Greene on the shoulder. "You did mighty well. I was beginnin' to wonder if we'd ever find anything."

"I'll go bring the train here," Missy offered.

"Think you can find it?" Chris asked.

"I'll go with her," Asa spoke up importantly. "Can't have a woman runnin' around loose."

"Might be best to have a man along, Missy," Chris told her, giving her a wink that Asa missed.

"I suppose that's best," she agreed solemnly.

"They're about ten miles over there. Go slow, now; your horses are pretty well spent. It'll take a while—maybe till midnight. Get along, now."

After they left, Chris looked at the pool. It was about seven or eight feet across and stretched in a rough shape about fifteen feet long. "Pretty shallow," he remarked to Sky. "Time we fill our water bags and water the stock, won't be much left."

"Asa did well," Sky commented. He looked around and said, "Maybe something will come for water—maybe an antelope."

Chris gave him an approving look. "Wasn't thinking of that," he admitted. "If we get back behind that rise, we might get something. Gettin' to think like a real hunter, son!"

Sky ducked his head and turned to lead his horse away. Chris followed him, and they tied the animals up far enough away that game would not be alerted to their presence.

Making their way back to the rise, they carefully picked across an outcropping of broken shale. Right across the middle of it was a gully nearly five feet deep. Sky scrambled down into it, followed by Chris, and tried to climb up the other side, but the sides were steep and the boy slid back to the ground.

"Need a boost?" Chris asked, stepping forward to help—and they both froze. The noise of a dry rattle sounded nearby . . . very close by!

"Look out!" Chris yelled, spotting the huge head of a dusty rattler rise from beside a rock on the gully ledge, not two feet from where Sky stood. It was a monstrous snake with its fangs out, poised to strike. There was no time to take a shot, and Sky could not move—paralyzed at the sight of the snake's gaping jaws on a level with his face.

Chris lunged, whipped his right arm around Sky's neck, and threw him violently to one side just as he saw the flash as the snake struck. Falling to the side, Chris felt the sharp stab in his right forearm and the weight of the snake as he hit the ground.

Hearing Sky's terrified shriek, Chris reached out with his left hand, caught the rattler behind the head, and jerked the fangs out. With his right hand, he whipped out his long knife and, pinning the thrashing body to the ground with his heel, severed the head. He stepped back to allow the body, thick as a man's leg, to writhe across the rocks. Then he threw the head away from him with a shudder.

With enormous eyes Sky watched his father pull the sleeve back and study the two red punctures on his forearm. He raised the knife and slashed one, then the other, with an X that instantly welled up with bright crimson blood. He raised his arm and sucked the blood, spitting it out often.

More than once, Sky had seen what happens to those bitten by rattlers. His best friend, a boy of nine named Otter, had been bitten by a very small rattler. Sky never forgot the screams of agony he heard as the boy died, nor the sight of his friend thrashing on the ground until he was held down by four strong men.

Horrified, Sky's mouth was dry with fear, and he could not speak. He had spent months hating this man—the man they said was his father—and now he was going to die. Many times at night he had pictured the death of Bear Killer, but now that it was here, his legs trembled and his mind swam. Aloud, he cried the only word he could think of:

"Father!"

Chris's head jerked up and he met the boy's grief-stricken eyes. Despite the pain, his heart sang. *I may die here—but my son has called me "Father."*

He caught sight of the snake again—it was the largest he'd ever seen. The sight of the massive head and the memory of the enormouse fangs caused his chest to constrict with fear. His breathing grew short and a feeling of lightheaded nausea seized him; he walked away from the snake and sat down with his back to the bank, fighting to stay in control. *It's not the poison working—it's just shock and fear,* he forced himself to think.

Sky had followed him, trembling so badly he staggered and almost fell. His face was washed pale. "I'll go for the doctor," he managed in a shaky whisper.

"No time for that," Chris said. Even if a doctor stood before him, there would be little he could do, and Chris knew it. Taking a deep breath, he forced his mind to stop racing by a mighty act of will. Closing his eyes, Chris concentrated.

"Sky, you know about snakebites?"

"Y-yes."

"Then you know I may die?"

The boy squeezed his lips together and did not answer for a moment. He swallowed hard and nodded. "Yes, Father."

Chris looked up quickly. "It's good to hear you call me that, son. It means a lot to me." Then he said, "If I die, you tell your mother that I love her."

Sky lifted his head and for the first time Chris saw tears in his son's eyes. "I have watched you. I didn't think you would love her now that she is sick. They told me the white man would use the Indian woman and throw her away—but you did not."

"No. I would have come for both of you long ago—but I thought you were dead." Chris felt a strange sensation creep along his arm and knew that the poison was working. "I wish I could be around to see you grow up, son. But God will watch over you and your mother."

Sky hesitated; then he moved closer to Chris. "I have listened to you talk. You say that Jesus loves the Christian."

"Yes, that's true."

"Then—why do you not ask Him to help you now, my father?"

Chris blinked his eyes at the boy's simple question. Sky's face pleaded for an answer, but Chris hesitated. "Well, son . . ." he faltered, "God can do anything, but—"

"You told a story once about a man who got bit by a snake, and you said he shook it off in a fire—and he did not die. Can't your Jesus do this for you?"

The story of Paul being bitten by a viper returned to Chris in a flash, and he winced at the unspoken rebuke. *Ye have not because ye ask not.* Feeling death creep through his bloodstream, he thought of all the reasons why he could not pray for life. It was too late, now! *Ye have not because ye ask not.* And then, a second passage he had not thought of for years:

And these signs shall follow them that believe; In my name shall they cast out devils; they shall speak with new tongues; they shall take up serpents; and if they drink any deadly thing, it shall not hurt them.

He had studied that passage at Yale. It had been an intellectual exercise at the time, something to write a paper on, perhaps. Now as he sat there with his veins full of venom, it was no longer a bookish matter. While Chris was not a man given to mysticism—he had seen some go off into error on passages much like this one— the sight of his son's face and the simplicity of his question went straight to Chris's heart. Pushing aside his misgivings, he said grimly, "Son, God is able. There is nothing that He cannot do."

Sky stared at him. "You believe your God will save you?"

Chris said as much to himself as to the boy, "Yes, I do believe!" Then he bowed his head and prayed quietly, "Oh, Lord, there is nothing you cannot do. In the name of Jesus Christ, I ask that you deliver me from this poison."

Sky waited for more, but his father sat quietly, his eyes closed and his lips moving. The silence grew thicker and a cloud moved across the sun, throwing a shadow over the scorched land. From somewhere afar off came the single cry of a bird, thin and reedy.

When Chris finally opened his eyes Sky saw tears brimming there, but confidence as well. "God has heard my prayer, Sky," he told him. "I won't die." He looked down and saw that the wounds from the knife had almost stopped bleeding. "I'm cut pretty deep and I'll always have scars on this arm—but they'll just remind me of what happened today. And that Jesus Christ is the only true God."

"You won't die?" Sky asked cautiously.

"I may get sick," Chris answered. "Don't know about that. But God has assured me that I'll live."

Sky's eyes traveled from his father's face to the wounds on

his arm. "Your God is strong, my father!" he whispered.

"Come here, son. Sit down by me." Sky sat down, and Chris put his arm around the boy's sturdy shoulders. Neither of them spoke for a long time. After several hours, they heard the sound of the wagons approaching.

"Don't tell them about the snake," he warned Sky. He had vomited twice, and once he had a spasm of trembling in his body; but through it all he had simply praised God for sparing his life. "This time was for you and me, Sky," he said.

"I won't tell," Sky promised. "I—I am glad you will be all right. And I'm glad you are my father!"

Chris reached out and took the boy in his arms, and he felt Sky's arms slip around his neck. "I missed out on your babyhood," Chris said huskily. "You're growing up, son—soon you'll be a man. So I'll tell you this now, and if I never say it again, you remember it: I love you very much!"

The boy's face was pressed against his chest, but Chris could just make out the muffled response.

"I love you, my father!"

Everyone soon knew about the cuts in his arm, but Chris passed it off lightly. "Just cut myself with my knife."

Dr. Spencer took one look at the twin lacerations on the arm and looked up in alarm. "Snakebite? Was it bad, Chris?"

"God healed the snakebite, Doc," Chris replied. "Just put something on the cut—and forget what you saw." He noted the puzzled look on Spencer's face, and added, "It was something just for me and my son, John. Just for us!"

CHAPTER TWENTY-THREE

TWO PROPOSALS

★ ★ ★ ★

"Nathan!" Julie ran down the road, waving an envelope in her hand, her face beaming with excitement. "A letter from Christmas!"

"Is he all right?" Nathan dismounted his horse in a swift movement and took the envelope. "You haven't opened it?"

"I wanted us to read it together. It's cold outside—let's sit at the table where we can both see it."

Fall had held fast to Virginia that year, but now the hint of snow was in the November sky, and the wind had sharp teeth that bit at the face. Nathan followed her inside and they sat down at the table, both of them anxious as he broke the seal and pulled out two letters. "One from Chris and one from Missy!" Julie exclaimed, peering at the handwriting. "Thank God they're both all right!"

"Which one should we read first?"

"You choose."

Nathan picked up the thinner of the two, smiling nervously as he did. "Just like always—a woman talks more than a man." She noticed that his hands were not as steady as usual and her own heart was beating fast. They had heard nothing since the exodus of Chris and the Greenes, and both of them were well aware of the high mortality rate of westward movers. He unfolded the single sheet of paper, laid it flat on the table, and Julie put her arm around him, moving closer and peering at the writing.

13 September, 1811
Knox Mission

My dear Parents,

I know you will rejoice to hear that we made the journey safely. It was a difficult trip, but our God is good! There were many hardships, but the Lord protected us, and by His grace none of us were lost. Blessed be His name!

We arrived at the Yellowstone on the last day of August, but after prayer, we concluded that a better place for the mission would be on the banks of the upper Missouri. I submitted to Brother Small, the head of the work, that the fort Knox and I had built there on our first trapping expedition would be more central to various tribes, and he agreed to my suggestion. We moved on to the old fort, and I asked that it be named Knox Mission, in Knox's memory, and that was acceptable also.

The large central building was gone, but the walls were still in place. We put new gates on and worked like madmen to get winter quarters up. As I write this, the shakes are going on what will one day be our church and school. This winter it will be our living quarters as well, for bad weather is on its way. We have partitioned it off into two sections—one for living quarters, the other to serve as school, church, and a hospital for Dr. Spencer. Come spring, we will build cabins for the families, and I think we should build another structure for trade. As I have told you, the Indians are robbed blind by traders, and I want to start a place where they can get a fair price for their furs.

I am well, though a bit thinner than when I started out. Missy, Caroline, and Asa did well on the journey, and seem to be very happy.

You will be pleased to hear that Sky has come out of his shell! We are inseparable now, and I thank God every day that I have my son back once more—in the truest sense!

I regret to say that Dove is very ill again. The trip overland was too hard for her, and she has been confined to her bed since we arrived. Dr. Spencer offers little hope, but I know that God is our healer, so I ask both of you to continue to pray for her—as I know you do.

Frenchie Doucett came by yesterday with a load of furs. He will take this letter to St. Louis, and see that it gets to you as quickly as possible.

Missy has added her own letter, which I enclose. She has been a constant nurse and companion to Dove; I do not think Dove could have lived if it had not been for Missy's care.

Your loving son,
Christmas Winslow

Nathan stared at the letter for a long moment, taking it all in. Finally he said, "Thank God they made it!" He opened the other letter and handed it to Julie. "Writing's too small—you read it out loud." Julie took the small sheaf of papers and began to read:

"Dear Mr. and Mrs. Winslow,

"I know that Chris has not told you much about our trip. He is not one to speak a lot of himself, but I want you to know that without him, we all would have died on the trail. He was the only one of us who knew how terrible it would be, but when the decision was made, he chose to go along. Let me tell you how he saved the wagon train. . . ."

Julie read steadily, and Nathan leaned forward, absorbed, as the terrible ordeal came to life. Missy was a gifted writer, and the stark hardships of the last days of the harrowing journey seemed to leap before his eyes: hunger . . . thirst . . . dying cattle . . . the courage of some and the fears of most were all recounted. By the letter's end it was clear to his parents that Chris had been the single driving force that got the wagon train started in the mornings. Finally Missy ended her letter:

". . . .As much as Chris did to save us from death on the trail, I must tell you that his faith bolstered our sagging spirits even more. We have had services for the Indians since we reached the Yellowstone, and he is a wonderful preacher. I cannot understand the language, of course, but the Indians never take their eyes off him! He is well known among all the tribes, and they cannot believe that a mighty warrior would preach of a gentle God of love. Many have trusted in Jesus under his ministry.

"He is willing to interpret for the others, and I suspect (you must never repeat this!) that many of the sermons he interprets into the Indian language are 'improved on' greatly from the original!

"I close with a plea that you pray for White Dove. We have become sisters since she accepted Christ. I had learned to love her even before this happened, but now it is doubly hard to see her going down with this dreadful sickness! Pray much!"

Julie smoothed the sheets out carefully. She knew Nathan, too, had been touched deeply. Without looking at him directly, she leaned her head over to rest on his shoulder. "I'm so proud of him!"

Nathan put his arm around her and drew her close. "So much has happened since I held that little morsel of humanity in my arms for the first time!" She nodded, and he mused, "Been a long road since Valley Forge, Julie. Lots of times I've doubted—but you never did. You always said that God would make a preacher out of our boy."

She pulled away, brushing a few tears from her eyes. "We must pray for Dove," Julie said slowly, "and we must also pray for Missy. She's done a brave thing, Nathan."

He sighed heavily. "Never heard of a woman doing what Missy's done, the way she loves Dove. Giving up her man to another woman—then loving her like a sister."

"Let's pray—I don't know what to ask, but the Bible says that 'the king's heart is in the hand of the Lord.' If He can move the heart of a king, He can bring good out of this, too!"

Snow was falling as Missy made her way down the path from the mission to the river. The skies had been steel gray all day, and now the flakes fell gently to earth as if a giant had dumped a mammoth basket of tiny white feathers from somewhere high in the heavens. The chilling blasts of wind kicked up, taking Missy's breath away and sending the flakes swirling like miniature tornadoes of white dust, embalming the dead land in a thin coat of white. By the time she reached the river, the snow was coming down hard. Flakes as big as the tip of her forefinger fell heavily on her face, biting her skin with hot-cold sensations, and she was glad to see Chris standing beside a big tree, staring out at the river.

"Christmas!" she called out, emerging from the line of trees. He turned at once toward the sound of her voice. Snow lay thickly on his reddish hair, for he had removed the round trapper's cap that he usually wore. He came here almost every day to pray, and she knew that the body of his brother lay buried somewhere nearby, though there was no marker.

"What's wrong?" He picked up his rifle and came to meet her, his eyes searching her face.

"Running Wolf is here. He's brought one of his young men with him who's sick. I think his name is Little Crow."

"I know him. What's wrong with him?"

"Dr. Spencer can't make it out. He wants you to come and interpret."

"All right." He fell into step beside her, and they made their way away from the river, their feet making no sound on the soft snow. He listened as she told him what little she knew of the Indian's problem, at the same time his eyes never ceased scanning the area as they walked through the forest.

When she finished, he was silent for a moment and seemed to be thinking about something else. At last he said, "We'll be snowed in for a time—hope we don't get cabin fever. I shared a cabin with Bill Sublette one winter. Always liked Bill, but in such close quarters, by the time spring came I was ready to scalp him!"

"Why was that?"

"He cracked his knuckles all the time," Chris grinned. "Guess by the time spring comes, I'll know all your bad habits, Missy."

"I already know most of yours," she shot back.

"My bad habits?" he asked in mock surprise. "Didn't know I had any."

"Come spring I'll have brought them all to your attention." She thought about it, then said, "It's going to be hard—all of us living together. Like a big family, I guess, but even that's not always easy."

"We'll be all right."

They said nothing more for a quarter of a mile; it was a silent world they moved in. A doe suddenly sprang up from where she'd been lying, startling Missy. Chris had been carrying his rifle cocked and loaded. Now he swung the weapon up with a hunter's instinct, following the beautiful bounding flight of the animal, and pulled the trigger. "No!" Missy cried, pushing his arm with all her might. The weapon exploded, sending the ball whistling harmlessly through the dead leaves of an oak. Chris whirled and looked at her angrily.

"Why'd you do a fool thing like that?" he demanded indignantly. "We could have used the meat!"

Wide-eyed, Missy watched the deer disappear into the underbrush, and then put both hands over her face. He saw with a shock that her shoulders were heaving, and the sound of her muffled sobs broke the quiet of the forest.

"Why, Missy—it's nothing to cry about!" he protested. She didn't move and though he was concerned, he didn't know what to do about it. Uncertainly, he laid the rifle against a small tree, walked softly to where she stood, and tipped her chin up with his finger. Her lips looked very red against her cold skin, and tears glittered on her long lashes before they fell and ran down her smooth cheeks. "Missy, you don't have to cry," Chris soothed quickly. "It's not important—one deer."

She reached up and dashed the tears from her cheeks, taking a deep breath. "It's not that, Chris. When I eat deer steaks, I know where they come from." Then she shook her head. "It's not the deer—it's Dove."

"Dove?" Chris asked, confused. "Is she worse?"

"She's worse every day!" Missy cried out, and there was a streak of anger and frustration in her voice. "You know it's so—we all do! Every day she gets a little weaker. I was with her before I came to get you, Chris, and it broke my heart! She's so frail!"

Not knowing what to say, wisely Chris said nothing. "Let's go back," she sighed. They made their way back to the grounds and passed through the gates to find the two Indians along with Running Wolf's squaw, Still Water, inside with the doctor.

Running Wolf nodded, the puckered scar on his face giving him a twisted smile. "Bear Killer is here."

"What's wrong with Little Crow?" Chris inquired. He glanced at the young Indian, who was holding his stomach as he sat in the handmade chair.

"He got some bad whiskey from a trader." Running Wolf reverted to speaking in Sioux. "At first he said he got some bad meat—but my woman got the truth out of him." He turned to Little Crow, "You are a big fool."

Little Crow nodded miserably. "No more whiskey for me!" he vowed.

Chris, realizing that the sick Indian was only Running Wolf's excuse to make a visit, explained the problem to the doctor, who shook his head. "Can't do much for a hangover. Some of that whiskey is enough to make a man go blind!"

Chris spoke to his Indian friends in Sioux. "I brought down an old buffalo day before yesterday. You two can stick around and try to chew a little."

The snow continued to fall, and the women busied themselves with cooking dinner as the men fed the animals and cut more wood. "Let's have a meeting tonight," Chris suggested to Small. "Won't hurt to get a little of the Word of God into the chief."

"I can't preach to them," Small grumbled. "They've all got faces like stone! Can't tell what they're thinking. You take the service."

The snow piled up and the temperature dropped outside, but inside it was warm and cheerful. Chris carried Dove to the eating area, placing her in a chair and wrapping her with blankets. "You and Still Water can gossip before we eat." He told her affectionately, then hesitated before he asked, "Do you feel any better?"

"I'm all right—and it's good to be here with you and the others."

Instinctively, he knew she was feeling very bad, but he touched her hand, saying, "I'll see you get some good broth."

The room was barely large enough for them all, but there was a festive air as the meal preparations were completed and they sat down—elbow-to-elbow—to eat. Running Wolf and his woman sat side by side across from Missy and Brother Small. When the minister asked the blessing, the Indian listened carefully, his eyes never wavering from Small's face.

After the meal, the women cleared the dishes away, and the men made a small space at one end of the room. Barney Sinclair produced his fiddle and began to play, and soon the rich tenor of Robert Tennyson filled the room as he led them in many hymns. After Brother Small led in prayer, Chris got up and announced with a twinkle in his eye, "Brother Sinclair will read the Scripture."

Barney, who had been sitting with his Bible on his lap, turned pale as paper at Chris's words. He shot an agonized look toward Caroline, shaking his head, but she was forming the words with her lips: "Read, Barney!"

He got to his feet, and Chris said, "Our text will be the first sixteen verses of John three." He suppressed a grin and winked at Barney, for he had heard Sinclair reading this passage over and over until he had it memorized.

Barney read it and sat down, glancing covertly at Caroline, who was beaming at him with pride. Then Chris preached a simple gospel message from the text just read. He avoided looking directly at Running Wolf as he spoke of how Jesus had to take the old man out and put a new man in. "Ye must be born again," he repeated over and over, praying that some of the truth would break through his friend's stolid countenance.

Afterward there was a time of talk, for it was early and there was no other place to go now that the weather had closed in. Soon the young ones were sent to bed, protesting, and those who remained divided into small groups.

Dove was tired, so Chris took her back to their tiny room, and she was asleep almost before he left the room. He went to sit beside Running Wolf, who gazed at Chris through inscrutable eyes. "There is trouble, my friend," he murmured. "I have heard that Black Elk has vowed to kill you and take back White Dove and the boy. He says you are a thief and he will have your scalp."

"I will not kill him," Chris responded firmly. "It is not the will of my God that I kill anyone."

"You will kill him—or he will kill you."

Chris could think of no way to explain his position as a Christian. To Running Wolf, it was all very simple.

"I will ask my God to bring peace with the Pawnees," Chris said at last. "That would be good for your people, Running Wolf."

"That will be the day I believe in your God, Bear Killer," Running Wolf replied slowly. "The Pawnees and The People have always been enemies."

Missy had been sitting on a stool between Ellen Schultz and Lorene Spencer. Their conversation wound down, and the married women got up and went to their tiny cubicles. After they had gone, Missy was surprised to find Aaron Small beside her. "May I join you?" he asked.

"Why, sit down, Brother Small." She began to talk of her plan to help Lorene Spencer start a school for Indian children, but he seemed preoccupied, and she noticed that he only half listened. She stopped talking and waited for him to speak. He shifted in his chair, mopping the perspiration from his brow before he began—haltingly, nervously.

"I—I've been meaning to see you alone for some time, Missy, but it's been hard to find any privacy, when we could talk privately, that is."

With a sinking feeling, she realized what was coming. She wanted to get up, to run out of the room. That was impossible, so she frantically racked her brain, trying to form an answer for the question he was about to ask.

For a few minutes he stumbled about the difficult life they were engaged in; then he cleared his throat and clenched his fists. "I wish there were more time," he said in a firmer voice, "but I will say what is on my heart now. I wish to marry you, Missy."

Her hand flew to her throat as she breathlessly tried to speak. "Oh, Brother Small, I—!"

Sensing what she was going to say, he interrupted. "I know you were engaged in the past. I can't give you what the other man could, but I can promise you I'll always be faithful. You'll never know unkindness from me." He paused and tried to make a better case for himself. "I know you think of me as a stern man—but in time I hope to show you another side of myself."

Then he waited, his eyes fixed on hers. In the awkward silence that followed, her thoughts seemed to flutter wildly. Finally she looked him in the eye and spoke quietly. "You've just paid me the highest compliment any man can give a woman—and I thank you, Aaron. But I don't think I shall ever marry."

"I was afraid that would be your answer. I will not bother you anymore with my attentions, but if you change your mind, please tell me."

He got up and left the room, and Missy was so shaken that she left as well. She had suspected he would speak to her, and he had done so with such simplicity and dignity that it had hurt her to refuse. For a long time that night, she lay in bed fighting the unhappy tears forcing their way to her eyes, finally spilling over onto her cheeks.

Barney's sharp eyes had missed none of the little drama. When the two had gone, he lifted his eyes from the Bible he was reading aloud to Caroline and murmured, "Well, that takes the rag off the bush!"

"What?" Caroline stared at him, puzzled by his country jargon.

"Your sister just got a proposal—and turned it down."

Caroline looked quickly across the room, failed to find Missy, and demanded, "Who—?" then, "Oh, yes . . . I thought Brother Small was thinking that way."

"He's a better man than he was when we left Missouri," Barney said. "He took his lumps real well." He looked down at the Bible on the table and studied it, still thinking of Aaron and Missy. "Yep, he took it real well. Guess he knew he'd get turned down—but he made his play like a man. I admire Aaron for that."

Caroline's heart stood still. She looked at Sinclair's gangling form, thinking of how he had blossomed under her teaching. Though he had never said so, she had known for a long time that he loved her. Now she knew instinctively that he would never speak of it to her. She trembled, but with a sudden burst of courage, she put her hand on his and spoke softly. "Barney, do you have less courage than Aaron Small?"

It was as though her words turned him to stone. She felt his big hand clench under hers, and he began to breathe as raggedly as if he had run a mile uphill.

Then he lifted his eyes and met her gaze. Taking a deep breath, he protested, "Caroline—I'm nothing! I'm ugly and ignorant, and . . ."

She put her other hand on his and whispered what she realized had been on her heart for weeks.

"I love you, Barney!"

He gasped and began to tremble. Slowly he took her hands, struggling silently against some unknown fear. Finally he looked up and said simply, "I love you more than I love anything on God's green earth, Caroline Greene! Will—will you marry me?"

"Yes!"

A great joy welled up inside Barney, and he had to fight to keep himself in his chair. Clearing his throat, he commented, "Goin' to be real interestin'—our young'uns."

"Our children?"

"Yep." A grin of pure happiness swept across his face, and his eyes mirrored a joy she had never seen in him. "Yep. With you so good-lookin' and smart—and me so dumb and ugly, we gotta pray a heap that they all take after their momma!"

CHAPTER TWENTY-FOUR

THE LAST BATTLE

★ ★ ★ ★

Spring came to the land with a swift blow that year, breaking the paralyzing grip the late February snows held on the earth. A week later the snow was gone, and tiny spears of grass pierced the thawed ground like green tongues.

The winter had been a time of waiting, and as Chris had warned Missy, they had to learn to live with one another's bad habits. Barney and Caroline announced their intention to marry as soon as he could get a cabin built in the spring, and the pair were teased considerably. "It's given them something to talk about—a little fun," Caroline said privately to Barney. "I don't mind the joking, but I hate to see Brother Small always looking so miserable."

"Can't fault him for that," Barney grinned. "If I hadn't got you, I'd have gotten the sulks myself. He'll just have to make it on his own—or maybe go back east and get a bride."

Except for Dove's illness, there was no serious tragedy during the cold season. She had both good and bad days; but over all, she grew weaker. Chris kept hoping that good weather would bring her around; and on the first day of March, he bundled her up and carried her outside. She felt almost weightless in his arms, though he did not let his fears show on his face. Instead, he kept up a running commentary as he moved around, carrying her from place to place like a child.

"There's where the new store will be—and look, Dove! Barney's already piling up logs for a cabin for him and Caroline!"

"She says they will be married as soon as the last shake is on," Dove replied. The sunshine brought a faint flush to her cheeks, but her eyes were deeply sunken and she seemed to have no energy left. "We didn't have such a nice cabin as they'll have, did we, Chris?"

"It was all we needed." He smiled at her, remembering. "If Barney is half as happy with his bride as I was with you, he'll be a lucky man!"

He took her out to the fields and put a blanket down for her, and for an hour she rested there, enjoying the warm sunshine and the wildflowers he brought her. Finally he rose, saying, "Wind's getting chilly. We better head for the house."

She sighed and looked around fondly. "It's been such a good day!"

"We'll have lots of them."

He picked her up and she laid her cheek on his chest. "Not very many," she said.

"You'll get better now, Dove," Chris tried to reassure her. "The winter's been bad, but now it's over. When you get strong again we'll have lots of days like this. You'll see." She looked at him doubtfully, and he forced himself to sound cheerful. "Why, I'm planning to take you and Sky all the way to the Big Falls soon as you get a little better. You just mind the doctor and he'll have you well by midsummer!"

Still she didn't answer, and he spoke rapidly to cover his own misgivings. After he put her back in bed, Missy came by and commented, "I bet you two had a nice walk—Oh, my! What beautiful flowers! Let me put them in water." She left the room and returned with a pottery vase. "Everyone's looking forward to the big meeting at the Flathead village, Chris. When will it be?"

"Just been waiting for a break in the weather. Guess we ought to go in a couple of weeks." He leaned back and added, "Brother Small has quite a burden for that tribe."

"I know," Missy returned. "It was an article about the Flatheads in a Boston newspaper that got him interested in mission work to begin with. Do they really bind the skulls of babies, Chris?" She frowned and set the vase of wildflowers on the table beside Dove's bed. "I saw the pictures and they looked awful!"

"Well, some of them do. They tie the babies tightly to a board and put a hinged board over their foreheads—as they grow it slopes the skull back. Not many do it anymore." He shrugged. "I hear the Chinese bind the feet of baby girls till they're real small. All sounds bad, but it's their souls we've got to think about. Get them converted and customs like that will die out."

"I heard you say once that the Flatheads are a much more gentle people than the Sioux or the Pawnees."

"Sure. That's one reason why I agreed with Brother Small on starting a work there."

Dove spoke up. "Their village is close to Black Elk's people—" A fit of coughing seized her, so severe that Chris and Missy exchanged helpless glances. The fierce coughing tore at her tiny frame until she lay there gasping for breath, nearly unconscious.

"I'll have Spencer come by," Chris said. "He mentioned something about a new cough syrup he's concocting."

He left, and Missy sat down to bathe White Dove's face with a damp cloth. Dove lay so still that Missy thought the woman was asleep, but then her eyes opened, and she said weakly, "I wish Chris would not go to the Flatheads. Black Elk is a cruel man—a great warrior. He will try to kill Chris to save his own honor."

"We will pray for Chris's safety."

"I am afraid . . ." Dove clutched Missy's hand. "Not because I must die, but for my husband—and for my son! Black Elk will kill Chris—and take Sky!"

"No!" Missy cried, covering Dove's frail hand with her own. "God will take care of them. You must believe, Dove."

Dove lay still but tense, her eyes filled with anguish. Gradually she relaxed a bit and lifted her other hand, laying it on Missy's cheek. There was a note of wonder in her feverish eyes as she whispered, "You believe that God will take care of them?"

"Yes!"

The certainty in her voice seemed to satisfy Dove. She did not move her hand, seeming to draw some strength from the touch. The silence ran on and then she said, "You love Chris."

Missy's heart throbbed, and she said in a shaky voice, "Of course, Dove. I—I love both of them—Chris and Sky."

"He will need much love when I am gone."

"Don't—don't say that!" Missy begged, falling on her knees beside Dove's bed and throwing her arms around the small woman. Dove held her as she began to weep; and despite the fact that she was much larger than Dove, Missy felt so small and helpless—like a child.

Finally she grew quiet, and Dove said gently, "You have been faithful, my Missy. I am so happy that God gave me a friend for this time. Jesus God—He is good!"

Then her eyes fluttered shut and she abruptly dropped off to sleep. This suddenness always frightened Missy. After watching Dove's breathing for a while, Missy got to her feet and tiptoed outside. The young ones were playing some sort of game with a ball, filling the air with their happy and carefree cries. She watched Sky in the midst of the fun, laughing heartily as he sent Max Schultz rolling along the ground. *He's going to be all right,* Missy consoled herself. But despite the warm spring sights and smells, she could not repress the foreboding in her heart.

"I hate to leave her," Chris said, striking the side of the house with his fist in a helpless gesture of frustration. The others were all waiting for him; he had delayed departure as long as he could. But it was now the middle of March, and Brother Small insisted that they must go. "Let me stay here," Chris begged. "My wife's too sick for me to be away."

Brother Small looked up at Chris, who was standing on the porch. "I know it's hard, Chris, but we'll be gone only a few days. This is just a preliminary visit into Flathead territory. After this, I'll feel more confident—but I would feel much better if you went along on this first effort." He shifted his feet and added, "Caroline and Dr. Spencer will be here. I won't order you to go, but I—I would be most pleased if you would."

This is not the old Aaron Small, Chris realized. The short preacher's humble appeal was impossible to refuse. "All right, I'll go, Aaron," he agreed, and jumped off the porch. He had already said goodbye to Dove, so the two joined the others who were waiting. In addition to himself and Small, the party included Sinclair, Neal Littlejohn, Lorene Spencer, and Missy. They mounted and rode out through the gate, and soon the mission was a distant blot.

It was a two-day ride to the Flathead village. The first night they stayed at Running Wolf's lodge, and were warmly greeted by The People. The next morning as they got ready to leave, Running Wolf and fifteen of his braves mounted and prepared to accompany them.

"Why are you doing this?" Chris asked in surprise. "Didn't know you had all that much interest in the Flatheads."

Running Wolf's face was passive, but there was a glint in his eyes. "Good hunting that way—and we like to hear Bear Killer preach."

Chris knew there was more; he also knew that Running Wolf would never admit to it. They made the trip easily, coming to the Flathead village just before dark. Chief Many Horses met them as they rode in, saying, "The Black Robes have come." Chris, who had heard the expression before, knew the chief was referring to the Catholic priests who made infrequent trips through the territory. He did not correct the man, however, for he felt that it was not the right time to explain doctrinal differences. Instead, Chris introduced the party as Small stared at the chief, speechless.

Many Horses was a fine specimen of a Flathead warrior, nearly six feet tall and well proportioned. He had large, expressive eyes and high cheekbones—but it was his forehead that drew Small's attention. He had heard of the custom observed by these people that caused them to bind their children's foreheads, but he had never seen the result of this practice until now. Many Horses's forehead was a flattened slope that extended from the man's eyebrows to his hairline. It gave him a rakish appearance, and made him look unfinished somehow.

"We will hear the medicine of the white eyes," Many Horses

announced, glancing at Running Wolf and his warriors. "The People are here. We will smoke together."

"Preaching will have to wait, Aaron," Chris said. "Got to get through a few formalities first."

"We won't be asked to do anything against our convictions, will we?"

"All you have to do is sit around and take a puff on a pipe and listen to 'em jabber. Don't know where people get the idea Indians are quiet. They talk like magpies when they meet in this way. Just have to let 'em run down."

The council continued far into the night, and then they all gathered for a feast. Small liked the stew he was given until he inquired what it was. Chris asked a Flathead brave across from him, then turned to Small with a straight face. "Puppy stew."

Aaron Small, a product of the upper levels of Boston society, turned pale at the answer. But he had come a long way since leaving Boston, so he grinned and took another bite, saying, "No worse than eating snails, I suppose."

They slept where they could that night, and the next morning the entire tribe met to listen to the preaching. Barney had brought his fiddle and was an instant sensation. He played and they all sang for the better part of an hour until Chris said, "We better get to the preaching, Aaron. They can go on like this all day."

"Maybe you should preach," Small suggested uncertainly. He looked out at the sea of dark faces and strange foreheads, feeling completely alienated.

"Just tell them about Jesus—how strong He is! The gospel will work here just like it does in Boston."

Small took a deep breath and stood up. With a rather desperate expression on his face, he began to speak, careful to avoid the pulpit mannerisms he had mastered in seminary, and the abstract theological terms he was so fond of. For the first time since he had been a very young preacher, he spoke very simply of the love of God for all men, and the hope of salvation found in Jesus Christ.

When he finished, Chris told him quietly, "That was real fine, Aaron. They may look hard to you, but I can tell. It meant something to them—it may well be that they'll come to the Lord because of the words you spoke today."

Many Horses stood up and said, "We will have more of this—after we eat."

The meeting broke up and the visitors were welcomed into the lodges, where the women were initiated into the secrets of Indian housekeeping and cooking. The men and boys wandered off late that afternoon for footraces and other games in a large field adjacent to the village. Chris was thrilled to see Sky easily outstrip the other boys in a long foot race. Running Wolf commented with a smile, "His grandfather was like that—he could almost catch a deer!"

Later Chris joined in the races, losing to the striplings, but he was able to wrestle every challenger to his back. He was larger than any of the Indians and more agile than most.

They were just ending a contest with bow and arrow that Running Wolf easily won when suddenly a shout went up: "It's the Pawnees!"

Chris turned to see Black Elk leading a group of at least fifteen warriors to the edge of the clearing—and he knew instantly why they had come.

"Does Black Elk come in peace?" Many Horses was in a difficult place, for if he took sides with either tribe, the other would bring war to his people. And he could not ignore the invasion of his territory by what appeared to be a raiding party.

Expressionless, Black Elk looked across at Running Wolf, who had notched an arrow, and saw the Sioux fanning out on either side. He had not expected to find the fierce warriors of Running Wolf at this camp, and he said to Many Horses, "I come for a thief. My heart is good toward my brothers; but that one has stolen my slave—and there is my son!" He pointed at Sky. Despite the terror that shone clearly in his eyes, the boy did not move from where he stood.

"I came for my wife and son—as you would do for yours, Black Elk," Chris replied.

Fire raged in the Pawnee's eyes and he cried out, "I will have your life!"

The Pawnee warriors, watching Black Elk, saw that he was

ready to fight, and they snapped their rifles up, cocking them with a deadly sound. From the corner of his eye, Chris saw the bow of Running Wolf rise, and other Sioux followed his example, ready to let fly. It was an explosive moment, and Chris knew that he could not let it happen.

"Wait—I will fight you for the woman and the boy!"

His cry stopped the Pawnee, who demanded, "What weapon, coward? Knife—gun?"

"Knife for you—hands for me."

"No!" Sky protested, running to his father. "He is too good—that is his favorite weapon!"

"He is a woman, my son," Chris said with a smile at Black Elk. "I will take the knife from him and cut his ears off."

The taunt did exactly what he had hoped: It drove Black Elk almost to madness. The Indian tumbled off his horse and threw his rifle to the ground. "I will cut your heart out!" he yelled, and a circle of warriors from both tribes formed around the two men. Such a fight was intoxicating to them, and they circled like wolves with glittering eyes.

Chris threw up his hand and challenged, "I doubt you can keep your word, Black Elk; but I want your worthless promise that if I beat you, you will never again seek my life—nor my wife and son."

"I do not have to promise anything!"

"I would like to hear if your word is good," Many Horses requested immediately. And Running Wolf echoed, "I also want to know what you are: a man—or a liar."

Black Elk hesitated, then laughed. "What difference does it make? The white dog will be dead in a few minutes—so I give my word. But I will say also—"

With a single catlike motion the Indian whipped a knife from his belt and threw himself across the short distance separating him from Chris. He almost succeeded in catching Chris off guard. The tip of his blade ripped through the cloth of Chris's shirt and the flesh underneath, soaking it through with crimson blood.

If Chris had not fallen backward, the cut would have killed him. But the fight had only begun: as Chris lay there, stunned,

Black Elk crowed triumphantly and threw himself forward. He would not have dared do this if Chris had been carrying a knife, but the chief had no need to protect himself as long as his victim lay helpless before him.

Chris reacted instinctively; there was no time to roll away, so he drew his feet up and caught the oncoming Pawnee full in the face with a fearsome kick. The velocity of the heavy man added to the force of the blow, and Chris's heel struck Black Elk in the mouth, driving his head back and jarring his front teeth loose.

Chris scrambled to his feet—as did Black Elk, spitting out blood and teeth, his eyes still glazed. But the force of Elk's hatred was not spent, and as he stood up, the weaving blade in his hand forced Chris backward. Moving relentlessly forward, the Pawnee feinted, nearly drawing Chris out of position, then lunged forward again.

Hoping to disarm his opponent, Chris's left hand struck out, but missed the wrist; and the angry blade raked his palm, ripping the inside of his forearm. His hand was slippery with blood, and the cut burned like fire. *Got to get him!* he thought wildly, retreating. He knew he could dodge only so many stabs of the knife, and felt sure that he'd used up his quota.

As Black Elk lunged forward, Chris turned sideways and clubbed down with his forearm, catching the Indian on the back of the neck and driving him to the ground. He kicked at the knife hand and missed, which gave Black Elk the chance to grab Chris's foot and throw him heavily to the ground.

A cry of victory went up from the Pawnee braves, for all Black Elk had to do was reach out and take Chris. If he got a grip with his left hand, there was nothing Chris could do to save himself.

The chief's hand shot out. In desperation Chris scooped up a handful of sandy dirt and small gritty stones, throwing it in Black Elk's face. A cry rose from Elk's throat as the pain made him grab involuntarily at his eyes with his free hand. In an instant Chris was on his feet, and with one hard kick to the Pawnee's forearm, sent the knife spinning. With a frantic dive, Chris snatched it up and stepped behind Black Elk, who was still rubbing his eyes. Throwing an arm around the thick throat, Chris whipped the knife around with the point over the Indian's stomach. "Is Black Elk beaten?" he challenged.

The Indian was in bad shape. His mouth was bleeding, and the sharp gravel that was packed into his sensitive eyes caused a terrible pain. Chris's steely arm was cutting the man's air off, and he sensed the knife point poised over him. He choked and cried out, "Enough!"

Chris dropped his hold and moved back, and Black Elk staggered around the circle, trying to clear his eyes. The dead silence echoed until he was finally able to see enough to stumble back to his horse. He painfully pulled himself on the animal, completely drained of any pride. The other Pawnees followed him as he slowly walked his horse away, and every Indian there knew that he would not be war chief for long. No warrior could be beaten in such a humiliating fashion and keep the respect of his band.

"My father is a great warrior!" Sky ran to him, trying to keep back the tears. Running Wolf glowed with admiration, and the rest of the camp let up a wild cheer.

"I hope I never have to fight another battle as long as I live!" Chris said vehemently. "I'm not a warrior—I'm just a simple preacher."

When the Pawnees had ridden up, Missy and the other women had come out of the lodge and watched the whole thing. Now Missy hurried to him. "I think you're God's soldier, Chris," she told him, putting her hand on his arm, pride shining in her eyes. "And I think God made you to be just what you are, Christmas Winslow—a holy warrior!"

CHAPTER TWENTY-FIVE

"YOU HAVE BEEN TRUE TO ME. . . !"

★ ★ ★ ★

Chris's injuries were more painful than serious, but Missy had seen the symptoms of blood poisoning too often to take them lightly. For the next two days she insisted on cleaning the wounds and putting on fresh bandages.

She was carefully washing out the gash in his palm when they both heard the sound of a horse coming into camp. "Somebody's sure pushing that horse," he remarked. Then he heard a commotion and someone called out, "Chris! Chris!"

"It's Tennyson!" he exclaimed, and pulled his hand back, wrapping it hastily as he ran out of the lodge. Tennyson was talking to Barney, and both Chris and Missy knew immediately what it was.

"Dove?" he asked.

Tennyson's handsome head nodded reluctantly. "She got worse last night, Chris. Doc Spencer wants you to come quickly."

"Is she dying, Bob?"

Tennyson bit his lip, then nodded again. "Doc Spencer said to hurry."

"I'll go with you, Chris," Barney offered.

"No, you're needed here." Chris looked at Sky, seeing that he had heard the whole conversation. "Get your horse, son."

"I'm going, too," Missy announced, and ran to where Thunder was hobbled. She had the stallion saddled by the time Barney had saddled Chris's mount, a tough buckskin. She mounted and came to where Chris and Sky waited. Chris looked at her, warning, "This will be a tough trip."

"Let's go," she nodded, and the three of them left the camp at a gallop. "God be with you!" Aaron Small called out, and then he said to Sinclair, "Spencer told me before we left this might happen."

They rode steadily, keeping the horses at an even gallop, stopping once every hour to rest them for ten minutes. At noon they stopped at a creek, watered the horses, and let them rest for half an hour. "Should have brought you something to eat," Chris said to Sky.

"I'm not hungry." They mounted again, and by three o'clock the horses were too tired to do more than walk. It was after seven that night before they arrived at the mission. Schultz opened the gate and offered, "I vill take the horses, Chris."

"How is she, Karl?"

"She ist alife—but ver' bad."

"Come on, Sky," Chris said, and the two walked across the compound and entered the large building.

Missy followed, but found walking difficult after the hard ride. Her legs were trembling, so when she reached the porch, she sat down. Her mouth was parched, and she wanted to get up to get a drink, but could not find the strength to move. It was almost dark, and part of a moon was hiding behind a canopy of rippling clouds that caught the last light of the sun.

Someone came outside, and she looked up to see John Spencer. "You look beat, Missy," he observed.

"How is she?"

"No hope."

She stood up, licking her lips. Watching her, Spencer said, "There's some cool water here—and after that some coffee. You eat anything on the way?"

"No."

He led her inside, and she downed three dippers of water before her thirst was slaked. He seated her in a chair and handed her a cup of scalding coffee.

"We thought Dove would be all right till we got back from the Flathead expedition," she said sadly.

"I did, too—but yesterday afternoon she had a terrible coughing fit, and it brought on a hemorrhage. Lorene was with her last night. There was nothing I could do. Chris mustn't blame himself for leaving her—he was only following orders."

"But he will," she insisted. "And I do, too."

"Don't be foolish, Missy," Spencer protested. "We all knew it was a matter of time."

"I've prayed so hard!"

Spencer put his hand on her shoulder. "So have we all, but our God is sovereign. And this is Dove's homecall."

He got up. "Stay close by, Missy. She's asked to see you several times—and try to eat something."

"Will—will she die tonight?"

He paused and bit his lip, then answered gently, "I think so. She's very weak. I think she kept herself alive till Chris and Sky got back."

He went back inside, and Bessie Moore came out. The large woman had a sharp tongue, but trouble brought out the best in her. She comforted Missy and urged her to wash and have something to eat. Then she suggested, "Why don't you lie down, child? I'll be right here when Dove wants to see you."

Missy obeyed meekly, and for what seemed like a long time she lay there, praying. Her exhaustion allowed her to drop off into a fitful sleep, but she awoke instantly at Bessie's touch. "Missy! Dove's calling for you."

She rose and hurried to the small room, passing Spencer as he left. Dove's eyes were on Sky, who crouched beside his mother, his head resting near her hand. *He's only eleven,* Missy thought, watching the painful scene from the shadow of the doorway. Chris turned and saw her. "Dove? Missy is here."

His face, Missy noted as she went to kneel beside Dove, was drawn and pale, and his firm lips were clenched tightly.

"Missy?" Dove shifted her eyes from Sky and smiled faintly.

"My Missy . . . I'm glad you are here."

Tears scalded Missy's eyes, and she groped blindly for the hand that Dove extended. Her throat was constricted so that she could not say a word, but held the thin hand tightly to her face.

"You must not cry," Dove murmured. She felt the girl's tears and slowly lifted her other hand and let it fall on Missy's hair. At her touch, Missy could not help but sob, though she tried to control herself.

"No—no. Don't cry," Dove whispered. "I am happy."

Missy lifted her tear-stained face and saw the look of peace on Dove's countenance. The lines of suffering that had been etched into her brow were gone, and her eyes were gentle and calm.

"I can't bear to lose you!" Missy cried.

"Sky?" Dove said, turning her head.

"I am here." Sky rose and Dove reached inside her gown, pulling the pearl ring free. "This is what your father gave me, my son. Take it. When you get a fine young bride—it is for her."

With trembling hands, Sky took the pearl from around his mother's neck, but could not say a word.

"My husband?"

"Here, Dove—here!"

"You came for me—no other man would have had the courage—but you came! And you loved me . . . in spite of what I was . . . no matter what they did to me . . ."

Chris blinked back the tears, took the hand that she held out to him. He tried to speak, but his throat was so tight he could not.

The minutes passed as Dove continued to hold Chris's hand in one of hers and Missy's with the other. Dove's strength was ebbing, and they saw the light in her eyes dim. At the end she did not speak, but for one moment summoned all her strength and drew their hands together. She put both of hers over theirs, and smiled at them.

"You have been faithful to me. Now . . . you must be . . . faithful to . . ." She faltered, her eyes closing. They leaned forward and once more Dove opened her eyes, smiling.

". . . .be faithful . . . to one another."

Then she sighed and relaxed. A tremor shook her body—and her hands went limp.

Gently Chris arranged Dove's thin hands to lay comfortably across her chest, then bowed his head and began to pray. His voice was thick as he struggled to keep from breaking down. "I thank you, Lord Jesus, for coming to take Dove to be with you . . ." He looked once more at her face and finally motioned to Sky and Missy. "Come outside."

When they opened the door, Spencer met them and knew what had happened without their telling him. "I'll take care of her, Chris."

"Thank you, John."

The doctor touched Chris's shoulder and moved inside. Sky asked timidly, "Can we—walk a little?"

"Of course, son."

Without talking, the three of them moved away from the house to the gate. Chris pulled the bar, and they went outside the fortified area and walked along the trail to a path that led to the river. The moonlight filtered through the lacy branches overhead, making fantastic patterns on the ground.

When they came to the creek where the women did their washing, Chris stopped. "She always liked this place." He sat down on the big stump, pulling them down, Missy on his left and Sky on his right.

The bright sliver of a moon was out, gliding toward a tattered cloud. "Let's see if the moon hits that cloud," he said quietly.

The sliver vanished, and for a few minutes the world grew darker, but then the moon peered around the cloud as if she were smiling. Chris turned to look down at Sky, his face filled with pain, but with peace in his eyes. "No boy ever had a better mother."

"I know. I will miss her." Then he hesitated. "Tonight she told me something."

"What?" Chris asked.

"I—I am afraid to say."

Chris did not press him, but he ducked his head and said, "She said I would not always be without a mother."

Chris's hand tightened on Missy's shoulder, and she bit her

lip. He turned toward her, keeping one hand on Sky, and his eyes searched her face. Her thoughts tumbled wildly as she returned his gaze. Then his lips formed the word: "Yes?"

She sat there, bathed in the warm moonlight, and thought of the love that had always been there for him—even when she had been a child; and almost without a thought she nodded, and a smile curved her lips. *Yes! Chris, Oh, yes!*

He read her eyes, and his hand lifted and touched her face as he directed his words at Sky. "Your mother was a very wise woman, son. I think you can believe anything she told you."

Sky slowly lifted his head. He leaned forward, his eyes resting on Missy, studying her face carefully. He looked very young—and very frightened—but Missy reached out and took his hand, smiling as only she could, as a rush of love for the boy swept over her.

Sky Winslow began to breathe deeply as a peace such as he had never known in all his eleven years filled his heart.

"Let's go back now," Chris suggested. And as they walked, hand in hand under the silver moonlight, the three shadows behind them melted into one.